'Martyn Waites at his dark and chilling best'
EVA DOLAN

'Martyn Waites is already crime fiction royalty. Tom Killgannon is one
of the best new characters in modern fiction'
STEVE CAVANAGH

'An excellently woven crime novel, with a captivating setting and a brilliant
lead character, from master storyteller Martyn Waites'
RAGNAR JONASSON

'A compulsive and creepy crime novel, brilliantly atmospheric and original.
It's one of those books you keep saying to yourself – just one more
chapter – and then realise you've been up all night.
One of the best books I've read this year'
STAV SHEREZ

'Deeply unsettling and hauntingly realistic'
SUSI HOLLIDAY

'This is a great read – dark and disturbing, a novel that's gripping
from the first page to its incredibly satisfying climax'
KEVIN WIGNALL, AUTHOR OF *A DEATH IN SWEDEN*

'Crime noir at its finest. Gritty, claustrophobically
tense and deeply emotive – unputdownable!'
STEPH BROADRIBB, AUTHOR OF *DEEP BLUE TROUBLE*

'Dark and twisting'
A. K. BENEDICT, AUTHOR OF *THE EVIDENCE OF GHOSTS*

'A twisting, atmospheric, scary tale that introduces a terrific
new character in troubled Tom Killgannon'
ANYA LIPSKA, AUTHOR OF *THE KISZKA & KERSHAW SERIES*

Praise for

MARTYN WAITES

'Waites brings all his storytelling talent and experience to this chilling tale. Superb'
LEE CHILD

'Waites is one of the very best crime writers we have, simple as that.
I'd been looking forward to this for a long time and, boy,
it was worth waiting for. I don't know if I devoured
IT or IT devoured ME . . .'
MARK BILLINGHAM

'Martyn has written another raw, deftly-plotted thriller with a
dark heart and a real emotional punch'
SIMON KERNICK

'Authentically spooky, thrillingly atmospheric and unnervingly relevant.
The Wicker Man for the Brexit era'
CHRIS BROOKMYRE

'Reading Martyn Waites is a guaranteed thrill-ride. His characters
sing off the page, his plots keep you guessing until the end, and
I always read his books in a day'
SARAH PINBOROUGH

'A joyous new series with an adorable hero. Waites has come
thundering back with all his talent intact'
ALEX MARWOOD

'A chilling slice of country noir. Great stuff'
MICK HERRON

'One of those books you start reading and feel it envelop you like a
second skin, meaning you can't put it down. Deliciously creepy.
I loved it. Every word. Superbly written, creepy as hell, and
chilling to the bone. I can't recommend it highly enough!'
LUCA VESTE

'A superbly atmospheric book full of menace and secrets'
TOM WOOD

Martyn Waites was born in Newcastle upon Tyne. He trained at the Birmingham School of Speech and Drama and worked as an actor for many years before becoming a writer. His novels include the critically acclaimed Joe Donovan series, set in the north-east of England, and *The White Room*, which was a *Guardian* book of the year. In 2013 he was chosen to write *Angel of Death*, the official sequel to Susan Hill's *Woman in Black*, and in 2014 won the Grand Prix du Roman Noir for *Born Under Punches*. He has been nominated for every major British crime fiction award and has also enjoyed international commercial success with eight novels written under the name Tania Carver.

Also by Martyn Waites

The Old Religion

THE SINNER

Martyn Waites

ZAFFRE

First published in Great Britain in 2019 by
ZAFFRE
80–81 Wimpole St, London W1G 9RE

A CIP catalogue record for this book is
available from the British Library.

Hardback ISBN: 978–1–78576–549–0
Trade paperback ISBN: 978–1–78576–550–6

Also available as an ebook

1 3 5 7 9 10 8 6 4 2

Typeset by IDSUK (Data Connection) Ltd
Printed and bound in Great Britain by Clays Ltd, Elcograf S.p.A.

Zaffre is an imprint of Bonnier Books UK
www.bonnierbooks.co.uk

To Chrissie and Beth, always

Part One
GHOSTED

1

Manchester, May 2014

A night far enough in the past for stories to be told. But recent enough for those stories to matter.

An old industrial estate and lorry park in the badlands of Stretford. The buildings mostly empty and vandalised, the tarmac potholed, refilled with debris, broken glass and excrement, canine for the most part. The remaining lights stretched so far apart they looked stranded. The kind of place no one went to voluntarily. It was perfect.

Dean Foley sat in the passenger seat of the BMW X5. Its gleaming, black carapace stood out against its surroundings, as inconspicuous as an intellectual at a UKIP meeting.

Foley turned to the man in the driver's seat. 'What's the time now?'

The driver checked his watch, tried not to look irritated. 'Just gone ten to ten. They'll be here. Don't worry.'

'Yeah,' said Foley. 'I know they will, I know they will.'

The tension in the car was palpable.

Foley looked like a bouncer on Love Island. Short and stocky, he wore expensive clothes that were all label and no style, his hair well-coiffed, teeth the colour of Egyptian cotton, skin the colour of mahogany. His muscle showed he could handle himself and he had a lightness of step that surprised many. He also had a charismatic, salesman's smile that made you feel like you were an instant friend for life. But that smile could turn on a breath, become so fierce and snarling it would be the last thing you'd want to see. And for quite a few it had been.

Foley sighed. Tried not to pretend he was nervous. 'You know,' he said, resisting the urge to check his own watch again, 'I don't know why we bother with all this cloak and dagger shit. Meetings in the dark in shitholes like this. We should just do it in broad daylight. Get it over with. No one's bothered anymore.'

'You think?' said the driver.

'Yeah,' said Foley, warming to his theme. 'I mean, protection I've got, the amount of people on my payroll, I could walk into a pub on Deansgate – if they hadn't all been turned into fucking wine bars or craft beer places or some shit – pull out a gun and kill someone. Right then and there. Bang. In front of thirty witnesses. And you know what? I'd get away with it. That's how untouchable I am. That's why all this is just bollocks.'

'Yeah,' said the driver, 'that's what the Krays said. Look what happened to them. And that was before CCTV.'

Foley turned to him, his smile a vicious slash in the streetlight. He snorted. 'You're a bundle of laughs tonight, aren't you?'

The driver stared straight ahead. 'Why would you want to murder someone in a pub on Deansgate?'

'I wouldn't unless they were asking for it, would I?' said Foley, 'Then I'd have to. Because that's what it is. You cross me, that's what you get.'

'If they've crossed you they wouldn't hang around drinking on Deansgate.'

'Then I'd track them down, wouldn't I? Get revenge. They wouldn't get far.'

'You know what they say about revenge,' said the driver, 'you go looking for it you'd better dig two graves.'

Foley stared at him. Then threw back his head and laughed. 'Brilliant. Just brilliant. Mick, mate, if I go looking for revenge, I'll need a damned sight more than two.'

Mick lapsed back into silence. Foley fidgeted, flicked looks like lit matches all round the lorry park. His gaze came to rest on Mick once more.

'Why are you so miserable tonight, anyway?' asked Foley. 'It's like watching Man U when Moyes was in charge.'

Mick sighed. More from professional exasperation than boredom. 'Just want everything to go right. That's all.'

'Everything's cool,' said Foley, knee bouncing up and down. 'It'll go down fine. Why wouldn't it?'

Silence once more. Both resisted the urge to check the time.

'Hey,' said Foley, eventually, 'Just think if my old man could see me now . . .' He shook his head at the thought.

'Sitting in some shitty lorry park in Stretford? He'd love that.'

'No, you prick, if he could see what I've done, you know, built. Achieved. One of the most successful businessmen in the North West. If not the country. Respected. And I've done it all myself, haven't I?'

Mick nodded. 'You have, Dean.'

'Yeah. I have. If he could see what I've achieved . . .'

'He'd still be a miserable bastard.'

Foley stared at Mick, the smile falling sharply away. Eyes as hard as stone. No one talks ill of Foley's father, everyone knew that. Foley might have hated him but that didn't give anyone else the right to join in. He was still Foley's father.

Mick didn't know which way the situation would go. He thought he was close enough to Foley, but the man was so unpredictable that he could have made a misstep. He tried to smile his way out of it.

'Well he would be,' said Mick. 'You know he would.'

Foley kept staring.

Mick tried to shrug. 'Just you and me here, Dean.'

Gradually the harshness left Foley's eyes and the smile reappeared. He started to laugh, building up to a roar, the kind of coarse, loud laughter you only hear in films when the bad guy tries to convince everyone he's a decent human being with emotions like everyone else. Mick smiled along.

'Oh,' said Foley eventually, mirth subsiding, 'good one, Mick. Good one.'

Mick looked to the front, knowing he had dodged a bullet. Through the windscreen he saw activity.

'They're here, boss.'

An articulated lorry with a shipping container payload was turning into the park, headlights temporarily blinding them, playing along the buildings, making the shadows give up their secrets. Foley's team suddenly visible.

Mick saw the cars too. Four by fours, like the one they were in. Predatory darkling beetles waiting to pounce. Dotted between buildings, waiting. Filled with Foley's men. Mick looked through the windscreens, knew them all by name. Then, heart jumping, saw one person in a passenger seat who shouldn't have been there.

'What's she doing here?' he said, pointing at the vehicle that had slipped back into darkness once the headlights moved on.

'Who?' said Foley.

'That girl, in the front seat, over there. What's she doing here?'

'Oh, Hayley. Yeah, she's a good girl. Been proving very useful to the team. Very useful.' Another kind of smile. The kind that turned Mick's stomach.

'She shouldn't be here. She's—'

'Hey, what's your problem?' said Foley. 'We make the trade, we go our separate ways, we head off somewhere and celebrate. Yeah, maybe Foxy shouldn't have brought her but she's a good kid, it's cool. No problem.' Another smile. 'She'll be around for the party afterwards. Maybe Foxy'll let you have a go, if you want.'

Mick felt his anger ramping up. 'She shouldn't be here. What if something goes wrong? What if—'

Foley stared at Mick, eyes crinkling. 'What you trying to say?'

'Nothing. Nothing at all. Just, she shouldn't be here. That's all.'

Foley shook his head. 'Right.' He smiled. It didn't reach his eyes.

The lorry pulled up, stopped dead with a hiss of air brakes. The sound dissipated to a tense silence.

'Here we go, then,' said Foley, opening the car door.

Mick did likewise.

Foley went round to the back of the car, opened the boot. Waited while the hydraulic door silently moved upwards. Then leaned in, brought out a huge duffel bag.

'Jesus Christ,' he said, handing it to Mick. 'Carry that mate, bastard thing's heavy.'

'Thought they said it had to be you handing over the money in person?'

'I'm here, aren't I? Get moving. Haven't got all bloody night.'

Another four by four pulled into the car park, kept its lights on. It parked next to the lorry. The doors opened. The backlit silhouettes of two men emerged.

'Here's the Romanians, right on time.' Foley laughed, moving forwards. 'Should get a quote for my new bathroom.'

Mick didn't respond. They walked towards the two men. Stopped halfway between the two vehicles. The other men continued towards them. Stopped also.

Mick handed the duffel bag to Foley. He stared back at Mick.

'Just put it down, what the fuck's the matter with you?'

'You take it,' said one of the Romanians. 'We want you to give it to us. So we know who we are dealing with.'

Foley's eyes glittered in the dark. Clearly unhappy about being told what to do. But he picked the bag up, put it in front of his feet. 'There. Now where's my stuff?'

'In lorry. We will get it. When we have checked money.'

He bent down, opened the bag. A smile returned to Foley's face. 'Doing it old school, yeah? Notes and that. Unmarked. Thought you'd be all electronic transfer these days. You lot and your cyber-crime.'

'We like old school,' said the other Romanian. 'Face to face. Know who you're dealing with. Less to go wrong.'

The first Romanian stood up, satisfied that the money was all there. He nodded towards the driver of the lorry who went round the back, opened the double doors. They waited in silence while the driver came to join them, a clingfilmed bundle in his arms.

'The good stuff,' said Foley. 'Let's have a look.' He took the bundle from the driver, took out a knife, dug it in. 'It's not like the films,' he said. 'I'm not going to put this up my nose. If it's as pure as you say it is I'll be off my tits for days. But I'm sure you won't cross me. If you do, I'll know where to find you.'

'We not cross you. We want to deal with you. Deal?'

Foley put the package on the ground. 'Deal.' He stretched out his hand. The Romanian took it. They shook.

'We all happy?' asked Foley.

'One more thing,' said Mick.

Foley turned to him, irritation on his face.

'What?'

'Speaking of crossing . . .' He reached behind his back, brought out a pair of plasticuffs, slipped them onto Foley's wrists, pulled them tight. Foley was too surprised to react.

'Dean Foley, I am arresting you on the charge of obtaining class A drugs with intent to sell. You do not have—'

Foley found his voice. 'What the fuck are you doing? Mick? What the fuck are you doing? What's . . . what's happening? Mick, what the . . .' He turned to the Romanians. 'Fucking do something . . .'

'We're with him,' said the first Romanian, voice now more Manchester than Bucharest. He drew his automatic from his side holster, pointed it at Foley.

Foley looked around, tried to see his men in their cars but he had been cuffed out of their eyeline.

The second Romanian spoke into a mic hidden in his jacket lapel. 'Target apprehended. Letting you out now.' He trotted round to the back of the truck, began opening the double doors.

Foley struggled in Mick's grip, managed to turn and shout at the cars.

'It's a fucking set-up! They're law!'

Foley's men were on hair triggers. In response to his call they jumped out of their cars, pulling their guns from within their jackets. Mick dragged Foley to the ground as his men started running towards them, firing as they came.

'Where's that backup?' Mick yelled to the back of the truck. He saw the second 'Romanian', an undercover firearms officer, swing the first of the double doors open, then spin and fall, face creased up in pain, as a bullet ripped through his side.

'Shit,' shouted Mick. He looked at the first Romanian. 'Get him out of the line of fire, get those doors open. Get the men out, move . . .' Mick's training kicked in. He took his gun out, grabbed Foley, dragged him back to the BMW. Keeping covering fire going all the while. Turning on men who until seconds ago had been his closest friends. Or thought they were. Not thinking, just acting, reacting.

The fake Romanian ran round to the back of the truck, pulled at the door. Armed body-armour-clad police began disgorging. They assessed the situation quickly, found spots to shelter behind, take aim.

Then it was free fire.

The fake Romanian managed to drag his wounded comrade behind the car, knelt and returned fire.

The police outnumbered Foley's men and outflanked them in professionalism, but Foley's team were vicious, desperate. They had the chance to be the outlaws they'd always imagined themselves to be and they weren't going to go down easily. At least not without taking out as many coppers as they could.

Mick ran, dragging Foley across loose gravel and broken glass, keeping up the covering fire, head down, dodging overhead bullets. He didn't have the benefit of body armour like the uniformed officers did. He just concentrated on the task at hand, didn't allow himself to be drawn into the firefight. Foley screamed all the way, kept up a litany of threats as to what would befall Mick when he got free.

The police were winning. It was an uneven fight. They found positions, attempted to pick off anyone who came at them. Foley's men were reckless and young, brought up on a diet of video games and self-aggrandisement. They believed they were the indestructible heroes of their own stories. The officers, guns used sparingly, clinically, were proving them wrong. Foley's men were the cannon fodder.

Some of them ran back to their cars, tried to get away. They wouldn't get far. The police had stationed cars at all the exits to the estate. Armed response officers alongside.

As the fighting died down, Mick and Foley reached the BMW. Mick opened the hatchback boot and lugged a protesting, kicking, swearing Foley inside where the duffle bag had previously been.

'You put me in here where you'd put a fucking dog? Would you?'

Mick ignored him.

Foley stopped shouting. He calmed slightly, panting from the exertion. Started asking questions.

'So you're law, are you, Mick? Fucking law? Since when?'

'Since always,' said Mick, getting behind the wheel and shutting the door.

'What the fuck?' Foley still had difficulty comprehending what he was hearing. 'You're my right-hand man, Mick. We did all this together. You've been with me fucking ages. How can you be law?'

'Because that was my job. I played the long game, Dean.'

Foley fell silent. When he spoke his voice was more reflective. 'Was it worth it? All the shit you've done? That we've done together? Brothers in fucking arms, was it worth it?'

Mick didn't answer.

Foley's voice took on a plaintive tone. 'I trusted you, Mick. I trusted you . . .'

Mick couldn't reply, couldn't listen to any more. It sounded, if Mick concentrated hard enough, as though the man was almost crying.

He locked the car, walked towards the lorry, pulled a red bandana out of his jacket pocket, the previously agreed sign to mark him as police.

Bodies everywhere. Mainly Foley's men, but a couple of police officers had been wounded beyond the reach of their body armour.

He found the duffel bag. It was where it had been left along with the block of cocaine. He stood beside it. It was clear to see who had won.

'He's in the BMW,' he said to an armed uniformed officer striding over to him. 'What's the damage?'

'Couple of them badly injured, couple of fatalities. The rest have either run or given themselves up.'

Mick nodded. 'Good night's work.' Then remembered something. 'There was a girl in one of the cars. Where's she?'

Sadness always looked worse on the face of a professional. 'Driver tried to get away, sir. Looks like she was in the line of fire. Got hit running, apparently.'

'Who by? Who hit her?'

'Don't know, sir. Stray bullet, probably.'

'What's happened to her?'

'Sorry sir, did you know her?'

Mick's heart skipped a beat. Then another. His legs became water. He didn't answer. 'Get an ambulance, get her seen to . . .'

He tried to run over to where she had been. The officer tried to push him back.

'You don't want to see, sir. Believe me. It's a mess.'

Others joined the officer, kept Mick away from the girl's body. He fought them all the way but they were too many for him. Eventually the adrenaline rush subsided. His shoulders slumped. He felt defeated.

'Was she important to you, sir?' said the first officer.

'My niece. And she shouldn't have been here. She wasn't supposed to be here.'

'I'm very sorry sir.' The officer looked around. He was being called. 'Excuse me sir. I'm needed over there.'

Mick didn't know whether he had replied to him or not. He just stood there, staring at the carnage. Ambulances were arriving now, their flashing lights adding to the chaos all around. He walked away, back to where he'd left the duffle bag. Stood beside it once more. Looked down at it.

He felt so, so tired.

Of everything.

1

Now

He was on the wrong side of the door. And he hated it.

Movement buffeted him from side to side. He tried to stay still. The room was small, less than one metre all round, and he could easily touch the walls if he wanted to. He didn't. Previous occupants had left their mark in several ways: mucus smeared on all surfaces, graffiti, hardened phlegm on the plexiglass door. Other, darker smears and trails. And the smells: sweat – yes obviously, that's where the name of the vehicle, the sweatbox, came from – shit, piss. Like the worst broken down lift in the worst tower block in the world. He thought of all the diseases the room might harbour. Then tried to forget it. Couldn't.

There was a gap under the door where a drink could be slid in if he was thirsty. Or a box if he needed to urinate. Beyond that, he was on his own.

But not alone. Another man either side of him, another three men opposite them. Each in his own little room. Unable to talk to each other, almost unable to think, the driver having pushed Kiss FM up to near earbleed levels. A small act of sadism or something to keep the driver awake? He didn't know. But he could guess.

The sweatbox, a miniature jail on wheels, moved through the night.

He knew where he was going. That didn't make the journey any more endurable. His destination was just as bad. Worse, even. Not for the first time he wished he was home. Or the place he was learning to call home. Building his new life, working on his future. And he could go back to doing that. As long as he did this one thing. And it worked out. Simple.

He shook his head. Yeah. Simple.

The sweatbox juddered, shook, turned to the left. He tried to look out of the window, twisting his body nearly ninety degrees to do so. No use. Couldn't make anything out. The glass, or the night, too dark. But he had a feeling they would be arriving soon. He sat back, tried to think about anything other than where he was, where he was going. And more importantly, tried not to touch anything.

It didn't take long to reach his destination. He may have nodded off, although given the circumstances he didn't know how. He jolted forwards as the sweatbox came to a standstill. Then remained still, trying to listen for anything above the blare of the radio.

Nothing.

The sweatbox pulled forwards again, came to its final resting place. The radio was silenced. The ringing in his ears was deafening. He waited. It wouldn't be long now.

He was wrong. He sat there for nearly an hour before anyone came for him. He heard voices, the other men in their cells, trying to talk to one another, size each other up, glean information, explore camaraderie, even. With varying degrees of success. He listened, but didn't join in.

Then his door was opened. A prison officer stood there, big and doughy, stretching his uniform, the seedy yellow light in the van making him look like a rancid marshmallow.

'Come on, then. Haven't got all night.'

He picked up the four big plastic bags, made his way out of the cell. Followed the officer along the van's narrow corridor and down the steps to the outside world. The air hit him. So cold it woke him immediately. He looked around, tried to make out his surroundings. Saw only dark grey stone against grey sky. Floodlights lit the way towards a door.

'You'll have plenty of time to admire the view,' the officer said, pushing him forwards.

He gave no resistance, went where he was instructed.

He was marched through to a holding cell. Inside was a row of plastic chairs. Five men sat on them, trying not to touch each other. The others from the sweatbox, he assumed. He sat down on the nearest chair, dropped his bags in front of him. The door clanged shut as the officer left, the key turning in the lock. He hoped he wouldn't have to get used to that sound. He sat back, head against the wall. Processing. He knew the procedure. Make as little fuss as possible, try to get a cell to himself.

He didn't know how long he was kept there. Time moved at a different rate inside prison. The artificial light told him nothing. Could have been morning by now. Or even afternoon.

The man next to him kept looking at him, attempting eye contact, wanting to talk. He ignored him. The man persisted.

'Nice reception committee, innit?

'I mean I've had worse,' the man continued, oblivious to his silence. 'First time in this nick?'

He gave only the slightest of nods.

The other man took that as encouragement. 'Not that bad, really. Not as bad as it used to be, anyway. Jesus, should have been here then . . .'

He looked at the talking man. Small, grey-haired, features like carved, well-oiled leather. Eyes that weighed odds, made calculations, did deals while he spoke. The speaking, he now saw, just a cover for thinking.

The man looked at him. 'Clive,' he said.

He didn't answer. Clive smiled.

'Right, I get it. One of those silent types. Fine by me, mate. We all have our own way of coping.' He kept looking at him. Kept smiling. 'Mind you, with that hair and that beard, they should call you Thor.'

15

He almost smiled at that. It was true he had let his hair and beard grow, and that the sun had lightened it a little. But Thor? That was a stretch. The key turned in the lock. The door opened.

'You're up.' Clive nodded as the officer beckoned.

He picked up his plastic bags, followed. The door clanged shut behind him. He was escorted to a reception desk. He stood, bags in hand, before the desk, waiting to be spoken to.

The officer behind the desk looked like she had never smiled in her life. Or had used up her supply long before she'd met him. Hair scraped back from her face, uniform rendering her neither masculine not feminine. She stared at him, her gaze stern.

'Name?' A question that sounded like a statement.

'Tom Killgannon.'

She looked up at him once more. 'Welcome to HMP Blackmoor, Killgannon.'

2

'We don't like doing this either, if that's any consolation.'

It wasn't. Tom had been taken to yet another room, told to strip naked by the prison officer, and searched. His bags had been gone through thoroughly, his personal items examined in minute detail. The officers had stopped at the photos, scrutinised the images, scrutinised him in turn. Guessing relationships, keeping judgements to themselves for now. Mentally filing the images away as potential leverage at a later date. It was intrusive, having his life dismantled and put on show, but nothing compared with what was to come.

'Take a seat,' the officer said, pointing to the BOSS chair. The Body Orifice Scanner.

Tom had heard about this and had dreaded experiencing it for himself. Grey and functional looking, it was a full body scanner that checked every cavity for contraband. Humiliating in the extreme, but he had no choice but to submit.

'I've got nothing to hide,' said Tom.

'Then you've nothing to worry about.'

The chair was switched on. It was something Tom hoped he would never have to endure again.

The experience over, he was told to get dressed and take a seat. He was tired, ready for whatever sleep he could get, but no one seemed in any particular hurry. He sat. The officer opposite him picked up a file from his desk, opened it. He was tall, grey-haired. Thin, with large glasses and a mournful expression. He looked more like a funeral director or an unsuccessful dentist than a prison officer. There was no cruelty about him, no harshness. Just a tired professionalism. Then the questions started.

'Where've you come from?'

He had decided to answer questions as monosyllabically as possible. Inmates tried different things when they first arrived. Some played hard, set themselves up as a challenge, tried to intimidate. Others went for cocky, unbreakable. Some, especially the older hands, tried to be chummy with the officers at first, make themselves seem likeable, get privileges in the bank. Tom gave little of himself away. Let them come to him if they wanted something.

'Where've you come from?'

'HMP Long Lartin.'

'How long you in for?'

'Two years.'

'How long you got left?'

'Eighteen months.'

'What level were you on?'

'Enhanced. Yeah. I worked for my privileges. Don't intend to lose them.'

The officer read the rest of the file in front of him. Tom waited silently. Eventually the officer looked up. 'You'll do all right here, probably. Keep your head down, your nose clean. All of that.'

Tom inclined his head to demonstrate he'd heard and understood.

The officer closed the file, studied Tom. 'How did you get on in your last prison?'

'Should be all there in the report.'

'It is, but I want your opinion.'

'Fine,' said Tom, talking as if words were difficult, precious things to extract from him.

'No problems with other inmates? Officers?'

'Don't think so. Unless someone's said anything I don't know about.'

'No.' The officer opened the file once more. 'Model prisoner. Says here you're well-educated but you didn't want to go to education classes.'

'Couldn't see the need. I've done all that stuff. Didn't want to do art either. Not good at drawing. Or creative writing . . . I don't like making up stories.' The irony, thought Tom.

'So you ended up working in the laundry. Why was that?'

'I like wearing clean clothes.'

The officer sat back, studied Tom once more. Took in his hair, beard. The tattoos poking out from his rolled up sweatshirt sleeves. The way Tom held his body, still but not relaxed, like an engine at rest.

'If I may say so,' said the officer, voice dropping, 'you don't seem like many of the men we get in here. I'm not saying you don't belong because clearly you do, otherwise you wouldn't be here.'

The statement seemed to invite a response so Tom gave a small shrug.

'It says in your file that you committed assault.'

'That's what it says.'

'A troublesome customer in the pub where you worked.'

'You know all this. Why are you asking?'

The officer looked up from his notes. Smiled. Tom's first question. A breakthrough.

'I just want your opinion on what happened, that's all.'

Tom shrugged once more. 'Lairy customer got a bit too handsy with the boss. Needed putting in place, that was all.'

'And that's the way you see it, is it?'

'What other way is there?'

'Well according to the trial notes, this lairy customer, as you describe him . . .' He verbally placed quotation marks around the words '. . . was attempting to rape your boss. He had followed her outside to the back of the pub, pinned her up against the wall and was attempting to sexually assault her when you happened upon them.'

'Yeah. That's right.'

The officer regarded Tom over the tops of his glasses. Like peering out from behind a shield. 'Should have got a medal, really.'

Tom shrugged. 'He needed to be taught a lesson.'

'Which is where, it says here, it stepped over the line to assault.' The officer nodded. His tone became warmer, conciliatory. 'Thin line, that. Very thin. Better barrister, different judge in a different mood on another day . . . there but for the grace of God, isn't it?'

Tom said nothing.

'Anyway, you're here now. My advice? Make the best of it.'

Tom nodded.

'Just another couple of questions before I send you along to the medical department. Have you had any suicidal thoughts since you've been in prison?'

'No.'

'Dark thoughts? Depression?'

'I'm on anti-depressants. Long term.'

'Are they working?'

Tom shrugged. 'Still here, aren't I?'

'Mental health's a big problem inside. If you feel you can't cope or you need someone to talk to, speak to your personal officer. He'll introduce himself on the wing tomorrow.'

Tom gave a small nod.

'Anything else?'

'I want a cell to myself.'

The officer smiled. 'Don't hold your breath.'

Tom nodded.

The officer wrote something in the file, closed it. 'Right, that's you done. Off you go to medical. Best of luck.'

He sat in his cell, on the bed, staring at the wall. It was painted a shade of yellow that looked like a dying, sick sun. The door, huge and riveted, took up most of one wall. On the opposite wall was a barred window, the plexiglass strips, pitted and melted from cigarette burns, gave only the barest of openings to stop inmates from stringing a line from cell to cell in order to pass contraband or reaching through to take whatever had been brought in by drone. The bed was against one wall, opposite that was a cheap table with a small, greasy-screened TV, a plastic chair, a metal, seat-free toilet and matching metal basin. His bags sat on the floor, unopened.

Whoever had lived in the place before him hadn't been one for cleaning. The floors were dirty, the walls smeared. It stank. That would be one task he would have to undertake immediately.

Medical had presented no problems. He had been passed fit and healthy, ready for work or education. After that he was given his non-smokers welcome pack – a small carton of orange squash and a few cheap biscuits – and directed to his cell. But not before his allocated phone call.

One call, a duration of two minutes, then cut off whether he had finished or not. Made from the wing phone with everyone else around, not knowing who was listening, both in the vicinity and beyond. Knowing someone could use your words against you if they wanted to. Choose carefully who you want to talk to, what you want to say, he had been advised. Make every second count. He should call Lila. Tell her he was OK. Not to worry. Or Pearl, even. But both of those calls would have to be longer than two minutes. Infinitely longer. And full of things he couldn't say. Instead he dialled another number, one he had learned by heart.

'It's me,' said Tom. 'I'm in.'

'Any problems?'

'None.'

'Good. Then get to work.'

3

Five weeks before

The end of October. Halloween mists and denuded trees. A day that, to all intents and purposes, had started like any other. But Tom, in hindsight, felt it was anything but.

A staunch rationalist, he had always dismissed the slightest hint of superstition. But as he looked out of his bedroom window that morning, part of him – the part that had been awakened by and responded to the untamed, isolated world around him, the part that had allowed the beliefs of locals to influence or at least commingle with his own – was tempted to think there were no coincidences, only omens.

The crows had returned.

Always present to some degree, they now circled the house cawing and screeching, swooping and diving, as if singling Tom out for special treatment. Sitting in the leafless autumn trees, charcoal against the grey sky, like the backdrop to a folk horror movie. The rational part of him dismissed such thoughts as pagan, as voodoo nonsense. But it was a hard unease to shift. The crows were reminding him of what happened seven months before. And with that memory came the unnerving feeling that he had somehow escaped censure for his part in those events. Or at least deferred it. But payment, he felt, would fall due.

He tried to dismiss such thoughts, or at least reduce them to an irritation, noise at the back of his mind. He went downstairs to get on with the day.

Lila was up and about before him. He came into the kitchen to find her eating a slice of toast with butter and Marmite, drinking a mug of tea, and packing her rucksack at the same time.

'Just look after yourself,' he said, 'don't mind me.'

'What d'you mean?' she said through a mouthful of bread, 'you're never up at this time.'

'Neither are you. Is this a college day?'

'You know it is. Why you even asking?'

Tom thought for a second. 'Sorry. Bad dream. Dragged it into the morning with me. Can't remember what day it is.'

'You're getting old,' she said, taking a gulp of tea. 'Right. Got to catch the bus. Laters, taters.'

She ruffled his hair as he sat down, picked up her rucksack, and was gone. He smiled as she left. It didn't last long. The slam of the door echoed away to nothing.

His dream. He couldn't remember what it had been about. Just that feeling that something dark and foreboding was gathering like storm clouds. And he was caught in the middle. Then on waking he had seen the crows. Or maybe the crows had wormed their way into his dream, darkening it, wakening him. Omens, Pearl would say. Don't mess with the omens.

He stood up, shaking superstitious nonsense out of his mind and put the kettle on to make coffee.

Seven months since he had come back from work on a freezing, wet night and found the seventeen-year-old Lila shivering, starving and soaking in his kitchen, on the run from an abusive family, a vicious boyfriend, in genuine fear for her life. Seven months since he had made a decision to help her, putting his own life in danger. Seven months since those events led to the village he had come to call home losing its collective mind in the grip of a murderously deranged demagogue. Tom had helped to pull things back from the brink, but life in the surrounding area wouldn't be the same for a long time. Not now that neighbours had glimpsed the skulls under their own skins.

In the aftermath he had asked Lila to move in with him. She needed safety, stability and had nowhere else to go. In doing so, the pair attempted to create some kind of functioning family unit from their mutual dysfunction. On the whole, it had been a positive experience, Tom trying to take his position as the girl's surrogate father, or at least uncle, as lightly as possible. They were a good fit; both damaged, both trying to move forwards, hoping in doing so it would help the other. Keeping each other's demons at bay. For the present.

Lila was now taking A levels at Truro College. Tom still worked the bar at the Sailmakers pub in St Petroc. Trying to live as normal a life as possible. He hoped it would last but suspected it wouldn't. In his experience nothing good did.

He was right.

It happened before lunchtime, before he was due to leave for work. A knock on the door. Tom was sitting in an armchair reading a book, listening to music, a mug of tea by his hand. He stood up, went to answer it. Heard a crow cawing outside.

'Mister . . . Killgannon?' The pause just long enough to inform him: I know your real name. And to give an implicit order: don't play games.

'Who are you?' A shudder went through Tom.

The stranger smiled, stepped aside. There were two of them, one man, one woman. Both wearing the kind of plainclothes that marked them out as just another uniformed branch of the police. The man held up his warrant card. 'Detective Sergeant Sheridan. And this is Detective Constable Blake.' He gestured to the hallway. 'May we?'

Tom knew he had no choice. He stood aside.

He followed them into the living room. Sheridan was tall, brown haired, grey suited. Neat looking, like a daytime TV host. Every centimetre the modern, management-trained police officer. Blake was smaller, more lithe, with dark bobbed hair. Her features, while plain, were remarkable. She had the blankness of film stars, gave nothing away, allowed a viewer to superimpose their own opinions on what she was thinking, read what they wanted to see. Good trick for a copper.

'Sit down,' said Tom, pointing to the sofa.

They did as Tom turned the music off, sat back down in the armchair. Not wanting to speak first, knowing they were waiting for him to do so, that his question would be their way of gaining the upper hand. He had done it himself enough times.

Sheridan took a laptop out of his briefcase, opened it up. 'I expect you're wondering why we're here, Mr Killgannon?'

'The fishing? Very good this time of year.'

Sheridan gave a brief smile. 'In a manner of speaking, yes.' He found what he wanted on the laptop, gave his full attention to Tom. Blake was looking round the room, making silent judgements.

Tom waited. He hadn't asked if they wanted tea. Neither had suggested it. This wasn't a social call.

Sheridan shot a quick glance round the room. 'Nice place you've got here. Not everyone gets this kind of opportunity.'

'The price is commensurate with what I was earning previously. Those are the rules. And you should know what I was earning since I was one of you lot. Plus I've put a lot of work into it.'

'Yeah, and it's paid off. Very nice.'

Tom felt anger rising within him. 'Did you just come here to compliment my decor or did you want something else? And how d'you know I'm here?'

'Has your liaison officer talked to you, Mr Killgannon?' Still saying his name but the tone changing, the pretence of the game slipping. Getting down to business.

'I'm kind of between liaison officers at the moment. I'm sure you know what happened to the last one.'

Sheridan said nothing. He was well aware of the events of seven months ago.

'You stuck your head above the parapet,' said Sheridan. 'Could have been nasty. Left your new identity in tatters. All that work for nothing.'

'Well you've found your way here. My identity seems to be an open secret.' His anger rose a notch.

'You've been given a fair degree of leeway in the past. Had several blind eyes turned when perhaps they shouldn't have.' Something crept into Sheridan's voice. Bitterness? Jealousy? Tom couldn't make it out. 'You must have been quite an asset back in the day.'

'Can't have been that good if you two have heard of me.'

'We've been given your name by the department handling you.' Sheridan gave a small laugh. 'And you wouldn't believe the hoops we've had to jump through, the forms we've had to sign, the briefings we've had so Tom Killgannon doesn't get given away.'

'So it should be. This is my life we're talking about here.'

'Oh, absolutely. But you're still down as an active asset. As and when you're needed. And you're needed now, buddy.'

Outside the crows continued to caw. This was the call he had always expected. Always dreaded. 'What's the job?'

'Noel Cunningham. Know the name?'

Tom frowned, thinking. 'Rings a bell.'

'Convicted child murderer,' said Blake. 'Known as The Choirboy Killer because he was a choirmaster. Local to the South West. Killed seven, but only five bodies have turned up. Won't say where the other two are.'

'Until now,' continued Sheridan.

'What d'you mean?'

'He's been making noises that he's ready to talk,' said Blake. Her tone of voice gave as much away as her features. 'Ready to give up the locations of his final two victims. We want someone there to help him along.'

'Why would he do that? Presumably he's never going to be let out so nothing he could say would make any difference.'

'His mother's got cancer. The terminal kind. He wants to visit her, be there when she goes, he says. It would be too politically sensitive to let him do that, especially for the amount of time he wants. So we've suggested a bargain. The two dead bodies for the right to be with his mother.'

Sheridan nodded. 'We've tried getting people from our own team next to him undercover, but without success. They're too well known. Put half of them that's inside there.'

'Inside being . . .'

'Blackmoor,' said Blake. 'Prison. Cunningham's a local boy. The bodies are buried somewhere on the moor. He requested a move to the prison. Said it would jog his memory. He's been there a while now. And nothing's changed.'

'So we're going to put someone on the inside,' said Sheridan. 'Cunningham's not good with authority. Doesn't want to just come out and say it. Plus he's a tricky bastard. We thought it would be more likely for him to open up to one of his peers.'

Prison . . . Tom's stomach lurched. He had previously worked undercover with criminals, in gangs . . . But not prison. He had drawn the line at that. Too confined, too easy for something to go wrong. To be found out. And if it did, he'd be stuck there. Or worse.

'Presumably you've read my file, or been briefed on me.'

'Yes,' said Sheridan.

'Then you'll know I don't do prison work. Never have.'

'You've been given a lot of leeway in the past like DS Sheridan said,' Blake's voice hardened. 'You've had it easy here. Been left alone when someone else wouldn't have been. And that's OK. Give and take, isn't it? But you knew you'd have to pick up the tab one day.'

'I don't do prison.'

A ghost of a smile crossed Blake's face. 'You do now.'

'Don't worry,' Sheridan said, trying to head off any further conflict, 'we'll move you in at night so as not to arouse suspicion among the staff and inmates. Ghosting, it's called.'

'Just a minute. The staff? They won't know why I'm there? Who I am?'

'The fewer people the better. Need to know only. I've read your file. That's how you've always chosen to operate. One person in control on the outside, you left on your own. Said it got you the best results.'

Tom could say nothing. Sheridan had clearly read his file thoroughly.

'We'd provide you with a cover story, a good one that you'll be able to corroborate and stick to. We could even use this identity to give it a bit of extra reality. Then once you're inside, get close to Cunningham. Once he talks, your job is done. Relay the information to me, we'll get you out of there. Handshakes all round.'

Tom thought before answering. 'So *if* I do this . . .' 'He looked at Sheridan. From the expression on his face, Tom didn't think he had a choice. 'The debt you mentioned.'

'What do you mean?'

'I do this and I'm left alone? For good?'

Sheridan smiled, looked directly at him. 'Obviously that decision isn't mine to make, but honestly? I don't see why not.'

Tom sighed. He knew what Sheridan's words were worth. Had even been on the same training course that taught him how to lie to another person's face without giving himself away. The room felt claustrophobic, suddenly. Like he was already jailed. 'When do I start?'

Blake stood up. Sheridan followed. 'No time like the present.'

And that was how Tom Killgannon ended up in HMP Blackmoor.

4

Five weeks before

It was late afternoon but the darkening sky made it more like night. The sea wind hit the cliff tops around St Petroc announcing the arrival of November. The St Petroc stone circle stood out against the flat horizon, dark grey on light. Lit only by the distant street-lights of the village, a sodium sunset on the horizon.

Two figures sat on a fallen stone, sharing a torch between them. The stone had been worn flat over the centuries. Local legend stated it was once used for sacrifices. During the madness seven months ago it almost had been. Now Tom and Pearl sat there, huddled close. For warmth only, they would have both said had they been asked.

Tom had something to tell her.

'So why have we come up here, then?' Pearl laughed. 'Crap idea for a date.'

Tom didn't know how to reply. He pretended he hadn't heard her. Nominally she was his boss at the Sailmakers Arms, the pub he worked in. But over the months they had become more than employer and employee. What that was hadn't been fully explored. They weren't lovers but they were more than friends. There was a connection Tom had felt only rarely. Once that might have delighted him. Now the thought scared him.

'Neutral ground,' he said. 'You know what the pub's like for gossip.'

She nodded. Their relationship was often a subject for speculation.

'So you've got something to tell me,' she said. 'That's what you said in the text. What's all this secretive stuff for?'

He sighed. Thought. Knew he had no option but to tell her straight. 'I've got to go away for a bit.'

She just stared at him. 'Got to?'

'Got to.'

'What d'you mean?'

He looked at the ground, checking for any remaining scorch marks in the grass from that night seven months ago. They were barely there. The seasons had covered them. He looked at her. She was very attractive, he thought. Slightly younger than him, dark hair kept quite short, intelligent eyes, a mouth ready to laugh. Trying not to let the recent past define her. She had become so important to his life. He didn't dare believe she would be thinking the same.

'I've got to go. You know my . . . background? How I ended up here?'

Pearl nodded. She was one of the two people he had told the truth to. The other being Lila.

'Well, as part of my deal with them I have to be on call. When they need me.'

'And they need you now.' Disappointment in her voice.

He nodded. 'They've got a job for me.' He turned to face her. 'And they want you to have a place in it too.'

'Me?'

'They've given me a cover story. I just need you to corroborate it for me. If anyone comes looking, you know.'

'Might that happen?'

'I doubt it. But don't worry. I've been in touch with an old mate. He's going to be around to keep an eye on things. Just in case someone comes around trying to poke holes in the story.'

Her eyes widened. She looked scared. 'What the hell's going on? What are you talking about?'

'It's just a precaution, that's all. Standard procedure, the way I used to operate. I'm being doubly safe. It's silly, really. But I have to tell you. Please say if you'd rather not be part of it and they can think of something else.'

'What is it?'

He told her. Blackmoor Prison. Noel Cunningham. His plausible cover story and her part in it. And how he would get it done as quickly as possible.

'I'll be back by Christmas. Promise.'

'You'd better,' she said, grateful for something she could cling to, 'or you'll get the sack. Busiest time.' She looked at the ground. Her voice became smaller. 'I need you there.' She tried to smile. It could have broken his heart. 'Isn't it dangerous?'

He shook his head. 'Not really. I just do what I'm supposed to, get out. Simple as that. It'll be fine. Honestly.'

She stared at the ground. He was sure she wasn't looking for scorch marks.

'Never trust anyone who uses the word "honest".'

'Good advice,' he said.

She shook her head. 'It's just . . . it's a lot to take in. It's . . .' Another shake. 'I don't know. It's like normal life has stopped suddenly. And now there's . . . this.' She looked up at him, eyes direct, locking. 'Do you really have to do it? Isn't there anyone else?'

'I don't know. I seem to be the best qualified, according to them. It's fine. The pub'll keep going.'

'It's not the pub I'm worried about.'

A wave crashed against the cliff behind them. The sea wind intensified. She moved towards him. Tom stayed where he was. She took his hand in hers.

'Tom . . .'

'Why do we have to meet out here? Where it's freezing? What's wrong with the living room or the pub?'

They both turned, hands dropping. Lila stood behind them.

'I asked Lila to join us,' said Tom. 'She needs to know as well. Both of you do.'

'Need to know what?' asked Lila. 'What's all this about?'

Tom noticed a slight buzz of anger on her words. Was that because she had had to walk all the way to the stone circle or because Pearl was here too? Or was it something else?

'You two announcing your engagement or something? Should I buy a hat?'

Lila sat down on the stone. 'Budge up, then. What's happening?'

'Come and join us,' said Tom. He smiled but it dissipated quickly. 'I wanted you here as well.'

'It's freezing.'

'OK, then.' He looked between the two of them. His gaze settled on Lila. 'I've told Pearl about this. Now it's your turn.' He sighed, hesitant, as if his next words would make something notional real. Both to them and himself. 'I've got to go away for a bit.'

It looked like something had juddered to a halt inside Lila. 'Why? Where?'

'It's . . .' He leaned forwards, concentrating on his hands rather than looking at either of them. 'You know who I am. Or who I used to be.' Lila looked like she was about to be told a loved one was terminally ill. Pearl looked like she'd just received the same information.

'I thought this might happen. I dreaded it, to be honest. And it seems I've got no choice.'

Lila stared at him. 'They're making you work again, aren't they? They've got you a job.'

He nodded. 'Undercover.'

'But you've retired. You told me that.'

'Yeah, I have. But I also told you that I have to be available when they want me. Price I pay for being left alone. After what happened here.'

'That's not fair. Tell them no.'

'I wish I could. I can't, it's not like that.'

'Just tell them . . .' Anger and sadness fighting it out with Lila. It looked like a part of her was detaching, drifting away. Tom found it heartbreaking to watch.

But you're coming back, aren't you? It's not going to be for long.'

Tom smiled. 'I'll be back as soon as I can. Believe me.'

'For Christmas?'

'A long time before then.' Hopefully, he thought.

'So where you going then?'

He told her. Everything he had just told Pearl. In as quiet and reasonable a voice as he could manage. Pearl watched Lila, checked her responses. Concern in her eyes.

Time passed. Eventually Lila looked up. 'They won't let you in without a cover story. Have you got one?'

'He has,' said Pearl. 'It's me. A customer overstepped the line and Tom had to put him right.'

Anger rose again in Lila. 'When did all this happen? When did you decide this and why didn't you tell me earlier?'

'Pearl's just found out now. I had to check with her first, make sure she was OK with it.' He glanced across at her. There was something heavy in that look. 'Not everyone would have agreed to it. Thank you.'

She shrugged, returning a gaze full of unsaid words.

Tom sat back. Looked at Lila. Reached for her hand. She pulled it away.

'No,' she said. 'Not yet. You don't get to do that yet.'

'D'you want to ask me anything?'

Tom could see Lila was angry that he had told Pearl before her. Even if he did need to discuss it with her first. And annoyed at him keeping secrets from her. 'Why didn't you tell me sooner?'

'It only happened this week. The plans were advanced before they brought me in. The cover story was already there. They just needed me and Pearl to fit round it. And I wanted to tell you in a place where no one could overhear. Both of you.'

Lila tried to take it all in. Didn't reply.

'You're still going to be safe, still living in the house. Nothing's changed.'

'Maybe I could move in as well,' said Pearl. 'Girls together. Might be fun. Or at least company. We could—'

Lila stood up.

'What's the matter?' asked Tom.

'Shut up,' she said.

'But—'

'Just shut up.' Tears welled in her eyes. She looked angry with herself for allowing that to happen. Tom knew she had felt safe, secure with him. For the first time in a long time. Possibly for as long as she could remember. And now, to her, this safety was gone.

Tom stood up too. Reached out to her. 'Lila . . .'

'Leave me alone.'

She turned and ran back towards the village, stumbling as her tears blinded her.

Tom and Pearl watched her go.

5

Quint stepped back, admired his handiwork. The tent looked sturdy. As deeply pegged as he could manage, it wouldn't take off at the first gust of wind. It might even keep out some of the cold, and the inevitable rain. It was the first time he had pitched a tent for years and he was rather proud of himself.

Slaughter Tor was near the south east of Blackmoor, all open land, rough rocky outcrops and at least one standing stone. Quint was always surprised when he encountered something like that. A part of the past intruding into the modern world, reminding people that for all their wifi, electricity and vehicles their lives were brief. But stone, that would endure. Or maybe it was just him. He didn't get out into the country much.

Not that there was much in the way of wifi or electricity where he was. Quint felt more alone than he had done in ages. He knew people came to the country for a break, for contemplation. But he couldn't have cared less. This wasn't a holiday, it was work. And until it was completed that was all he would focus on.

He had read up on Blackmoor in advance. On where and when he could camp and park. Campsites were to be avoided. The sight of a single black man in a tent was liable to arouse suspicion, if not at the time then afterwards. It was the way of remote places, of the kind of people they attracted. Hikers and campers liked camaraderie. Drinks and shared dinners, swapping stories. And they would overcompensate because of the colour of his skin against theirs, try to be extra chummy, show they weren't racist by inviting him to join. They wouldn't keep in touch, though. Holidays were one thing, the rest of their lives quite another. He had experienced it before, the casual racism of the middle classes.

So he kept himself to himself. It suited his temperament, suited his needs. Suited the work. He wouldn't crop up in the memories of other campers. He had enough provisions for a few days. He had pitched his tent well away from the roads, out of most people's sight. He could be alone and wait.

Quint walked up to the brow of the hill he was camped under, put his binoculars to his eyes, looked around. Smiled.

There it was. In the distance, but not too far away.

The prison.

6

'Killgannon. Get your things together. You're moving.'

Tom had barely slept so the words didn't wake him. As soon as he lay down on the narrow, uncomfortable bed the room seemed to get even smaller, the walls closing in. Fears ran round his head, fears he hadn't expected to experience.

The door is locked. What if there's a fire? Or some kind of catastrophe and I'm locked in here for ever? What if they don't let me out? Or I'm rumbled and they decide to teach me a lesson?

On and on, his doubts spiralling and deepening, until he stuffed the thin, lumpy pillow into his mouth and stifled a scream.

Everyone has a fear, a defining phobia. Heights, snakes, spiders, illness, whatever. For Tom it was confined spaces. Closed, locked spaces. He'd been claustrophobic ever since he was a small boy. When his sister had taken him on shopping expeditions into Manchester city centre he had hated getting into department store lifts. Expecting them to break down and become suspended tombs as the air ran out and no one came to save them. Crowding on to buses, trams or tube trains had been an ordeal, closing his eyes and holding his breath, blocking his ears and pretending to be anywhere but there. Even taking dares from other kids, to explore old, abandoned pipes and factories, in the wasteland beside the estate where he grew up. He'd always avoided it. But he didn't want anyone else to know, to see it as weakness, so he hit the first person to question his bravery, ensuring that no one else would.

Although he had tried to conquer his fear as he got older, his commando training brought it all back to him. On exercise with a full pack, trying to pull himself through caves and tunnels that he was barely able to squeeze inside without the pack. He tried to channel that fear, use it to motivate him, and hide from the others how terrified he was. Be a leader. And it had worked. This had taught him a valuable life lesson: no one knows what they're doing. Everyone just hides their fear and keeps going.

But now, after one night, those fears had returned. He wished he had never agreed to do this job. No matter the consequences.

It was too late for that now. As the prison officer stood at the door waiting for him, Tom struggled off the bed, his muscles aching from the prone calisthenic workout he had given his body instead of sleep.

'Get your stuff.'

'Where am I going? I only just got here.'

'This is the induction wing. You stay here till you've been properly allocated. Come on.' Sighing as he spoke. Just one more thing on his to do list.

Tom complied, gathered up his meagre belongings into bin bags once more, followed the officer out. Relieved to be stretching his legs, if only temporarily.

On the wing, the rest of the inmates were already up. Clad in regulation blue tracksuits, they were being herded to the kitchen to queue up for what smelled like the poor relation of hospital food and looked like slabs of beige stodge designed to keep them full, placid and pliant. Or that was the theory. Once served their meal they would take their trays back to their cells to eat. And wait to see whether they would be allowed out for the morning jobs or education.

Tom looked at the queueing men but didn't make eye contact with any of them. He didn't want to be seen as issuing a challenge. The men came in all shapes and sizes, mostly with short hair, some with arms and faces full of spidery, home-made tattoos. Drug-sunken features, always-alert eyes, fear hiding behind the threat of violence in every movement.

Tom was led off the wing and through the prison, pausing at every gate, facing the wall and waiting while the officer unlocked and then re-locked as they went. He walked along corridors in silence, the officer's attitude discouraging him from questions or small talk. He used the time to process as much about his surroundings as possible. Orient himself.

His training kicked in: mentally checking for angles where he could be attacked, hallways where he wouldn't be safe, vantage points where he could defend himself if he had to. Committing the layout to his memory, or as much as he could manage.

As they walked the prison became older, like travelling back in time. Walls turned from painted plaster to old brickwork. Light fittings and power points looked less integral to the architecture, more like later additions. The caging and gates they walked through looked over-painted, layered up to disguise and discourage any rust. Cell doors were heavily riveted, reinforced, immovable.

The officer led him up some metal stairs. Tom looked down to the level below. Netting partially obscured the view but he could see one or two tracksuited prisoners carrying buckets and mops, pretending not to be interested in this new arrival.

'Here we go.'

The officer stopped before a cell door, took out his keys. Tom glanced at the cell's whiteboard telling the name and number of the occupant.

'Cunningham.'

Really? Was it that simple?

The officer opened the door. 'Stand up, move away from your bed. Got some company for you.'

Tom was ushered into the cell.

'Your new home,' announced the officer.

Cunningham was on his feet. 'I said I didn't want to share. Want to be on my own.'

'And I want Beyoncé waiting for me when I get home. Can't always get what you want.'

Anger blazed in Cunningham's eyes. 'But I said—'

41

'Take it up with the Governor.' He walked back through the door, closed it behind him. The sound reverberated away to nothing.

Tom tamped down the rising fear inside him. Locked up again. He turned to Cunningham who was still staring at him.

'Who the fuck are you?'

7

Cunningham's fists were clenched, rage flaring. He was big, bulky. Thick arms, stout legs, but from the way his stomach undulated a few seconds after the rest of him, Tom guessed he hadn't been keeping up his exercise routine. His face was round and red, purple-veined, hair clipped short, stubbled chin, eyes black, deepset. Like an angry gooseberry past its best.

'I wanted to be on my own, too,' said Tom, unmoving, 'but here we are.'

Cunningham took a step towards him. Tom remained where he was. He was in better shape than Cunningham but didn't have his rage. In a confrontation that wouldn't necessarily be a bad thing. For emphasis he flexed his biceps, his chest. Cunningham didn't move.

The two stared at each other, Tom breathing quietly, Cunningham raggedly, wheezing. Maybe he'll die of a heart attack before he gets the chance to confess, thought Tom. Or even speak.

'Don't think we have much say in the matter,' he continued.

Cunningham didn't reply.

'But I've just arrived and I've been put in here. I'm on Enhanced. I worked hard for that. And I'm not going to lose it for anyone.' Tom opened his arms. 'So give it your best shot, big boy. Here I am.'

Cunningham stared, but Tom's words had penetrated. The fire burned out of his eyes. He looked away, round the cell. Trying to find some way to back down yet still save face.

'Just ... stay away from me.' The words gurgled out quietly. Drained away. Cunningham's mood seemed to have changed completely. Where there had been anger, all Tom could see was wariness, fear perhaps.

Tom regarded him quizzically, noting the change. As if Cunningham's anger had been a learned response from being inside. If in doubt, confront.

'But I still have the top bunk.' Sullenly, like a stroppy child.

Tom didn't want to argue. 'Your shout, mate. You've been here longest.'

Cunningham nodded, honour seemingly satisfied.

The Choirmaster Killer. That's what the tabloids had dubbed Noel Cunningham. And they had played that up in every photo they printed. Round faced, cherubic, like the stereotype of an overgrown choirboy. Living with his aged mother. Dressed and groomed by her, by the look of him. Pudding basin haircut and bow tie. Photographs published and studied. Everyone looking for evil behind the jowls.

Tom didn't recognise his new cellmate from the person the tabloids claimed he had been. It was as though being caught had stripped him of whatever camouflage he had used to exist in the real world, sloughing that skin, revealing the pathetic individual underneath. More damaged than dangerous.

He had started by abusing boys in a cathedral choir in Devon. A figure of respect in the local community, an odd one, but nevertheless thought of as harmless. Then children in the area started to go missing. The children were never from the choir. Too dangerous for him to do that. Too many questions asked. But the church did outreach in the local community. And that involved taking underprivileged kids away for weekends and during school holidays. Usually camping on Blackmoor. That was when he had first met them, sized them up. Moved in with a predator's cunning. Picked off the weak, the fragile, the not easily missed. From there, simply befriend them, see them back in town, tell them about other trips to Blackmoor if they were interested. Then take them away with him. Never to be seen again.

The local police eventually put together a pattern that trapped Cunningham. He admitted his crimes, confessed easily, but still refused to say where the bodies were. Or how many there were.

44

But he had always tried to be friendly with men who fitted Tom's description. Tall, rugged.

'Always looking for a father figure, according to the psychological profile,' Sheridan had told Tom. 'To replace the one he never had. You fit the bill. You should be just his type, so to speak.'

The tension in the cell had eased. Tom placed his bags on the floor, pointed to the wall. 'This shelf mine?'

Cunningham shrugged.

Tom opened his bag, began to unpack. It didn't take him long. Clearly Cunningham was on Enhanced too, having the privileges that came from playing along with the rules. Colour TV. Play Station. A shelf of toiletries. A framed photo of an older woman, smiling.

'That your mother?' said Tom, unpacking his own toiletries.

Cunningham nodded, grunted.

'She looks happy.'

Cunningham didn't reply. He had decorated the area round his bed with pictures torn from magazines and newspapers. They were all of beautiful boys who seemed younger than eighteen. Apart from their posing and pouting they had two other things in common. They had crude, swan-like wings drawn on their backs. And their eyes had been clipped out. They looked like dead-eyed angels.

Unnerved, Tom looked away, unpacked a couple of books, placed them spine out next to his toiletries. Took out some underwear, spare joggers, the shirt and suit he had been wearing when he entered the prison. Folded them all up, found a drawer for them. All the while Cunningham affected not to watch him.

Finally he took out a framed photo of himself and Lila, placed that on the desk by the bed. Cunningham became interested then, couldn't help himself. Tom saw him staring at the photo, unblinking.

'Who's that? Daughter?'

'Niece,' said Tom. 'She lives with me.'

'Does she now.' Cunningham didn't – couldn't – hide the leer on his face.

Tom stared at him. 'Yeah. She does.' The tone of his voice warned Cunningham not to pursue that train of thought. Cunningham complied. At least outwardly. Tom sat down on his bunk. 'How long you been here?'

Cunningham grunted. 'Six months. She looks very young.'

Tom ignored the comment. Wondered instead about the etiquette of asking other prisoners what their crime was. Before he could speak, that decision was taken away from him.

'What you in for, then?' Cunningham leaned forwards.

'Actual bodily harm.'

'How come?' Cunningham's expression changed. Like he was waiting to be told a story.

Tom obliged. 'I work in a pub. Punter got too handy with my boss. Had to be taught a lesson.'

Something crept across Cunningham's face. Tom couldn't describe it. 'How handy?'

'Very handy,' said Tom in a voice meant to discourage any further investigation. It didn't.

'You mean like trying to . . . you know?'

Tom didn't answer. Cunningham took his silence for agreement, became more excited. 'How far did he get?' Then he shook his head as if to dislodge the thoughts growing there. 'No, no . . . don't . . . no . . .' He looked up. 'Did he get his hands on her . . .' He couldn't say the words, gestured to his chest, mimed breasts. 'Did he?'

Tom stared at him.

'No,' said Cunningham, once more, to himself, 'No. That's wrong. Don't think it. Don't think about the, the dirty things . . .' His face contorted, struggling. He looked up, a lascivious smile in place. 'Then what? Did he force her down?' He clamped his hand over his mouth, eyes wide, as if he couldn't believe what he had just said. 'No, it's not right . . . You've been told, Noel, been told . . . you know what happens if you have those kind of thoughts . . .' His voice had changed. Become older, more feminine. He closed his eyes, shook his head once more. Leaned forwards, body rocking to and fro. Opened his eyes only when he had finished violently shaking his head. His voice dropped low, scared to say the next words aloud but also defiant. He gave Tom a long, leering smile. 'Did he fuck her?'

Years undercover had taught Tom to stay in character, play along with the target rather than impose his own values on a situation. Out of practice, he thought. He swallowed down his revulsion, tried to ignore the thought that this face was the last thing Cunningham's victims ever saw. Kept his eyes hard, his cover intact.

'No one fucks her but me. He learned that the hard way.'

His tone of voice had clearly been authoritative enough. Cunningham backed down from any more questions.

'What about you?' The ice was well and truly broken.

Cunningham made a noise that sounded like liquid gravel on the move, but Tom realised it was a laugh. 'You don't know me?'

'Should I?'

'You should. Famous, aren't I?'

'Tell me, then.'

'I'm a murderer.' Cunningham simpered, his eyes shining. Like a child trying to impress by saying the worst thing imaginable.

'Right.' Tom's face was as still as stone.

Cunningham looked deflated. Expecting a bigger reaction from Tom. 'Who'd you kill, then?'

Cunningham's features became evasive. 'Well, that's the thing. That's what they all call me. Murderer. Here. On the wing. Murderer.' Said in an angry whisper, followed by a giggle. 'Keeps them away from me. Let's me be on my own.' He did it again. 'Murderer ... Don't go near him, he might murder you too ...' Another laugh. 'They leave me alone then. Scared. Scared of me.'

Tom had seen the other inmates. Cunningham was deluding himself if he thought they were scared of him. He could imagine them leaving him alone, though. Too irritating to bother with.

'So you're not a murderer?'

Cunningham's expression changed again. Sharply. Tom couldn't gauge what it meant but something behind his eyes unnerved him. 'Oh, I'm much more than that. Much more . . .'

'Like what?'

Cunningham shook his head, a blissfully sick look on his face. 'You wouldn't understand. It's . . . you just wouldn't.'

He took his attention away from Tom, went back to the photo of Lila. Stared at it. 'You wouldn't understand . . .'

Tom's first impulse was to jump up, hide it. Then smack Cunningham round the head. But he tamped it down. Kept in character.

'So why aren't you on the VP wing?'

Vulnerable prisoners were housed on a separate wing. Usually child killers or paedophiles but not exclusively. Anyone whose life was in danger, a suicide risk or even an ex-copper, they were all put in there.

Cunningham smiled as if he knew something Tom didn't. 'Who knows? Maybe they want someone to hurt me here.' He leaned forwards. 'Are you going to hurt me?'

The sick light in Cunningham's eyes told Tom that he might not find that so unappealing.

Tom ignored him, took a paperback out of his bag, lay back on his bunk.

Cunningham just giggled.

Silence fell. Following his outburst Cunningham zoned out, sat slumped, staring at Tom's photo of Lila, a smile twisting the corners of his mouth. He began to sing to himself. Tom couldn't identify it but knew it was something holy. Something befitting an ex-choirmaster.

Tom tried to read but his mind was whirring too much.

8

Dean Foley closed his eyes. Tried to relax. Or relax as much as he ever could. Sentries were posted, screws paid off, no one could get to him. No one would dare. But still, the rational part of his brain was telling the other half that this would be the perfect opportunity to attack him. With his guard down. With everything down. The other half of his brain told him to chill. Enjoy it. He tried to listen to that side of his brain. But it didn't really matter. Because at present, a completely different part of his anatomy was doing the thinking.

He opened his eyes, looked down. Kim was doing a grand job. Working his cock with her mouth and hand like a pro, head bobbing up and down like she was nodding to the beat of something only she could hear. She was half in, half out of her prison officer's uniform, enough that she could pull it together if she needed to, but also enough for him to see her magnificent tits as she worked.

Or magnificent for in here. Maybe on the outside he wouldn't look at her twice. A five or a six, probably. But in here everything changed. In here she was a ten. Prison did that to people.

He felt his legs stiffening, breathing becoming harder, harsher. He was coming. Kim sensed it too, bobbed, pulled quicker. Building him up until he couldn't hold it anymore.

He came, gasping and grunting. Kim tried to pull away, get her face, her mouth out of shooting distance, but he was having none of it. He forced her head down onto his cock, pushed his body up towards her as he bucked and spasmed.

Eventually the wave passed and his body eased, moving his hand from her head. She fell backwards, red-faced, gasping for breath, chin and mouth wet. He looked down at her, slumped with her tits hanging out, anger, shame, self-loathing in her averted eyes. Christ, what did he see in her? Was she really the best he could do?

He knew the answer to that one.

She stood up, crossed to the sink, rinsed her mouth out, began to gather her uniform around her.

'How's Damon doing?'

'Fine,' she said.

'Did you get him into that special school?'

She nodded. 'Thanks,' she said, eyes not going anywhere near his. 'For the money.'

He sniffed, sat up. Wiped himself off with a tissue, pulled his jeans back up. 'When you next on?'

'Got two days off. Back on Thursday.'

'See you then.'

She crossed to the closed cell door, knocked. It was pushed inwards from the outside. She stepped over the threshold and was gone.

Foley stood up. Got his breath back, sniffed once more. 'Baz.'

The door opened and a young man stepped inside. In another life he might have been good-looking but not in this one. His face looked like it had suffered severe punishment. His nose had been broken so many times it looked like a useless appendage. His skin was flecked with healed cuts and scars and there was a strange symmetry about his features, like one side was a perfect but unnatural mirror of the other. Despite the damage his once handsome features could still be glimpsed underneath. His face was a roadmap of where he had been, the underlying handsomeness the path not taken.

'Close the door,' said Foley, sitting down in a wooden chair.

The cell was well-equipped. A large screen TV in the corner, curtains at the window. The mattress and duvet were a long way from standard prison issue and there was framed artwork on the walls. It wasn't very good art, all landscapes and sunsets, but it was original and it was all signed in the bottom right corner: D Foley.

Baz stood, waited.

'Everything alright out there?'

'Yes boss.'

'No problems while she was in here?'

'No boss.'

'Good.' Foley relaxed. But only slightly. Baz was the best right-hand man he'd ever had. But in prison everyone was vulnerable to attack. 'How's business?'

Baz crossed to the table the TV stood on, emptied his pockets. Grubby, creased, screwed-up bank notes fell out, a few coins. He straightened the notes out, piled up the coins. Foley looked across.

'Hardly worth bothering. But every little helps. The next shipment should be in a couple of days. Keep it quiet, I don't want anyone getting tipped off again. Hopefully we've scared off the opposition.'

Controlling the supply of drugs in a prison was like controlling the air they all breathed. Everybody wanted it so there was a demand, which was good. But nearly everybody had a way of getting it, which meant there was more than one method of supply, and that made Foley's job even more difficult.

Supply was easy, especially with drones cutting out the hassle of the mules, no longer running the gauntlet of sniffer dogs and body searches, but as he knew, it meant anyone could do it. So if he was to hold on to his monopoly he had to do it the old-fashioned way. Put the fear of God into them. God being him. And Baz his representative who carried out the Lord's work.

When he arrived he had let it be known that he was in charge. And if anyone didn't like that they could challenge him. But he came inside with money and favours owing and challengers were few and doomed. Now it was well known that no drugs entered

51

the prison without his say so. But that didn't mean everyone stuck to that rule: he still had to get his foot soldiers to teach a lesson or two.

He looked at the pile of money. It was dwindling, no doubt. It always got like that before a new shipment came in. And then it was boom time again. The fact that the prison was privately run helped Foley immeasurably. The entry requirements for these officers were lower than state ones and they consequently attracted a lower quality of officer. Easier to manipulate, bribe. Corrupt.

It was no bother to have a hole cut in a security fence and send one of his runners to the perimeter to pick up packages droned and dropped there. The private officers didn't have the training or the pride in their work. It was easy to get them to look the other way. Or just to have stuff droned right to the cell window. Even better.

Foley had contacts all the way up the North West to Manchester, which meant he was able to source and supply high quality product. Demands and tastes changed. He was happy to accommodate them. Where it would have been heroin and weed a few years ago, now it was spice, black mamba and the bastard daddy of them all, annihilation. Super strong synthetic cannabis, that didn't just mellow you out, it sent the user on a psychotic trip. True escape for the mind, even if it was often difficult to come back from. They weren't called zombie drugs for nothing.

Yeah, it fucked people up, but so what? Foley only cared about profits. And that was something he needed now, more than ever.

A knock on the door.

Both Foley and Baz turned. Foley stayed where he was but Baz moved to the side of the doorway, fists ready. They shared a look. Foley nodded.

'Yeah?' said Foley.

'Someone to see you.'

'Who?'

A pause. 'Says his name's Clive. Got something for you.'

Foley frowned. Did he know a Clive? He searched his memory. Clive . . .

The only Clive he knew was some greasy little scrote from Oldham.

Foley sighed. 'Send him in.'

The door opened and a hunched little weasel of a man entered. 'Hello Mr Foley,' he said, hands wringing as if holding a cap in Dickensian times, 'how are you?'

'All the better for seeing you, Clive. What d'you want?'

Clive smiled, missing the sarcasm. Then he noticed Baz. Frowned, trying to look beyond the ruined face. 'I know you, don't I?'

Baz stared at him. Unnerved, Clive turned back to Foley.

'I've . . . I've got something for you, Mr Foley. Something you're going to like very much.'

'What?' A statement rather than a question.

'Well. You'll never guess who I've seen coming into this prison . . .'

9

The cottage was small, but Lila thought it felt even smaller when Tom wasn't there to share it with her. Stifling, even.

She had been studying stuff like that in her Psychology A Level at Truro College so she knew why it was. The same reason that unhappy people don't become miraculously happy when they move somewhere new. They don't change as people. They just take their unaddressed problems with them. That was how it was without Tom to distract her. She was alone with herself and her thoughts. Her doubts, guilt and fears. And they grew to fill the space. Or the space contracted around them.

That was why she had been so angry when he announced he was going away. Or one of the reasons.

Things had calmed between them before he left. She began to accept what he had to do. Knew he was only doing it reluctantly. He also knew how much he had hurt her by having to go. But he had no choice and deep down she knew that.

So now she was alone. She hadn't really made any new friends at college. Unsurprising, given what she had been previously. The fact she had turned her life around to attend college at all was astounding enough. Tom had encouraged her to think that what she had endured wouldn't happen again and she could look to the future with confidence. She wasn't sure she believed him – or that he believed it himself – but she was trying. And struggling. Her peers at college all seemed so happy and sure of themselves, their world, their place within it and their life maps, unaware that things could take a sudden turn for the worse and those rock-solid beliefs could come crashing down. She couldn't be like them, think like them, feel like them. 'Just do your best under your own terms,' Tom had said. 'And if you're worried about not fitting in, just pretend you do. That's what they're all doing. You might not think it but they are. Everyone does it. If there's a secret to life, that's it. Fake it till you make it.' So she tried. It had been difficult. Now even more so in his absence.

Meeting Tom had changed her life. And, although she had felt she was being presumptuous, or even tempting fate, she had taken his surname for college enrolment.

'I never found out what your real one is,' he had said.

'Killgannon,' she had said, smiling. 'Like yours.'

He had understood.

She made herself a cup of tea, looked out the back window. Autumn had dismantled summer, leaving drifts of wilted leaves and carpets of rotten flowerheads around the garden. Leave it all on the ground, Tom had said. Good compost. Make things grow bigger and stronger come the spring. Lila had dutifully done so, watched as those beautifully lush green branches turned into spider scrawl against the heavy grey sky, waited for those green buds to return. But for now it was the quiet period before the end of the year and winter fully hit, the earth gone into lockdown.

The water boiled, the kettle clicked. She turned away, took a tea bag from the jar in the cupboard.

A knock at the door.

Lila couldn't stop the involuntary shiver that ran through her. No matter how comfortable she got in this place, there was always that threat of a knock at the door. It had happened to Tom. She feared that she would be next.

Another knock.

She turned, headed down the hall. Took a deep breath. Opened the door.

'Just me.'

Lila smiled in relief. Another bullet dodged.

'Hi Pearl.'

'I was just passing and . . .' Pearl stopped speaking. 'No I wasn't actually. I came to see you.'

Lila stood back, let the other woman through. 'I was just making a cup of tea.'

'Brilliant timing.'

They both made their way to the kitchen. Lila took out another mug, another bag. Poured in the water. Tea made, she took it to the table. Pearl had already taken off her coat, sat down.

'Thanks.'

Pearl was over ten years older than Lila, with dark hair where Lila's was mousy blonde, smart jeans as opposed to Lila's attempts to bring back grunge, and with a poise and self-confidence Lila thought she could never hope to emulate. But the woman was Tom's boss, perhaps more. And they had been through a lot together.

'How you coping?' asked Pearl.

'Fine,' said Lila, sitting down opposite her. While it was true that they had shared a lot, Lila was still wary of opening up to her.

'You heard from him?'

Lila shook her head.

'Me neither.' Pearl took an experimental sip of her tea, found it too hot, placed it back on the table. 'He said it might be difficult.'

They sat there in silence. Both, for their own reasons, not wanting to be the first to speak.

'Look,' said Pearl, 'That offer still stands. Me moving in here.'

Tom had asked her again before he left. She had told him she would be fine on her own. Neither had believed her.

'Did Tom ask you to come round?'

'He just wants me to keep an eye on you.'

Lila felt anger building inside her at Pearl's words. 'What does he expect me to do? Have wild parties? Get into trouble? Run away again?'

Pearl shook her head slowly. Her voice was low, calm. 'He was worried about you out here on your own. Just wanted to make sure you were looking after yourself.' She smiled. 'That you weren't just eating pizza and burgers and drinking coke all the time.'

Lila felt herself redden with a kind of angry amusement. 'He said that? Those words?'

Pearl laughed. 'Yeah. Is that code, or something?'

Lila smiled. It was the last thing he had said to her before he left. They had gone through the anger and heartache, tried to come out the other side and joke about it. No pizza and burgers and drinking coke all the time. And no boys in your room after ten thirty. Yes sir, she had replied, giving him a mock salute in response. 'That's all he said?' she asked.

Pearl shrugged. 'Something about boys as well.'

'Right.'

'I didn't think you needed to hear that bit.'

'It's OK. He's already given me that speech.'

'Right. But how are you holding up, really?'

Lila took a sip of tea. It was still too hot but she wanted to drink it anyway. A psychological thing, she thought. 'OK. I'm used to looking after myself.'

'I know you are. But that's not what I meant. And I don't think it's what he meant, either. He just wanted to make sure you felt safe here.' Pearl paused, looked straight at Lila. Hoping her unspoken words would be understood.

They were. Lila had been in trouble when she met Tom. And despite his insistence that those troubles were gone, she still woke up screaming at the things she had done to gain her freedom. The nightmares had become less and less frequent as time went on, but they hadn't completely left her alone.

'I'm OK,' said Lila then felt something else was needed. 'But thank you.'

'No worries.' Pearl looked round the kitchen, clearly thinking. She found her tea, drank. 'Listen. I've been thinking. Instead of you being here on your own, you could move into the pub with me.'

Pearl looked at Lila expectantly. Lila said nothing. Pearl continued. 'There's plenty of space since Mum and Dad moved out.'

Pearl tried to keep her voice as neutral as possible while she said those names, but Lila knew what kind of pain was behind those words. At that moment she felt a kind of kinship with her. A sisterhood of pain and disappointment. Of being let down by those you should have been able to trust absolutely.

Pearl continued. 'I mean, you're on your own with no one to talk to—'

'I want to stay here. This is my home. This is where I live.'

Pearl nodded. 'Fair enough. OK. I understand.' She looked round the kitchen once more. 'But you know, it's not just you. On your own, I mean. I am as well.'

Lila looked at her curiously.

'I miss him. Lots.' She reddened. 'He's my friend too, you know.' She placed a strange emphasis on the word 'friend'. 'And it's lonely in the pub without Mum and Dad around. And him especially.'

Lila knew what she was saying. For the first time since she had met this woman, Lila felt as though she understood her.

'I said I don't want to move into the pub.'

Pearl nodded. 'Right. Sure.' Head downcast.

'But . . . you could move in here if you like.'

Pearl looked up at her. Smiled.

Lila felt her own cheeks redden. 'I mean, just while he's away. For company. And that. You know. Like you said. Safer together.'

'That's great. Girl's nights in. Drinking tea, watch Netflix. Whatever.'

'You'll be lucky to get Netflix here,' Lila told her. 'We barely have electricity.'

Pearl laughed. 'Thank you. Look, I know you're still not sure about me, for whatever reason, because of what happened, and yeah, I understand that. But . . .' She sighed. Continued. 'We're on the same side. Always have been.'

Lila looked at Pearl over the table. Remembered what Tom had said about looking to the future with confidence, trusting things to grow again.

'It gets cold. Better bring some warm jumpers. And some wood for the burner.'

Pearl smiled. 'Deal.'

'And some boxsets.' Lila smiled too. 'Got to find some way to fill these long dark winter evenings.'

'You can count on it.'

They both drank their tea. And chatted. Like new friends just getting to know each other.

10

The doe was lined up perfectly. Grazing, away from the rest of the herd, which was usual in this cold weather. Just walking in the woods, coming in and out of the trees, head down looking for food. Then a few quick upward jerks, around, left, right, then, satisfied she was alone, back to foraging.

Quint had spent most of the morning waiting. He had built a blind for himself out of ferns, twigs and branches. Now he sat inside, unmoving, barely breathing. Wearing his weather-resistant camo gear. Just watching. Waiting. Like he had been trained to do.

Looking down the Schmidt and Bender scope atop his Tikka TX3 Hunter. Perfect in low light, which was all there was in this winter forest, even in the middle of the day. It had a range of nearly half a kilometre and he was well practised in its use. Nothing escaped him when he was hunting.

He looked at the deer once more. Lined her up in his sights. That thin black cross, its apex coming to rest on her neck, then moved up ever so slightly, gently, to rest on her head, just behind the ear . . . a clean shot – only one – and it would be over for her. The sound would ring out around the forest, scare away birds, other deer, but it would echo away to nothing. Fading as quickly as the deer's life. Just one shot.

His finger tightened on the trigger.

Just one shot . . .

He took his finger away. Breathed in deeply. Not today. She was lucky. She would live. Go back to the herd, her children, oblivious to how close she had come to the end of her life.

Quint still watched her. Observed her movements. A hunter could learn more about their prey by watching them than by killing them.

It made the conclusion of the hunt more satisfying, more complete. A single bullet wasn't always the correct way to do things. Each hunt was individual, it called for an individual kill. Some called for involvement, some for distance. Some led to that incomparable feeling of emotional nourishment, others, unfortunately, not. Most of them didn't, if he was honest. But that didn't stop him hunting. It just made that rarefied high all the more intense when he finally experienced it. And that was what drove him on.

Sometimes, like today, it wasn't necessary to kill. It was enough just to know that he could, that the power of life and death was within him, to use when he wanted to.

A gust of cold wind blew through the forest, moving debris on the forest floor, the branches in the trees. The doe looked round, suddenly skittish. As if sensing her own vulnerability she turned, moved quickly back to the rest of the herd. Quint took his eye away from the sight. Looked up. Rain was on the wind, slanting in towards him, hitting him side on.

He stood up. There was nothing else to be gained from sitting here now. He had proven his point to himself, and anyway, the moment was broken. Slinging his rifle over his shoulder, he walked back to his tent.

He completed his security tests to ensure no one had tampered with anything. He examined his motorbike. No one had touched it. He walked all round the tent, checking that the patterns of branches and twigs he had arranged hadn't been disturbed. They were still intact. Then finally he opened the tent. Inside was everything he needed to survive in the wild. The large metal box was still locked. He took the key from around his neck, opened it, inspected its contents. Two handguns. One assault rifle. Ammunition. It was all there. And a manila folder on top. He took the folder out, lay the contents on the bed. Two photographs with names attached. He placed them side by side, studied them.

Pearl Ellacott.

Lila Killgannon.

He nodded to himself, gathered up the written information that went along with them. Read it once more, familiarising himself with it. Then, once he was sure it had sunk in, he picked everything up, put it back in the file, placed the file back in the box and locked it.

The rain hit the outside of the tent like hard pellets fired from an air rifle. Quint was hungry. Thirsty. He took out the camping stove, went about making himself something to eat and drink.

Once more way of measuring out time's passing.

11

Night fell early in prison, at any time of year. The thick, brick walls and tiny barred windows on Tom's wing made daylight's attempts to penetrate feeble so its absence wasn't greeted with much fanfare. If it hadn't been for a certain shift in the attitudes of the inmates, the passing of time would have gone unnoticed. Even in the short while Tom had been inside he had noticed it. The same shift animals feel at the zoo after the visitors have stopped staring and left. A collective stillness, not calming or tranquil but tense, coiled. A tightening of muscles, a hardening of features. Eyes looking beyond what could be seen. The inevitable realisation that, assuming you'd been allowed out of your cell that day, your tiny bit of freedom was about to be taken away. The cell doors would once again be locked, and you would be back on the wrong side. And when the lights went out, the talking stopped, the cries and shouts died down, you would lie there, locked in the even deeper prison of your own head, alone with only your thoughts, emotions and fears for company.

Tom understood why there were such high rates of mental illness amongst prison inmates.

He looked out of his cell window. Blackmoor stretched out onto the horizon, uninviting and bleak. The perfect place to build a prison. Just looking outside was an escape deterrent. A challenge: *think prison's tough? Get out and come and meet me.* A direct counterpoint to his claustrophobic cell. But no less frightening.

He turned away. Cunningham lay on his bunk. The cell door was open and out on the wing other inmates were having their evening association time. Tom had decided not to join in.

The day had been all about his induction. Tom, as part of a group of new inmates, had sat through lectures and presentations about prison rules, behavioural guidelines, visiting information and the courses that were on offer. Cleaning, cooking, business accounting, none of these appealed to him. He filled in a questionnaire for the education department listing his qualifications and what he might want to study while he was there.

The irritating inmate from the sweatbox, Clive, had been in Tom's group. He had tried to attract Tom's attention, nodding and waving. Tom had replied with a stoic nod, but Clive persisted. He contrived to sit next to him through it all.

'Thought that was you, Thor. How you settling in?'

'Fine.'

'What wing you on?'

'Not sure yet.' Something about the man made Tom not want to trust him.

'I'm on Heath.' He shrugged. 'Not bad. Least it's one of the newer ones.'

Tom said nothing. Clive, trying to break the silence again, looked down at the questionnaire Tom was filling in.

'Know what you want to do, mate?'

'What?' Tom hoped his irritation was showing.

'Put down art. That's a good one in here. Lot of privileges attached to that. Trust me, it's worth it.'

Tom just stared at him.

'It's good, mate, makes the days go quicker. Very therapeutic. And there's competitions. National ones. You can win things. Get out for the day. Get some decent food.'

Tom ignored him. Put down astronomy instead, looked at Clive, a challenge in his eyes.

Clive couldn't look directly back at him. His eyes dropped away. Tom relaxed, placed his pen on the table. Clive quickly picked it up and, too fast for Tom to stop him, ticked the box for art on Tom's questionnaire. Tom stared at him.

Clive gave a simpering smile. 'Trust me, you . . . you'll want to do it.' Nodding, desperate to be believed.

Tom didn't know what Clive's game was but didn't have time to do anything about it. The questionnaires were collected. Clive slunk away back to his own seat.

'See you later,' he said.

Tom stared at him, wondering what had just happened.

Rounding the day off was a visit to the prison chaplaincy where a vicar talked to them. He had short grey hair and a wide smile on his weathered, suntanned face. His shirt fastened at the cuffs but didn't hide his tattoos or his well-muscled frame. Ex-army or ex-biker, was Tom's guess. He explained about religion in prison, how all the major ones were catered for. Tom knew that. Also knew how inmates had miraculous conversions if it meant extra time out of their cells on Sundays.

After that Tom was returned to the wing. With Cunningham away doing whatever it was he did during the day, Tom went back to his cell. He tried to make use of the time, so he went through Cunningham's belongings. There wasn't much there. Toiletries, clothing, underwear. All prison issue. A couple of well-worn tabloids left on his bunk, crosswords attempted with letters heavily gone over and altered. No books or magazines. No notebooks, diaries, letters. Nothing. Tom had more stuff with him.

He lay back on his own bunk, thought of home. Of Lila and Pearl. Hoped they were looking after each other. Tried not to miss them too much, told himself it wouldn't be long before they saw him again.

Tried to make himself believe it.

Tom turned away from the window. Cunningham still lay on his bunk, eyes staring at his wall of angels, lips moving with words only he could hear, reciting prayers or hymns to them. He looked again at the open cell door, went out on to the wing.

It was what he had expected it to be. Victorian, he guessed. All worn red brick and heavy metal pipes. Small barred windows looked out onto darkness. The top level that he was on was separated by a metal walkway and landing. A net strung between it and the ground floor.

Men milled about in grey or maroon joggers and sweats, chatting with others. Broken features, wounded eyes hardened with cataracts of fear and violence. All sizing Tom up, giving him a provisional place in the wing hierarchy.

Someone nodded at him. He nodded back. Another couple looked up from the game of cards they were playing as he passed. One bald and covered in tattoos crafted by an artist more enthusiastic than talented, the other tall with greying blonde dreadlocks.

'Just got in?' the tattooed one asked him.

Tom nodded. 'Overnight yesterday.'

The dreadlocked guy looked towards the cell Tom had just left. 'Put you in with him, have they? Moaning Myrtle?'

'What d'you mean?'

They smiled between them. The dreadlocked one's teeth seemed to have been assembled from other people's cast-offs. 'You'll see. Well, you'll hear.' Another look round then as if by secret, tacit agreement, Tom was asked if he wanted to join the game.

'Yeah.' He pulled up a chair, sat with them. He wasn't a natural card player, had always dismissed it in the army as a waste of time, but he knew how important it was now. Bonding, sizing each other up. Isolation on the wing could be dangerous.

They asked him questions, he stuck to his script. He asked them questions in return and received equally rehearsed replies. Life stories edited down to short stories, learned off by heart. Painful pasts minted into polished anecdotes. He didn't learn anything of interest but it did him no harm to mix.

He watched the steady stream of inmates queuing to use the wing phone, wondered whether he should call home as well. Decided not to. Lila would be missing him. He was missing her too. And he didn't think it would help to be reminded of the outside world. Not just yet. So he stayed with the card players.

Eventually it was time for lock-up. They all got up, and with a minimum of argument, went back to their cells. Tom did the same.

The door slammed shut. Echoed away to nothing. Tom sat down on his bunk.

'Where'd you go?' asked Cunningham.

'Onto the wing for a look round.'

Cunningham grunted, turned towards the wall.

'Didn't want to join me?'

Cunningham grunted. 'Nothing out there for me. Nobody I want to talk to.'

'Because they're scared of a murderer?'

Cunningham didn't answer.

'Just thought it might pass the time. Make things go quicker.'

'Things don't go quicker or slower,' Cunningham told him. 'Things are what they are.'

Tom detected a quaver in Cunningham's voice. He dismissed it, picked up his book to read.

'I'm going to read till the lights go off,' said Tom. 'Goodnight.'

Cunningham didn't reply.

It wasn't long before the cell was in sudden darkness. It took Tom by surprise, but Cunningham audibly gasped. His breathing became heavier, more agitated. Tom closed his eyes. Tried to go to sleep.

The whimpering and sobbing woke him. He had no way of knowing what time it was, how long he had been asleep. From the uncomfortable position of his neck and the heaviness of his eyes, he didn't think it had been too long. Cunningham was thrashing about on the bunk above.

Tom had no idea if the other man was asleep or awake but he knew now why the other inmates had called him Moaning Myrtle.

Tom closed his eyes, tried to ignore him. But all he could hear was Cunningham's crying, his pleading with whoever was in the dark with him to go away, leave him alone.

Tom again tried to tune out.

As he eventually drifted off into a disturbed, uncomfortable sleep, a thought struck him: how long would he be in here before his own night terrors struck?

12

The cold cut through Tom as he made his way along the tarmacked path. He pulled his sweatshirt around him, turned up the collar on his cheap denim jacket. Mist had settled all around. He could barely see as far as the razor-wire-topped high fences, certainly no further. The prison looked foreboding and abandoned. A sprawling old mansion ripe for a haunting.

He was amongst a group of prisoners being escorted to the education block, ready for the day's lessons. Two officers hurried along with them, clearly wanting to be done as soon as possible, to get back on the wing with a hot cup of tea inside them. The weather stopped much conversation. Tom liked it that way.

Most of the men he had seen and spoken to the night before were there. He seemed to have been accepted by them, or was at least on friendly nodding terms. Good. He didn't need any unnecessary complications.

The dreadlocked guy, Darren, walked alongside him.

'Moaning Myrtle keep you awake?' he asked, displaying his random teeth.

'You could say that.'

Darren laughed. 'Say the word, mate, and he's taken care of.' He tapped the side of his nose. 'For a price, mind.'

Tom tried to smile. 'I don't think it's come to that. Yet.'

Darren shrugged. 'Whatever. You'll get a good night's sleep, 's'all I'm saying. Important thing in here.'

Tom smiled. 'I'll bear that in mind.'

They walked on.

Cunningham had woken up before Tom, although Tom hadn't had much sleep. A combination of Cunningham's night terrors and

Tom's claustrophobia had seen to that. It seemed like he had only started to drift off as the thin morning light began creeping through the barred windows. And the cell was so hot. He had thought he would be cold initially, seeing how sparse the bedding was, but he had figured without the heating. He knew it wasn't done out of concern for the inmates' welfare, it was at that level to keep them pliant and docile. Same with breakfast: Tom had never eaten such poor quality, carb laden food in his life. Even in the army.

'Sleep alright?' Tom had asked Cunningham, hearing again in his head those screams, expecting what the answer would be.

Cunningham merely grunted.

Tom persisted. 'Not a morning person?'

Another grunt. Cunningham swung his legs off the bunk, farted, made his way to the toilet. Tom turned away towards the window to give him some privacy, and also because the smell was atrocious.

'Where d'you go during the day?' asked Tom. 'Education?'

'Business Studies. Accounting. I'm good with numbers. On Sundays I go to church. I sing in the choir.'

'Right.'

Cunningham finished his ablutions, flushed the toilet. Didn't wash his hands, Tom noted.

Tom was also aware that Cunningham was avoiding looking at him directly. His night terrors, thought Tom. He knows I heard it and he's waiting to see if I'm going to mention it, make something of it. Tom had already decided that if Cunningham introduced the subject Tom would talk about it, but he wouldn't bring it up himself. Cunningham was making every effort to avoid it.

And now, thanks to weaselly Clive, here he was on the way to his first day as an art student.

The education block was a brick building of indeterminate age but certainly well into the last century. As they approached the officers looked at one another, smiled, then one of them turned to address the group.

'Lot of new faces here, who's just arrived?'

A few grunts, small hand gestures in response.

'Let's go this way, then. Quick detour, bit of history.'

Instead of letting them into the main entrance, the officers led them over to a door on the left that looked as though it led into another building. A couple of the inmates raised their eyebrows, knowing what was coming next.

They were taken through a heavy wooden door which was then locked behind them. Tom felt relieved to be out of the cold. The relief was short lived.

'This way.'

They were led through another door into a circular room with a tall vaulted ceiling with wooden beams and supports. Stacking chairs and flat tables were piled against the walls, showing that it was a storeroom. It had once been white but it seemed no effort had been given to its upkeep. It felt colder than – or just as cold as – the outside. The wind sang a mournful, plaintive song through gaps in the walls and roof. The officers kept the lights off.

'Think yourself lucky,' the first officer said, 'that you were never here earlier. Because this is where you'd have ended up, probably.'

Tom immediately knew where he was. Something more than cold chilled him.

Some of the other inmates weren't as quick as him. They looked confused.

The other officer spoke. 'This is where, until fairly recently, certainly in my lifetime, the executions were carried out. Hangings.'

'The topping shed, we call it.' The first officer took over, unable to keep the relish from his voice. 'The gallows stood here,' he said, pointing to the centre of the room, 'took up most of the space. The condemned man would be marched along, through the door you all came through, into here where he'd stand in front of it, looking at it. Just him and the chaplain, if he wanted him. On his own if he didn't.'

'And the executioner,' continued the second officer, 'would stand at the side here, ready to throw his lever when his victim was in place. He'd walk up to the middle there . . .' He pointed, his gestures becoming as expansive as a tour guide's. '. . . have his hood put on him, and then . . . bang.'

'The trapdoor would open and he'd be gone. Neck broken.'

'If he was lucky.'

'Yeah. If he was lucky. If the executioner had worked out his weight correctly and the height of the drop, otherwise he'd just hang there, slowly strangling and choking to death.'

From their tone it was clear which method the officers preferred.

'Anyway,' the first one said after a pause, 'count yourselves lucky we don't do that anymore.'

'Even though it mightn't be a bad idea.'

'Very true.' They both laughed. 'But we can't stand here reminiscing about the good old days. These gentlemen have to get to their classes.' The final word a sneer.

There was silence all the way to the education block.

The art room was surprisingly large. The walls were covered with artwork of variable quality, but most of it was better than Tom had expected. Their teacher, Mike, a small, middle-aged man wearing grey overalls, greeted them all and guided them to their workstations.

'Got some new faces, that's nice.' His voice was soft, non-threatening. 'Brushes are over there, pencils there, paper there. Let's stick the radio on, enjoy yourselves while you work. I'm here if you need to ask anything.'

The regular inmates made their way to a block of files at the back of the room, took out their work to continue. Mike came over, stood next to Tom.

'New here?'

'Yeah,' said Tom.

'What you interested in, then?'

Tom looked around. There was another delivery of men from a different wing. Just a couple this time. Tom studied their faces then looked around for Clive. Annoyed that he had made him come here. He couldn't see him.

'I don't know. I've never done this before.'

Mike smiled. Began to explain the mediums he could work in, the styles he might like to try, the subjects that might inspire him. 'We get a lot of lads want to draw landscapes, the outside world. Then take them back to their cells, give them something pretty to look at. That's popular. Or if you want to bring in a photo of a relative or loved one, a son or daughter, perhaps, do a portrait of them. Anything like that. Have a think.'

Tom said he would. He thought of the photo of Lila, wondered if he should do a portrait of her. It didn't feel right, somehow.

He was thinking about it as the door opened and another lot of inmates were let in.

'Busy today,' said Mike.

Tom watched them enter, looking once again for Clive.

But Clive wasn't there. Instead Tom saw someone who he had believed he would never see again. *Hoped* he would never see again. Not living, anyway. Someone who hated Tom and had vowed to kill him if their paths ever crossed again. And Tom didn't doubt him. Someone who had forced him to move to a different part of the country, get a different name, lead a different life.

Dean Foley.

13

Tom wanted to stare, but he knew he couldn't give himself away so cheaply. He kept his face devoid of emotion, his eyes fixed on the paper in front of him. He picked up a pencil, twirled it through his fingers, made out he was thinking.

He stole glances when he could. Foley seemed to be well known. Mike scurried up to him, treated him like a valued friend. Guided him to his workspace, asked if he wanted anything. Foley behaved as if this near deference was what he was used to, didn't expect anything other than that. He told Mike he just wanted to get on with what he had been working on. Mike then brought his work over and set it before him. Foley looked at the half completed painting and with that Mike was dismissed.

Tom kept studying him. He was older than the last time he had seen him, obviously, but beyond that he didn't look much different. Perhaps bulkier, although prison often did that. Once one of Manchester's most feared drug barons. A man who was never attacked or challenged by his enemies, whose presence was so terrifying that he had the confidence to appear in public without bodyguards. A man who believed he had legitimised his empire, had respect, or the veneer of it, from the community at large. A man who was ultimately betrayed by one of his closest lieutenants when he was revealed to be a police officer working deep undercover. He still carried himself as if his empire was intact, as if his downfall had never happened. As if the person who had betrayed him wasn't at the opposite end of the room.

Tom doodled, making scratches on the paper, head down, his mind – his body – wanting to be somewhere else entirely but knowing he had to keep all his mental and physical receptors open. He was bearded now, his hair longer, but he doubted that would be enough to stop Foley recognising him. Not with a hatred that deep.

'Need inspiration?'

Tom jumped, looked up. Then quickly down again, hoping he hadn't attracted any attention. 'What?'

Mike. Hovering at Tom's side. Smiling, a pleasant, open face.

'I'm . . .' Tom's voice dropped too. If Foley didn't recognise his face he wouldn't miss his voice. Tried to disguise it, neutralise it. 'I'm just getting going. Yeah.'

'There's books over there,' he said, gesturing to a shelf on the other side of the room, the side where Foley sat. 'Different kinds. Landscapes, nature. Photos, all of them. Some of the class like to copy them to get going. Want to help yourself?'

'I'm . . . fine at the moment.' His words a whispered near hiss. Bent over, he made himself as closed off as possible.

'Well, if you're sure, I'll leave you alone. Anything you need, just ask.' Mike walked off.

He must be used to people talking to him like that, Tom thought. They were all prisoners, damaged men. He couldn't imagine anyone being pleased to be there. He pushed everything else from his mind, tried to think. Ran through possibilities as quickly, analytically, as his thumping heart would allow.

What was Foley doing in Blackmoor? And why was he in the art room at the same time as Tom? How big a coincidence was that?

Tom froze. The understanding, the answer to his question made his heart skip a beat. He couldn't believe it but it had to be. The question wasn't what was Foley doing there, it was what was he doing there? Or rather, how did he get there?

Clive.

That ratty little bastard. That's why he had so many questions for him when they arrived. He must have recognised him. Then told Foley.

So who was Clive? And since Clive knew who he was, why hadn't Tom recognised him?

He sneaked another glance at Foley who seemed to be in his own world, happily painting, a smile lifting the edges of his lips as he concentrated.

Tom wasn't fooled. He had seen that look before. Too many times. Up close. Masking what was really going on in the man's mind. Disguising his true intentions. Letting his prey believe they were safe before swooping unexpectedly, violently. Sometimes terminally. Then his face showed a completely different expression. The memory of which still unsettled Tom.

He looked at him again. The man was giving nothing away.

He risked another glance round the room, this time seeing if Clive was there. He wasn't. His absence just added weight to Tom's theory. He felt his anger at Clive rise, competing with his fear of Foley. Tried to tamp down both emotions. Fall back on his training. He couldn't let either of them get the better of him.

So he drew. At first he had no idea what he was doing, just making trembling marks on the paper. But gradually a picture began to emerge. A young woman's face, drawn from memory. Not brilliant or particularly competent, he didn't think, and perhaps the features were only recognisable to himself, but it was heartfelt. Honest. It was what was in his mind right now.

Hayley. His real niece. The one whose death he still felt responsible for.

He glanced up again, that familiar anger mixing with that familiar fear. Foley. He was the one who should be blamed for her death, not him. But that would be too easy, that would give himself a free pass from the pain his actions had caused. And it wouldn't help right now, in this place. So he put his head down again, worked.

Eventually the bell went. It had been one of the longest hours of Tom's life.

Everyone reluctantly stood up, began to tidy their work away. Tom didn't know what to do. Move first and be left waiting for the officers to arrive, mingling with inmates from other wings. Or be last, risking the possibility of attracting attention to himself, have all eyes on him as he dawdled. Perhaps even get a name for it. So he stood up when the rest of them did, tried to hide among the mass of prisoners. But there was a greater problem. To put his work away he had to walk past Foley.

Foley hadn't moved. Head still down, as though the room was his and he was waiting for everyone else to clear so he could have some peace and quiet. Tom edged past his desk, trying not to even acknowledge the man but at the same time not to make it obvious that he was turning his face from him.

He risked a glance as he passed. Foley's gaze didn't seem to have changed but Tom wasn't so sure. There was an infinitesimal flicker at the corner of his eye, like he had been looking but didn't want to be caught. The expression on his face remained the same. Or was the smile deeper?

Tom's stomach lurched. He knows, he thought. He knows it's me.

Hands shaking, he put his work away, made for the door where he tried to lose himself amongst the other inmates.

Soon their escort arrived and he fell in with the men coming out of the classrooms, going back to the same wing.

He didn't look back.

Once on the wing Tom, along with everyone else, was herded into the queue for lunch. Instead he went to the small glass office where most of the officers sat.

'Oi,' an officer said, behind him. 'You. Over here.'

Tom held up his hand. 'Just a minute.'

The officer didn't want to give up. Tom tried to make his body language unthreatening, but urgent. He kept moving towards the office. The officer inside looked up.

'I need to call my solicitor,' Tom told him. 'Now.'

14

He didn't get his call. Not until later the next day during association time. There were no special rules, no privacy. He had to queue
up along with everyone else, take his turn on the wing phone, put
in his PIN, remember the number he had to call and hope he had
enough credit. Since the mobile number for Sheridan had been
given as his solicitor the wing staff weren't allowed to listen in. But
that didn't preclude inmates. Not for the first time Tom wished he
had set the terms for this job. Or put up more of a fight not to take
it at all.

He had spent the rest of the day avoiding the education block,
keeping to himself during association time. The ever-present tension on the wing fed into Tom. Made him nervous, kept him tense.
Loss of face, loss of reputation was everything inside, so men concentrated to hear any slight against them, imagined or otherwise,
and make restitution for it. Violence and the threat of violence were
constant. A wrong look, a wrong word was all it took. Sometimes
not even that. A punch, a kick, a headbutt for no reason. Inmates
would hide behind their pad doors with homemade weapons, waiting to attack the next person who appeared. Didn't matter who.
And those attacks had to be avenged. If someone was the victim
of an unprovoked attack, they had to attack someone else or risk
looking soft, weak. It didn't matter who. The wing staff treated this
as any other day at the office.

After lights out, Cunningham experienced a new night's terrors.
But that wasn't what kept Tom awake. His claustrophobia hadn't
abated. He felt panic rise through the darkness. He had tried to reason it away, tell himself he was safer inside the room than outside.
But it was what – or rather who – awaited him beyond the door that

really kept him awake. The next day he stayed on the wing, even though it meant being locked up all morning. He thought he was safer in his cell.

He had tried to find something he could use as a weapon. He knew inmates could make weapons out of anything, like a malevolent episode of Blue Peter, but he didn't have any tools on hand to help him. No lighter to melt his toothbrush, push a razor blade into it. Or even better, two, side by side. Stripe an attacker, make the wound harder to stitch back together. No paperclips either, or blu tack. Same principle: break down the paperclips, sharp edges out, push them into blu tack, carry it between his knuckles like a scared suburbanite would a car key. Swing a punch, make a lot of painful mess. Especially if he aimed for the eyes. But he had nothing like that. A hot cup of tea overloaded with sugar was useful when flung in an attacker's face: the sugar helped the heat stick and burn. But he couldn't carry that around with him all day. So he stayed in the cell, only venturing out to use the phone.

He dialled the number, waited. Looking around all the time, trying to work out who Foley could have contacted, paid to do him damage. Who was avoiding eye contact, or whispering, trying not to look at him. Any other time he would have thought he was being paranoid but he had spent enough years undercover to know that there was no such thing. Paranoid feelings had saved his life more than once.

The phone was answered. 'I've got a problem,' said Tom, trying to keep his head down, turned away from the majority of inmates, his mouth covered just in case anyone could read his lips.

A sigh at the other end of the line. 'What?' DS Sheridan's exasperated voice. 'I thought I said no communication until you'd got what we needed.'

'As I said, there's a problem.'

'Well it's down to you, then. You have to make Cunningham talk. So work round it.'

'It's not about Cunningham.'

'What then?' Sheridan couldn't have sounded more bored and irritated if he tried.

Tom put his mouth even closer to the phone. Covered the side of his face with his hand. 'Dean Foley.'

'Can't hear you.'

'Then listen closer. Because I'm not going to speak any louder. Dean Foley. He's in here. And he's made me.'

'So?'

Tom tried to keep the anger and desperation out of his voice. Struggled to keep calm. 'Read your fucking case files, Sheridan. Find out why him and me don't get on. Then you'll see why we have a problem. A bloody big one.'

Silence. When Sheridan eventually spoke there was no hint of his earlier irritation. 'You sure about this?'

'Why have I got a new name? Why did I go into hiding? Dean Foley.'

Another sigh from Sheridan. Tonally different. 'Shit.'

'Yeah. Right.'

'You sure he's made you?'

'Definitely. And you need to get me out of here. Now. Otherwise I won't be coming out. Ever.'

'Leave it with me. I'll see what I can do.'

Tom felt that anger, that desperation rise within him once more. 'That's it? That's your answer?' He grasped the receiver so hard his knuckles turned white. 'My cover's blown and I'm in danger. Don't you understand? We've got to abort. Now. Get me out.'

Tom became aware of someone standing next to him. He looked up. One of the inmates from the art room was standing next to him. Staring at him. Tom stared back.

'You goin' to be long?'

'Solicitor,' said Tom, mouth suddenly dry.

The inmate gave him an intimidating, unblinking stare.

'I'll be as quick as I can be,' said Tom, not backing down but not wanting trouble.

'I'm waitin' as well. Don't be a cunt.'

Tom turned. There were several people behind him. All watching to see what he would do next. He turned back to the receiver. 'Just do it,' he said. 'Get me out.'

Without waiting for a reply he put the phone down, broke the connection. Turned to the inmate. 'All yours.'

He walked slowly back to his cell. Aware all the time of the others around him.

He needed to get out. He needed to find a way to speed up his job, gain Cunningham's trust, get out. He needed—

'Alright, mate?' Dreadlocked Darren.

Tom looked up, reverie broken. 'Yeah, fine.'

Darren scrutinised his face. 'Look tired, mate. Myrtle keeping you awake?'

'No it's . . .' Tom looked at the cell, knowing Cunningham would be in it. Looked back at Darren. 'Yeah. He is.'

Darren smiled. 'Want me to do something about it? Cost you, mind.'

'What?'

'Twenty Marlboro. Going rate.'

Tom looked round, checked no one was listening. 'Come over here. Let's talk.'

15

Dean Foley wasn't, by his own admission, a subtle man. Or an overly cautious man. That wasn't to say he was an unintelligent man. Quite the opposite.

Many of his enemies had thought that, given his temperament and proclivities, he was some ignorant Neanderthal who only knew to strike out. How to hurt, not to think. They had used that assumption against him, underestimated him. They were no longer around to rue that mistake.

He preferred to think of himself as Alexander the Great faced with the Gordian knot. Taking a sword to the most complex puzzle, splitting it down the middle, moving forwards. He knew that some would be surprised he even knew who Alexander the Great was, let alone what he had achieved. He had been to school once. And seen Hollywood films. A couple of people had laughed and pointed out to him that Alexander the Great had been gay. They too were no longer around to contemplate their error of judgement.

So when he saw the man who was now calling himself Tom Killgannon in the art room, he did not confront him. Foley was, in his own mind, responding the best way he knew. Injuries came later. Thinking came first.

He sat slumped in his armchair, watching daytime TV. Endless property programmes, shows about moving abroad or to the country. He would have dismissed them as care home viewing before but now he was inside. If he was honest with himself, he was becoming hooked. Colour images of long white beaches or rolling, bucolic countryside. He even liked the interiors. The freedom to walk from the living room to the kitchen then out onto the patio. Imagining himself taking a long, leisurely stroll round spacious interiors with the presenters, sometimes thinking of stopping off in one of those bedrooms too. Those presenters were tasty. Young, fit, enthusiastic. But that was secondary. It was the homes he'd grown to love. He'd gone as far as to paint them, hang them on his cell wall.

Looking away from the screen and the paintings around the rest of his cell, and that familiar depression would hit once more. The weight of where he was. Yes, he had everything he could possibly get in here but he was paying for it. And the money wouldn't last for ever. He knew that. He just hoped it would be there for as long as he was here. He was never going to be released. He just had to make everything as enjoyable as he possibly could. But he knew he would never be able to walk round some spacious country house and call it his own. He'd never drink wine in the kitchen or lounge, potter around in the garden, feel the sun on his face. Not anymore. And that hurt. Those feelings could curdle into anger. Well now he had someone to take it out on.

Tom Killgannon.

The beard had been a surprise. And the long hair. He had always been close cropped, ex-army. Now he looked as though he'd been living in the wild since they last met. But the eyes were the same. He couldn't hide them. That green. Overly sensitive for a muscle-bound thug, showing a depth of intelligence that was rare in the people Foley dealt with. That was why he had recruited him. Knew him to be more than just a physical threat. And he had been right. Tom Killgannon quickly rose up the ranks of Foley's empire until he was one of his most trusted advisors.

Tom Killgannon – ridiculous name – Mick Eccleston was the name Foley knew him by. And the fact that Foley's empire went down so hard and so fast, was all down to Eccleston's testimony. After the trial, Mick had disappeared. He had tried to look for him, spent money and manpower on it, used every contact on any side of the law, but Mick Eccleston was nowhere to be found. The man was a ghost. Then he discovered Mick had a sister. And that

Mick wasn't his real name. He kept the sister under surveillance for months, thinking he might contact her, but no. Nothing. Eventually Foley began to believe he was dead, so successfully had he vanished.

He remembered the conversation they had the night Mick betrayed him. About crossing Foley, about running. About revenge. About digging more than two graves. Foley smiled at the memory. This was more than just revenge though. He believed Mick had taken something belonging to him. And now he had the perfect opportunity to ask him where it was. And yes. Revenge. He smiled. Too good. Too good.

He deliberately hadn't said anything in the art room. He knew Mick had recognised him. He had watched him surreptitiously, taking great pleasure as his expression changed from near boredom to abject fear. Mick had even walked past Foley while he was painting and Foley, so good, hadn't even looked up, acknowledged his presence. Perfect. So now he would be back on his wing, terrified of what Foley was going to do next.

A knock at his cell door.

'Who is it?'

'Baz.'

'Come in, then.'

Foley flicked the remote at the TV, turning the screen to black. The young man with the wrecked face entered. Foley looked up at him from his easy chair. 'What you got for me?'

Baz began to empty his pockets on the table, taking out crumpled notes, coins. He smoothed out the notes, stacked up the coins. Stood back, waiting for his handiwork to be admired. Foley looked at it.

'Jesus, that it? New shipment not arrived yet?'

'Any time now. We're making do with what we've got, stretching it as far as it'll go.'

Foley took the money, pocketed it. Sat back, regarded Baz once more. 'Got a job for you.'

'Yes, Mr Foley.' A statement, not a question. Baz would do whatever was asked of him, he was a good, loyal soldier.

'Is Kim on today? Can't remember.' Before Baz could answer Foley continued. 'Doesn't matter. If not her, one of the other ones. Skippy'll do.' He leaned forwards, wrote something in a notebook, tore out the page, passed it to Baz. 'I want him to find out everything he can about this bloke here. What wing he's on, what he's in for, where he comes from, everything. In fact just tell him to print off his file and bring it along to me. Can you do that?'

'Yeah, Mr Foley. Course.'

'Good lad. Oh, and be subtle. Know what that means?'

Baz nodded. Face impassive. 'Yes, Mr Foley.'

'Good. Then tell him to come straight back to me when he's got everything, yeah? Soon as.'

'Right, Mr Foley.'

Baz waited for his official dismissal then left.

Foley sat back, looked at the black screen, not wanting to put the TV on again. Not just yet. He thought of Alexander the Great, taking his sword to the Gordian knot. Yeah, he could have done that with Mick Eccleston or Tom Killgannon. Had someone take care of him straight away. Have him bleeding out in the showers or the dinner queue by now. But that wouldn't give him anything he wanted. Not the satisfaction he craved, and, more importantly, not the answer to his questions. And that, if he tried to look at the situation objectively, was more important. Or equally as important.

He sat back, smiled to himself. That was the thing about knots. You couldn't always cut through them. Sometimes the joy was in unravelling them slowly.

16

DS Sheridan stared at the screen on his desk. Didn't see what was on it. Instead he thought about the phone call from Tom Killgannon.

He looked over at Blake. She was sitting at her own desk opposite him, peering into something, reading glasses on the end of her nose. She wasn't given to displaying much frailty, knowing how difficult it still was for a woman to be treated equally in the police force. So this admission that she couldn't see perfectly was, Sheridan had always believed, a huge one on her part.

He hadn't told Blake or their superior DCI Harmer about the call. He had tried to, but couldn't decide on the best course of action. For both the assignment and Killgannon. He needed help to reach a decision.

He gestured to Blake. 'You busy?'

She turned round, closing her screen, taking her glasses off straight away. 'Why?'

'We need to talk to the boss.'

She frowned. 'What about?'

He stood up, looking round the office. 'Tell you in a minute. Come on.'

Keeping the frown in place she followed him as he knocked on Harmer's door, waited to be summoned, entered. DCI Harmer sat behind his desk. He looked like a squash player in a suit, or a well presented hedge fund manager, about as far away from the rank and file as it was possible to be. He also bore an unfortunate resemblance to a red-haired Muppet. Hence the nickname Beaker.

'DS Sheridan. DC Blake. What can I do for you?' He gestured for them to sit.

The office looked like it was waiting to be featured in Middle Management Monthly magazine. Sheridan imagined Harmer standing against a filing cabinet, file open in his hands, trophies and framed certificates in shot behind him, smiling sideways at the camera. His mass of red hair untameably unruly, undercutting the confidence he tried to exude. All he needs is googly eyes, thought Sheridan.

'Got a problem, sir.' Sheridan was aware of Blake looking at him, still frowning.

'What kind of problem?'

'The Killgannon assignment. Operation Retrieve. He's been compromised.'

'What?' said Blake.

Harmer leaned forwards. His action was swift but designed not to crease his freshly laundered shirt. His voice serious. No doubting he was a copper now. 'In what way?'

Sheridan addressed the two of them. 'He worked undercover in Manchester a few years ago. Infiltrated Dean Foley's gang. Got high up, the right hand man. His testimony put Foley away.'

'I know. And a shipment of money went missing, didn't it?' said Harmer.

'It did,' said Sheridan. 'But the drugs that were due to hit the street were all impounded. The money was never found. Foley swore he didn't have it. Didn't matter. We still made the case against him. Thanks to Killgannon's hard work. The whole network collapsed.'

'Commendations all round, yes. So what does this have to do with Operation Retrieve?'

'Foley's in the same prison as Cunningham, sir. And he's made Killgannon as the man who put him there.'

Harmer sat back, let out a stream of air, eyes narrowed, face pinched. It was as extreme as he got in showing emotion. 'Shit.'

'When did this happen?' asked Blake. 'Why didn't I know about it?'

'Phone call. Not so long ago,' said Sheridan, covering up the fact that it wasn't just immediate and he had been trying to decide what action to take and had not come up with anything. 'I couldn't tell you in the office. Sorry. Anyway, he says he thinks he was recognised, sold out to Foley.'

'Is he safe?' asked Blake.

'He doesn't think so. He wants to come out now.'

'What about Cunningham?' Harmer this time.

Sheridan shrugged. 'We'll have to try again later. Use someone else. Or get Cunningham transferred, take Killgannon with him.' He stopped talking, realising how ridiculous that sounded.

Harmer stared at the desk. 'All that work, all that planning . . .' He looked up. 'Why didn't we know this? Wasn't there a risk assessment done? Surely this should have been looked into. Rule one stuff.'

'Absolutely,' said Blake. 'It was done thoroughly. Then I went through the whole thing myself. Double checked. Nothing, no one was flagged.'

'I checked since I got the call,' said Sheridan. 'Current prison population for Blackmoor. Foley's been there a while.'

Blake looked between the two of them. 'I don't know how that happened. It shouldn't have happened. Seriously, there's no way that could have happened. No way.' Incredulity was giving way to anger.

Harmer sighed, shook his head.

'Look, I know this is all cloak and dagger and stuff,' said Blake, 'And we have a strict set of guidelines to comply with before putting an operation like this into motion. But could someone have hidden Foley's name from us?'

'Why?' asked Harmer.

'I don't know. Is there some reason he wouldn't show up? Is he some kind of asset? Something going on above our pay grade, perhaps?'

'I don't know,' said Harmer. 'There shouldn't be. We'd have been told about it before we launched this operation. I'll look into it.'

'What do we do in the meantime, sir?' asked Sheridan.

'We've got to get him out,' said Blake.

Another sigh from Harmer. 'Let's see. How close has Killgannon got to Cunningham?'

'Physically very close. They're sharing a cell.'

'Brilliant. Perfect.'

'But Killgannon's in fear for his life now. Foley's recognised him. He's just waiting to see what he does next.'

'Who in the prison knows that he's one of ours?' asked Harmer.

'No one,' cut in Blake. 'We didn't want his cover blown or for him to be compromised in any way.'

'So you two are his only line to the outside world?'

'It's the way he's always operated, sir,' said Sheridan. 'He insisted we didn't change that. He's always got results in the past doing it this way.'

'So if we got him out, how long would it take to get someone in the same position with Cunningham again?'

'Killgannon is a perfect asset,' said Blake. 'Might take us months to find a replacement as good. But he's compromised.'

'And he might only have a small time to live if Foley gets to him. I've just called a couple of detective mates who know more about Blackmoor than me. Apparently Foley pretty much runs the place. He's still in charge of what's left of his empire, runs it from his cell. And no doubt he's got everything inside sewn up as well. It's his caged city. Killgannon's just a tenant.'

Harmer almost smiled. 'You should have been a writer, Nick.'

Sheridan felt himself redden.

Harmer steepled his fingertips. Thought. 'I say we keep him where he is,' he said eventually.

Sheridan and Blake exchanged glances. '*What?*' said Sheridan.

'We may never get a chance as good as this again,' said Harmer. 'Not this close. Not without a lot of work. Let's see what Killgannon can get for us. If he gets what we need and we get those locations sooner rather than later, great. We get him out.'

'And if Foley gets him first?' asked Sheridan.

Harmer sighed. 'It's regrettable, but . . .' He shrugged. 'He knew the risks. He's deniable. Like you said, Nick, no one but us knows he's in there. And Blackmoor's one of the privately run prisons. At arm's length from the Home Office if there should be a death. They could take the blame, not us. I'm thinking operationally here.'

'Or we get him out,' said Sheridan. 'Start again with someone else. Keep an asset intact to be used again.'

Harmer stared at the desk. 'No, we keep him in.'

Sheridan frowned. 'Sir?'

'Monitor the situation, get regular status reports, updates. If it looks like Foley's getting too close then we'll pull him out. Straight away. But we have to weigh everything up.'

'So what do I tell him?'

'To stay where he is for the time being. We appreciate his situation, but we're at too crucial a juncture to jeopardise the operation. If he does his job efficiently, he'll be out in no time.'

Would you like to tell him yourself, sir? thought Sheridan. But he said nothing. Instead he stood up, knowing he was dismissed. 'Right sir. I'll do that.'

'Good.' Harmer gave a smile. It was the kind Pontius Pilate would have made.

Blake was already out of the door and on the way back to her desk. Sheridan watched her go. He went back to work. Knowing that the next phone call he made to Killgannon he might be sentencing him to death.

17

Tom had tried, with his limited phone time, to contact Sheridan again but there had been no reply. It was like he was holding his breath. He was still here, in the cell with Cunningham, waiting for Foley to act. Waiting for Cunningham to talk. Waiting for something to happen.

Dinner time came and he and Cunningham queued up alongside everyone else for beige carbs. They stood with their plastic trays, plastic mugs. Not speaking to each other or anyone else. His senses were heightened because he knew what was about to happen. It was risky, but he felt he had no choice. He needed to demonstrate to Cunningham that he was on his side. That he could be trusted. And this seemed like the most direct way. And all it would cost him was a packet of Marlboro. Tom didn't smoke but he always carried a few packs with him. They were valuable currency in prison.

Darren came charging out of nowhere, swinging for Cunningham. This wasn't the kind of prison fight in films or TV. There was no warning, no build up. One second he wasn't there, the next he was. And he wasn't backing down. It was the prison way: get as many hits in as possible until everyone else stops staring and catches up, takes action against him.

The suddenness even took Tom by surprise. And he was expecting it.

Darren's fist connected to the side of Cunningham's head. Cunningham, almost too surprised to scream, held his arms up. Darren kept hitting. One side, then the next, not pausing for breath. Getting as much hurt in as he could.

Cunningham went down, curling into a foetal ball, whimpering. Darren stepped in to follow up. He brought back his fist, ready to transmit as much energy as he could down the knotted muscle of his arm and into his fist. And on, to Cunningham's head.

Everyone else, those in the queue, those serving, the officers standing around, stared, too shocked to move. Tom was the first to regain his composure. He stepped up to Darren as fast as he could, grabbed hold of his swinging arm, forced it down by his side.

Darren looked at him, confusion on his face, about to speak.

'Changed my mind,' said Tom, so low only Darren could hear, if the blood hadn't been pumping in his ears so much.

Anger blazed in Darren's eyes. He tried with his other arm to swing at Tom. But Tom was ready for him. He placed his foot behind Darren's heel, pushed him backwards. He was in mid punch, his body not expecting the sudden change of direction. He stumbled, fell backwards. Went sprawling on the floor.

Tom turned to Cunningham, tried to pick him up. 'You OK?'

Cunningham looked terrified, didn't seem to trust himself with words.

The guards had come to life and were piling on the prone body of Darren. Tom helped Cunningham to his feet.

'He needs medical assistance. Now.'

Guards escorted Cunningham away, found a seat for him to sit on, assess the damage. Tom held his hands up, he was no threat. The two men were hauled off separately, Darren kicking and screaming, swearing and cursing in Tom's direction.

Tom gave no resistance. Allowed himself to be led away.

That went about as well as could be expected, he thought.

He was taken to one of the wing classrooms, questioned by staff. He could hear Darren's cries echoing off the walls as he was led off the wing.

'What happened?'

Tom shrugged, made out he was as surprised as they were. 'Don't know. We were just standing in line and he comes straight for Cunningham. Starts hitting him. Hard. So I just . . .' Another shrug. 'Pushed him away.'

The officers stared at him, before going back to their office to check the CCTV, then their bodycams. Everything supported Tom's version of events. He asked what had happened to Darren. He had been sent to the seg – the segregation block. A spell in solitary might calm him down, they said. Eventually they allowed Tom to go back to his cell.

Cunningham was curled up on his bunk. He jumped when the door was opened.

'Only me,' said Tom, as the door closed behind him.

Cunningham slowly sat up. Looked down at Tom. The left side of his face was swollen and red.

'Have you had that seen to?' asked Tom.

Cunningham nodded. 'They said it would be fine. But it'll hurt tomorrow.' He sighed. 'Hurts now.'

'They given you painkillers?'

Cunningham nodded.

'Good.' Tom sat down on his bunk. 'Well that was a bit of excitement, wasn't it?'

Cunningham nodded. Still shaken.

Neither man spoke.

'Thank you,' Cunningham said eventually, voice small and whispery.

'No problem,' said Tom, aiming for lightness. 'What friends are for?'

Cunningham moved about as if agitated. 'Friends?'

'Yeah. We're stuck in here, with each other. We have to make the best of it. And that means being friends. Don't you think?'

Cunningham didn't answer straight away. The bunk started to move. Tom knew he was crying.

Tom lay back. This is what he was again, how he had to act, to live. He had used Darren, lied to him, given him extra, unnecessary hardship to contend with. And now he was lying to Cunningham, all to gain his trust and then drop him afterwards when he had what he wanted. Yes, Cunningham was a child murderer but he hadn't started out that way. His life had been shaped and twisted until he had become that. If someone had intervened earlier he might have been stopped. And now here Tom was, the latest in a long line of people letting him down when he needed help.

This wasn't who Tom wanted to be anymore. Years of being undercover had taught him to weaponise his humanity. Make friends, take lovers. Fake sincerity. Be liked by the right people. Like them in return. And then betray them. Walk away. Tell yourself it didn't affect you. Keep telling yourself that. Then do the whole thing again. And again.

He could truly hate himself for doing this again if he allowed himself to. But he had to keep going. Tell himself – as he so often had in the past – that the end justified the means. Try to believe it this time.

'She's an angel,' said Cunningham, breaking his reverie.

'What?'

'Your niece. She's an angel. I'm just looking at her picture now.'

He felt something inside him curdle. Swallowed it down. He hated to use the photo of Lila but if it got Cunningham talking, especially now, then he would. And worry about how it made him feel later. 'Is she now?'

'Yes. She's pure. Her hair, like angel dust . . .'

'And you like purity, Noel? Yeah?'

'Yes . . . purity. Children have it. It's . . .' Tom felt him moving about on the top bunk, getting in to his story. 'Fleeting. You have to catch it, capture it. Then it's gone. So fleeting. But beautiful while it lasts. Oh yes, beautiful . . .'

'And what happens when it's gone, Noel?'

Silence in response. It went on so long that Tom thought he had asked the wrong question. But Cunningham had been weighing his words carefully. 'It's gone.' His voice had changed. Empty of creepy passion, devoid of anything approaching common human-ity. Like a different person had entered the room. 'Gone. And you have to dispose of it. You see, you take that purity, keep it, let it nourish you and then . . . it's no good. You have to get rid of it.' He laughed. 'I can tell you this, now that you're my friend. You can understand.'

'Right,' said Tom. 'And that's what you did, yeah? Got rid of the purity?'

No reply, but from the rocking of the bunk Tom could feel Cunningham nodding. Or at least he hoped that was what he was doing.

'And where did you do that?'

Cunningham gestured towards the window. 'Out there . . .'

Tom felt something shift within him. Like he was on to some-thing. 'Where in particular?'

Silence. Tom waited.

A sigh from the top bunk. 'I'm tired now. Want to go to sleep. Thank you for being my friend, Tom.'

And that was as much as Tom could get out of him.

18

Night in Blackmoor. And again Tom couldn't sleep.

The sounds of unhappy men drifted along the wing, slipping under the heavy metal door like ghosts on wires. Wailing, crying. Sobbing. Pleading. Other sounds too, harsher ones: calls to shut the fuck up, threats of what would happen if they didn't. Back and forth until they tired themselves out, wore themselves down until some form of sleep claimed them. At least some of them.

Tom didn't scream, didn't shout out. He kept his fear locked up inside. Now it was around two in the morning. Cunningham was engaged in his usual nighttime activity. Crying. Tom didn't need to hear the rest of the wing, there was noise enough in this cell. Cunningham had the same dream, or a variation of it, every night. Always apologising to someone for something. Sobbing that he was sorry. Tom knew he had a lot to apologise for.

'I'm sorry . . . sorry, I . . . I won't . . . I didn't mean to . . .' Then breaking down once more.

All night, it seemed like. Every night.

Driving Tom mad.

Cunningham's constant confessing was getting to Tom in other ways. It made him think of apologies he wanted to make but knew he never could. Especially to Hayley, whose death he would always blame himself for.

His niece, the daughter of the sister who had brought him up in their mother's absence, had started running with a bad crowd, thinking it was an easy way out of her impoverished background, getting involved with a local drug dealer. One who worked with Tom's then target, Dean Foley. And it all came to a head the night that Foley had finally been arrested. Hayley had been where she wasn't supposed to be and had paid the ultimate price. And Tom, knowing it was his operation, blamed himself for her death, even though he hadn't pulled the trigger.

He hadn't been able to contact his sister during or after the trial; it was too dangerous for her. Foley's men were hunting him and he knew they wouldn't hesitate to kill her if it meant getting to him. So he stayed away. And now he was in Witness Protection. He had never spoken to her since. Something else to hate himself for.

It was a part of the reason he had taken Lila in when she was in trouble. Trying to avoid another death, another lost soul. But no matter how many people he helped, it would never remove the guilt. And Cunningham pulled that guilt into focus once more.

Tom tried to push it all to one side, concentrate on his mission. Tried to square the crying with what he knew of Cunningham's past.

'No, please, I . . . I . . .'

Tom sighed and swung himself out of bed. Enough.

'Hey,' he said, touching Cunningham on the shoulder, rocking him gently and trying to wake him. 'Hey.'

Cunningham jumped, startled, almost banging his head on the wall. In the darkness, lit only by the perimeter lights, Tom could see Cunningham staring ahead, eyes fixed on something he couldn't see.

'Cunningham . . .'

Cunningham jumped once more at Tom's touch. Kept staring ahead.

'Give it a rest, mate,' Tom said, not knowing what other words would reach him. 'I'm trying to sleep down here. Yeah?'

Cunningham didn't blink, just kept staring.

'You OK?'

Cunningham raised a pointed finger, aimed it at the shadowed corner of the cell. 'There they are . . .'

'What?'

'There, in the corner . . . can you see them?'

Tom turned. He could make out shadows on the wall. They were substantial, they had depth. It looked like two figures, one standing in front of the other.

'You can see them can't you? The choir?'

Tom blinked. The figures disappeared. Saw only the silhouettes of the chair and the desk. The outline of the TV against the wall. Cunningham's grinning, eyeless angels. He blinked again. The figures didn't return.

'It's the middle of the night. Your mind's playing tricks on you.'

Cunningham turned his head towards Tom. His eyes were lit by a strange, penetrating light. For the first time since he arrived, Tom was afraid of what his cellmate might be capable of.

'You saw them,' Cunningham said. 'I know you did. You saw them.' He pointed again, his hand shaking. 'They're here all the time. With me. They hide in the day but come out at night. They sing to me. My requiem. I can never get rid of them. Never. They won't go away . . .'

He screwed his eyes tight shut. Tom saw tears squeezing from the corners. He looked again into the corner of the cell. Saw nothing out of the ordinary.

'Hey mate,' he tried again, 'get some sleep. You're not alone here and they won't get you while I'm here.'

Cunningham slowly turned to look at him once more. A desperate kind of hope in his wet eyes. 'You . . . really? Protect me?'

'Yeah, sure.' Tom hoped he wouldn't regret what he was saying. Knew he was taking a chance doing this. Didn't know which way it could go. 'Go to sleep. I'm here.'

'Thank . . . thank you . . .' Cunningham's words sounded so pathetic. He laid himself down again, breathing heavily. 'You don't know what this means to me . . .'

'Just go to sleep.'

It took a while, but Cunningham eventually did. Tom lay there, feeling revulsion at having befriended the man, or having pretended to. But he had done it for the assignment. And more importantly, so he could get a good night's sleep.

Except he couldn't. He lay there listening to Cunningham snore, staring at the corner, watching until those shadows dispersed in the pale morning light.

Trying not to let his own ghosts haunt him.

19

Quint could see why Tom had chosen the house he lived in. It had good vantage points on all sides, anyone approaching it would be seen. If they were watching.

Nestled in a bay beside the village of St Petroc, the house was one of a few dotted around a shingled slope that led down to the water. The bay itself was quite narrow, curving out to the sea, not wide enough for surfers, barely deep enough to launch any craft. A winding, steep, switchback road led to the cliff top. Anyone approaching came down very slowly.

The other houses were mostly summer holiday lets, appealing to urbanites who wanted the pretence of being cut off from civilisation for a week, the inconvenience of getting supplies in and the novelty of terrible wifi. They were empty at this time of year, adding to the haunted, desolate feel of the bay. The only house with any lights on was Tom's. The last house on the bay.

Quint had thought long and hard about how to approach it. He thought covert surveillance best, only to find precious little in the way of camouflage. He was sure his motorbike's engine would alert the house's inhabitants. So instead he stayed at the top of the hill, looking down, a discreet pair of binoculars pointing towards the house.

Dawn struggled to rise and the light within the house was a boon for him. He saw silhouettes move behind windows. Caught glimpses of two different bodies, making their separate ways sluggishly from room to room. He guessed they would be Lila and Pearl. The names in the file. They moved in together while Tom was away. That made sense. Quint could see why Tom would do that.

The front door opened and a figure emerged. Young, female, blonde. Lila, he thought. He looked round for somewhere to hide, realised there wasn't anywhere. He was exposed. If she looked up he would be seen. The girl began to walk towards the road.

He stowed his binoculars in a leather saddlebag, readied himself to put the bike into gear, ride away. Then looked down again. She had disappeared.

He checked on all sides. No sign of her.

Panic rose in his chest. An unfamiliar sensation. Usually he was the one that induced panic in others. Among other emotions. He thought quickly, tried to reach a decision. He would have to go. Come back later, find somewhere he could hide – construct it if necessary – and observe the house more fully. He still had his tent pitched on Blackmoor, perhaps he could bring everything over here and camp out? Would that be more or less conspicuous?

He didn't get any further in his thinking. Because there, right in front of him, was the blonde girl. Walking towards him. He immediately put his head down, trying to hide his identity from her, make out there was some mechanical fault and he couldn't get his bike moving.

She paused in her walking, looked at him. 'Trouble with your bike?' she said.

He looked up, couldn't avoid it. He had the visor of his helmet up. She saw his face and he saw hers. She was wary of him, suspicious even. He had to do something to counteract that, prove he was no threat. Act.

'Yeah,' he said. 'I'm camping down the road, I just came for a ride, was looking for shops, stopped for the view . . .' He gestured over the bay where the sun was rising. He shrugged. 'Then this happened. Must be the cold, or something.'

'Right,' Lila said. Her voice still unsure but giving his story the benefit of the doubt. 'You want to give it another go?

'Yeah,' he said. He took her in from the corner of his eye. Dressed in a parka and boots, a bag slung over one shoulder, files and books poking from the corner. College. Another quick glance round showed him the stepped footpath, cut into the side of the rock, the lonely looking bus stop she was headed to. 'I'll just . . .'

He put his foot down. Hard. The bike sprang into life.

'There you go,' she said.

'Yeah.' He smiled.

She didn't move.

'I'll be off, then.'

'Right.' She still hadn't moved.

He put the bike into gear, rode away.

Down the road, deserted at this hour, he glanced behind in the wing mirror.

She was still standing there. Watching him go.

20

Tom was too tired to get up. He had barely slept, only drifting for a couple of exhausted hours when the dawn arrived. Now, he just wanted to roll over, stay in bed all day. He didn't even mind having the door locked. At least he would be safer that way. Probably. But he had to get up. He was working, things to do.

He didn't want to open his eyes, though. Or his nostrils, for that matter. Cunningham was sitting on the toilet. From the smell, his body was in as parlous a state as his psyche. The lack of privacy, or dignity, was something Tom didn't think he could ever get used to. He had been in the army and was used to living up close to other men in regimented conditions, but this was worse. He tried to block out the groans Cunningham was making too.

Instead he retreated once more inside his own mind. Tried to think. Plan.

No news from Sheridan and no way to call him until later. He expected to be pulled out any second but until that happened he had to come up with a way to keep himself safe.

Clive. No surname yet, just that. And he didn't recognise him either. He had tried to place him, gone through as many faces as he could remember from undercover operations, villains he had crossed, but he came up with nothing. Yet it seemed that Clive knew him. Or knew who he used to be. And that kind of knowledge was currency in prison. He couldn't see any other way Foley knew he was here.

The art class. He was supposed to be attend again this morning. He couldn't risk it. If Foley said something, did something, it would jeopardise more than just this operation.

The cell door was opened.

'Breakfast. Up you get. Outside, line up.'

Tom threw back the covers, got up. He pulled his joggers on, slipped a sweatshirt over his head, laced up his trainers. His day clothes barely differed from his night clothes. And showers were a rare commodity on the wing. He had begun to smell like every other inmate. A mixture of poorly washed and dried clothing, cheap soap and sweat. Prison cologne.

He had a quick wash, still holding his nose, brushed his teeth, made his way to the door, looked out at the wing. All the other prisoners were lining up to receive their food from the kitchen. He joined the queue. Face as neutral, as slack, as possible, his eyes on full alert all the time. He didn't know if Darren had any friends on the wing who wanted retribution for what he'd done to him. And that was without the threat of Foley. The food smelt like bad school dinners. Tasted even worse. But it was that or starve. Again, he thought of the army and was unsurprised that so many ex-squaddies ended up in prison. There was little in the way of life-style adjustment to make. Only downwards.

Then he stopped dead. He hoped his expression hadn't changed but was sure it had. What he saw threw him off guard. There, about ten people ahead of him. Clive. Queuing up for breakfast.

Tom's mind whirled. Why was Clive on his wing? When had that happened? Must have been overnight. Why the move? Could be any reason. But he knew the main one: Foley wanted Clive to keep an eye on him. A few days ago he might have dismissed that as fanciful but not now. It wasn't a huge leap of the imagination to think that Foley could do something like that. He still had influence, power, money. Enough to pay off a few officers, for sure.

Tom could do nothing, say nothing. So he just pretended he hadn't seen him. Tried to look from the corner of his eye, see if Clive was watching him.

He reached the counter, chose his food, took it back to his cell to eat.

Cunningham came in after Tom, sat down, started to eat. The door was closed behind him.

'Another day,' Cunningham said, trying for a smile.

'Yeah,' said Tom.

Cunningham finished his food, placed the tray on his bunk. Stood up, hovered over Tom. It was clear he had something to say and Tom knew it had to do with his behaviour during the night. Tom said nothing. Waited.

'It's hard sometimes,' Cunningham finally said. 'You know. At night.'

'Yeah,' said Tom, as noncommittal as he could manage.

Cunningham sighed. 'It's hard.'

'Yeah,' Tom said again. He waited, wanting to grab Cunningham, scream at him: *Just tell me where they are!* But he didn't. Instead he said, 'Do you tell the psychologist about these dreams?'

'Sort of. No, not really. She might . . . I don't know. Laugh or something. Or send me somewhere worse.'

'She won't do any of that. Just tell her. She'll understand.' And hopefully make my job easier, he thought.

Cunningham nodded, said nothing more.

Tom turned on the TV. Breakfast television. Brightly painted presenters in a brightly painted studio. Compared with the drabness of the cell it hurt Tom's eyes. He blocked it out, tried to think.

Clive had forced him to put down art on his education choices. Or rather made the choice for him. But what had Clive put down? He had seen Clive's form. He tried to visualise the paper, Clive holding the pen in his hand. There were marks against certain subjects. If he could only remember . . .

He opened his eyes again. Got it.

The door opened once more. An officer stood there, clipboard in hand.

'Right. Killgannon, Art. Cunningham, Bookkeeping. Get ready, you're going now.'

Tom stood up. 'I've made a mistake. Can I change it?'

The officer stared at him, face impassive yet angry at the same time. The majority of them seemed to have perfected that look, he thought.

'Please,' Tom said. 'I'm not trying to cause trouble or make your life difficult. I've just put down the wrong thing. I went to art the other day and hated it. Can I go to the carpentry workshop instead? Please.'

'You're not supposed to change like that. You have to do it properly.'

'I know. But I don't know who to talk to. It's my first time in here. Please. I'm not messing you around. I've made a genuine mistake.'

Tom waited. If that didn't get through to the officer he would have to try another way. But he wasn't going to the art class today under any circumstances.

The officer sighed, looked at his clipboard. Erased a mark, made one somewhere else. 'Go on. Put it down to clerical error. Wouldn't be the first time.'

Tom smiled. 'Thank you. I appreciate it.'

'Get moving, then.'

He did.

On the wing the inmates were lining up, getting ready to go to their respective classes and workplaces. Their names and destinations were called out and they left with their officers. Tom saw Clive standing near the back of the line.

'Carpentry shop, this way.'

The group started to follow the officer. Tom stepped in with them, coming up next to Clive.

'Hello, Clive. Surprised to see you here. Changed wings, have you?'

Clive jumped. The colour drained from his face and it took him a few seconds to regain his powers of speech.

'What . . . what you doing here? You're, you're supposed to be going to art.'

Tom smiled. It was a lot less pleasant than the one he had given the officer. 'Change of plan, Clive old son. I'm doing carpentry now.'

'But . . . you can't . . .'

'Can't I?'

Tom moved in closer. Grabbed Clive's arm, gave it a squeeze. Clive winced.

'Going to be spending all morning together. I think it's time we had a little chat. Don't you?'

From the expression on his face, Clive clearly didn't agree.

21

The same two officers who had given the tour of the topping shed escorted them to the workshop. There was something different about their attitude, Tom noticed. As though they had been told a secret about him and it had changed their opinion. They weren't scared of him, but they were apprehensive. Tom couldn't decide if they wanted to rush him, or back away from him. But they were definitely watching him more closely.

On Foley's payroll.

His closeness to Clive on the walk was making them take even more note. Clive tried to telegraph his fear to them, show them in his eyes and body language that something wasn't right. Tom countered this by seeming as cheerful as possible. The officers were given no excuse to intervene.

As they walked, Tom noticed another inmate coming in the opposite direction. He was unescorted but that wasn't the most unusual thing about him. His face was covered in scars but strangely overly symmetrical. Like he had placed a mirror too close to one side of his features. He noticed Tom and Clive walking together. Clive just stared at him, as if silently begging him for help. The scarred man ignored him, kept looking at Tom. Then he smiled and was gone.

Tom tried to shake the encounter from his mind. He didn't know what had just happened but he knew it wasn't a positive development.

They arrived at a prefabricated hut. One of a number erected on a patch of land by the furthest perimeter fence. Some had been turned into offices, some classrooms. Tom entered with the rest of the group. Gave his name, number and wing to an officer inside, looked around.

It was like being back at school. Workbenches dotted the room, tools hung in locked cupboards on the walls, felt tip outlines of each so missing ones could be easily spotted. A couple of full-size lathes. The teacher wearing a grey overall, waiting for everyone to enter.

It was the same as the art room. The regulars went to their benches, took out their work. Went through the procedures to be given tools to work with. Everything counted off, ticks on clipboards. Tom, being new, didn't know what to do or where to go.

'You'll need an induction,' said the teacher. Sour looking, middle aged. Nose wrinkled as if perpetually smelling something unpleasant. Talking like he might expire before he's finished his sentence. 'There's always a few new ones every week. Just wait there till I've sorted everyone out with work to do.' His worn-out features and bitter eyes seemed to resent not only the inmates being there, but the officers and himself as well.

He walked off, made a cursory circuit of the room, nodded at what he saw then returned to Tom and the other two men with him. They were then given a tour of the room, had the machinery and tools explained to them, given warnings about what would happen if they misbehaved or even worse, misused the tools in any way. He asked whether any of them had experience of working with wood. The other two put their hands up. The teacher took them away, got them started. Tom was once again left on his own.

He saw Clive at the other side of the room, sanding down a small box. He checked to see if anyone was watching him. They weren't. He went and stood next to him.

'What you making?' Tom kept his voice as loud and cheerful as possible, as though he and Clive were old mates.

Clive had no option but to respond. 'A box.'

'I can see that.' Laughter from Tom, the funniest joke in the world. 'What kind of box?'

'For my granddaughter. Something for her to keep. To remember me by.'

'Nice,' said Tom, voice still loud. Then he let it drop. Moved in so no one else could hear. 'I know you're only a small bloke, but I mean. Bit tiny for a coffin, isn't it?'

Clive stared at him.

Tom, unblinking, kept on. 'I could work with it, though. If I had to.'

He straightened up, smile in place once more. Clive's eyes darted round, hoping someone had heard, but knowing they hadn't.

'So what's going on, Clive?' asked Tom, his voice as conversational as possible. 'You set me up with the art class. And you know who with. Now I'm guessing you're not bright enough to pull that one yourself. So why do it?'

'Don't know what you're talking about, mate.' Trying desperately not to look at Tom, concentrate on his box.

'Yeah you do. You filled in my form. And I know who you're working with. Or rather for. Want me to say his name?'

Clive said nothing. Just kept sanding away.

Tom bent in again, pretended to be admiring Clive's handiwork. Even pointed at a dovetail joint. 'You set me up. With Foley, Clive. Didn't you?'

No response.

'I'd go so far as to say that you recognised me as soon as I arrived here. That right?'

Clive kept sanding.

'Then you went straight to Foley, told him I was here. And Foley told you to get me to the art class. How'm I doing so far?'

'Nice . . . nice story.' Clive's voice as uneven as his handiwork.

'Yeah. Lovely. And then after that, Foley managed to get you sent over to my wing. Spying on me, Clive? Reporting back? Surely Foley could have got someone else to do that. I'm sure you're not the only one on the payroll.'

No response.

'But there's something niggling at me, Clive. You see, I could well believe you capable of all that. Well believe it. But here's the thing.

I've never seen you before in my life, Clive. I'd remember a weaselly little face like yours. Might have even slapped it around a few times. But I've racked and racked my brains and got nothing. So tell me, Clive, where do you know me from?'

Clive stopped sanding, looked up. 'You don't scare me,' he said, the words barely coming out in between swallows, his Adam's apple bobbing up and down so much it was quivering.

'Your voice says otherwise.'

'I'm protected. You're not. Not in here.' Voice stronger.

'You're only protected as long as you're useful, Clive. And at the moment you're useful. But only while Foley wants you. When that changes you'll be tossed aside. If you're lucky, that is. Might be worse. Then what'll you do?'

Clive stared at Tom. A weird intensity began to grow in his eyes. As though he was developing bravery.

'You haven't a clue, have you?' said Clive. 'Not a clue.'

'About what, Clive?'

'About what's going on here. About you. Not a clue.' He was on the verge of laughing. A giggling, unhinged laugh. 'Have you?'

Tom wanted to keep pressing, find something out, anything that would give him a clue. But his interrogation was cut short.

'Killgannon,' shouted a voice from the door.

Tom looked up, startled. 'Yeah?'

'Solicitor visit.' An officer had come to the door, a slip of paper in his hand.

Tom straightened up. His heart began to beat faster. This was it, he thought. He didn't have to question Clive about anything. That wasn't important now. All that could be dealt with later. When he was on the outside.

Because this was it. Sheridan had come through.

He was going home.

22

The officer left the room with a combination of reluctance and relief. Maybe he wanted to listen in, thought Tom, but it was too much to break those rules even for Foley.

The room they met in was part of the admin block, near the Governor's office, away from the main body of the prison and any ears or eyes. Solicitor meetings were private, but Sheridan had another reason for the secrecy. As a detective he was no doubt responsible for putting away plenty of the inmates so his cover would be blown the second he walked onto a wing.

Sheridan was already sitting at the desk. Files and briefcase in front of him. Props and set dressing for a solicitor. Tom pulled up a chair to join him. He tried to gauge the detective's face, but Sheridan kept his head down, looking at the desk.

'Thanks for coming,' said Tom. 'Glad you're taking this seriously.'

Sheridan nodded.

'So this is it, then? I'm walking out?' Tom allowed hopefulness to enter his voice.

Sheridan looked up. Tom saw his eyes. And hope died.

He knew that look from his time in the force. The expression an officer assumed to impart bad news. Usually when informing a relative of a death. But any bad news would do. Such as telling an innocent prison inmate his appeal had been turned down. Or an undercover officer that he had to stay where he was, even if there was a good chance it would lead to his death. Something like that.

Sheridan sighed. 'I thought it better if I came to see you, tell you face to face.'

Tom stared, quelling the conflicting emotions rising within him, keeping his voice steady. 'I think you've already said it. What the fuck is going on?'

Sheridan leaned across the desk, hands clasped. He looked pained, sounded sincere. If it was just his training showing then he was very good. But he looked like he meant it. 'It's not my decision. Honestly.'

'Yes it is, you're in charge of the operation.'

'There's . . . I talked to my superior. He wants you to stay. Thinks the threat isn't too great.'

'He's not the one inside, though, is he?'

'No, he's not.'

'He's not the one whose testimony put someone away for life. A someone who threatened to hunt him down and kill him. And the threats were taken so seriously I was put into witness protection. And now that person is here, inside with me. And he's running this place. And he could have me killed . . .' Tom clicked his fingers. It echoed round the room. Made him realise how low, controlled his voice was '. . . like that.'

'I know.'

'So why am I not out of here?'

'Because . . . they want you to make progress with Cunningham. That was the prime directive of the operation.'

'But I won't make progress with Cunningham if I'm dead, will I?'

Sheridan looked up, startled. Tom's voice had risen louder than he intended. Tom hoped no one outside had heard that.

He settled back, tried to regain control of his emotions. 'Will I?' he repeated.

'Look,' said Sheridan, hands raised in a gesture of useless supplication, 'I'm on your side. Honestly. I've done a few jobs like this in the past. Never on your scale, obviously, but I know what you're going through.'

Tom opened his mouth again. Sheridan cut him off.

'OK, OK, I don't know what you're going through. Not like this. But I can appreciate the pressure you must be under. And I argued your case. I honestly did. I don't think you should be here any more than you do. I want nothing more than for you to walk out with me right now. But—'

'Then do it.'

Sheridan stared at him.

'Do it,' said Tom. 'Stand up, walk to the office, flash your badge, tell them who you are, who I am and that this operation's been compromised. There'll be a bit of complaining on their part but they'll let us go. They have to.' Tom stared at him, unblinking.

Sheridan tried to return the stare. Couldn't. He sighed. 'I can't.'

'Why not?'

'You know why not. I'd be disobeying orders. I'd—'

'We've gone way beyond that.'

'I can't do it.' Sheridan's voice began to creep up in volume and shrillness. 'I'm sorry. I want to. If it was up to me I would. But I can't. You know the way these things work.'

'Yeah, I do.'

'So you'll know that I can't just stop it now. I don't have the authority.'

Tom stared. Deciding what to say next. Sheridan said nothing. Had nothing more to say.

'You know why I was so good?' Tom said at length. Sheridan didn't reply. 'At what I did. Working undercover. You know why? Because I knew when to dig in. And I knew when to get out. And my handlers respected that. They let me run things my way. Trusted me.' Tom leaned forwards. 'Trust. That's the main thing. That's why I was successful. Because I had trust from my handlers. They knew I was the one on the ground, risking my life. They knew I would do the best damn job I could. Get results. And they trusted me to do it. But they also trusted me when I said I had to be pulled out. If I said a job was going wrong and to get me out, I was out within hours. And that's the difference here. Trust. That's what these kinds of operations are fuelled on. And I'm getting fuck all of that from you.'

The words hung in the air. Time dragged, prison slow. Eventually Sheridan spoke.

'Like I said, I want you out of here. Right now. But I've been overruled. And there's nothing I can do. I'm sorry.'

'So you keep saying.'

'I know. And I wish I could do something more.'

'Then do something more.'

'I can't just walk out of here with you. You know that.'

'Then go and talk to your superiors. Tell them I need to get out. Not that it would be a good idea, not perhaps, tell them I *need* to get out. Or I will be killed. Tell them that. Then get me out of here. Straight away. Do it now.'

'I will. I promise. But . . .'

'No buts. Get me out of here. I'll try and look after myself until that can happen. But make it quick.'

'What are you going to do? How will you protect yourself?'

Tom thought of Darren. Of the scarred man who had stared at him. At the danger he was now in. An idea entered his mind. A stupid, desperate idea that might not even work. But he had nothing better. 'Leave it to me,' he said. 'Just go to your boss and get me out.'

Sheridan nodded, then stopped. Like something had just occurred to him. Something unpleasant.

'What?' said Tom, picking up on it. 'Something wrong?'

'No, I . . .'

'What? Something's going on. You've just thought of something.'

'No . . . leave that to me. I have just thought of something. Let me sort it.'

Tom stared at him once again. Trying to appraise Sheridan, work him out. 'Is there something you're not telling me, Sheridan?'

'Like what?' Sheridan seemed suddenly shifty.

Tom wasn't going to trust his answers. 'I don't know. But something's just occurred to you. And you're not going to tell me.'

'It's nothing.'

'Even if you think it's nothing, tell me.'

'If you can get a confession out of Cunningham that would be great. Your ticket out of here straight away.'

'Yeah. That's not going to happen overnight. Just get me out.'

'I will,' said Sheridan, resolve in his voice.

Sheridan stood up. 'I have to go. Please trust me. I'm working to get you out of here. In the meantime, do what you have to do to survive.'

'I always do.'

The officer escorted Sheridan out, another took Tom back to his wing.

No one tried to stop him, assault him, impede him on the journey.

Back on the wing he checked his watch. Dinner in a couple of hours.

Then he could put his plan into action.

23

Tom spent the rest of the afternoon banged up by choice. He had long missed lunch by the time his meeting with Sheridan had ended so he was given a cold coagulated mess on a tray to eat. It remained uneaten. He no longer had an appetite. Cunningham was off the wing, so he remained in his cell alone.

He couldn't read, saw only words dancing on the page, couldn't watch TV, saw only mouths moving but nonsense coming out. Couldn't do anything. Except go over the conversation he had just had with Sheridan, then think about what he was planning to do.

It was a ridiculous, stupid plan. And worst of all, it might not even save him. But it was that or nothing. And nothing would definitely get him killed. Whereas this could buy him a little time. Then it was down to Sheridan.

He was starting to warm towards the detective. He didn't think that would have been possible after their first meeting. Sheridan had been cold, arrogant. But that mask had slipped to reveal a conscientious copper trying to do his job as best he could.

Further thoughts were cut short by the sound of the key in the lock. The door opened.

'Dinnertime,' said an officer, walking away before the word was out of his mouth.

Tom stood up. Took a deep breath, exhaled. Another. Exhaled. Ready.

He stepped outside. The walkway of his upstairs cell was narrow, the metal steps downstairs to the food queue clanging and clattering with the footsteps of inmates all moving at once. He looked around, tried to catch sight of the person he wanted. Couldn't see him.

'Hello.' Suddenly Cunningham was by his side. Smiling.

'Hey,' said Tom, continuing to scan the wing.

Cunningham smiled. 'I've been thinking about things.'

Tom didn't reply.

'I've been to see the psychologist this afternoon.'

'Good for you.' Distracted, eyes on the crowd.

'And she says I should open up more. I told her about the night terrors, like you said I should.'

Had he? He couldn't remember.

'And she said I should talk to you about them. Especially if you're there to share them. I told her you'd been a friend.'

The word still jarred, even though Tom had used it first. 'Right.'

'Yes.' Cunningham was nodding earnestly, the smile still on his face. 'A friend. My friend. Because you stopped me getting hurt. And you helped me during the night. And we talked. Remember?'

'Right.'

'So she said—'

Tom was aware of a movement on the walkway above him. He looked up. There was the scarred man once more. Smiling the way he had that morning. But now he was joined by someone else.

Dean Foley.

As Tom stared, Foley cocked his finger and thumb, made a gun. Fired. Laughed.

Tom looked round, mind moving quickly. Message received and understood. He was in danger. Immediate danger. He needed to do something about it if he wanted to stay alive.

He looked again at Cunningham. The man had been about to say something. Might it be about the bodies? Could Tom risk it? And what would he do if it was? How would he get the information to Sheridan then?

Then he saw his target. Looked between the two men below, the two above, making his mind up on the spot. 'Just a minute,' he said and walked off.

Clive was lining up along with the rest of the men returning from the carpentry workshop. Tom pushed in alongside him.

'Oi,' came a voice from behind, a huge threat implied for such a small word.

Tom turned. 'Won't be a minute. Just want a word with my mate here.'

Clive's eyes darted round the room like a swallow trapped in a barn.

'Don't I, Clive?'

'We got nothing more to say.'

'We were in the middle of a conversation, weren't we? When I was dragged away. Now what were we talking about?' Tom pretended to think. 'Oh yes. You were telling me I didn't have a clue what was going on. Isn't that right, Clive? Yeah?'

Clive looked round once more. If he expected someone to come to his aid he was going to be disappointed. Others were curious about what was happening, but not enough to intervene.

'So tell me, then,' continued Tom. 'Tell me what I don't understand.'

'There's nothing.'

'Oh, come on, Clive. Don't be like that. You've gone all shy. Come on. Tell me.' Tom put his arm round Clive's shoulders, began to squeeze.

'Get off me. I'll call one of the screws over. I will.'

'Do it,' said Tom. 'Because I really don't care anymore. I've had enough of this place, of your shit. You think you're protected? We'll see.'

Clive turned to him, tried to squirm out of his grip. 'I am protected. But you're not.' That sick little smile again. 'Your days are numbered, mate. Numbered.'

'I know that. And I've got nothing to lose. Nothing at all. So if I'm going down, you're coming with me, Clive. Now tell me. What's going on in here? And why are you involved?'

'Oh, that's the thing that really annoys you, isn't it? You don't know me. You don't know what I'm doing here. You're so used to having everything your own way, having every angle thought out that you can't take it when that doesn't happen, when someone pulls one over on you. You hate it, don't you?'

Tom was really beginning to get angry now. He no longer bothered to hide it. 'Then tell me. Enlighten me.'

'Enlighten you? Oh, la di fuckin' dah. Enlighten you.' Clive laughed. Heads began to turn.

Tom felt his face redden with anger. He knew how this conversation was going to end but at least he could try to get something from it. He made one last attempt. 'Just tell me, Clive. What's going on. You've got nothing to lose. Just tell me.' Hoping that his raised voice was one of anger not begging.

Clive just giggled. Then, with a quick lick of lips, he stopped. Thought. And spoke. 'How's your niece, Mick? How's Hayley doing?'

Clive stood back, pleased with his retort. Even more pleased with Tom's reaction.

Tom staggered back as though he had been punched in the heart. Staring all the while at Clive who kept giggling, a small, frightened man enjoying his moment.

He cocked his fingers into a gun, pointed. 'Hayley,' he mouthed. And Tom lost it.

Part Two
ISOLATED

Manchester, 2014
Later that same evening, long into the night

Foley was finally alone.

The holding cell in the police station looked and felt exactly the same as it had when the teenage Dean Foley had been repeatedly banged up for finishing too many conversations with his fists. And for starting them that way too. He thought he had come too far to be back but clearly that wasn't the case. And he would have at least the rest of the night to decide how he felt about that.

His high-priced brief had been and gone. Arriving with his usual anger and arrogance, throwing profanities and threats around the interview room like grenades, telling the detectives they would just get up and walk out, that they had nothing. His usual tactics, but this time they didn't work. They just stared at him, watched the show. This noted, he shifted his approach. Argued his case, Clarence Darrowed himself through every loophole. Like the well-paid legal whore he was, thought Foley, he tangoed nimbly round every tenuous legal definition, contorted himself into every possible position to dazzle them. Nothing. He didn't scare them anymore. They had Foley bang to rights. His brief was a sideshow distraction. He could huff and puff as much as he liked, no way was he blowing their house down. Once he realised that he checked Foley was being looked after to the letter of the law and left.

No joy catching the eyes of his payroll boys and girls either. They wouldn't look at him, speak to him, from which he drew two conclusions. Firstly, they didn't want to give themselves away, secondly and most importantly, he was fucked and they weren't going down with him.

So, back in the cell, belt, shoes, watch, money, everything gone. Stripped of his assets. No special privileges. Alone. With only his thoughts for company.

Get used to the solitude, Mick had said through the flap in the door as he'd passed by earlier, you're going to have plenty of it.

He had shouted in return, given a full rundown on what he would do to him once he got out of here – and he would be getting out of here – then what he would do to his family and . . . But Mick was long gone by then. So Foley, spent and exhausted, slumped back down on the bench.

Now he had time to think. Plenty of time to think.

Mick Eccleston. Betrayed by Mick Fucking Eccleston. Betrayed.

'Betrayed . . .'

The word sounded overly dramatic spoken aloud. Like Shakespeare or Game of Thrones or EastEnders or something. But it was the right one. The only one. Betrayal. And by someone he trusted. No, not someone – the person he trusted more than anyone else. The one person he believed would never betray him. It was unreal. Like his life had skipped the rails and he was in some upside-down dream world. He wanted to wake up, for everything to go back to normal again. But that wasn't going to happen.

Betrayed by a man he had come to regard as a brother. Again, that sounded dramatic but it was true. His own brother – his real one – was long since gone. Spirited away into foster homes and adoption, where their father couldn't get at him anymore.

Dean had gone into foster care too, separated from his brother, because it hadn't been determined whether he had helped his father with the abuse or been trying to prevent it. But Dean didn't want to live in foster homes. Or with his father. So he set out on his own.

His mother had left when he was little. Well, not left, because he could never remember her being there much. Just kind of drifted away. He could remember her smell: dead flower perfume and economy gin. Her taste, when she pushed her face up against his and gave him a great slobbery kiss: sweat, hardened powder and thick cheap lipstick. He would always rub it away when she had gone. Remove any mark of her, open the door of any room she had been in to get rid of the fumes. She was always going out, always looking for something his father could never provide, she said. One night she went out and didn't come back. Nine-year-old Dean felt plenty of conflicting things about his mother. When she disappeared he just felt relieved, but mostly because his dad had told him that's what he should feel.

'Gone off with a fancy man,' said his dad at first. That changed over the years to, 'Gone to live in Spain', 'Went to see her sister and never came back', 'Just didn't want to know us no more'. It wasn't until years later that Foley realised his father had been interviewed repeatedly by the police about his mother's disappearance. Sweated for as long as they could legally hold him. Assaulted with telephone directories and rubber pipe in places that hurt but didn't scar. Then let go, only to be brought in again and again, whenever they thought they could turn the screws on him. She never turned up. Dead or alive. Being able to prove nothing, they eventually, reluctantly, left his father alone to get on with his life.

'Never trust the police, son,' his bitter father's bitter mantra. 'They're a bunch of cunts.'

Young Dean took those words to heart.

His father had plenty of other words for Dean too.

'You're fucking nothing. You'll always be fucking nothing.'

'Best part of you dribbled down your mother's leg.'

'Should have drowned you at birth.'

Years later, Dean had driven his Bentley to his father's house to show him what he had made of himself. His father wouldn't let him in. 'You're still a fucking nobody. Always will be.' Slammed the door on him.

He was the only man Foley couldn't hurt. So he hurt everyone else instead.

Dean Foley was an angry kid. He made that work for him. Eventually he learned how to channel it and became an effective, angry man.

His empire was quickly built. And he needed a right-hand man.

Enter Mick Eccleston.

Mick was perfect. Hard when he had to be, clever when he had to be. Deaf, blind and dumb when he had to be. He became the brother Dean had lost.

They did everything together. Everything. And now this. That's why it hurt so much. More than he could show. He had never had a meaningful relationship with a woman. Sometimes he saw one who made him feel things he couldn't articulate, connected on some lizard level. Put images in his mind of what he wanted to do to her body. So he would. And sometimes pay her afterwards. But nothing more than that. Nothing that would get in the way of his work. Or his relationship with Mick.

He thought of what he had said earlier. About shooting someone in a Deansgate bar and getting away with it. About digging more than one grave for revenge. About what Mick had done to him. About what he would do to him as a result of that.

And he thought.

And he thought.

And he thought.

And when the morning arrived and the officer opened the door for his hearing and looked at him, both of them pretended not to notice the tears.

24

Lila stirred her coffee, stared ahead at nothing. Morning in the refectory-cum-coffee shop on Truro College campus and she was taking a break from her classes. Alone. As usual.

She crumbled her double chocolate muffin into pieces, popped one in her mouth. The campus was still busy this close to Christmas, local day students on pre-degree courses, just like she was doing, reluctant to say goodbye to their friends and go home. Degree students still doing the rounds of Christmas parties before they disappeared. Lila was apart from all that.

She was invited to parties, drinks in the town with her classmates, and had attended a few. But she still felt she had little in common with them. Because of what she had been through, she couldn't share their self-assurance and certainty about the future. So she went along with them, joined in as much as she could, but found them, for the most part, too young for her. Or at least too naive.

Tom had encouraged her to mix, get to know them. They might not be as bad as she thought. And she had made an effort, but she still preferred her own company at breaks rather than hearing their opinions on the latest vacuous American TV show they were all watching on Netflix. And not just because she and Tom couldn't get Netflix.

But as the term had progressed she had reached something of a conclusion. Maybe it wasn't them. Maybe it was her. Yes she was different to them, had had a different set of life experiences, felt older than her years as a result. But maybe she just wanted to fit in and couldn't. Maybe she wanted to be carefree and laugh at everything like they did. To care about dumb stuff like TV shows and Instagram celebrities. To have certainties instead of nothing. Maybe. And the closer she got to that, the harder the divide was to navigate.

Whatever. She sat on her own, drinking her coffee, eating her muffin. Thinking that maybe she should just accept that distance if she couldn't change it. She tried to think about other things. Like the motorcyclist she had seen a couple of days ago at the top of the hill.

Why couldn't she get him out of her head? He had been lost, he said, that was all. Looking for somewhere. Seemed simple enough. So why did she feel like he had been watching her?

She hoped it wasn't because of the colour of his skin. True, there weren't many people of colour in her part of Cornwall and the ones who were there tended to stand out. But with his Belstaff motorbike jacket and good boots he hadn't looked like a local. Or a tourist for that matter. He looked like he had been working. And that made her uneasy.

Since then she had checked for him while she was on the bus, when she was home, even during the night, getting up to peer into the darkness. She found no trace of him, no evidence he was watching her or the house, but that unease still wouldn't lift. She was glad Pearl was with her most of the time, just for security.

She wished Tom were there. He would know what to do. Or if he didn't, she could comfortably imagine that he did. He was that kind of reassuring presence in her life. She just wished she could talk to him. Maybe she could go and . . .

'Hey,' said a voice, 'mind if I join you?'

Lila looked up, startled. A girl was standing in front of her. Dark skinned, pretty, smiling. Lila thought for a moment, recognised her from her sociology class.

'Uh . . . yeah, sit down.'

'Looked like you were miles away,' said the girl, sitting down opposite, putting her coffee on the table.

'Yeah, I was.'

'We're in sociology together, aren't we, with good old Guru George Hearn?'

'Yeah.' Lila smiled then looked perplexed. 'Guru? Is that what he's called?'

'Yeah the whole class calls him that. Don't you?'

'I'm . . . I hadn't heard.' She smiled again. 'Guru. Suits him.'

'I'm Anju. Don't know if you knew or not. You're . . . Lola?'

'Lila.' She said it. Couldn't help herself. There was something about this girl's openness that made her put aside her normal reticence.

'Lila. Right. Where's that from?'

'What d'you mean?'

'Lila. Does it mean something?'

'Dunno.'

'Your parents didn't give you that name because of any deep meaning or anything?' Anju laughed as she spoke.

Lila smiled again. It felt like the most smiling she had done in ages. 'Obviously you've never met my parents.'

Anju laughed again. It sounded so refreshing, unforced. Infectious, even. There was no way this girl had an agenda. No way someone had sent her over to talk to her. At least Lila hoped there wasn't.

'Mine gave me this name, Anju, because it's Hindi for beloved.'

'So you're Hindu?'

Another laugh. 'No. Muslim. My parents wanted to show just how progressive they were by giving me a Hindi name. I told them, if they really want to show how progressive they were, they should have called me Alison or Sandra, or something like that. They didn't think it was funny.'

Lila was starting to enjoy herself for the first time in ages. She made eye contact with Anju. Anju's gaze was direct, intense, even. But not in an unpleasant way. The opposite. Like she just really wanted to see her and be seen by her. So honest Lila dropped her eyes to her crumbled muffin.

'Sorry,' said Anju. 'I'm stopping you eating.'

'No.' Lila shook her head, 'You're not. I was just having a coffee. The muffin was just something for my fingers to do while I drank.'

Anju laughed, again unforced, uninhibited. Lila was really warming to her. 'Why are you on your own? You waiting for someone?'

'No,' said Lila. 'Just . . . dunno. Just on my own.'

Anju sat back, regarded Lila inquisitively. 'I've been watching you.'

Oh God, thought Lila, here it comes. She's mental. I've attracted another mentalist.

'Not like that,' said Anju, almost reading her mind, 'Not in a stalkery way or anything. Just, you know. I've seen you in class and round here. And you're always alone. Well, most times. But you don't really look lonely.'

'What do I look like, then?'

Anju thought, tried to find the right word. 'Apart. Separate.'

'Yeah?'

'Yeah. Like you're different to the rest of the class. You're mainly in psychology, right?'

Lila nodded. 'And Sociology. But mainly Psychology. So you think I don't fit in? I'm a misfit, is that what you're saying?'

'No. You just seem like you know something they don't. And they might never know it. It's interesting.'

Lila sat back, stared at the other girl. Wary now. Not wanting to give up any more of herself. 'I know something? Like what?'

A look of worry crossed over Anju's face. 'I'm sorry. I'm really sorry. I've spoken out of turn. I get like that. I don't have . . . whatever other people have. A filter? I don't know. I just . . . say things. What I'm thinking. Some people say it makes them uncomfortable. I've done it to you now. Sorry.' Anju's face reddened. She picked up her coffee cup, made to go. 'I'll leave you alone. Enjoy your muffin.'

Lila watched her rise. Something told her if she let her go she would regret it. She thought quickly, made a decision. She would trust her feelings.

'No wait. You don't have to go.'

Anju paused, looked back at her.

'Sit down. We were getting on all right.'

Anju sat back down. 'Sorry. I'll make small talk instead. Promise.'

Lila smiled. 'Who the hell wants small talk?'

Anju smiled too.

And they both laughed.

25

Foley stood by the door, waited patiently for it to be opened. Looking at the floor, his feet, showing a deference, a nervousness even, he never would on the wing.

The door opened. A young woman greeted him, hand on the edge of the frame, looking round, smiling, long hair falling to one side as she did so. 'Hello Dean. Come in.'

The accompanying officer nodded at him to enter then walked away. No longer visible, but somewhere nearby. Dean Foley entered the room. The door was closed behind him.

The room was like no other in the prison. It didn't even feel a part of the prison, which was the point. A desk at one end, bookshelves and files against one wall. Modern furniture. Tasteful, not the usual institutional kind. Even some decorations, paintings, flowers. A coffee maker on top of a filing cabinet filling the room with welcoming aromas. Recognisably branded supermarket milk and biscuits in their packaging gave a comforting but slightly melancholic glimpse of the outside world. In the centre of the room two comfortable Ikea armchairs.

Foley knew the procedure. He sat in one. Waited.

'Coffee, Dean?' Doctor Louisa Bradshaw knew the routine. She had established it.

'Please,' he said.

She poured a mug of coffee, added milk and one sugar. Foley smiled inwardly at her remembering. She passed it over as she seated herself opposite him.

'Thank you,' he said. His voice changed in here, layers of hardness stripped away, revealing something softer. He knew he did it but couldn't help it. Now he no longer wanted to help it. He took a sip of the coffee, placed it down at his side.

'So how've you been, Dean? How's your week?'

He picked up the mug, took another mouthful. 'Interesting, I suppose you might say.' Replaced the mug. She was waiting for more. He knew she would be patient with him, wait until he found the right words.

He had never thought he would actually tolerate a visit to the psychologist. Not just tolerate, actually enjoy. Look forward to it, even. It had been one of the terms of his sentence. A reduction in time served if he agreed to address his underlying anger issues. With no choice, he'd agreed. It was the approach his barrister had taken during his trial. Dean Foley wasn't a villain – not as such – just an angry man trying to make a living the only way he knew how. If he didn't have the anger he might be a more useful member of society. All bullshit and he knew it. But if it reduced his sentence, he would play along.

And it worked. So when he was transferred to HMP Blackmoor he was told that he would be having regular weekly sessions with Doctor Louisa Bradshaw. Fair enough, he thought. He would find a way round that.

But he didn't. He had taken one look at this young woman – pretty but not making the best of herself – and thought she would be a pushover. So he took charge, told her he didn't need all this bollocks, that he was going to use these sessions to contact associates on the outside, check how his empire was running. He'd see she was handsomely compensated.

But this doctor, this young woman, had stood right in front of him and said no. You're not going to do that. You might have your own way everywhere else in this prison but not in this room. And if you think you can try that then I'll refuse to hold these sessions with you and whatever concessions you've managed to achieve for sentence reduction will be null and void and you'll be back at the beginning. If you're in here you do what you've come for. Or you don't come at all and take the consequences.

Foley had been shocked. No one had spoken to him like that in years, certainly not a woman. He didn't know what to do, how to respond. So he just looked at her speechless. And then did what she told him to do.

And it was the most difficult thing he had ever done in his life.

'In what way interesting?' she said.

'Someone turned up. From my past. Turned up in this prison. The person who's responsible for me being in here, you might say.'

Louisa's eyes widened, then quickly regained her professional composure. 'Before you say anything else, Dean, I have to remind you of my position here.'

'I know. If I confess anything you have to pass it on. But other than that, everything in here stays in here, right?'

'That's right.'

'Well it's no secret. I was betrayed by my right-hand man, who turned out to be an undercover cop. And now he's in here. Supposedly for assault.'

'Why d'you say supposedly?'

'Because he's an undercover cop, isn't he? Got to be working on something.'

'Not necessarily. He might actually be in here for assault. It was a long time ago. His life might have changed. Have you spoken to him?'

'Not as such.' A smile crept onto his face. 'But he's seen me. He knows I'm here.'

Louisa picked up on the smile straight away. Knew it wasn't a positive development. 'And have you attempted to do anything? Take revenge against him?'

She looked at him directly. He tried to avoid her penetrating, unwavering gaze, but couldn't. He could see beyond those eyes, knew decisions were being made about him. Like she knew and understood him better than he did himself. It used to unnerve him. Not anymore. Just made him want to find out what she knew, how she knew it. Wanted to understand himself as well as she seemed to understand him.

'No,' he said, eyes dropping away. 'I haven't.'

'Do you intend to?'

He picked up the mug, took a mouthful of coffee. Tried to hide behind that before answering.

'I . . . don't know.'

Louisa sighed. 'Your honesty's commendable, at least. But I've got to remind you . . .'

'I know. I'm just trying to tell the truth.' He leaned forwards in the chair, hands clasped, engaged. 'I mean I looked at him, went onto his wing to see him for myself. Made sure he saw me.'

'And?'

Foley shrugged. 'He kicked off. Got taken to the seg.' He held his hands up. 'Nothing to do with me. Honest. Didn't touch him.'

'And now what? Are you waiting for him to be released back into the general population?'

He frowned. Twisted his hands in his lap. 'I've been thinking about this. For years, really. And honestly? I don't know what I want to do. I mean, I know what I should do. And I'd do it in a heartbeat if I was on the out.'

'And what's that?'

'Make him pay. Slowly. Then make sure he couldn't do anything like that again. To anyone.'

'And would that satisfy you?'

'Yeah.' Quickly, without reflection.

Louisa frowned. 'Would it? Really?'

Foley thought. Again, he wanted to be honest with this woman. She demanded it of him. Deserved it. 'I . . . It used to. In the past, like. You know? When someone does you a wrong turn you make them pay for it. Don't think about it, it's just the way it is. You have to do it, it has to happen.'

'Why?'

'Because you look weak if you don't. And if you look weak, others'll think you are weak. And they'll attack you. Image, innit? Got to project a strong image or your enemies'll find a way to get you. Like Chinese whispers. Word gets round. Before you know it everyone's left you for the other side – because there's always another side, always someone who wants to be where you are – and you're on your own. And you won't last long like that. So yeah. You've got to take revenge.'

'But you haven't answered the question. Does doing that, taking revenge, satisfy you?'

'I . . .' Foley thought. Hard. 'I don't know. I never look at it in those terms. Just what has to be done, you know? You do it without thinking. It's what you have to do.'

She gave that penetrating gaze once more and he felt himself shrinking. Sometimes he wanted to shout: 'What can you see? What am I really like? To you? To everyone? To me? Tell me . . .' But he never had. Or at least not yet. But he never stopped thinking it, wanting to do it. He might do it one day. But he probably wouldn't. He was too scared to hear the answer.

'So you get no satisfaction from it, is that right?' Her voice calm, as though she had all the answers to the questions she was asking and was waiting to see whether his measured up.

'I've never . . . I don't know. I suppose I must do. Yeah, I must do.'

He tried to imagine times in the past, draw those memories out and examine them in front of her. It was what she had taught him to do in these sessions and he found it so damned painful. Reliving his life. All the pain, tears, hurt, everything. But it was necessary, she had told him. To try and understand who he was now, where he was going from here, he had to discover and acknowledge how he had come to be here. And that meant opening everything up. Everything.

His father. The beatings. The childhood taken away from him by one man's singular cruelty. Making himself so pathetic in front of his father he would turn his vicious, abusive attention to his younger brother. Letting his relief, his silence become complicity. Reliving all of that once more. Stripping himself emotionally bare in front of her.

And the life after that, in care. Foster homes. Institutionalised neglect. Abuse. That anger building up inside him, all the time, waiting for an outlet. Detention centres. Young offenders institutions. Feeling something within him die, something fragile, knowing once it was gone it could never be reborn. Then trying to harden himself round it. Not wasting time mourning the man he could have been but embracing the man he had no choice but to become.

Which led him here. And now this question. Did he enjoy his revenge?

He thought back on all the punishment beatings he'd orchestrated, the ones he'd carried out himself. Bones breaking bones, turning flesh into something unrecognisable, getting high off the screams, the prayers and the pleading. Seeing other faces on the bodies he hurt, older faces. One in particular. Hitting again and again until he had no strength left, until his arms were carved from jelly, until that face disappeared. And that would suffice, that exhaustion. That sense of accomplishment. Until the next time. And the next . . .

'I . . . suppose so.' He had tried lying on previous occasions and had been found out straight away. He had done it to look good in her eyes. But he soon realised the only way he could do that was by telling the truth.

'How did it make you feel?'

'Like . . .' Back there again, in some anonymous warehouse or lock-up. Punching a hanging body like he was tenderising a side of meat. Blood pounding in his ears, the air rank with coppery blood, shouting all the while, drowning out the screams of his victim.

Trying to get rid of that one face.

'I had to keep going,' he said, eyes closed, mind somewhere else. 'Had to make sure that face went away.'

'Which face?'

He opened his eyes. What had he said? He was suddenly sweating, shaking from more than the coffee. He stared at her.

'Which face?' she asked again.

He hadn't known he had said that. She had done it to him again. Forced him to admit something about himself that he hadn't realised he was thinking or feeling.

'You know which one.'

'You need to say it.'

His voice had shrunk to near a whisper. 'My father.'

Louisa nodded, as though her hypothesis had been confirmed. There was no triumph in her gaze though, just acknowledgement.

'So all the time you were taking revenge on people you thought had done you wrong, you were trying to attack your father.' Not a question, a statement.

He nodded.

'So what are you going to do about this new person? The one you claim is responsible for you being in here?'

'He is responsible.' The words whiplash quick, coated in anger.

'Is he? Aren't you ultimately responsible for your own destiny? That's what you've said previously.'

Foley didn't answer. He knew to answer either way would incriminate him.

'Dean?'

'I trusted him. And he betrayed me. That's the facts.'

'So how did you feel when you saw him again? Did you want to take revenge on him for what he did? Are you planning on doing that? And if you do is it because of what he did to you or who he represents?'

'I . . . I don't know. I really don't know.'

'Were you and he close?'

He couldn't look at her, didn't trust himself to speak. He nodded.

'Very close?'

'Brothers,' he managed.

'And if you do decide to take revenge on him, this brother figure, for betraying you, how would you do that?'

He frowned at her.

'You've just said that when you administered punishment beatings before you did them personally. Would you do that this time? Could you do that? To someone you considered a brother? Or would you have to get someone else to do it for you?'

He looked at her, frowning.

'Come on, Dean, I'm not stupid. I know the sway you've got in this place. The hold you have over people. You say the word and something would happen to this man.'

'That's not—'

'Yes it is true, Dean. We both know that. What I want to know is, what would be the point? For you, I mean. You could have him beaten up, even, I don't know, killed. But what would be the point? He's been out of your life these past, what is it, four years? I'm sure you don't regard him as someone close to you anymore. So what would you gain?'

Foley said nothing.

'Or do you think it's something you have to do yourself? Are you trying to prove something? I mean, you wouldn't be trying to hurt someone who can never be hurt again. It wouldn't be your father. Not this time. And it wouldn't be to save face on the out. So ask yourself. Why would you do it? And what would you gain?'

Foley stared at the floor. The coffee had gone cold. The room felt dark, as though a thunderstorm was about to hit. He felt tired. So, so tired.

'I want to go back to the wing now, please.'

He was escorted by the same officer. Neither attempted conversation.

He felt like he had just done six rounds in the ring. The sessions did that to him. On other occasions he had screamed and thrown furniture. Other times he had curled up into a foetal ball and sobbed his heart out. But this time he just felt . . . different. Exhausted, but like a door had been opened inside him and he didn't know which way he should go. All he knew was that he had better regrow his shell by the time they reached his cell.

Public persona back in place, he stepped onto the wing. And almost immediately ran straight into Clive.

Foley took in the other man's dishevelled appearance, reddened features and black eyes. 'Well, well, well . . . Killgannon's done a number on you, hasn't he?'

'Yeah,' Clive spat through missing teeth. 'Got solitary for it, though. Bastard.'

Foley laughed. 'Come into my room.'

The officer led the way to Foley's cell, let them in, then, dismissed, drifted away.

'Tell me what happened.'

'I reckon Killgannon thought he was being clever,' said Clive. 'Attack me, get put in solitary. So you can't get to him. Or so he thinks, anyway. But you can get him anywhere, can't you, boss?'

Foley said nothing. Heard Louisa's words rattle round his head, spinning so fast they gave him a headache.

He blinked them away. 'Why?'

Clive frowned. 'Why what?'

'Why did Killgannon go for you?'

'Like I said, so he could get put in solitary. For protection.'

'I know that, Clive. I was on the wing and saw it happen. He could have gone for anyone. Why you and not someone else?'

Clive became suddenly impatient to be away from there. He could sense the mood in the cell had changed. 'Because I led him to you. And he was angry because of it.'

'And that was all?'

'Yeah,' said Clive, nervously, 'That was all.'

Foley stared at him, unflinching. The kind of gaze Louisa had given him.

Clive wilted. 'Well, I may have said something to annoy him. Nothing really.'

'Like what?'

'Nothing, just . . . to spark him off, see what he would do.'

Foley felt his anger rising. 'Like what?'

Clive knew he had no choice but to tell the truth. 'I mentioned his dead niece. That's all.'

Foley turned his back on Clive, walked as far away from him as he could in the cramped space. Clive kept prattling on.

'Shut it.' Foley turned back, eyes blazing.

Clive shut it.

Foley's voice, when he spoke, was dangerously calm and low. 'That was a bad thing to do, Clive. A very bad thing.'

'Yeah, I realise that now, Mr Foley, but—'

'Don't interrupt. You did a stupid thing. An unnecessary thing.'

Clive shook. 'I'm . . . I'm sorry . . .'

'So you should be, Clive. And you will be. But first you need to be taught a lesson.'

Clive was almost sobbing now. 'Why?'

'Because . . .' Foley thought. About his session with Lousia. About what had been said, what he had experienced. The conclusions about himself he had reached. 'Because it's what I have to do. Because you've done me wrong and I have to punish you for it. Simple as that.' The words said like a learned piece of church ritual. He sighed, felt something slip away inside him.

Clive was openly sobbing.

'Baz.'

His right-hand man stepped into the cell.

Put something into it, he thought. 'Little task that needs attending to, if you don't mind. Clive here's been a naughty boy and spoken out of turn, upsetting someone very badly. As such he needs to be taught a lesson. Nothing too major, just so he won't do it again.'

'What about a fall?' asked Baz.

'Yeah. A high one. With some stairs for a bit of variety.'

Baz nodded. Smirked.

'Please, Mr Foley, no, please . . .'

Foley turned to Clive. Regarded him with contempt. 'We're all responsible for our own destinies, Clive. Be a man. Accept responsibility for yours.'

Baz dragged Clive out of the cell. Foley heard him pleading all the way up the stairs until, after a little while, his pleading crescendoed into a scream, then silence fell across the whole wing.

He sighed once more. Felt, in his mind's eye, Louisa giving him that stern gaze.

Seeing right inside him.

Even when he closed his eyes she was still there.

26

DS Nick Sheridan liked to think of himself as a decent man. Conscientious and diligent in his work, always putting in as much effort as he could, a staunch friend and supportive colleague. One of the good guys, making a difference by catching the bad guys. Or women. Or however they preferred to be referred to. He didn't differentiate. At home a loving husband to Carrie and a great father to Chloe and Baxter. He also refereed non-league football matches. Just a hobby, but one he took seriously, bringing his rigorous sense of right and wrong to bear on the pitch. He saw it in part as an extension of his police work: creating as fluid and exciting a game as he could while at the same time not allowing impropriety to go unpunished. Rigorously enforcing fair play in all things. So to have doubts about his colleagues and their attitude towards an investigation was no small thing for him. And to actively take steps to investigate for himself was unheard of. It challenged every belief he had been brought up with, the very bedrock of his existence. Nevertheless, something told him to persist. And he listened to that voice.

No police station was ever silent and Middlemoor, the Exeter headquarters for Devon and Cornwall, was no exception. With its flat-fronted red brick façade and pitched roof, it resembled anything from a redundant Territorial Army base to a factory in an old Norman Wisdom film. Inside it had been gutted and renovated according to the best practices of every generation of police commander, every Home Office initiative. Currently the Serious Crimes Squad worked out of a large open plan first floor office, all workstations and access cards.

Sheridan was still at his desk even though the rest of his shift had long since gone home. He was waiting for an unobtrusive time to start investigating, when he wouldn't attract too much attention from the night shift.

The office was still well lit, the overhead strip lights and desk lamps turning the windows into mirrors against the darkness beyond. Night shift tended to be on call more than day shift, reactive not proactive. As such he found himself alone in the office. He had made small talk with the few officers he had encountered, telling them he had reports and court documents to finish before he could go home. Trading weak jokes and bonhomie, they left him to it.

He had thought of working from someone else's computer in case anything was logged but decided that his own would be secure enough. There was a legitimate reason he was searching for these things, after all. He logged into the Police National Computer. Quickly found who he was looking for.

Dean Foley. Plenty on him and what led to his subsequent imprisonment. But it was less informative than he'd been expecting. Sheridan knew all the facts already. There was only a mention of Killgannon by the pseudonym 'Witness M' and a note that nothing more could be revealed about his identity for fear of being compromised in the field. It stated that Witness M had infiltrated Foley's gang under the name of Mick Eccleston and was reporting back to his handlers. It was his first-hand testimony that led to Foley's arrest and imprisonment for drugs, people trafficking, assault, robbery, intimidation, extortion and anything else they could find to throw at him. And it had stuck.

As he read through something caught his eye. The fact that there had been another undercover officer involved in Foley's gang. 'Witness N'. Witness N had been placed first but hadn't been as successful as Killgannon. For some unspecified reason there was no mention of Witness N anymore. Sheridan tried a search under that name. Came up with nothing.

That was as much as he could discover. The rest he knew, even down to which prison Foley now resided in. Which made Sheridan wonder. Had Harmer not known Killgannon was really Witness M when he assigned him to cosy up to Cunningham? Or had the information somehow slipped through the net? Or the line of thought Sheridan didn't want to pursue but knew he had to: had Beaker known about Foley's presence and still assigned him? Or even worse, assigned him because of Foley's presence?

It made no sense. Or none that Sheridan wanted to countenance. He sat back, came out of the PNC.

What next? He looked over at Harmer's closed door.

He knew what he had to do. And he didn't relish it one bit.

He stood. And caught his reflection in the glass. He looked furtive, a criminal about to commit a crime. Felt immediately guilty because of it. Maybe that's all he was. An untrustworthy sneak spying on his colleagues. In a way he hoped so. He wanted to be proved wrong. But there was that niggle again. Telling him that he was right. That there was something wrong and he had to find out what it was. No matter how unpleasant the outcome.

He crossed to Harmer's door, tried the handle. Unlocked. He knew he should feel pleased about that but it just made what he had to do all the more unpalatable. He looked round once more even though he was the only person in the office. He felt he was being watched through the night-mirrored windows. Or maybe that was just his sense of guilt again. He stepped in Harmer's office, opened up the screen, tapped in Harmer's password. Finding it had been easy. His porn name. Name of first pet, mother's maiden name. The team had played that game one night in the pub. Harmer, not wanting to appear standoffish, contributed his. Then, still drunk later, let it slip he would use it as his password. Sheridan, good copper that he was, had filed the information away. He never thought he would need to use it, especially under these circumstances.

When requested he typed in 'LolaCraddock' which he supposed could have been a real porn name given some adjustment or imagination, and he was in.

But he didn't actually know what he was looking for. He just hoped he would recognise it when he saw it. If he saw it. He still hoped that he was imagining things.

And yet . . .

He scanned the files for anything that looked out of place, anything alluding to the current investigation. Nothing looked out of the ordinary. Everything seemed in order. He was going to leave things at that, reluctant to delve further into a superior's work, when something caught his eye. A file. No. Two files. He checked their names.

Witness M.

Witness N.

Sheridan sat back, heart hammering away.

He had been right. Damn it, he had been right.

He didn't know whether to congratulate himself or commiserate with himself.

He did neither. He opened the files.

27

Tom heard the key turn, the sudden noise resonating round the empty cell. Even though an opened door usually signified the beginning of something, that deep, heavy metal sound seemed more suited to an ending. Maybe it was time for him to leave solitary, Tom thought. Or knowing this place, maybe it was just lunchtime.

Tom sat up on the rudimentary bed, regarded his visitor. A young woman, quite well dressed, looked back at him. She smiled. The gesture seemed more about showing she was no threat than any kind of kindness. Prison wasn't a place where kindness flourished. Or if it did, it was swiftly punished.

'Hi,' she said, dismissing the officer who had opened the door for her.

'Have to stay with you,' the officer said, unmoving. 'Hostage risk.'

She turned towards Tom. 'You're not going to take me hostage, are you?'

Tom frowned. 'Why would I do that?'

She turned to the officer. 'I don't think there's anything to worry about.'

The officer clearly didn't want to move. 'Will you state you're taking full responsibility for your own safety, then?'

'I will.'

The officer reluctantly left, but not before saying he'd just be down the corridor.

'Hi,' she said again. 'I'm Dr Bradshaw. Louisa.'

He nodded. 'Tom Killgannon.'

'I know.' She looked round. The only piece of furniture in the room was the bed. 'May I sit down?'

'Be my guest. Didn't know I was getting visitors. I'd have run the vacuum round.'

She laughed. It sounded genuine. She sat down at the far end of the bed, away from Tom. He didn't move. The only other seat was the toilet in the corner. 'How've you been?'

The question invited a full answer, one Tom was unprepared to share. He had been dragged off the wing as soon as he assaulted Clive. The officers were on him straight away, hitting the alarms for backup and using the kind of restraining techniques he had used in his previous life. Some of them had got in body shots while he was restrained, the clever, sadistic kind that left little or no mark but instantly debilitated him and hurt like hell for ages afterwards.

He was dragged straight off to the CSC, the Close Supervision Centre or Seg Block as the inmates called it. The place was a prison within a prison, no natural light in the corridors, no way to tell day from night. Once the key was turned and he was left alone, he could have been deep underground for all he knew.

He'd paced the tiny floor until the adrenaline rush wore off then lay on the bed as the pain the officers had inflicted replaced it. And there he had remained. His claustrophobia, already bad in his usual cell, went into overdrive. It was like a cheap public toilet in some brutalist car park, tiled walls, disinfected floor, stainless steel pan and washbasin. A bed that provided the barest minimum of comfort. A small window of reinforced glass in the cell door so wing staff could observe him, shattermarked and blood smeared by the force of a thousand fists and headbutts. If his injuries hadn't been so debilitating he would have screamed himself hoarse. Instead he just lay on the bed, trying to hold himself together, eyes closed.

Sometime later that night – he thought it was still night – an officer brought him a tray of food. His first instinct was not to touch it. Foley had people all over the prison – why not the kitchens too? Could it be poisoned? Or worse, could someone in the kitchens have tampered with it just because he was in solitary and they assumed he was a paedophile or a rapist? He knew from urban legend the kinds of things that were put into prison food. Everything from excrement to broken glass.

He had no appetite. Left the tray by the door.

Later, after a fitful spell of sleep, he was awakened by the key in the door and an officer telling him it was time for exercise. He was led out to a small cage, still inside the prison within the prison, and told to walk round it for half an hour. If he wanted a shower now was the time to do so. He did so.

There were other inmates in the exercise cage, some walking, others just standing, staring. All kept apart from each other by the officers. They ranged in looks from the damaged to the dangerous but all seemed to have one thing in common: something missing behind their eyes. Either as the result of their segregation or the reason for it, Tom didn't know. But he avoided eye contact with all of them.

He took his shower, alone, then it was time to go back to his cell. Another tray replaced the untouched one from the night before and he looked at the unappetising food in its compartments. Some cheap white sliced bread. Something which could have been porridge or wallpaper paste. Two overcooked, shrivelled sausages. At least he assumed they were sausages. A plastic cup of milk. He ate the bread, one of the sausages. Left the rest.

And that became his routine. He thought he had been on the Seg Block for at least three days, judging by the number of times the lights had gone out and the number of times he had been allowed out to exercise in the cage. Other inmates came and went, making as much noise and trouble as possible: banging on cell doors, shouting threats, making promises. Like once powerful jungle animals having their agency forcibly removed, reacting the only way they knew how. Their bravado failing to disguise their fear.

Tom had managed to keep his claustrophobia under control by congratulating himself on escaping Foley's attentions. Hoping Sheridan would manage to get him released. But the silence dragged on, the loneliness crept up on him. And with it paranoia. Justified para-noia, he felt.

He wasn't safe here. The door could be opened at any time and anyone could enter and he had no way of stopping them. They could take him somewhere, even beat him up in the cell. Or worse. Alone, Tom imagined it all.

It wasn't just the fear that got to him. There was the enforced time spent with only his psyche for company. Time to re-examine every single event in his life that had led him to this point, every wrong or right move he had ever made. Not just re-examine, but relive. In as much detail as his memory could muster. And, with nothing else to expend its energy on, it could muster a lot. His emotions were in constant turmoil. All he relived were the wrong moves. The costly ones. And no matter what he did, he couldn't get his mind off that track. He understood why so many people in solitary attempted suicide. His claustrophobia ramped up, made him want to throw himself at the walls, batter his way out, scream the place down. But he forced it down, kept it trapped inside him, as he was trapped in the cell. It made him shake constantly. He didn't know how much more of this he could take. Lights out on the wing in a locked room was bad enough. But lights out inside him was a whole new level.

Then the door had actually opened. And Dr Bradshaw had entered. At first Tom was relieved to see someone who wasn't in a uniform, someone smiling. But that meant nothing. Someone could have sent her. And that whole hostage thing might have been to lull him into a false sense of security. Or was he just being paranoid? He gave himself the benefit of the doubt.

'So,' she said again, 'how are you?'

Tom shrugged, not wanting to give anything away to a stranger. Tried to keep his trembling under control.

'Must be difficult for you in here,' she said. 'I've had a word with the officer outside, said you should at least have something to read to pass the time. Any requests?'

'Sorry, but who are you and why are you here?'

'My mistake. I thought you'd know. I'm the prison psychologist.'

'And why have you come to see me?'

She smiled once more but Tom sensed nervousness in that smile. Her eyes darted away from him, down to the right. She's about to lie, Tom thought.

'I do this with everyone who ends up on the CSC. It can be a harsh environment. It's my job to see you're coping. And if you're not, suggest ways which might help.'

'Right.'

'So how are you coping?'

Tom shrugged.

She said nothing, she was working out another approach. 'Noel Cunningham. You know him, right?'

Tom nodded.

'He's been acting out since you've been in here.'

'So?'

'He's a . . .' She thought. Seemed to be deciding how much she could say to Tom. Or how much she should say. Or maybe just pretending to do that to get Tom onside. 'He's an interesting person. I see a lot of him. When you were brought here he wanted to see me. Said it was urgent. Said it was about you.'

Tom waited. Tried not to show any eagerness in what she had to say.

'I think he misses you. He seemed to function better when you shared a cell with him. Said you answered his questions, talked to him. Tried to help him with his night terrors. He seems to have taken a few steps backwards since you've been here.'

'What d'you want me to do? I thought anything like that was frowned upon in prison?'

She leaned forwards, sharply. 'Anything like what?'

'I don't know. You said he misses me. That sounds like a red flag if you're thinking of putting me back in with him, don't you?'

'Or it sounds like you were a positive influence on him. Someone who could help make his time inside more bearable.'

Tom didn't know what to say next. He didn't know whether to trust this woman – his instinct said not to – but she seemed to be smoothing the way for him to return to the wing and resume his place in a cell with Cunningham. Let him complete his mission, get out. That mission, however, had now taken second place to survival. Stay alive by any means necessary.

Before he could reply she spoke again. 'His mother is very ill, you know.'

'Cancer. I know.'

'He wants to get out and see her.'

Tom said nothing.

'He's made a kind of deal with the Governor. Has he mentioned it to you?'

Tom was wary now. If she wants to know something, make her work for it. 'Would he have?'

Dr Bradshaw sat back, regarded him again. Seemed to be making up her mind. She leaned forwards again. 'He's agreed to give up the whereabouts of the graves of his final two victims on Blackmoor. If he does that and it checks out, he can visit his mother.'

'Right. And you're telling me this why?'

'When you're returned to the wing I can arrange for you to be his cellmate once more.'

'Why would you do that?'

'As I said, you're a positive influence on him.'

'And you want me to get him to open up about these graves, is that it?'

She smiled. Nodded.

'What about me? What do I get?'

She paused, seemed to study him. 'You were in therapy for PTSD before you came in here. On anti-depressants. Yet you've not asked to see me or anyone else on the mental health team. Why is that?'

Tom didn't reply. Just felt his heart hammering.

'I think I could help you.'

'With what?'

No smile now. Only seriousness. 'I saw how you looked at me as I entered. I've observed how you've behaved while I've been in the room with you. I've seen those looks, those reactions before. Prison can be a harsh environment even for those who are used to it. There's help here if you need it. And I think you'd benefit from it.'

Tom said nothing.

'Would you like me to recommend you return to the wing? Back with Cunningham? Inmates are usually only here for a few days when they've done what you've done.'

'And I be your spy, is that it?'

'It would certainly help in your parole.'

Tom thought. The walls of the cell pushing in on him, suffocating.

'OK,' he said.

'Good.' She crossed to the door, knocked on it a couple of times. It was opened. She turned back to Tom.

'Thank you for talking. I've enjoyed it. I hope you have too.' She smiled. 'And thank you for not taking me hostage.'

The door slammed shut behind her.

28

Lila had finished her coursework and had no exams but still went into college. Not because she had to, just because she wanted to. She was beginning to enjoy the routine. Having had no structure in her life for so long, to willingly embrace it was quite exciting. Almost an act of rebellion. Pearl and she had settled into a routine of sorts at home too. Lila going to college, Pearl running the pub, both coming home, taking turns cooking, watching TV together. Pearl being the better cook by far but tolerating the meals Lila came up with. Becoming comfortable in each other's company.

However Lila had another reason for still coming into college. To meet the girl who had sat next to her and couldn't make small talk.

Anju had been on Lila's mind a lot since they met a few days ago. The thin, Asian girl with the ready smile and the sparkling, I-know-something-you-don't eyes, the dark, shining hair. The way she picked up her coffee cup, those long, sensuous fingers curling round it, bringing it to her lips, enjoying drinking in slow, languid mouthfuls. She'd barely stopped thinking about her? *Couldn't* stop thinking about her.

Lila had tried to explore and understand her feelings for Anju, so strong, so sudden, but wasn't given to that degree of self-examination. She usually pushed everything as far inside as possible where it couldn't hurt her. Tom was the only person she had come close to opening up with. And he wasn't here to listen to her.

Then there had been the text last night:

Coffee tomorrow? Anju X

Yes, she had replied. Oh yes.

She reached the café. There was Anju, sitting at the same table they had sat at last time, two coffees, two muffins in front of her.

Her head propped on one hand as she read a book. She looked up as Lila approached, gave a wave and a smile.

Oh God, thought Lila. Why is my heart racing?

'Hi,' said Anju, straightening up and closing her book.

'Hi back,' said Lila, returning her smile too. She felt suddenly awkward.

'You going to sit down? I got you a coffee. And a muffin. Waited for you to get here before I started on mine.'

'Thanks.' Lila put her bag on the table, sat down next to her. The move, bringing her into such close proximity to the other girl, felt exhilarating yet natural. She looked at her once more, aware she hadn't stopped smiling since she saw her. Noticing Anju doing the same thing.

Lila forced herself to look away. 'What you reading? Something for the course?'

'Nah,' she replied, picking up the paperback and showing her the cover. 'Something for me.'

Lila took it, looked at it. '*On The Road*, Jack Kerouac. I've heard of it. Any good?'

'Nah,' Anju shook her head. 'Supposed to be the kind of novel everyone has to read when they're our age. Meant to open our horizons and make us rebel against our parents and take off looking for art and creativity the rest of our lives.'

'And it doesn't?'

She laughed. 'Fake as fuck. This guy admits he borrowed money off his mother and took off when his exams were done. Drove round a bit with his mate then wrote it down. It's like what he did in his Easter holidays. And he hates women. Or at least is terrified of them.'

'Well that's off the list then.' Lila put it down on the table.

'Yeah. I'm not at the end yet, so maybe it all changes. But I doubt it. It's like that other one you're supposed to read and love. *Catcher In The Rye*.' She shook her head. 'World's moved on, mate.'

166

'Yeah. I read *The Great Gatsby* a couple of years ago,' said Lila. 'It's really not.'

They smiled at each other. Eyes held for that beat too long, neither wanting to be the first to break. But Lila did.

'Thanks for the coffee.'

'You said.' Anju picked up hers, took a sip. Lila watched those long, delicate fingers at work. Fascinated by them.

'What's up?' asked Anju.

'Nothing.' She took a sip of her own coffee. She wished she could have matched Anju in the finger stakes but with her bitten, unvarnished nails and her red, scarred hands, there was no way. Those scars told a story. One of desperation and escape. One she didn't want to talk about.

'So, what you been up to?' asked Anju.

'Oh, nothing much. The guy I live with . . .' She stopped herself. 'That's wrong. The guy I share a house with is away at the moment. And his . . .' She paused, unsure how to describe Pearl. 'Well, friend, I suppose, she's moved in.'

'Why?'

'Company, I guess.'

'He's not your dad or anything though, is he?'

She shook her head. 'Just a guy I share a house with.' She looked at Anju once more. Differently this time. 'You think it's weird, or something? It's not . . . you know, anything funny.'

'Nah, I don't think it's weird. You're in Cornwall, remember. Weirder things than that round here.'

Lila definitely interested now. 'Like what?'

'My dad's a child psychologist. Some of the things he's seen out in the really remote villages . . .' She shook her head. 'I'll tell you about it sometime.'

Lila was surprised at how warm a feeling those words gave her. It meant she would be seeing more of Anju. And she really liked the sound of that.

'What's this guy you live with do, then?' asked Anju.

'He's . . . well he sort of runs a bar in the village. St Petroc.'

Anju looked immediately more interested. 'St Petroc? Where there was all that trouble a few months ago?'

'Yeah, that's where we live. Just outside, anyway.'

Anju leaned forwards. 'Did you see any of it happening? There were human sacrifices, weren't there?'

Yeah, thought Lila. It was meant to be me.

'Oh, it's all over now.' She sighed. 'I think the village's trying to put it in the past. Good for the tourist trade, though. Apparently.'

Anju sensed Lila didn't want to talk about it. Sensed there might be something more to her reluctance, let it go. 'So,' she said instead, 'he's not running his bar now? He's away.'

'Yeah.'

'Coming back for Christmas?'

'Hope so.'

Anju sensed the weight behind Lila's words. Leaned in closer. 'Something up?'

Lila turned to her. She hadn't known this girl long – barely knew her at all – but she felt there was some kind of connection between the two of them. A deep connection. She felt she could talk to her. But more than that. Tell her secrets that wouldn't be used against her.

'Can I tell you something?'

Anju shrugged. 'Yeah. Sure.'

'I mean, really tell you something. It's important. You can't tell anyone else. And I mean that.'

Anju began to look a little nervous. 'What are you saying here, Lila?'

'I just don't want you to tell anyone else. No one. This is really secret. D'you understand?'

'Yeah.' She smiled. 'I'm not going to say that you can trust me because I've found that everyone who says that turns out to be an untrustworthy little shit. But go on, you can tell me. I don't lie.'

Lila thought. There was something about Anju that seemed trustworthy. Honest. She hoped she was right.

'He's in prison.'

Anju nodded. 'Right. I thought it might be something like that.'

Lila jumped forwards, lowered her voice. 'No, not like that. It's . . . he's working in there.'

'A prison officer.' Anju's expression said she wondered what the fuss was about.

'No, not like that either.'

'What, then?' She laughed. 'Is he a spy or something? Working undercover?'

Lila didn't answer. Her expression did the talking for her.

'Seriously? Really?'

Lila shushed her. 'Keep your voice down. Yes. He's . . . he does jobs for the police and people. He's doing one now.'

Anju sat back. 'Wow. Just . . . wow. I was only joking, you know.'

'I know. But you've got to keep that a secret. Please.'

'Yeah, course. Who'm I going to tell?'

Lila believed her. She had wanted to tell Anju so much, share something important with her. And she had feared that if she did so she would regret it afterwards. Hate herself for it. But she didn't. Telling Anju had felt like the most natural thing in the world. The right thing to do.

'D'you go and see him?' asked Anju after a silence.

Lila shook her head. Took a sip of coffee.

'Why not?'

'I dunno, I . . .' Another sip of coffee. 'It's selfish of me. I know it is.'

'What d'you mean?'

'I just don't want to see him in there because I know it'll depress me. Sitting in that room, behind bars . . . I don't think I could take that.'

'But doesn't he want to see you?'

169

'Yeah, probably. And that just makes it worse. Because then I feel even more guilty. And I feel like such a selfish cow. I hate myself for it.'

'Couldn't you go with someone? That friend of his who's staying at yours?'

'I think she feels the same. But she can't go because she's part of his cover story and doesn't want to blow it.' She sighed. 'I just hope he gets his job done and comes home soon.'

Another silence.

'I'll take you,' said Anju suddenly.

'What?'

'I've got a car. I mean, I won't come in with you, I'll wait outside, but at least you'd get to see him. And you'd have someone to bring you home so you wouldn't feel lonely.'

Anju placed her hand over Lila's. Lila's heart skipped a beat. Neither moved.

'OK, then,' said Lila eventually. 'Thank you.'

'You don't have to thank me. We're friends. It's what we do. Now eat your muffin. Then let's go do something.'

Lila smiled. She wanted to eat her muffin. She wanted to drink her coffee.

But she didn't want to move her hand away from Anju's. Ever.

29

Sheridan could barely sit still. Back at work, at his desk, staring at the screen, but hardly seeing it. Mind otherwise occupied with what he had discovered on Harmer's computer.

DCI Harmer had given the go-ahead for Operation Retrieve with Killgannon. But he was also the one who had dismissed Sheridan's concerns for his safety. And now there was this. Harmer was compromised, but Sheridan couldn't say or do anything about it to anyone higher up the chain of command. Especially not concerning how he had come across the information. It would be a huge black mark against him, potentially even a demotion or suspension.

So there he sat, unable to progress until he knew what to do. But he had to do something, tell someone. And the natural person would be Blake.

He watched her working at her computer, her face expressionless, nearly angry. He had heard of this thing called resting bitch face. One of his kids had said it at home over dinner describing a girl at school, the other had laughed. He had been angry at first. It sounded insulting and he questioned why one of his own children would use language like that. They had laughed in response, told him what it meant. A face in repose that looked angry or cruel. A part of him felt bad thinking that about her. Especially since he felt he had something like it himself.

He reached his conclusion. No choice, really. He had to talk to her. But not here, not now.

He kept working, one eye on his screen, the other on her until eventually she rose from her seat, picked up her lanyard and a box of cigarettes from her desk, made her way to the door. Sheridan rose, followed her out.

She was standing in the self-appointed smoking area, outside the back door by the vans. The gulag, it was called. A uniform lit up, nodded to her. She nodded back, her expression telling him she didn't want company. He sauntered away. Sheridan took his place.

'Can I have a word?'

She looked at him, suppressed a smile. 'Come over to the dark side, Nick? Didn't think your fitness regime would allow it.'

She proffered her packet. He saw a cancerous mouth on the side, winced as he shook his head.

'It's about work,' he said. 'I didn't want to say it in the office. Thought it was best when we were on our own.'

She looked round the car park. Officers and detectives were coming and going all the time, cars and vans on the move. 'And you chose here?' she said, smiling once more.

'Better than inside.' He paused. Gathered himself for what he was about to say. 'Look. There's no good way to say this. The Killgannon thing. I . . .' He sighed. 'Harmer hasn't been straight with us.'

She froze, dead as a statue, cigarette on the way to her lips. Slowly, she turned to face him. 'What d'you mean?'

'I . . . hacked his computer.'

'You did what?'

'Just listen. He's got stuff on there about Tom Killgannon and Dean Foley that he shouldn't have. Or at least should have shared with us before we sent Killgannon in there.'

'Like what?' She glanced sideways at anyone who might be listening in, made the movement as natural as possible. Her face gave nothing away.

'I think he knew Foley was in Blackmoor when we sent Killgannon inside. He knew their history, what Killgannon had done, how he'd got him in there.'

She took a huge lungful of smoke, let it percolate within her, slowly blew it into the air. Then let the cigarette fall from her fingers, stubbed it out casually but firmly with the toe of her boot. 'I don't know what to say, Nick. I'm as confused as you are.'

Sheridan looked round. Shook his head. Then looked back at Blake, mind made up.

'We've got to go and see Harmer.'

'When, now?'

'Why not? We've got to know what's going on.'

Blake looked unconvinced. 'It's risky. Let's think about it.'

'We don't have time. Come on.'

He walked back into the building. Blake watched him go, then followed him.

'Come in.'

Sheridan walked into Harmer's office, Blake running along behind him. Harmer sat back, regarded the pair of them.

'What can I do for you?'

'It's about Operation Retrieve,' said Sheridan. 'We've been doing some digging and—'

'Is this about Foley and Killgannon?'

'Yes, sir,' said Blake.

Sheridan was pleased she was speaking up, backing him up.

Harmer nodded. 'Sit down. And make sure the door's shut.'

They did so.

'I was going to talk to you both. After your visit the other day I looked into the Foley case. And there are some . . . irregularities. To be honest, I don't know how we didn't see this earlier. This could be a real mess.'

'How so?' asked Sheridan.

'Like I said, I looked into Foley's file. And I think there's something else going on here. A huge amount of money went missing the night Killgannon busted Foley. Foley's money. And the last person to see it was Killgannon. Or Mick Eccleston as he was then.'

'So?' said Blake.

'Everyone was questioned. No one saw anything. No one knew what had happened to it. Like it had just disappeared into thin air. But someone had taken it. And the suspicion was always on Killgannon.'

'How much went missing?' asked Sheridan.

'Over two million.'

'What?' Sheridan again. 'And we think Killgannon has it?'

'We don't know. We don't know anything about this Tom Killgannon, do we?'

'He's got a good record.'

'For doing underhand, dangerous things. Not always on the right side of the law, either. For all we know he could be dodgy, shall we say? In fact I think he might be.'

'What d'you mean?'

'As I said, I've been doing some digging. And Killgannon wasn't the only one undercover in Foley's gang. And that other one didn't have such a good ending as Killgannon.'

'What, he's dead?'

'May as well be. Poor bastard.'

Sheridan flinched. Harmer hardly ever swore. This must be serious. 'What, Killgannon sold him out?'

'I'm trying to find out. So we've got more to go on. It's not easy.'

Sheridan thought. 'But none of this changes the essential job, though, does it? Whether he's taken money or not, it doesn't matter. He's there to do a job and he's been compromised. We have to get him out.'

'He's safe where he is at the moment,' Harmer replied, voice hardening. 'He's in segregation, away from the wing, from Foley. Let's think about this.'

'What's to think about?'

'This could be a major complication, DI Sheridan. We have to proceed carefully. As I said, he's fine where he is. I need to think about this.' He sat up straight, looked at the door. 'I have work to do.'

Sheridan reluctantly stood. Blake also.

Sheridan walked slowly back to his desk, Blake to hers. Neither spoke. He stared at his screen once more. Thought.

How did Harmer know Killgannon was in solitary? Who had told him? Sheridan was waiting to hear from Killgannon. And what about this other undercover officer? What had happened there? It sounded like Harmer knew more than he was letting on. And not sharing it. This wasn't how Sheridan did things. This wasn't fair play.

He tried to work. Think what to do next.

But he couldn't concentrate.

30

'God, it looks awful,' said Lila. 'Like a haunted house or something.'

'Or a concentration camp. Look at all that barbed wire . . .'

They had driven to HMP Blackmoor in Anju's Citroen C3, that her parents had bought her for passing her GCSEs and to bribe her to keep studying. She had laughed as they drove off, asking Lila what they would think if they knew she was using the car to drive her friend to see someone in prison. Lila had laughed along, but apprehensively. Parents buying gifts like cars for their children and nurturing their education was completely alien to her. A world she had never been in and could never be part of.

The morning was crisp, the winter sun shining and the sky a pale robin's egg blue. Consequently the drive had been pleasant, Lila almost forgetting the purpose of the trip, feeling instead they were just out for the day. She felt slightly guilty about Tom for thinking that.

She also felt very nervous about seeing him again. It had been over two weeks since he had set off on this assignment and she hadn't heard from him at all. While she admittedly hadn't tried to contact him, he had told her not to. If he could, he'd said, he would phone her. She hadn't expected him to, not really. And he hadn't. She knew it would be difficult for him and talking to her would make it even worse. That was the reason she hadn't reached out either. She felt he would understand. Or hoped he would. But now she was changing all that by coming to see him. She just hoped neither of them would regret it.

They pulled into the car park. Looked at the prison once again. It seemed to suck all the light from the sky into itself, making the day darker, colder. Lila felt her stomach turn.

'Here we are, then,' said Anju turning the engine off.

The mood in the car changed, reflecting the prison, turning from light to dark. No more laughing or singing along to music, no more convincing themselves they were on a carefree day out. This was it.

'Well,' said Lila, 'time to go in.'

She looked over at the main gate where other visitors were beginning to gather. Dressed against the cold they resembled a huddled, sad mass of broken people in Primark clothes, their urban dress at odds with the surrounding countryside. Blank-faced women, old before their time, holding on to small sullen children, their hard eyes counting down the years until it would be their turn inside, their tiny fists clenched to demonstrate how they would get there. Older relatives beaten down by time and circumstances, their prematurely aged features roadmaps of wrong turns and dead ends. A few wild-eyed, gap-toothed crackheads trying to pretend they hadn't taken anything before coming, hoping they wouldn't be turned away.

Lila knew she would have to join them. Be one of them.

'It's hard to tell,' said Anju quietly, 'whether they're like that because visiting the prison made them that way, or it's the end result for them being like that.'

'We do sociology,' said Lila, equally quietly, 'I think we know the answers.'

Anju said nothing.

'It's like stepping back in time, going to join that lot,' said Lila.

Anju frowned, turned to her. 'What d'you mean?'

A hard sigh from Lila. 'I used . . . I wasn't always like this. Student, regular life, all of that. I used to . . .'

'Don't. You don't owe me anything.'

'No, I . . . I feel like I should. I didn't used to have a . . . what could you call it? A life like yours. It was more like theirs.' She gestured to the crowd.

Anju smiled. 'So what? Doesn't matter. You're here now. You've come a long way from . . . wherever you were before. And you

178

fought hard to get there. I can tell.' She placed her hand on Lila's knee. 'It doesn't matter. It's not who you are now.'

Lila felt a near electric charge from Anju's hand, the warmth penetrating through her jeans. She looked up, straight into Anju's eyes. 'Who am I now?'

Lila would think back on this moment, try to remember who had moved in first. She couldn't remember, didn't know. Sometimes it had felt like her, others like Anju. Most of the time it had felt mutual, both at the exactly the same time. But the result was the same. They kissed. Long and with increasing passion, hands gripping the other's body, each pulling the other towards them, getting as close as the car would allow. Lila's heart hammering like it was about to explode, shaking from everything. Fear, lust, desire, love. And things she couldn't name too.

Eventually they pulled apart. Eyes wide, chests heaving, as though they had both run marathons. Both still staring at each other.

'That's who you are now,' Anju said eventually.

Lila just stared. Couldn't find any words.

From out of the corner of her eye she saw the gate open, the mass of visitors move forwards.

'You'd better go,' Anju told her.

Lila nodded, not trusting herself to speak. She didn't move.

'Quick, before they shut the gate.'

She nodded, got out of the car, closed the door, her movements seemingly done by someone else.

She made her way to the gate. The words, questions, in her head bursting like fireworks before they could properly form.

She tried to pull herself together. Prepare herself to see Tom.

31

'Visitor. Off your arse, come on. Lucky you're about to go back to the wing. Wouldn't normally be allowed this.'

Tom was still on the seg block when the door opened and an officer stood there. He was barely squeezed into his uniform, more angry bovine than human, face like a shaved bull, ready to charge at the merest excuse of a red rag. Tom stood up slowly, not wanting to do anything that could be misconstrued as a violent attack. This guy wasn't just ready, he was hoping for it.

'Out here.'

Tom left the cell.

'Face the wall.'

Tom did so. The officer locked his cell door, turned to open the door off the wing.

'Go on.'

Tom walked through it, waited at the other side.

'Get moving.

He did as he was told, not minding the deliberate dignity-sapping instructions. This is it, he thought. Sheridan's come through. He had to stop himself from smiling as he walked.

They reached the visitor's room.

'Face the wall.'

Tom did so.

The door was opened.

'Go on, then.'

Tom scanned the room. Strip lit from above and painted a colour of green that only existed in institutionally depressing paint charts, it had official posters on the walls warning of expected penalties for smuggling contraband, breaking contact laws or attempting to pass gifts. Everyone sat at tables, leaned in, hunched together, trying to create invisible bubbles of privacy. Wives, parents and children desperately trying to reconnect with increasingly distant husbands, fathers and sons. Like the most depressing restaurant ever. Officers took the place of waiters, watched and listened. Reminded everyone where they were. Not that anyone would forget.

Tom's heart sank. He couldn't see Sheridan.

Then he saw who was there.

Lila.

And a completely different set of emotions overtook him.

She looked up, smiled. No, beamed. So pleased to see him. She stood up as he approached, attracting the attention of a prowling officer. She hugged him.

The guard broke them up. 'Come on, enough of that.'

They both sat down at either side of their table, just like everyone else. Tom's initial euphoria at seeing her drained swiftly away. He didn't want her to see him like this. In here. Subjugated. Powerless. It was like something had shifted inside her too, like she was experiencing something similar.

They both gave each other tentative smiles, both not wanting to be the first to speak. Unsure how to proceed.

'So here you are, then,' he said eventually.

'Yep. Here I am.'

'So . . . how you doing? At home. Everywhere.' Like English was no longer his first language.

'Fine, yeah.' A nod and a quick look round. Hoping no one was listening in, not wanting to make eye contact with anyone else. Not sure she could believe she was actually here. Then trying for honesty. 'Missing you.'

The words hurt as much as he had expected. Reminding him why he hadn't been in touch with her. He tried another smile. It didn't disguise what was in his eyes. 'You too.' Then, before either of them could linger on that, he went on. 'How's things at home? You managing?'

'Yeah. Pearl's moved in.'

Tom nodded. 'Good. Company for each other.'

'Yeah. We're getting on OK. She's . . . OK. Yeah.'

'I'm glad. I hope you two can be friends.'

'She's fine.' Almost a smile. 'We watch films together. The kind I can't watch with you.'

Tom smiled. Easier this time. 'Stuff about bursting into song over dying boyfriends?'

'It's not like that.'

'You know what I mean.'

'Yeah. And she's managed to get the wifi set up. Got me into *Riverdale* and *Glow* on Netflix. And *Dynasty*.'

'I take it back,' said Tom, properly smiling now, 'she's a horrible person and you shouldn't be friends with her.'

Lila laughed. The moment passed and died away to nothing. Silence fell once more.

'How did you get here?' asked Tom. 'Did Pearl drive you? Why didn't she come in?'

'No, I got a lift from someone at college. A friend.'

Tom picked up an undertone to Lila's words. 'A friend?'

Lila looked away, eyes down to the right. 'Yeah. A friend.'

Tom picked up on the gesture, what it meant. 'What's he like?' He smiled as he spoke.

Lila glanced up, then away again. 'She.'

'Oh. Right.'

Tom stared. So much he wanted to ask her but knew this wasn't the right time. Then arrows of sadness and regret. Anger. He should be at home with her, looking after her. Listening to her, trying to guide her. The pair of them getting ready for Christmas next month. Not here in this place.

'You look like you've been in a fight.'

Startled, her words brought him out of his reverie. 'Oh. Yeah. Nothing serious.' Playing it down. Knowing she wouldn't be convinced.

Her look told him she wasn't.

'It's a harsh environment. It doesn't mean anything. You've just got to stand your ground. Not get pushed around.'

Lila sighed. 'I worry about you in here.'

Tom tried to smile the worry away. 'You should see the other fella.'

'No thanks.'

He nodded. Another silence.

'Miss you.' She sighed. 'It's not the same without you at home.'

'But you can watch *Dynasty*.'

'Yeah, but it would still be better if you were there.' She was trembling behind her words. Tom realised that being here with him was hitting her harder than she had expected.

'It's not going to be long now. Don't worry. OK? I'll just . . .' He glanced round, conscious of ears everywhere. 'It won't take me long now. I'm getting close. I'll get that done and . . .' He shrugged. 'Come home.'

She nodded, eyes down. He couldn't tell how convinced she was by his words but he could guess. Not as convinced as he wanted her to be but desperately wanting to believe.

She looked directly at him and the fear, the pain was no longer hidden in her features. Tom's heart went out to her but he had to keep it together. She was the one walking out of here, not him. He didn't want to take all that back into a cell with him. Couldn't.

'How's everything else at home?' he asked again, not sure what else to say as everything felt unsure.

'I'm still going to college.'

'And you've a got a new friend. So everything's OK?'

'Yeah. Well, you know.' Lila leaned forwards, suspicious. 'Why?'

'Has anyone been around to the house?'

'What d'you mean?'

'Remember, I told you and Pearl that I'd asked someone to keep an eye out? On the pair of you, on the house. Just in case, you know, anyone came along trying to poke holes in my story.'

'So you're asking if I've seen anyone suspicious.'

'Well, I—'

'Yes.'

Fear came suddenly into Tom's eyes. 'What?'

'This biker was at the top of the hill the other day. Said he couldn't get his bike started but it worked first time. I watched him leave. Haven't seen him since.'

'What did he look like, this biker?'

'Tall, good looking. Nice leather jacket. Big boots. Black guy.'

Tom eased slightly. Sat back, a small smile on his face.

'What's wrong?'

'That's Quint. He's the old mate that I asked to keep an eye on you both. And the house.'

'Well he's pretty shit at it because I spotted him straight away. Crap liar. Bike's not working. Jesus.'

Tom smiled. 'You're good, aren't you?'

'Yep.'

A bell rang. 'Time's up,' shouted a guard.

They looked at each other, their faces unable to hide their respective sadness.

'Don't give you long, do they?' said Lila.

'Never long enough.'

The guards walked round the tables, forced goodbyes, checked for contraband. Some seemed genuinely sorry to be intruding in private moments, some seemed to enjoy it.

'I've got to go,' said Tom. 'Thank you for coming. I mean it.'

'Pleasure.' Lila realised what she had said. 'Well not a . . . well, you know what I mean.'

He smiled. 'I know. It's helped me, seeing you. Thank you.'

185

She gave a sad smile. They embraced under the watchful eye of a guard.

'Won't be long now,' he told her.

Lila nodded, trying to keep tears at bay. Then turned and made her way to the door.

Tom tried not to watch her go. Instead he walked to the doorway, ready to re-enter the main body of the prison, queued up alongside everyone else.

Tried, like everyone else, to keep his face as devoid of emotion as possible.

32

The Double Locks Inn stood on the Exeter Ship Canal. An old red brick pub, the kind of destination cyclists and walkers made for during the summer. Accessible by foot or cycle path from the quay, an easy-going place where people would while away sunny afternoons, drink beer, eat home-cooked food and let their dogs splash about in the canal. Still technically walkable from the centre of the city but due to the silence and surrounding greenery, it felt out in the countryside, far from anywhere.

Winter nights were different. The trees and bushes denuded, now screeds of arthritic branches gnarled against the darkening sky. No walkers. No dogs. The only cyclists those pedalling home late from work. Approaching by car spoiled the rural idyll. A drive round a warren-like industrial estate, then avoiding the potholes to cross a rusted, narrow metal bridge, the plates clanging and loosening further with the weight of each vehicle, down a minimally surfaced road to reach the pub.

Sheridan pulled his car into a shadowed corner of the uneven gravelled car park, turned off the engine. Sat there, unmoving. He and Blake had arranged to meet to discuss what Harmer had told them. Somewhere neutral, well away from the eyes and ears of Middlemoor.

He never thought his career would come to this. Secret meetings in pub car parks, with his own colleagues. Yes, this kind of thing happened with CIs and others, but not fellow officers. It just wasn't right. We're supposed to be better than them, he thought. We have the moral high ground, we shouldn't need to engage in this murky cloak and dagger kind of stuff.

When he had graduated from the academy he had felt bright, shining. Like the Christians would say, born again. So eager to fight crime, to make a difference, keep the streets safe, the first few weeks as a probationary constable were the happiest of his life. He might have annoyed his superiors, his peers even, with his earnestness, but that didn't matter in the long run. He just hoped some of his enthusiasm rubbed off on them, inspired them to try harder at their jobs. And he had hoped, as he continued with his career, that feeling would continue. That he would never become disenchanted.

But he soon saw things, experienced things that were so far out of his field of reference that all of his beliefs were challenged. When he witnessed first-hand as a uniform the depths to which one human being was capable of sinking in order to damage another, the shine soon wore off. Especially as he saw it repeatedly. He was then faced with a choice: go along with it, become like everyone else on the force, accepting of the status quo and develop coping strategies to get through every shift, or declare it wrong and fight against it. Keep that part of himself shining. He chose the more difficult way.

And he still believed it had been the right thing to do. Even now, sitting in this car park. Whatever happened, no matter how unpleasant, how repulsive, he would always find something within himself to keep going. To not accept things as they were, to use his position to make things better. He completely believed that. And to prove it, lived this personal creed every day.

A knock on his window jolted him from his reverie.

He looked up. There was Blake, leaning down. She gestured for him to get out. He did so, locking the car behind him.

'Have you just got here?' he asked.

'I saw you arrive. Came over to get you when you didn't emerge. Come on.' She turned, walked towards the pub. He followed.

A corridor with bare, uneven wooden floorboards gave way to a tiny bar with a fire roaring in one corner. The few people drinking inside barely looked up as they entered. Blake looked at the bar.

'What you having?'

'Sparkling water, please.'

She gave him a quizzical look.

'I'm driving.'

'One won't hurt.'

He shook his head, personal credo still intact. 'Sparkling water, please.'

She went to the bar, returned with a glass of red wine for herself and a bottle of sparkling water for him. Sat down opposite. 'Cheers,' she said.

She had changed her clothes from work, he noticed, and she looked very different. Now dressed all in black; tight jeans, boots, zip-up leather jacket with a scarf coiled round her neck. Heavy make-up. He had never seen her dressed like this before. He still wore his work suit, padded anorak over the top. He looked at his watch.

'Let's talk.'

She moved in, head close to his. They looked, he imagined, like a couple having an affair before returning home to their respective partners. He tried straightening up, not wanting to give that impression, but she spoke so quietly he had no choice but to lean in to join her.

'So. What are we going to do?'

Blake sighed. Nodded wearily to herself as if she been thinking hard, reached a conclusion. 'Well, first I've got something to tell you. Then we'll take it from there.' She took a mouthful of red wine. His water was untouched. It was only set dressing so he could sit in a pub and not look out of place. He didn't think it was fair to come into somewhere that made a living by selling drinks and not buy one.

'I was a uniform up in Manchester when Foley was arrested.'

'What? But how did—'

'Just listen, Nick. I was on the scene the night he was busted. The night that Mick Eccleston sold him out.'

'You were there?' Sheridan couldn't believe what he was hearing, or why he was only hearing this now. 'Why have you never told me this before?'

'I told Harmer. It was his call whether he told you or not. Apparently he didn't think you needed to know.'

'But—'

'Just listen, please. I was there when Foley was arrested. And when the two million quid went missing. For a while we thought it was going to throw the trial, that we wouldn't get a conviction. But Eccleston's testimony was more than enough to put him away.'

'And you thought it was Killgannon, I mean Eccleston? Why?'

'He was the logical suspect. The last one seen with it. But he was thoroughly investigated, and it seemed he was clean. He was at a loss to explain it as well. Claimed he had followed the chain of evidence with it back to the station. I don't know. Emotions were running high that night. It was a big bust. Would have been easy for something to slip through the cracks. Eventually we had to let it go. And it's never turned up.'

'So what has this got to do with what's happening now?'

'I'm getting to that.' Another sip of wine. 'You see, there was another guy undercover in Foley's operation that Eccleston didn't know about.'

'Witness N. I found that in Harmer's files.'

She nodded, a small smile playing across her lips. 'Right. And his career ended that night. He crashed the car he was driving trying to get away from the bust – on the orders of Foley's lieutenants – and bang. That was the end of that for him.' She sighed. 'He took the force to court for substantial damages but they fucked him over. He refused out of court settlements, expected a big pay-off. He lost. Got nothing. Not even his pension.'

'That's not fair,' said Sheridan.

'Who said anything about life being fair?' Another mouthful of wine. 'They dropped him. Not even a handshake. He tried to get work. But it was difficult. So long story short, he dug out all his old acquaintances from working with Foley. Went back to work with them. It was easy work, strong-arm, violence, extortion. But he got nicked. And sent down. For a long, long time.'

'I'm sure he deserved it,' said Sheridan.

Blake smiled. 'Everything's black and white to you, isn't it?'

'It has to be. There's good and bad. We're the good guys, they're the bad guys. We behave in a better way. We set an example. If an officer turns to the bad side I've got no sympathy. He deserves everything coming to him. We should be better than that. Have you read a writer called Ayn Rand?'

She shook her head, amused. 'No, and I'm not about to. Anyway, this guy who according to you should have known better was eventually transferred to Blackmoor and reunited with Foley.'

She sat back, looked at Sheridan, waited for him to speak. Sheridan just looked confused. 'So . . . what does that have to do with what we were talking about?'

'Everything. Because . . .' She leaned forwards once more, fingers toying with the stem of her glass, a look on her face that Sheridan could only describe as seductive. He had never seen her like this before. The straight-faced almost angry coworker was gone. This was a completely different person who sat in front of him.

'Because,' she continued, 'this is where you come in. You see, that guy in prison, the one you have no sympathy for, is an old friend of mine. We came through the academy together. Even had a bit of a thing going at one time. Both wildly ambitious, both on our way to the top. We were the golden couple. And now look at us. He's where he is, I'm playing second fiddle to you.'

The way she spoke that final word couldn't have sounded worse if it was the harshest swear word Sheridan had ever heard. He just stared at her.

'You play everything by the book, and that's your trouble. No imagination.' The words angry, hushed, at odds with the flirtatious smile and body language she was presenting to the rest of the bar. 'You believe in fair play. And because of that, you expect everyone else around you to as well. Don't you?'

'Yes, I do. You know I do.'

'You would never believe another copper would go behind your back, have secret meetings with her boss. Would you?'

'No.' His voice full of sadness more than anger. 'No I wouldn't.'

'Well I did. You see, I moved down here to kickstart my career. I became a DC but I don't think there's much higher I can go on the ladder. Not on this force. And time's running out for me. So I went to see Harmer. Had a word. Well, more than a word, actually. He's easily flattered, our boss. Especially by a pretty young officer, telling him how brilliant he is . . .'

Sheridan's throat was dry. He wished he could drink his water but his hands wouldn't move. 'You slept with him.'

She nodded. 'Not much sleeping went on.'

'But . . . do you find him attractive?'

'That's not the point. He finds me attractive and that's enough. Way it works, Nick.'

'So . . . what has this to do with our operation to get Cunningham to talk?'

'You think that's what this is all about? You poor, deluded man, Nick.'

'Well, what then?'

'It was never about that. It was always about the money, Nick. That missing two million. You see, I'm a good copper. No matter what you think of me. I've got good instincts. And they're never wrong. I think Eccleston, or Tom Killgannon, or whatever he's calling himself, now has it. I've always thought that and every year that goes by and it never turns up, I'm more and more convinced. So the next step was simple. I heard about the trouble in St Petroc a few months ago and recognised Killgannon as Eccleston straight away. So, I thought what if we can get Killgannon into prison next to Foley and Foley can persuade him to give up that money? I did my homework. Found out Cunningham was in there, wanting to confess to the right person in exchange for seeing his dear old mum again before she pops off. And of course Harmer came to see it the same way. The cherry on top, though, was putting you in charge. Because when the whole thing went tits up – as it's going to do – you'd take the blame, possibly a demotion and I wouldn't have to care about my career because I'd have enough money to invest in my future. Foley would see to that. And that would have been that.' She sighed. 'But you had to find out about it, didn't you? The one incorruptible copper on the force. Don't suppose there's any point in offering you a cut?'

Sheridan sat there, unable to move. He felt like his whole world had been rocked off its axis. He couldn't find the thoughts, the words, to express what he was feeling.

'Thought not.'

He looked round the bar, couldn't believe that the night was still going on as it had before, that nothing seismic had happened around him to match what had happened inside.

'So what are you going to do now?' asked Blake, taking another mouthful of wine.

'I . . .' What was he going to do now? He had to think. Sit quietly, let his inner moral compass find true north once more before he could even speak, let alone make his mind up. 'I don't know what I can do . . .'

She took another mouthful of wine, drained the glass. 'I'm empty. Time to go.' She didn't move. 'But before I do, I need to know where we stand. What are you going to do about what I've just told you?'

He just stared at her.

She shook her head, stood up. 'Come on. Let's talk about this outside. Maybe the fresh air'll wake you up.'

She put her arm within his, snuggled into him as they walked out together.

Through the door the cold wind hit them like ice. Sheridan looked around. Confused, like he had just woken from a dream.

'Let's walk to the car.'

Still arm in arm, she walked him through the dark night down to the unlit car park, their feet crunching on gravel the only sound. They reached his car.

'So,' she said, looking him straight in the eye, 'What are you going to do? Have you made up your mind?'

He looked at her face, like she was slowly coming into focus. And with that, so was his mind. 'Yes,' he said. 'I know what I'm going to do. There's no point talking to Harmer if you're both in it together. I'll find someone who'll believe me. You two won't be on the force anymore and Killgannon'll be out like a shot. I would never have been party to this if I'd known.' His voice had become stronger as he spoke. He was finding that shining part of himself once more. Being true to it like a good police officer should. Being better than the bad guys. Even if the bad guys turn out to be female colleagues.

Blake looked sad for a few seconds. 'Oh, that is a shame, Nick. I was hoping you wouldn't say that.'

Sheridan had found his voice. 'You knew I would never agree with you, so why tell me all this in the first place?'

'Because you found out about Foley, Nick. I really didn't want you to find out. Honestly, I didn't. For your sake, I mean.'

'What d'you mean, for my sake?'

'Because there's no going back, now. Sorry.'

Sheridan was about to ask her what she meant by that but he didn't get the chance. Unseen by him, a tall, black man wearing an expensive leather jacket detached himself from the shadows and stepped up behind him, put a restraining arm around his neck, pushed him onto the roof of the car, placed a silent automatic against the back of his ribcage, pulled the trigger and blew his heart away.

Sheridan didn't even have to time to acknowledge he was dying before his body hit the ground.

His phone started ringing.

33

Tom stood in the queue, waiting patiently. Three people in front of him, one already on the phone, turned away from the rest, trying to create what privacy he could.

He was back on the wing. He had been sitting in his cell on the seg block, staring into space, doing nothing. He had tried exercises, push-ups and sit-ups, until his arms felt useless, his stomach cramped. He could smell his own sweat, soaking through his T-shirt. Sour. Just like every other inmate in the prison. *I'm one of them now.*

And he was. Like he was ticking off a list of things he expected inmates to do. Get into trouble and be put into segregation. Be constantly on the phone. Have tearful, depressing visits with loved ones. His disguise was complete. He had become his cover story.

Tearful, depressing visits with loved ones. That wasn't how it had actually gone with Lila in the visiting room, but afterwards, alone in that Spartan cell designed to crush his spirit even more than the ones on the wing, he hadn't been able to stop himself. Tears came as he thought of Lila walking away from him, being able to breathe clean air and go where she wanted to. Able to go home, sit in the living room, watch TV. Go to bed when she wanted. He had come close to losing himself then, breaking down so much that he wondered whether it would be possible to pull himself back together, get into shape and finish this job.

It would have been so easy to just give in, lie there with the walls closing in on him and let himself go, acknowledge defeat. So he tried to bring himself back, compartmentalise his emotions. He used to be so good at this. Concentrate on the task in hand. Stay alive. Get the information out of Cunningham. Gradually he had done so, pushing his feelings about seeing Lila out of his mind, but it had been a struggle. Brought the old days back again. Reminded him that this line of work wasn't something a person could do for long, not without losing themselves to it, possibly for ever. He had started exercising then, pushing himself as hard as he could, hoping the pounding of blood round his system would drown out his thoughts. He kept going until he couldn't move anymore, slept that night on the floor of the cell.

And then the key in the lock, an officer looking in, telling him it was time to return to the wing.

He got up, went outside. He had expected to be told to stand and face the wall once more but the officer wasn't alone. Louise Bradshaw was there. As was a small, balding, suited man, staring at him.

'Hello Tom,' said Louise.

'Doctor,' he said, giving a formal nod.

'We're going to return you to the wing now,' she told him, 'put you back in general pop. We think you've served enough of a punishment for your action.'

Tom said nothing.

'Do you agree?'

'Obviously.'

'But I don't want to hear of any more incidents like this one, right?' It was the small, bald man who had spoken.

Tom turned his attention to him. 'Sorry, I don't think we've been introduced.'

Silence froze the group. It was clear the officer, the bovine one Tom had interacted with previously, wanted to teach him a lesson in respect. Or a lesson in anything, any excuse to inflict physical pain. Even Louise looked taken aback and Tom realised that, for all her talk and her offers of help, she would never be totally on his side.

'Governor Shelley,' said the small man. 'I run this place.'

'Right. I've never met you and I genuinely didn't know who you were.'

Shelley scrutinised Tom for any signs of sarcasm. Tom had been sincere. He said nothing more. Waited.

Shelley turned to Louise. 'You think this . . .' He searched for the right word to describe Tom. '. . . one is ready to return to the wing, then?'

'Yes, I do. I've talked to him and believe this won't happen again.' As she spoke her eyes alighted on Tom's, as if asking him to agree with her. Or at least not disagree. 'He's agreed to see me for sessions in how to handle his anger.'

Shelley turned back to Tom, squared up to him. 'You going to do that?'

'Yeah,' said Tom. He didn't elaborate. Didn't feel it necessary.

Shelley appeared to be making up his mind. 'OK, then. But if I hear of one incident involving you, just one, then you're back down here, busted down to basic, you got it?'

'Absolutely.'

'I've got a strict no tolerance policy for people coming into my prison and taking the piss. Play by the rules and you'll do all right. OK? Don't and you'll have to be dealt with.'

He's so much smaller than me, thought Tom, I could rest my arm on his head. Stretch my arm out and hold his forehead while he tried to swing shots at me. 'I understand.'

'Something funny?' Shelley was still staring at him.

'Just pleased to be going back to the wing,' said Tom, slightly annoyed that he must have let his feelings show.

Shelley stared once more. So did the bovine officer. They both looked like they were waiting for Tom to do something so they could keep him on the seg block. Shelley looked towards Louise, then back to Tom. And that look told Tom everything about Shelley's attitude. He was clearly a misogynist. The way he had been looking at Louise – dismissively, disrespectfully – told him that he didn't like psychologists, especially female ones, deciding what was best for the prisoners. *His* prisoners. But he knew he had to go along with it. Perhaps, thought Tom, this doctor might actually be an ally after all.

'Doctor Bradshaw's going to take responsibility for you,' said Shelley, 'But you're also to take responsibility for your own behaviour. I don't want to see you back here, right?'

Tom agreed.

Shelley walked off. Louise nodded to Tom, followed Shelley off the wing.

And now Tom queued for the phone. Only one person in front of him now. Not wanting to intrude, Tom looked away.

Some old faces had left the wing, new ones had arrived. And a different atmosphere. Towards him. He could feel all eyes on him as he was escorted back from the seg block. Like there was a sense of anticipation, waiting to see if he would kick off again. If they were hoping for that, Tom disappointed them. He did everything the officer told him, stood away from the doors, turned his face to the wall while they were being unlocked, everything. A model inmate. But he could still feel the eyes on him as he walked the length of the wing towards his old cell.

It was association time. Hard-eyed men standing and sitting, watching. Searching for an angle to everything, everyone, some leverage to be made, some advantage gained. Keeping up that level of vigilance was exhausting but necessary. No one could show weakness. No one could be seen to back down from a challenge. No one could show disrespect or accept it. It was a near silent battlefield, a war of attrition, of glances and muttered words, of body language and silences, all conducted under the eyes of the watching officers.

And now they were all watching Tom, taking the measure of him. Seeing what he would do now that he was back. Wondering whether to challenge his growing reputation as a hard man, like the Navajo warriors of old, believing if they defeated someone in combat they bested not only them but the souls of those they had in turn bested, advanced up the rankings, became a feared presence in their own right.

Or seeing him as a potential ally, someone to get onside. Barter favours with to keep them protected. Do whatever they could for Tom – contraband, sex – to get him to rid them of other predators. Tom ignored all those eyes, even Cunningham's, who had seen him approach, expecting him to enter their cell. Tom had nodded as he walked past. Made straight for the phone queue.

The person in front put the phone down, walked away. Tom's turn. He dialled the number by heart, waited. It was answered.

'Sheridan?' Tom asked.

'Try again.' It was a female voice.

Tom froze. So surprised by not hearing Sheridan's voice, he couldn't place it at first. Then he realised. Blake.

'What's happening, Blake?' Careful not to use her rank, give things away.

She laughed. 'Nothing. Nothing's happening.'

Tom was more confused than annoyed at her words. 'What d'you mean?'

'Nothing, Tom Killgannon. Or should I say Mick Eccleston?'

Tom froze again.

'This phone line is dead. Sheridan is dead. And so are you.'

She hung up. Tom was left staring at the receiver. He quickly dialled again. Nothing. And again. Nothing.

A dead line.

He stared at the receiver. Behind him, other inmates in the queue became vocal. He placed the phone back in its cradle, walked dazedly to his cell.

He was alone.

34

'Get rid of this.' Blake prised the SIM from Sheridan's phone, handed it to Quint.

'Glad to,' he said, taking it from her and pocketing it.

'Not around here,' she told him, 'I'll deal with the phone.'

They both looked at the body of her colleague slumped by the side of his car. Blood had sprayed all over the window and roof, and left smears where his body had slid down to the ground.

'What we going to do with him?' asked Quint. 'You thought of that?'

'Yep. Put him in his car and leave him here.'

'He'll be found.'

'He will. But not till tomorrow and I'll be involved in working his case. Now go on. Get him in there.'

Quint bent down, manhandled Sheridan into the driver's seat, careful not to get any blood on his clothes. Blake stood there, watching him.

'Don't bother to help,' he said.

'I won't. You're off back to Cornwall after this. I'm not. I don't want his blood on me.'

He finished his task, crossed to his bike, hidden in the bushes. Got on it, checked no one was watching them then roared away.

Blake watched him go. Looked at Sheridan's car. Tried to decide what she was feeling.

He was her partner. No, had been her partner. But that didn't mean she should be upset at his passing. Yes he had a wife and children who would be heartbroken at his death. And she would be lying if she said she didn't feel a pang of remorse for them. But it had to be done. *Had* to. Once he realised what had been going on it was either him or her. And it wasn't going to be her. He would never understand. That was the heartbreaking thing. If he had been any other kind of copper, more able to turn a blind eye or even, for a cut, help her, it would have been different. But he was straight by the book, boring Sheridan. Well, some of the things she had planned for him in death would put the lie to that. Tarnish forever his image as the perfect cop. Yes it was sad, but again, she had no choice.

She took out her phone. Not her usual one, a cheap pay as you go burner. Unregistered. Untraceable. Called a memorised number. Waited. It was answered.

'It's me. Sheridan's been dealt with. You can move on Killgannon.'

She cut the call, didn't wait for a response. Pocketed the phone and walked away.

35

The door slammed behind Lila. She placed her bag in the hall, keys on the hallway table. Unzipped her coat, hung it up. Same routine as always. Getting used to it. Even starting to enjoy it.

'That you?' a voice called from the living room.

She yelled a reply as she kicked off her boots, entered. Pearl was sitting in the armchair, flicking through one of her glossy magazines. Lila hadn't found the point in them at first, thinking they were a waste of time and money, just full of photos of emaciated, bored or angry-looking women in expensive clothes, and adverts for watches and handbags she could never afford, or even want. Then an interview with some celebrity who was using their platform – or so they claimed – to make the world a better place. If that was so, she thought, their platform didn't extend to Cornwall. Then more pictures of, and adverts for, shoes. But lately she had been picking them up when Pearl wasn't around, glancing through them at first, then looking more concertedly. Even imagining herself in the clothes, the feel of the fabric next to her skin, skipping along some tropical, white beach, smiling against the sun . . .

That's how they get you, Anju had said. And then it's a slippery slope to conformity. Bit ironic, Lila thought, a rich doctor's daughter lecturing her on the perils of conformity but, as she knew from experience, finding your own path in life took many forms, regardless of your background.

'Hey,' Pearl said, looking up from where she was sprawled over the armchair, legs dangling to one side. 'Good day?'

'So so.' She sat down on the sofa opposite her. 'Shouldn't you be at work?'

'Got Briony the new girl doing the dead zone. I'll pop over later when it's busier. Anyway.' She closed the magazine, sat up fully. 'I haven't seen you properly to talk to since you went to see Tom. How's he getting on?'

Lila thought of the visit. How Tom had tried hard to look like prison hadn't changed him, even in such a short space of time. How his wounded eyes and damaged face had given away that lie.

Or how she had fought back tears as she left. Sat in the car silently sobbing, Anju's arms around her, pulling her close. Crying on her shoulder. Anju stroking her cheeks, kissing away the tears. Feeling Tom's absence like a physical thing, but glad she had someone there to comfort her. It was a feeling she wasn't used to.

Afterwards she hadn't come straight home, even though Anju had dropped her off at the front door. Instead she had walked the cliff path, ignoring the cold persistent wind razoring through her too-thin coat, the rocks and mud underfoot making her lose her footing. Walking until it was too dark to see anything around her but the black, star-flecked sky, hearing nothing but the top line roar of the wind competing with the deep cymbal clash of the sea. Until she felt like she was alone in the universe, a tiny, galaxy-dwarfed speck clinging to a rock as it hurtled away through space. Completely insignificant yet somehow the centre of everything. She didn't move, didn't cry. Just stood there. Balancing. Holding on.

'How is he?'

Pearl's question bringing her back. 'Yeah, he's . . .' Lila didn't know what to say. Be honest? Be brave? 'He said he was doing OK. I don't know. He looked a bit . . . you know. Like he didn't want to be there.'

'That's a given.'

'He asked after you anyway.'

'What did you say?'

Her question a bit too quick, Lila thought. 'Asked how you were doing. How we were getting on. Told him we were watching *Dynasty* together.'

Pearl smiled. 'Sure he loved hearing that.'

'Anyway, he says he hopes that it'll all be finished and he'll be back soon. That it won't be long now.'

'I hope so. Not that I'm not enjoying being here with you and having some company . . . I'm glad you're here. I wanted to talk to you.'

'What about?'

Pearl dropped her eyes. 'I've had an email. From my mum and dad.'

'Oh.'

'Yeah. And I don't know what to do.'

Pearl's parents had been two of the main instigators behind the near murderous events that put St Petroc on the national news. Once the police had arrived they had disappeared, leaving the pub and hotel to Pearl. It had been a rough few months for her too. Lila thought with a pang of guilt, she didn't give her enough credit for that.

'Did they say where they were?'

'No, but they wanted to meet me.'

'Are you going to?'

Pearl looked straight at Lila. And Lila knew that no matter what she had thought of Pearl in the past, how she hadn't fully trusted her, their actions had bonded them. She may not be a friend by choice, but they were now bound by something deeper.

'I don't know.'

'What did they say?'

'That they were sorry. That I shouldn't worry about them, they were all right. They'd taken their savings and were trying to start again. They were abroad, didn't say where in case someone was monitoring these things. But they hoped I could understand what they had done and why and forgive them for it.'

Lila almost laughed. 'Forgive them. They'd have killed me if they'd been allowed to.'

Pearl said nothing.

'So what do they want? You to go and join them?'

'That was the impression I got.'

'And are you?'

'I wanted to talk to you first before I did anything else.'

Lila frowned. Thought of that night on the cliff path, balancing on the edge of the world, the universe. 'Why me?'

'Because you . . .' Pearl sighed, 'you've been through shit with your parents. And it's . . . I just . . . I don't know how I'm supposed to feel about it. About them.' Pearl seemed on the verge of tears.

Lila paused, thought hard. Pearl was reaching out as a friend; perhaps it was time to put any lingering doubts about her aside and treat her as a friend. It's what Tom would want her to do. 'Yeah, it's difficult. Conflicted. You're brought up to think you should love them no matter what. And that you should forgive them anything they might do to you.' Lila gave a bitter laugh. 'Sometimes you have to learn the hard way that life's not like that. Sometimes you have to just say "fuck you" and walk away from them.'

'And that's what you think I should do now?' Pearl sounded like she genuinely didn't know. It felt like Lila was the older, wiser one. And maybe, in terms of life experience, she was.

'Families aren't biological.'

Pearl smiled. 'Spoken like a psychology student.'

Lila also smiled. 'I've learned that the hard way. Living here with Tom, he's my family now. Or I hope so. It takes a lot to trust after . . . you know.'

'Yeah.' Pearl nodded. 'Part of me wants to write back, tell them how much I miss them and go and see them. Try and make things like they were before. But then I think . . . it won't be like that, will it? Because before was a lie. They were planning all this . . . this monstrous stuff that I never knew about and I was supposed to just go along with them. And I couldn't. And no matter what they say or do it won't make up for it. But then I think . . .' She shook her head. 'Oh, I don't know.'

'It's up to you,' said Lila after a while. 'I can't choose for you. I can only tell what I did. You might be, I dunno, different.'

'It's just so . . . hard. You never think these kinds of things will happen to you.'

Lila gave a harsh laugh. 'Tell me about it.'

Pearl fell silent. Neither spoke. Pearl eventually broke the silence. 'Thanks. For listening, anyway.'

Lila shrugged. 'What are friends for?'

Pearl smiled at that. Lila did also.

'Fancy an episode of *Dynasty*?'

'You're on.'

'I'll make some coffee.'

Pearl got up from the armchair, went into the kitchen. Lila watched her. Felt that balancing universe thing again. Realised she didn't have to cling on to the rock quite so hard now. That she could stand on her own.

Any further thought was cut off. There was a knock at the door.

'Can you get that?' called Pearl from the kitchen.

She got off the sofa, went to open the door.

There stood the black biker she had seen previously. He smiled at her.

'Hi,' he said. 'We've met before, remember?'

'Yeah.'

He smiled. 'I should have introduced myself properly. I'm Quint. A friend of Tom's?' His upward inflection made the statement into a question. 'Anyway, he said I should look in on you. You know, see you're OK. That OK? You must be Lila, yeah?'

Lila didn't answer.

Quint laughed. 'Least you didn't say no. So I reckon that must be yes.' The smile dropped. 'Can I come in? Want to talk to you.'

Lila's first reaction, her gut instinct, was to say no. But she overrode it. Tom had told her about him. She had kind of expected him to be in touch. But something still told her she didn't want him in the house.

'Please? Freezing out here.'

Lila reached a decision. She moved aside, let him enter.

'Thanks,' he said, going past her.

She closed the door behind him.

Part Three
HANGED

That same night in Manchester

'Shit . . .'

Foxy opened his eyes. Couldn't see anything, his vision all blurred and smeared black. He closed them, tried again. Wiped his hand across his face. That hurt, like dragging needles, but at least he could see, if not fully. He blinked again. There. Some kind of liquid in his eyes, thick, viscous. He blinked again. Put his hand to his face, looked at his palm. Realised it was blood. And something else in the pooled blood in his palm. Small, glittering shards. Glass.

He tried to pull himself into a sitting position and felt pain like he had never known before. His body wouldn't respond, his left side refusing to follow commands. Then he remembered. The crash. He looked up. Through the blur he saw the BMW wrapped around a lamppost, the windscreen shattered and himself in front of it. He worked out what had happened.

When the police arrived, everyone in Foley's gang had driven off straight away, looking for any exit the police hadn't covered. They all panicked, drove any which way. Foxy tried to keep a cool head. He tried to work out which exits the police would have blocked, come up with alternative routes around them. He could still get away with this, he thought. Still convince them he was on their side. That all the easy money and pussy, the drugs and the violence, hadn't turned him. Salvage something. He just had to get out of the estate to do it.

He pulled himself up using the front bonnet of the car and the lamppost. They were almost one since the crash. He gasped for breath, pain singing through his body like a choir of demons. His right arm hung uselessly at his side. His first thought: get away. Get help. He heard a noise. The passenger seat airbag had inflated, saving that half of the window from splintering. The cry came from behind it. He pulled himself round to the side of the car, looked in. The girl he had been with, Hayley, was still sitting there. Trapped.

'Oh god . . .' She began to move, coming round slowly, then faster as she realised what was in front of her face, fought with the airbag, thinking it was suffocating her.

'It's all right,' Foxy said, or tried to say. His mouth didn't seem to be working well. 'It's all right . . .'

She managed to fight her way through the bag and out of the car. Unsteady on her legs from both high heels and the shock of the crash, she was bloodstained but not to his extent. Her wide eyes told him that shock was setting in. He didn't have time for that. He had to get away. And her as well.

'Come on,' he said, letting go of the bonnet and reaching out his good hand, wobbling as a result, 'we've got to go.'

The night came back into focus for her now and she realised where she was, what must have happened. Then she looked at Foxy. And started screaming.

'Shut up, you stupid bint, shut it . . .' Anger straight away. He didn't have time for this.

'Your face, shit, what's happened to your face?'

He moved towards her, she pulled back instinctively. He could hear voices, see lights, getting nearer.

'A fucking car crash,' he said, or tried to. The words sounded fine in his head, mangled as they left his mouth. 'Now come on.'

He made to grab her, pull her with him. She flinched away once more.

'No,' she said, shaking her head, tears forming in her eyes. 'No, I'm not, this is . . . not fun anymore. I'm scared, Foxy . . . I'm scared . . .'

'Come on then.'

'No . . .' She refused to budge. The tears came freely now. 'I want to go home. I want my mum . . .' She kept shaking her head. 'This is . . . no . . .'

The voices, loud, angry, were getting nearer. He grabbed her arm, dragged her along with him. Unsteady on his feet, but determined. She refused to move.

'The fucking law's coming, come on . . .'

She didn't move. 'The law? The law . . . I'm going to tell them, Foxy. Tell them I wasn't involved, tell them it wasn't me. I'm going to tell them . . .'

'You're coming with me . . .' Another grab for her. He didn't have the strength to compel her to move and his words weren't helping. He had to impress on her the seriousness of the situation, just how badly and quickly they needed to get out of there.

His heart was hammering, pumping blood round his body, out of his body. He needed to move. He needed attention. With no other choice, he pulled his gun out, pointed it at her. He had never been firearm trained. In fact his Glock had barely been fired, except for practice in the Worsley Woods. But he was used to brandishing it in order to get attention, make someone follow his orders. That was usually enough.

'Now.' He pointed it at her.

She just stared at him. 'Foxy, what you doing?'

'We've got to go. I can't . . .' Weakening now, a different kind of darkness than the night dancing before him. 'Come on . . .'

'I'm not moving.' Her voice edging towards hysteria. 'I'm staying here. I'm not . . .' She closed her eyes, pretended she wasn't there. 'I want to go home . . .'

Anger overtook him once more. He couldn't leave her here, she would try and control the narrative – his narrative – close down his own attempts to come out of this any kind of hero. But she wouldn't come with him. And he couldn't hang around here any longer. He made one last attempt to get her onside.

He grabbed her once more. 'Come on.' Started walking, hoping he had enough strength to drag her with him.

'Get off me . . .' She shook off his grip easily.

He tried again, pulling at her. Again, she resisted.

Then came the shots from behind. The sound of bodies running towards him.

'I don't have time for this . . .'

He pulled her along beside him and she twisted her ankle, falling over her heels. She crumpled to the ground in a heap. He bent down, pulled her up.

Just as a bullet whistled past the side of his head.

'Shit . . .'

Crouching, he returned fire. Hayley dragged herself to her feet, began running. Towards where the gunfire was coming from.

'Stay here you stupid bint . . .'

Another bullet, even closer this time. He could see bodies in the distance. Moving slowly towards him. He raised his gun, fired blindly, unable to see clearly.

Later, he told himself that it was an accident. That he hadn't meant to hit her. He had just been desperate, blacking out, even. But he did hit her. Several times. Damaged nerves from the crash, he told himself later. His trigger finger must have spasmed.

He also told himself that pulling up a nearby manhole cover in a desperate display of strength and dropping the gun down it, waiting for the splash as it hit running water in the sewer below, then replacing the cover was just his instinct as a copper kicking in. Nothing more.

With no energy left, he collapsed next to her.

It wasn't me. I didn't do that. It . . .

The questions would have to wait. The voices and those bobbing flashlights were getting nearer.

When they found him, he was still alive. But he would never be the same again.

36

Foley was escorted through the prison once more. Not just by an officer but also by Baz. It wasn't that Foley didn't feel safe inside at the moment, just that he felt it best to have protection from someone he could trust. And he didn't trust the officers. They didn't just hate him, they despised him. His money paid for his life inside as well as keeping them onside, but it also meant that a higher bidder could turn them away from him. And things had been very fucking strange recently. Since Clive had arrived inside, in fact. And Eccleston. And until he could get rid of this feeling of unease, Baz would accompany him everywhere he went.

Outside the main building, round the corner, ignoring the drizzle and mist, the dankness from the moors, the prematurely grey day. Walking the pitted tarmac footpath by the perimeter fence, the razor-wire creating a double obstacle before the outer wall could be reached. The space between the fence and wall was a graveyard of failed escape attempts and contraband that never reached its target. Foley had seen it so many times he ignored it. This was his everyday life. His home.

He stood outside Dr Lousia Bradshaw's hut. Turned to face the wall, smiling, in a mockery of what the officer would have him do, waited for that same officer to knock on the door. It was opened.

'Come in,' said Louisa, seeing Foley standing there. Then she saw Baz, seemed confused.

'He's with me,' said Foley.

'I don't think—'

'He's waiting outside. He'll be no trouble.' Foley turned to the officer. 'You can go. Come back when I'm finished.' Like dismissing a servant.

The officer, disgruntled but knowing where his money came from, left.

'Right,' said Foley, summoning up a smile, 'let's go.'

He stepped inside. Lousia followed. Baz took up his sentry position. Tried to ignore the cold and damp.

Inside Foley walked towards his usual armchair, sat down. He could smell the coffee but it didn't have its usual siren call today. He had too much on his mind. A burden ready to be unloaded.

'So,' said Dr Bradshaw, settling down in the opposite chair with a notepad on her lap, coffee at her side. 'How've you been, Dean?'

Foley opened his mouth to speak. He often started with wit, barbs or charm. Only when he couldn't come straight out and say what he wanted to, had to work round it, circle slowly down. But not this time. Straight in.

'Not going to lie, things have been difficult.' He squirmed as if the chair was uncomfortable. 'Since I last spoke to you.'

'In what way?' Pen poised.

'I . . .' He had planned what he would say as they walked across. Before that, even, the night before. Rehearsed his words and even her anticipated responses, planned what he hoped the eventual outcome would be. But sitting there, facing her, the words wouldn't come. And he couldn't think of anything to say to talk round it. 'I . . . it's been difficult.'

She waited, gave him time, space, to gather his thoughts. Find his voice.

'It's this . . . it's what you said to me last time. Got me thinking.'

'About?'

'About . . .' He sighed, leaned forwards, agitating his hands. 'This ex-copper. This narc. I've thought about him for years. Wondered where he was, what he was doing, whether he was alive or not, was he fucking up someone else's business, pardon my French, you know? And I thought . . . what I would do when I got hold of him.

What I'd always threatened to do. Make him pay. All of that. And like I said he's here now, right in front of me . . .'

'And?'

Foley shook his head. Looked at his hands is if expecting to find the answer there. 'I don't know. Just don't know.'

She waited.

'I mean, last time we were talking about revenge.'

'We were.'

'And how good it felt when I took it into my own hands. Administered it myself.' His voice relished the word *administer*.

She nodded slowly, keeping eye contact, encouraging him to continue.

'Well . . . that's it, isn't it? Taking pleasure in punishment. Doing what's right. Letting everyone know you've done the right thing. A warning to anyone else thinking of starting. Don't mess. Don't take the piss. And, you know, the satisfaction of a job well done.'

'We talked about that. You said it was the way things had to be. What was expected of you.'

He nodded.

'Now you're saying you got satisfaction from it? From hurting surrogates of your father?'

Foley jumped at the mention of the name, like he had just been shocked. 'Surrogates.' He nodded. 'Yeah.' Another nod. 'I suppose . . . I've said it so it must be. But it's more than that, you know? You look at yourself and . . .' He stared at her, fists raised before his eyes. 'It's for its own sake.'

'Can you explain?'

He looked at his fists again. Rotated them before his gaze. Saw them in another time and place, glistening with blood and gore, knuckles sore and distended. Clenched so hard he couldn't immediately unlock them. And his body pumping with adrenaline, sweat and blood on his skin, soaking his clothes from both sides, lungs burning hot as a steam engine's furnace, arms just pistons, parts of a machine. But his mind content. At the nearest thing to peace he had ever known. Justice served. The natural order restored.

'I see,' said Dr Bradshaw.

Foley looked up, startled. Had he said all that aloud? From the look on the doctor's face it seemed he had. He said nothing, suddenly embarrassed.

'You've described a high that's certainly attractive to you,' she said. 'And attainable. But I suspect that violent euphoria becomes harder to attain the longer it goes on. Am I correct?'

Foley thought back again to the punishment beatings. How, even before Mick Eccleston had betrayed him, the highs were getting harder to reach, more difficult to maintain. Like they were further away and he had to grasp for them, strain to catch them. And when he did he barely held on to them. And that in turn made him even angrier. But it had been a weary anger. An unpleasant one.

'Yeah,' he said. 'Bang on.'

'And how d'you feel about that now?'

Foley didn't answer immediately.

'You said as soon as you heard this man had entered the prison you wanted to see him. And when you saw him you wanted revenge for everything he'd done to you. Is that correct?'

'Yeah, that's right.'

'But you didn't know if you would do it yourself or get someone to do it for you. And if you did, you feared it would sap the enjoyment from it. And now you don't know if you even want to do it at all?'

He nodded, shifting around once more. 'You see, I've been having . . . dreams.'

'What kind of dreams?'

'Bad ones. Ghosts, even. Like I'm being haunted. And I wake up . . . well. Not in a good state.'

'Tell me about them.'

Foley was reluctant to delve any further but knew that he had to. This might be his only chance to make things right with himself. To find some kind of peace. To know which way was forwards. 'There's me and him. And we're back in Manchester, the night it all went tits up. The night he betrayed me. And we're there again and . . .' He shook his head. 'It gets weird then. Like the whole thing starts to melt away. And I'm shouting at him, *You've done this! You've taken all this away from me!* And there's cars disappearing, and money . . . all of that. Until there's just me and him left.'

'And where is this?'

'I dunno. Like . . . nowhere. And it's like a western. Just me and him facing each other. And I'm armed, I've still got my gun, see. And he's got nothing. He's just standing there. And I try to raise my gun arm to take aim. I try to feel the anger inside me, let it do its job, let me shoot him, and I want to keep shooting him until there's nothing left of him and I'm all out of bullets. And I'm shouting how much I hate him and he's just standing there. And I try to bring my arm up . . .' He mimes the action. 'But I can't. Can't move. Can't do anything.' He sat back, panting.

Neither spoke.

Eventually Foley laughed. Unsteadily. 'Just a dream, eh? Can't go around reading too much into that bullshit, can you?'

'That's for you to decide, Dean. You've been talking about how you should take revenge against this person for what he's done to you in the past. Yes, it may be emotionally satisfying for a while but in the long term it may well cause more upset than not.'

'But it might not.'

'That's for you to interpret how you wish. Same with your dream. You tell me that you don't think you can take revenge anymore. That you won't get anything beneficial out of it, even though you've been thinking about him the whole time you've been in here and what you'd do to him if you saw him again. Does that sound about right?'

Foley nodded.

'And how d'you feel about that?'

'I dunno, honestly. I've got a reputation in here. Can I speak honestly?'

The question, asked abruptly, threw her off guard. 'No point in being here otherwise.'

'Right.' He nodded, making his mind up about something. 'My reputation. I know you know about it. And you maybe think of me differently because of it, I don't know. But somewhere like this, a reputation's all you've got. And if that goes you've got nothing. So I have to decide what to do. And it might not be the answer you want to hear. Or I want to hear. But I have to do something.'

'You know I have to report you if you're going to—'

'Yeah, I know all that. But you don't know who this bloke is. And I haven't said anything about him to you so there's no way you could tell anyone anything. It's just . . .' He sighed. Put his head in his hands. 'I get tired of all this. So tired. But I don't know what to do. What can I do?'

'I've given you all the help and advice I can. The tools to cope. You've got to make that decision on your own.' She looked at her watch. 'I think that's it for today, Dean. Sorry.'

He looked up at her like he had been cut adrift.

'I think you've got plenty to be getting on with, though. A lot to think about before our next session, don't you?'

Foley leaned forwards once more. Exasperation in his voice. 'But I need to know what to do. I'm . . . I can't just go on like this . . .'

'I'm sorry, Dean, this is all I can do here. If you need someone to talk to on the wing then I'll—'

Foley stood up. 'You haven't been listening, have you? I can't do that. I can't talk to anyone on the wing. Because they'd know then. They'd *know*. Everyone's going to be expecting me to do this, and if I don't, I'll be weak. And I'll have had it. So no. It's here or nothing.'

Louisa sighed. 'OK, Dean. Let me see what I can do. I'll juggle some things around and see you again this week. That's the best I can do, OK?'

Foley sighed. Looked round like the room was just another prison cell. 'Suppose it'll have to.'

'Leave it with me.'

He left.

37

DC Blake looked at the crime scene at Double Locks. Not the spot where her partner was murdered, not the place where she betrayed him. Nor where she had taken justified action to protect her investment. Just another crime scene.

She shouldn't have been there. By law, she was too close to the victim to be part of the investigation. But she had to find a way to control the flow of information, shape the way it was used. Guide it away from herself. So she had turned up at the scene, ostensibly to see if she could be of any assistance. Play the role expected of her.

The Double Locks crime scene was a few days old. The novelty for rubberneckers had worn off. Barely anyone gave it a second look now. The white tent and erected fence hid the car park from the towpath and the sight of white-suited officers going painstakingly about their business was now deemed boring. Once onlookers realised it wasn't like on the telly, and police work was as exciting to watch as any other job in the public sector, they drifted away and left them alone. The only aggravation came from the owners of the pub who were waiting for the all-clear to reopen, complaining of lost revenue. Blake knew what they really meant: come and see the site of the latest grisly murder! Follow the signs! Read the information placards! Then stop for food and refreshment! And bring your friends and family! She couldn't blame them, they had a business to run. But the investigation would take as long as it had to.

DCI Harmer was with her. 'Must hurt, seeing all this, Annie. Could get very emotional for you.'

'I just want to be on the team, Dan,' she said, deliberately using his first name, playing up the intimacy between them, her voice lowered, matching the words, 'Part of this investigation.'

His expression looked pained. 'Too risky. You were his partner.'

'All the more reason, then. Plus, I owe it to him.'

He didn't reply, just stared at the forensics going about their business in their white tent.

She kept working on him. 'Dan,' seductive now, the promise-laden tone one he could never refuse, 'come on. I knew him better than most.'

'Maybe you didn't.'

She frowned. 'What?'

He looked at her then, opened his mouth, closed it, then opened it again. Deciding whether to share something with her or not. 'They're going to question you, you know. This team.'

'They already have.'

'Another time, I mean.' Again, that indecision. She knew he would talk to her though. She waited. 'Listen, between you and me, there've been some irregularities discovered concerning Nick Sheridan.'

She frowned, barely suppressing a smile. Kept acting. 'What kind of irregularities?'

'Well . . .' He looked round, checked they weren't being over-heard. Leaned in closer. 'His computer was taken away, checked over. Looks like there was some . . . there's no way to say this gently. It looks like he was bent.'

She assumed a wide-eyed look. 'No . . .'

''Fraid so. It seems he was taking payments. From whom, we don't know. Or why. But the evidence is all there. It's being examined now.'

'Not Mr By The Book Nick Sheridan.'

'I'm as surprised as you are, Annie.'

'Then that's all the more reason for me to be on this team. You need me there. Someone has to make sure findings like that don't taint the rest of us.'

Harmer frowned. 'You think there might be more?'

'God knows. But if that's what they've found so far, we might need damage limitation.'

He nodded. 'You're right.'

She smiled and he looked at her as if just seeing her for the first time. 'You done something to your hair?'

She smiled, put her hands to the ends, fluffed it out, arching her back as she did so. 'You like it? You've always said how much you find redheads attractive.' She leaned forwards so he could get a good view of her cleavage. 'Haven't you?'

'You remembered.'

Of course I bloody remembered, she thought. Everything gets filed away for future use. 'I did. I also bought something to wear to go with it . . .'

Harmer could barely control himself. 'And . . .' He looked round, seemingly wishing he was somewhere more private. 'Do the collar and cuffs match?'

Blake felt a bit of sick in her mouth at the words. Harmer imagined his blokey badinage was the kind of thing women loved to hear. God, it was like being shagged by David Davis.

She giggled appropriately, leaned right in to him, mouth to his ear. 'Who said anything about cuffs?'

He just stared straight ahead as the meaning behind her words sunk in.

'Usual place, usual time tonight?' she whispered.

He nodded as vigorously as a cartoon dog.

'So I'm on the Sheridan investigation?'

How could he refuse?

She drove away from Double Locks, back to Middlemoor. Her official title was team liaison. She couldn't be seen to be working with the investigating team directly, but was privy to everything that went on. That suited her perfectly.

They were looking for the woman Sheridan had been seen with the night of his death, focusing on her as the lynchpin of the investigation. A drinking companion, dressed in figure-hugging black,

black hair scraped back. Leaning into him over the table, a suggestive smile on her face all the time they talked. No one had managed to trace her yet. Blake had been questioned, of course, but cleared. Figure-hugging black had never been her style. And no one would ever suggest an affair between her and Nick Sheridan.

Along with the DI brought in from Avon and Somerset to oversee the investigation, she had interviewed the other drinkers in the pub that night. Most of them had barely looked at her, just took her for the female sidekick of the leading investigator. And she was happy to let them believe that. The general public, bless them, were always eager to help an investigation, believing that they might hold the clue that could unlock the whole thing, bring a murderer to justice. So they would explain what they saw on the night in question in as much painstaking, boring, unwanted and unnecessary detail as possible. All the while never noticing that the woman they were talking about was sitting right next to them.

She should have been on the stage.

Inside Blackmoor was going to plan too.

Just the way she liked it. No surprises.

In control.

38

Down – hold – up again. Down – hold – up again. And again. And again. Tom was keeping himself fit. Sit-ups in a cell was cramped enough, in a shared cell just about impossible. But he had to keep himself fit, keep himself sane. Keep himself ready.

Evening. Association time but neither of them had left their cell. Cunningham lay on the top bunk, singing softly to himself. He had the kind of voice Tom would have expected given his choir background, high and clear, even at low volume. Something in Latin, Tom thought. Some religious piece or perhaps even opera. Nothing he recognised. Cunningham tuned out of the room when he sang to himself, and it was something he had been doing more and more since Tom came back onto the wing. So with Cunningham doing that and Tom doing his exercises, it was like two different worlds coexisting in the smallest space possible, or so Tom thought.

Everything was back to the way it had been. At least superficially. Cunningham's face had lit up when he returned. There were red marks and welts on his face and arms, they looked like they stung. Perhaps Tom's presence had stopped other inmates bullying and abusing his cellmate. Perhaps that was why he was so pleased to have him back.

Earlier, Tom had tried talking to Cunningham, with some success.

'So I hear you're looking to get out, visit your mother?'

Cunningham jumped as if he had been shocked. 'Who told you that?'

'Thought everyone knew. They're waiting for you to give up some information then you can go, yeah?'

Cunningham thought about Tom's words, smiled. 'Yeah . . .'

Tom saw, in that moment, why Cunningham hadn't given up the location of his bodies yet. The power it gave him. Not only over the police and prison staff, but the families of the victims themselves. He was enjoying it.

'Why not tell them? Then you can get out? Seems simple.'

'It's not. Not that simple. It has to be . . . I have to see my mother when . . . when the time is right.'

'What d'you mean?'

'She's still in the hospital. There's nothing they can do for her. They're going to send her home to die.'

Tom couldn't work out what kind of emotion was behind the words. But he kept talking. 'So you want to see her at home, right?'

Cunningham nodded.

'Why don't you tell them what they want to know, then arrange to see her when she's back at home?'

Cunningham stood up, his eyes angry little dots. 'Because I'm doing it my way. *My way.* Don't tell me . . . don't tell me . . .'

Tom held up his hands. 'OK, OK . . .' He waited for Cunningham to calm down. 'Hey, here's an idea. Why don't you tell me? Then I can tell them when you want me to?'

Cunningham looked at him, something like joy appearing briefly in his eyes.

'I mean,' Tom continued, 'that's what friends are for, helping each other out when they need to.'

Cunningham said nothing, but it looked as though a war was being waged behind his eyes. Like a cartoon character with a devil on one shoulder and an angel on the other. Tom waited.

Eventually Cunningham turned away, looking like he had lost his train of thought, or lost interest in the conversation. That was when he began to sing.

And didn't stop.

Tom, realising he wasn't getting anywhere but needing to do something in that small space, started his sit-ups.

As he exercised, he thought. The phone call. Blake. Anger and fear danced within him, each vying for prominence. He tried to tame the fear but couldn't. Too overwhelming, too all-embracing. He was stranded, in prison, alone. His only contact with the outside world gone. His life in danger.

He'd walked back to his cell, numb. Lain there all night, not knowing if he slept or not. Unsure even whether he heard Cunningham's night terrors. Just letting the enormity of his situation sink in. Trapped. Stranded.

The next day had been the same. Every movement around him became a potential threat. He was ready to retaliate, his body tensed and coiled, get the first punch in, make it count, make it dirty. Don't be fair, just win. Everyone from the inmates to the officers. They could come at him one at a time or all together. He just had to be ready.

He thought about pulling his razor apart, melting the blade into his toothbrush with a lighter. He decided not to risk it. If he was discovered with it he'd be busted down to basic, and he didn't need that. So he started exercising.

Push-ups, sit-ups, squats, anything he could manage in that cramped space to make his body harder, stronger. Focus his mind away from the ever-present fear. As he worked out, he planned. What to do next, how to get out of there.

Just walk up to the Governor and tell him who he was and what he was doing there. And be disbelieved. With no backup and no way to find out if Sheridan was working with anyone else besides Blake, his claims would make him the laughing stock of the wing and an even bigger target than he already was. Quint? There was nothing his old commando mate could do either. He was only insurance in case anyone tried to get to him through Lila or Pearl. No. There was only one way out that didn't involve serving his whole sentence.

Get Cunningham to confess.

Dr Bradshaw had said doing so would reduce his sentence. He wondered how sympathetic she would be to hearing his whole story. First though, he had to get results.

He finished up, having reached his number, rolled over on to his back, stared at the ceiling while he got his breath back, about to start on his push-ups.

He didn't get that far. An officer put his head round the door.

'On your feet, Killgannon, you're wanted.'

Tom frowned. 'Where?'

'How do I know? Just told to come and get you.'

'Not my turn for a shower, is it?' He was sweating profusely from his workout and beginning to stink out the cell. That was why after-shave was almost as valuable as tobacco in prison. 'Could do with one, though.'

'Come on.'

Tom got to his feet. Cunningham stopped singing to himself, lowered himself down from the bunk.

'Not you,' said the officer, pointing, 'just him.'

Cunningham wordlessly got back on the bunk. Tom frowned. That seemed odd.

'Come on.'

Tom was led off the wing. He recognised the officer as one of the two who had given the art group the tour of the topping shed. And that seemed to be where they were headed now.

Tom shivered from more than just the cold. He was off the wing, out in the open night air. The sweat dried to his body, turned suddenly freezing. This wasn't right, he thought. Something was going on. Then he realised. This is it. This is Foley's attempt on me. He steeled his body, ready for attack.

The officer reached the door to the topping shed, took out his key to open it.

'In there.'

Tom turned to face him. The officer flinched. 'You coming as well?'

The officer became tongue-tied. 'I . . . there's someone in there who'll, who'll tell you what's . . . Just get in.'

Tom stared at him, unmoving. Eyes unblinking. 'How much are they paying you for this?'

The officer turned away, unable to face him.

'Pathetic,' said Tom. 'Fucking pathetic.'

The officer said nothing.

'At least give me a weapon to defend myself.'

The officer looked up. Conflict in his eyes. But he had made a decision. 'Just get in there.'

He gave Tom a shove through the door, locked it behind him.

Tom looked round. Or tried to. The room was in darkness. His fingers played along the wall, searching for the light switch. He found it, flicked it on. The room was illuminated by the overhead striplights. It seemed to be as it was the last time he had been inside. Except for one thing. The makeshift noose and rope tied from the central roof beam. The chair beneath it.

Two shapes detached themselves from the shadowed piles of stacked chairs. Two huge inmates. Tom had never seen them before – or didn't think he had – but he knew the type. Prison enforcers. Big, covered in tattoos, both professionally done and prison marked, with the kind of dead eyes that only came to life when they were taking someone else's. One had a mohawk, one had a beard but a bald head. Other than that they were indistinguishable

'Come to give me a message?' he asked, body already tensing into a fighting stance.

'Yeah,' said Mohawk. 'It's behind us.' He pointed to the noose.

Beardy reached into his jogging bottoms pocket, brought out a cell-made shiv. Mohawk did likewise. They began advancing towards him. 'You going to give us any trouble?' asked Mohawk. 'Be easier if you didn't.'

Tom smiled. No humour reached his eyes. He looked round for potential weapons. Couldn't see any, except the stacked chairs. Better than nothing. But only just.

Beardy was making his way round Tom's back, attempting to come at him in the clumsiest pincer movement he'd ever witnessed. They were slow-moving but he didn't believe they would be slow-witted. Or that wasn't a chance he was going to take. He feinted to his right, made it look like he was going to run, put the two of them on the front foot, ready to go after him, then quickly darted to his left and the pile of stacked chairs. Before they could react, he had a chair in his hand. He brandished it at them like a lion tamer.

The two of them turned, smiled at him. 'That the best you can do?' said Mohawk.

'Come here and find out.'

They both moved slowly towards him. One of them had to break, he thought, make a sudden movement, attempt to get him. He just had to work out which one.

It was Beardy. He lunged at Tom, trying to get his knife arm around the metal legs of the chair. Tom brought the chair leg down onto his arm. Then again. It had virtually no effect.

Changing tactic he lunged with the chair, aiming it at Beardy's face. That produced a better result. The leg struck him just above the right eye. He recoiled. Tom struck again. This time he hit him right in the eye. Pushed as hard as he could. Beardy, hands to his face, screamed in pain and retreated.

Tom didn't have time to relish this triumph. Mohawk was now behind him, a shiv in his hand too. He felt rather than heard its swish, tried to dodge out of the way. The blade, small but vicious, connected with his forearm. He gasped in pain, looked at it. Blood sprayed out of his arm as it scythed away from the blade. He let go of the chair. It dropped to the floor.

Tom tried to ignore the pain, knew there were more important things to do. He could hurt later.

Looking around, he checked his options, quickly assessed the situation, looked for something that might give him an advantage. He jumped on the chair underneath the noose, grabbed for the rope and swung his body towards Mohawk. Both feet connected and the man went over. The shiv fell away. Tom jumped down, picked it up.

And felt a sudden pain across his right shoulder blade. Beardy, half-blinded, had got himself upright and swung at Tom with his shiv again. He felt the blood instantaneously soak through his sweatshirt. Tom dropped the shiv and turned, ready, trying to ignore the extra pain.

No time to think, he went in on Beardy's blind side, punching him on the side of the head. The man, already in pain, brought his hand up to defend himself. Tom kept punching, as fast and as hard as he could.

Behind him, Mohawk was getting up. Thinking fast, deciding Beardy wasn't the immediate threat, he bent down, grabbed the shiv and turned to Mohawk who threw a fist that was more hopeful than accurate. Tom managed to grab his meaty, muscled arm with one hand and, holding the shiv in the other, twist it down and round. The man pushed against him and Tom stumbled, losing his footing. He let the arm go. Mohawk swung again.

Tom managed to get most of his body out of the way but his right shoulder took a hit. Right where the shiv had already caught him. Mohawk was so big, his blow so powerful, that Tom felt like his arm had gone dead. Beardy, battered but still going, came up behind him, thrusting his knife. Tom just managed to twist out of the way, going to ground, feeling something in his knee pop as he did so.

He spun away out of the grasp of them both, looked round frantically for a way of escape. Couldn't see one. He turned back to them. Looked at the shiv in his hand.

'You want this? Come and fucking get it . . .'

Ready to take the fight to them and be finished, he stepped into the path of the half-blinded Beardy, swung the shiv at him. Backwards and forwards, as deadly and as quick an arc as he could manage, darting and dancing on his feet as much as his damaged knee would allow, becoming a hard target to hit. Beardy put his arm out and the shiv connected. He instinctively pulled his arm back as the blood started to spurt. Tom pressed forwards, swung again. Connected again. Same arm. Beardy grabbed his bleeding arm with his good one. Tom went for a third cut. The blood was now geysering.

He turned to see where Mohawk had got to. The attacker was wary now, standing back from him. Wondering why Tom hadn't followed the script. He came for him.

Tom scanned the room. In the far corner was a wooden handled mop standing upright in a bucket. He ducked away from the advancing Mohawk, made a grab for the mop.

Thinking he could leave Beardy for a few seconds, Tom turned to Mohawk who had stopped his movement and was regarding him uncertainly. Dropping the shiv, he swung the mop, hard as he could, feet braced as well as he could manage. The wood connected with Mohawk's head. He actually screamed 'ow', which Tom might have found amusing under other circumstances.

He swung again, but Beardy managed to grab the shaft of the broom. He followed through with his grip, pushing it towards Tom, forcing him back. He put both hands on the handle, ran Tom back to the wall, pinned him up against it. Wood against Tom's throat, pushing.

Tom knew he would choke if he didn't do something so, knowing one eye was already damaged, pushed his thumbs as hard as he could into both of Beardy's eyes. The man tried to pull his head back and away from Tom, which eased his grip, making Tom in turn press all the harder. And harder still. Beardy cried out in pain. Tom kept pushing, managed to get his thumb right in the corner of his left eye. He could feel the back of the eyeball, see it beginning to pop out of the socket.

Beardy screamed and pulled away, letting go of the mop, trying to claw Tom's hand away from his eye. Tom relaxed his grip, took hold of the handle and pushed Beardy back. He stumbled, ended up on the floor. Tom, not waiting to think, just acting on instinct, swung the wood until it connected with his head. Then again. And again. Until he was sure Beardy wasn't going to get up for a while.

He turned, quickly, looked to see where Mohawk was. He had found the shiv Tom had dropped and stood up, nursing his injured head while holding the shiv out towards Tom without much conviction.

Adrenaline was killing the pain. Tom stood his ground, held the mop handle like a weapon, snarled. 'What you waiting for? Eh? Come on, then, let's be having you . . .'

Mohawk just stared. Glanced at the doorway, down to his fallen comrade who was now bleeding profusely from his arm, the side of his head and ear, cradling what was left of his eyes, then back at Tom. He looked at the knife in his hand. It suddenly seemed very small.

'Come on you fucker, what you waiting for?' Tom's voice rising in pitch, in ferocity.

The other man held up his hands. 'Hey, mate, just a job. No hard feelings.'

He turned and made for the door, dropping the knife as he went.

Tom made to follow him. Before his attacker reached the door it was unlocked from the outside. A crew of officers in riot gear stormed in and stopped, staring at him.

Tom, blood-soaked, anger in his eyes, ready to take on the world just stared back, then yelled, 'Who's next then? Who's fucking next?'

And they were on him.

39

'Here we are again. We're going to have to stop meeting like this.' Anju smiled as she spoke, hands round her coffee for warmth.

Lila looked confused, distraught, even. 'Why?'

Anju frowned, looked closely at her. 'You being serious?'

'Erm . . .'

Her hands uncurled from the cup, wrapped themselves round Lila's. 'It was a joke. Didn't you get that?'

Lila gave a smile. It took a second or two. 'Sorry. Sometimes I . . . don't react to things the way everyone else does. It's . . . I missed a bit. When I was younger.'

Anju's smile widened, her grip on Lila's hands tightened. 'Don't worry. I'll help you get all caught up.'

Lila couldn't help but smile in return.

Anju took her mind off things.

But there were things she wanted to talk to her about.

They were in Grounded, a coffee shop in Truro's artisan quarter. It was an off-campus place where they had taken to meeting. Lila found the coffee good, if a little pricey for a student, but Anju didn't seem to notice. Coming from money will do that, Lila thought, but not in a cruel way. Anju couldn't change her background any more than Lila could. But only one of them wanted to.

They sat on the seats they always did. In front of the counter, smelling the fresh ground coffee and pastries, leaning forwards together, arms on the stripped reclaimed wood tabletop. The wooden stools were circular, their round, padded seats with holes in the centre, in brown and white. Like sitting on a doughnut, Lila had said the first time they went there. I think that's the idea, Anju had replied. Subliminal advertising.

'We had a visitor,' Lila said after taking another mouthful of latte.

'Is Tom home?' Anju had taken to calling him Tom too. Not Mr Killgannon or your friend, nothing like that. She just accepted Lila's home arrangement.

'No, not Tom. Still haven't heard from him. But someone turned up saying he's a friend of Tom's.'

'So he's got news from him?'

'Not exactly.'

'What then?'

Lila sighed. Told her all about Quint.

'This is Quint,' Lila had said to Pearl as the man followed her to the kitchen.

Pearl looked up, startled. Didn't know what to say.

'He says he's a friend of Tom's,' Lila said before anyone else could speak.

'I am a friend of Tom's.' Quint grinned. Cheerful, disarming. He stuck out a finger, pointed in a theatrical manner. 'You must be . . . Pearl. Am I right?' Still smiling. 'I'm right, aren't I?'

Pearl returned the smile. It was infectious. 'Yes, I'm Pearl. Hi.' She walked to him, shook hands over the kitchen table. 'I was just making tea. Want one?'

'Yeah, that would be great, thanks. Cold out there.' He began unzipping his leather jacket.

'Sit down. Please.' Pearl's sense of hospitality kicked in.

He did so, hung his jacket on the back of the wooden chair.

'So what are you doing here, Quint?' asked Lila, staying standing.

'Well, Tom's on his . . . mission, shall we call it. And before he went, he asked me to just keep an eye on you both.'

Lila said nothing. Waited for him to continue.

'I was trying to keep a low profile but after you saw me the other day, well . . .' He put his hands on the air, shrugged. 'Thought I may as well come and say hello. So here I am.' Another disarming smile, accompanied by a little wave this time. 'Hello.'

Pearl, once again, returned it. Lila didn't.

'I went to see Tom a few days ago,' said Lila, face not giving anything away.

'Yeah?' said Quint. 'He mention me?'

'He did, actually, yeah. I told him we didn't need anyone to look after us.'

Quint shrugged. 'Well, you never know.'

'So why would we need someone looking out for us?'

Quint's smile faltered. Lila stared at him, watching him all the time. The smile broke, his features regrouped, ready to take another approach. 'Nothing in particular, I don't think. But he and I go way back. We served together. We always had each other's backs. When he was recalled for active service, so to speak, he phoned me and like I said, here I am. I was camping first but it got a bit cold for that.' Another smile. 'Can't do it like I used to. So I booked into a B&B nearby. I was on the way there when you saw me the other day.'

Lila nodded, said nothing.

Pearl placed a teapot on the table, three mugs, milk from the fridge and a sugar bowl with a spoon in it.

'Help yourself,' she said. 'Although I'd give it a few minutes to brew.'

Quint thanked her. Lila sat down.

'So you were in the army, that right?' asked Pearl.

Quint shook his head. 'Commandos with Tom. Or, you know. What he used to call himself. I've got to get used to calling him that now. Suits him, I think. He looks like a Tom.'

'We've never known him as anything else,' said Pearl, lifting the pot and pouring. 'Sugar?'

'No thanks,' said Quint, then hit them with another dazzling smile.

Don't say it, thought Lila. Please don't say it.

'Sweet enough, that's me.'

Pearl laughed.

Prick, thought Lila.

With their mugs of tea in front of them, the conversation seemed to have wound down a little.

'So why are you here now? Tonight?'

Quint turned to Lila. 'Well, like I said. You saw me, and black people in this part of the world, we tend to stick out, right? So I thought it best to introduce myself.'

'So why does Tom think we need protecting? You still haven't answered me,' said Lila.

Pearl gave her a warning glance, *don't be unfriendly*. Lila pretended she hadn't seen it.

'Didn't he tell you why?'

'No. Could you tell us?'

Lila could remember exactly what Tom had said to her. She just wanted to hear Quint say the same thing.

Quint took in a breath, let it go. 'Well, as you know, Tom . . .' He placed emphasis on the name, like he was saying it in italics. '. . . made a lot of enemies. In his previous life. Led him to being here. So he just wanted to know that, if anyone tried to get to him while he was . . . away, then I'd be here to help you two. That's all.' Another shrug, palms open. 'Nothing sinister. Just that.'

'But we don't *need* protecting,' said Lila.

Pearl looked at her, startled.

'Well we don't,' she continued. 'No one knows Tom's here, no one knows we're here.' She pushed her thumb at Quint. 'Except him.'

'Lila, that's . . .' Pearl began but stopped herself.

'No,' cut in Quint, 'it's fine. It's bad enough that Tom's away doing what he's doing, that's stressful enough without some stranger popping up.'

Lila said nothing. It was Tom she was angry at. She knew that. Or the police officers who had talked him into doing this. Not Quint.

242

And she felt bad about taking it out on him. But not bad enough to apologise.

'Yeah,' she said. That would be as much of an apology as she was going to give.

'So what are your plans, then?' asked Pearl. 'Now that you've said hello.'

'Don't know that there's much I can do. I'll give you my number and if there's anything you don't like the look of, or anyone, give me a call. I'll come round. Sort it. And I'll keep popping in.' He looked at Lila. 'If that's OK with you?'

Lila shrugged. She couldn't find a way back down from her earlier hostility.

Quint smiled. 'Good.' He drained his mug, stood up. 'Well, I'll be off. Oh, one more thing. D'you mind if I just do a quick check of the house? See that no one can get in. That kind of thing.'

'Sure,' said Pearl. 'Go ahead.'

'Thanks.'

He left the room. Lila and Pearl looked at each other.

'He seems nice,' said Pearl. 'You didn't have to be off with him.'

'Couldn't help it. Everything that's happened since I came here . . . you can't blame me for being wary.'

'No, but . . . he's a friend of Tom's. And Tom mentioned him. So he must be OK.'

'Yeah.'

They heard him moving about upstairs. It made Lila feel uneasy. She stood up.

'Just going to the loo.'

'Lila . . .'

'Sorry. All that tea.'

And before Pearl could say anything else, she was out the door and up the stairs. As quietly as she could go.

At the landing she didn't head in the direction of the toilet. She walked slowly down the hallway towards the room she had heard

Quint in. Light was spilling from beyond the frame of the door. She peeped through. Spied. Quint had moved the bed and was kneeling in front of the fireplace, looking up the chimney, his arm in as far as it would go.

Lila didn't stop to think. She entered the room.

'What are you doing?'

Quint was startled. Pulled his arm down from the chimney. His eyes wide, then he composed his features. But just before he did, Lila was sure she saw something else flit across there. Something unpleasant. He stood up, dusted down his arm.

'I was ... these old houses. Some of the chimneys are wide enough to get a body up. Or down. Just making sure no one could get down there. Wouldn't want that, would we?'

'And can they?'

He smiled again. An everything was fine kind of smile. 'Nah. You're all right.' He looked round the room once more. Eyes lingering on the chimneybreast for longer than they should. 'Well, I'd better be off.'

Lila stood aside to let him out. Kept her eyes on him until he left the house.

Later, she would identify what had passed across Quint's eyes before his smile returned. Anger.

*

'And then he left?' asked Anju.

'Yeah,' she said. 'Haven't seen him since.'

'Wow.' She frowned. 'What was he looking for up the chimney?'

'I don't know. I had a look up there after he'd gone ...' She shrugged. 'Nothing there.'

Anju thought for a moment. 'Weird.'

'Something just felt off about him. Maybe ... oh, I don't know.'

'What?'

Lila paused. 'I think we should find out about this guy Quint. How would we go about that?'

Anju smiled. 'Are we girl detectives now? Wow.'

Lila didn't know what to say.

40

Night again, and the walls of Blackmoor prison seemed to absorb darkness, store it up, let it seep out through the crevices in the brick, the gaps in the metal, expel itself from the locks and under doors. The only thing keeping it at bay was the overhead strip lighting. Harsh, burning and unforgiving, those fluorescent tubes lit corridors and wings, spurs and classrooms, workshops and walkways, like artificial suns whose illumination couldn't be escaped. But there were always ways. And means. The brightest lights cast the darkest shadows. And if there was one thing inmates knew how to do, it was move in the shadows.

The hospital wing was never busy. Extreme cases were taken to the local hospital, handcuffed to their beds with a guard attached. But that was expensive and a drain on man hours and overtime. So everything was either dealt with as quickly as possible with the injured inmate back on their wing or, in rare cases, left to recuperate on the hospital wing. There was only one patient there now. And he had a visitor.

The officer on the door looked quizzically at this visitor. 'What d'you want?'

'Have a word with a patient. Visiting time, innit?' He leaned forwards. 'You know who I am.'

The words had the desired effect. The officer looked scared. Didn't want to disobey orders, but knew where the real authority lay. He looked quickly round, checked no one else was there. 'Go on, then. Inside. Quick.'

He unlocked the door, locked it behind him. Stayed where he was.

One patient in the whole wing. Raised leg in plaster, arm in a plastic cast slung across his chest. Head popping out of a neck brace.

Clive.

He sat on the edge of the bed, startling Clive to wakefulness.

'Well, you've been in the wars, haven't you? Look at the state of you.'

Clive quickly oriented himself. Fear immediately took hold. He tried to shrink away from him. 'What d'you want? Haven't you done enough? I'm in here, aren't I? I haven't said anything.'

'Clive, Clive . . .' He smiled. At least he intended it to be a smile. 'Just came to see how you are, that's all. Pay my respects.'

Clive stared at him, wary. Said nothing.

'We go back a long way, Clive, don't we? All the way back to Manchester. Those were the days, eh?'

Clive again said nothing. Watching, waiting.

'They were good times. You, me, Mick.' He sighed. 'Ah, Mick . . .' He shook his head. 'What a cunt he turned out to be.'

'He didn't recognise me,' Clive said at last. 'We both came in together. And he didn't recognise me.'

'Well to be fair, Clive, the years haven't been kind to you. Smack and booze'll do that.'

'I'm clean now.' A quivering pride, a strength in his voice.

'And well done you. No, I'm not here to talk about that. I'm here to reminisce about the good old days. And they were good, weren't they, Clive? Before that bastard took us all down.'

'Yeah,' said Clive, placated but still on guard. 'They were.'

'We lived like kings. We were kings.'

Clive tried to nod. Winced from the pain.

'All in the past now. All in the past. We lost everything that night, didn't we? I mean, some more than others. I mean, you ran, didn't you? Thought you'd get away. No money, nothing. No way of making a living. All gone. So what did you do? Hit the bottle. Big time. And heroin.' He sucked air in through his teeth. 'Bad stuff, Clive. Very bad stuff. Never get high on your own supply.

You should know that. It's all right for the punters but we don't touch it.'

'Yeah well, like I said. I'm clean now.'

'I know, Clive. I know. And you tried to get back into the good books. Well done.'

Clive tried to nod once more. Gave up. Just listened. Too tired to talk.

'But you weren't the only one to lose something that night. I lost plenty. I lost everything.'

'I . . . I know . . .'

'But mentioning Tom Killgannon's niece . . .' a headshake. 'That was out of order, Clive.'

'I . . . I know. And I'm sorry.' He tried to move his encased arm. 'But I've paid for that.'

'Well yes. And no. Because you've started him thinking. You've tipped him off. And when you get well again he's going to come looking for you wanting another chat. And you with your blabbermouth, Clive, you're going to tell him more. Aren't you? Who killed her? How she died?'

'I'm not . . . I promise . . . I won't . . .'

'Well, you say that Clive, but we both know that's not true. So I'm sorry Clive, it has to be this way.'

Clive started to cry.

He eased the pillow from behind Clive's head, cradled it and placed it tenderly on the mattress. He placed the pillow over Clive's tear-wet face. Clive tried to cry out.

'Shh. Come on, Clive. Be Brave. You know it has to be done.'

Eventually Clive stopped crying and his body went limp. He kept the pillow on until he was sure that Clive wasn't pretending, that he actually was dead, then removed it, looked down at him. Shook his head sadly.

He let the pillow drop onto the bed, turned and left the ward.

The officer was on the door.

'I was never here.'

The officer stared at him. Then looked nervously at the ward. Then back to the visitor.

'Never. Understand?'

The officer was too terrified to disagree.

He walked slowly back to his wing.

41

Dr Louisa Bradshaw had never fully made her mind up about Paul Shelley. As a prison governor he seemed competent but not spectacular. No standout schemes for rehabilitation or to cut reoffending. No brave trials, no particular vision, no rocking the boat. Just keeping on keeping on. Like he was only in the position for a short while and wanted to hand it over to the next incumbent as he found it. A safe pair of hands. And plenty of other clichés that he would no doubt employ when asked about his job. A remarkably unremarkable man. Or perhaps, she thought, that was just the impression he tried to give. Perhaps the truth was something else.

She sat beside him in his office, noticed just how hot it was. Not warm, hot. Uncomfortably so. Did he do that on purpose, to make colleagues and inmates alike feel ill at ease? If so, why? And how did he stand it himself? She didn't know, but wanted to shed her jumper she was so uncomfortable. The fact that she was wearing a T-shirt with the NASA logo underneath stopped her. Not work-appropriate. But then she didn't think it would ever be this warm.

The office itself was as expected. Framed photos on his desk of his wife and children. All as unremarkable looking as him, she thought, mentally chastising herself for judging on appearances. Surely working in this place had taught her not to do that.

The lighting was softer than in the rest of the prison and there were some framed certificates and photos on the wall. Diplomas and cricketing photos. Shelley dwarfed in pads and a helmet, holding the bat in an aggressive way, the ball nowhere to be seen. Shelley and others bundled up in rough weather gear, on top of a mountain, all smiling at the camera. Probably needs something like that, she thought, after spending most of his working life stuck in a place like this.

There was still something off about him, though, and Louisa couldn't quite place what it was. At one time she would have dismissed feelings and intuitions as something for the new agers, not specialists like her. But again, this place had taught her to respect her instincts. It always seemed like there was something he wasn't telling her. A secret he didn't want to share. Something to do with the way the prison was run. Her place in it. She might have imagined it but he had seemed to be on the verge of saying something to her a few times, breaking down whatever self-imposed barrier he had erected, testing to see if she could be trusted. Then changing his mind. She had said nothing at those times, just filed it away.

The door opened. An officer brought in Tom Killgannon.

Louisa was shocked, but hoped she didn't show it. That wouldn't be professional. However, the change in Killgannon since she had last seen him was more than noticeable. His hair was wilder, beard more unkempt. Bandages and plasters covered his arms, face and shoulder. Bruises and cuts grew round them. That was to be expected since his attack, but something in his manner marked him as different too. He seemed less like the man she had first spoken to and more like a hardened prisoner. The tattoos on his arms that she had previously dismissed now seemed more prominent. His body seemed harder, leaner. He might still have that softness, that intelligence in his eyes, but they were hooded now, hidden. She couldn't tell what was in there.

'Sit down,' said Shelley.

Tom sat.

Shelley leaned forwards, hands clasped together. Like an old headmaster trying to reach a bright but wayward child. Or bargain with one who was uncontrollable.

'Has a night in segregation given you a different perspective?'

Tom looked up. Louisa still couldn't see his eyes. 'On what?'

'On telling me why you were attacked. On why you think you were important enough for two very dangerous criminals to take the risk of further punishment and take you on?'

Tom shrugged.

Shelley looked down at his hands, back at Tom. Trying again. 'How did you come to be alone in that room?'

'Ask your wing staff. One of them escorted me there. Then locked the door after me.'

Shelley looked uncertain, unsure how to proceed. 'I won't hear any criticism of my staff, Killgannon.'

'Then stop asking me pointless questions. Because you'll hear a lot. This whole thing should go to adjudication. Your staff led me in there. There was a noose and two ugly bastards waiting for me.'

'How did your alleged attackers get into that room?'

'Ask them.'

'They're not here anymore. Their injuries were quite serious. They've been moved to other institutions where they can receive better treatment.'

'Colour me surprised. Scared of the lawsuit?' Tom hadn't raised his voice yet. All his words were in the same flat, weary monotone.

'So what had you done to annoy them?'

Tom shrugged. 'Never seen them before in my life.'

'But you must have—'

'Stop fucking about.' Tom leaned forwards quickly, spoke sharply. There was power in both of those things and Shelley was taken by surprise. Louisa too, to a lesser extent, but Shelley actually jumped back. 'You know what's going on. There was a noose in there. They were sent to either hurt me, intimidate me or kill me. They'd been paid to do it. And you know who by.'

Shelley stared at Tom. Tom returned the stare. Louisa saw his eyes for the first time. The intelligence was still there but no softness.

Shelley looked away, pretended to find something on his desk fascinating. 'You're making ridiculous allegations, Killgannon.'

Tom laughed, shook his head. He turned his attention to Louisa. 'Why are you here?'

She was shocked at the frankness of the question. This wasn't the man she had spoken to recently. Or if it was, something very bad had happened to him since then.

'I'm . . .' she began '. . . here to assess you. See if you're fit enough to go back to the wing.'

'Fit. You mean mentally? So I can do your investigating for you without attacking anyone else who comes to kill me, is that it?'

Louisa reddened. 'Something like that.'

'Investigating?' asked Shelley.

'Ask her,' said Tom, indicating Louisa with his thumb.

Louisa said nothing.

Tom turned his attention back to Shelley. 'Just tell Foley not to send any more people after me. Then I won't have to fight them off.'

'Foley?' said Shelley too quickly. 'Dean Foley? Why would he take an interest in you?'

Tom took his attention from Louisa, returned it to Shelley. He smiled, blurted out some kind of laugh. 'Ask him.'

'I'm asking you.'

Tom looked between the two of them. Louisa thought he was making up his mind about sharing something and was reminded again of Shelley. With Tom it seemed different. Not that he didn't want to share something, more that he was now almost beyond caring what would happen if he did.

Tom sighed. 'Right,' he said. 'I'll tell you. Do whatever you like with this information afterwards.'

They waited.

'Tom Killgannon's not my real name. I'm an ex-copper and I'm here undercover.'

Shelley laughed out loud. 'Bullshit. Any undercover operation in my prison goes through me. I'd never heard of you before you arrived and started causing trouble.'

254

'It was supposed to be done secretly so no one would know, especially not the target.'

'Who is?' Shelley asked, amusement in his voice.

'Noel Cunningham. I'm supposed to get near him, befriend him, find out where those kids' bodies are in return for letting him out to visit his mother.' He looked at Louisa who was about to speak. 'When you asked me to do the same thing I couldn't believe it.'

Shelley looked between the two of them. 'You asked him to do the same thing? Why?'

'Because they seemed to have bonded. And there was a good chance Cunningham would open up to him.'

Shelley sat back, smiled. 'So you tell us now that you're undercover. Taking this very seriously, aren't you? Very good. Keep going.'

Tom ignored him. 'I was the person whose testimony brought down Dean Foley. He knew me back in Manchester under a different name. I was undercover then. He made me, sent those two men over to me.'

'Is that right.'

'My contact, DS Sheridan of Devon and Cornwall Police is dead. He can't vouch for me.'

'Of course he can't.'

'But his partner, DC Blake should be able to.'

Louisa had wondered who Dean Foley's target was. Now she knew. She also noticed a change in Tom's demeanour when he mentioned the Detective Constable's name. Like saying something he didn't believe. She couldn't work out why.

'Well let's give her a call, then, shall we?'

Shelley picked up his office phone, found the number from his rolodex, dialled. It was answered. 'Governor Paul Shelley, Blackmoor Prison. Could I speak to a Detective Constable Blake? Yes, I'll hold.' He looked directly at Tom, still smiling. 'You're in luck. There is a Detective Constable Blake. They said they'd put me through to her.'

Tom watched him impassively.

'Yes,' said Shelley. 'DC Blake.' He introduced himself once more. 'I've got an inmate here called Thomas Killgannon. He says he's an undercover operative working for both yourself and DS Sheridan, is that true?'

Tom stared at him.

'Oh,' said Shelley, 'I'm sorry to hear that. My condolences. No ... you haven't. Right. Thank you. Sorry to waste your time.' He replaced the receiver, looked back at Tom, triumph in his eyes. 'Never heard of you.'

'Speak to her commanding officer.'

'Who would that be?'

'I don't know.'

'I'm sure you don't. You were right, though. About DS Sheridan. She says he's dead.'

Tom's face changed. Sadness tinged and desperation appeared on his features.

Shelley sat back, threw his hands in the air. 'Thanks for the entertainment. I suppose you're to blame for the death in the infirmary last night too, aren't you?'

'What?'

'Clive Bennett.' Shelley looked at something on his desk. 'Isn't that the inmate you attacked, that got you your first spell on the segregation block?'

'Bennett. Bennett. That's him. Looks different now. That's why I didn't recognise him . . .'

'I suppose you know him too.'

'He was one of Foley's gang back in Manchester. You can check that. He joked about my niece. She's dead. That's why I lost it and attacked him last week.'

A shadow passed over Shelley's features at the mention of Foley's name. 'Get him taken back to his wing.' He looked at Louisa. 'Can't win 'em all, Dr Bradshaw.'

Louisa didn't want to move, didn't want the conversation to end. 'I'd like to keep working with him.'

'What, treat him for being delusional?' Shelley laughed at his own joke.

Louisa was beginning to think Tom Killgannon wasn't delusional. Or at least there was more to his story than he was saying. She addressed Tom directly.

'Will you feel safe back in general population?'

Tom shrugged. 'As safe as I can in here.'

'Fine. Then I'll take you back there.'

She stood up. Tom did the same. Shelley just watched them go, the smile no longer in place.

42

'How are you feeling?'

Tom looked at Louisa, walking alongside him. She had set the pace and didn't seem to be in any hurry to get back to the wing. She seemed sincere but he still didn't want to engage her in conversation. He had just tried that and it had got him nowhere. He was aware of how much his most recent spell on the seg block had changed him, tipped him into a different character. He didn't feel like he was even Tom Killgannon anymore. He felt like he was becoming someone else. Someone harsher, harder. Even crueller, maybe.

'Are we in session now?' he said, his words virtually spat at her. 'Is this therapy?'

She seemed upset by his tone. 'It's a genuine question. How are you bearing up?'

Louisa stopped walking, looked round, checking for eavesdroppers. No one was in earshot. They could hear voices, cries echoing down the corridors, but no one nearby.

'I believe you, Mr Killgannon.'

'Not Tom anymore?' He couldn't take the sneer out of his voice. It seemed to have settled in permanently.

'I'll call you Tom if you like. It doesn't change what I'm saying though. I believe your story.'

Tom looked wary. 'Why?'

'Because . . . I shouldn't be breaking client confidentiality, but someone fitting your description was mentioned to me by another of my patients recently. Your description and background. And how it personally impinged on them and their situation. Then you say all this today and I just put two and two together. Am I right?'

'If by other patient you mean Dean Foley then yes, you are.'

Louisa fell silent, thinking before speaking. 'What if . . . bear with me here, what if . . . I were to get you two together. Somewhere neutral like my office, just so you can both talk to each other in a safe space? Have a conversation away from all the other pressures of this place, try and come up with some kind of, I don't know, way of going forwards for both of you? Would that be worth trying?'

'What, so he can do the job himself? Kill me, face to face?'

'The meeting will be properly monitored. He'll know not to step out of line. He won't. I'm sure of it.'

'Oh, you're sure of it, are you? You know him that well?'

Louisa reddened. 'Yes, I think I do. I've come to understand him quite well.'

Tom laughed. Something harsh escaping from a trap. 'Really? He's playing you. That's what he does. Plays people. Tells them what they want to hear. Until he gets bored of you. And you really wouldn't want to be around him then.'

'I think he's changed since he's been here.'

Tom held up his arms. 'I've got the scars that say he hasn't.'

Louisa shook her head. 'I think it's worth a try. For him as well as you. I've worked with him a lot. I don't believe he's the same person he was when he came in. People change. Especially in somewhere like this.'

She looked directly at him as she spoke. He felt the truth in her words.

'Don't they?' she challenged.

Tom didn't answer.

'Tom?'

'How can I trust you? What about the other stuff? Cunningham?'

'I asked you to do that in good faith. I knew nothing about why you say you are really in here.'

'"Say" I was in here. That's why I *am* in here.'

'And I believe you. Honestly I do, but you have to admit, it's easy for someone like Shelley to reach the conclusion that you're delusional.'

'And how does that help me?' Tom felt anger rise within him. He turned to face her, aware of how much he towered over her, how much more physically powerful he was. How much he could hurt her. 'The whole point of me being here was to get Cunningham to talk. My outside contact's been killed and for whatever reason my other contact is denying all knowledge of me. I have to get out. Never mind Foley, what are you going to do to help me?' Leaning over her, dwarfing her. Hands clenched into fists, ready.

Fear on her face, Louisa shrank away from him, pushed herself into the wall. Her hand went to the pocket of her jeans.

He moved backwards, away from her personal space. Unclenched his fists, averted his eyes from her. 'Sorry . . . sorry. That's not me. That's not me . . .'

Her hand stayed by her pocket. She kept staring at him.

'I'm sorry. It's . . .' He looked up, around, aware once again of just how enclosed he was, how much at the mercy of someone else's timetable. How his life was no longer his own. 'It's this place, it's . . .' He looked at her, briefly. 'Sorry.' His eyes darted away, didn't wait for a reply.

She nodded then slowly moved herself away from the wall. Her hand still hovered over her jeans pocket. 'OK.'

'It's just . . . I'm just . . .' He felt this new persona, the one the prison had forced upon him, the battle-scarred survivalist, crumbling away again. He was reverting to Tom once more. 'I've got to get out of here. I should never have accepted this job. Should never have said yes.'

Louisa made no response.

He looked at her again. 'You have to believe me. I'm not delusional. I'm not a liar or a fantasist. I know that phone call to Blake made me seem so, but I swear to you I'm not. Please. You have to believe me.'

She didn't answer straight away. 'You seem . . . certain. And Dean Foley's told me things that back up your story, like I said. But why would she deny all knowledge of you? Especially if her partner's just died?'

'She must be up to something. And I don't know what she's after. But I'm not going to find out in here.'

'Would Dean Foley know?'

Tom gave the question thought. 'If he's in on all this then he might do.'

'All the more reason for us to arrange that meeting.'

Tom didn't reply immediately. He weighed up his past, his future. Sighed. 'Looks like it's my only choice, doesn't it?'

Louisa nodded, more from relief than anything else, he thought.

'I'll get it set up,' she said. 'In the meantime, do you want me to find out about this DC Blake for you?'

Tom looked directly at her once more. There was none of the recent prison savagery in his gaze. Just hurt and honesty. 'Would you do that?'

She attempted a smile. It didn't quite come off. 'I said I believed you, no matter how ridiculous it sounds. I mean, I'm not much of a detective or anything, but let me try and find her. Talk to her.'

'I would really appreciate that. But be careful.'

'I will.'

'Thank you.' So emotionally fragile was he that he felt tears threatening the corners of his eyes. He quickly blinked them away, refused to acknowledge their existence.

But Louisa caught him. Pretended she hadn't seen them.

'OK.' Her voice was soft. 'Get yourself sorted. And I'll take you to your wing.'

Tom tried to harden himself up once more, ready to front it out on the wing.

It took him longer than he thought.

43

Louisa ushered Tom back into his cell, both of them trying not to make eye contact that could be read as significant by anyone else. Cunningham seemed to have barely moved. Even though it was well past breakfast Tom wondered if he was still asleep.

'Morning,' said Tom.

Cunningham came alive immediately. Jumping up, looking at Tom like he was a ghost. Staring at Tom but not truly seeing him. Then he noticed the state Tom was in.

'You . . . what happened? Where've you been?'

Tom sat down on the rigid chair, tried to look relaxed. Compared to where he had just spent the night this was beginning to feel positively homely. It was easy to see how inmates became accustomed to it and became scared to leave.

'I seem to have made some enemies since I've been in here,' he said.

Cunningham examined Tom's injuries with his eyes, let them rove all over him. Tom couldn't tell if Cunningham was excited by what he saw or appalled. Truth was, he didn't want to know.

Tom sighed, rubbed his face with his hands, trying not to reopen wounds, pull dressings off as he did so.

Cunningham was fully interested now. 'Have you been . . . what happened?'

Tom sighed, not wanting to go over it again. He was about to brush Cunningham's question off but stopped. This might be it, he thought. A way of sharing something, getting him to open up. He sat back. Took a deep breath.

'I was attacked. In the old topping shed. Two blokes. They came at me with shivs.'

Cunningham's eyes widened. He glanced nervously towards the door, as if expecting the blokes to come barging in.

'It's OK,' he said, 'they've gone now. I took care of them.'

'Two of them?' Was that fear in Cunningham's voice or admiration? Tom couldn't tell. Yet.

'Like I said, I seem to have some enemies.'

Cunningham nodded, his jaw slack. Thinking. He looked up. 'Was this because of me?'

'How d'you mean?'

'Because you stopped that man attacking me the other day? Did they come after you for what you did to him?'

Tom was about to say no, it was something else, but stopped himself. 'I don't know. Might have been. Dreadlocked Darren might have wanted me taken care of.'

Cunningham's eyes were off somewhere else. 'You did that for me . . .'

Tom nodded. 'Could well be.'

Cunningham's mind was off somewhere else. Tom waited.

'So you saved me from him and then they did this to you. Because of him. Because of me.'

'Looks that way,' said Tom.

Cunningham was nodding once more. 'So you are my friend, then . . . you must be my friend . . .'

'Told you I was.'

'Yeah . . .' Cunningham slipped back into his own world.

Tom waited. Was this the right time to ask him about the graves? Would there be a better one?

'How've you been?' he asked. 'Since I was away.'

Cunningham looked up again, confused by the question, not used to being asked by anyone not in a professional capacity. 'I . . . I've been . . . here.' His head fell, eyes darkened. 'I've been . . . lonely.'

Tom tried to contain his excitement.

'Well,' he said, 'No need for that. I'm back now.'

Cunningham frowned. 'Did Dr Louisa drop you off?'

'She did. She's good, isn't she?'

'She's helped me a lot. Since I've been in here. I told her about you.'

'I know. She said. Said it was good that we were friends. That we could help each other. Confide in each other.'

Another nod from Cunningham.

'She knows you want to go and see your mother and she's keen to arrange that. And you know what they want to know. But like I said, if you wanted to tell me, I could let them know as and when you needed me to. If that would help you.'

Tom said nothing, waited.

Eventually Cunningham looked up at him. Smiled. He opened his mouth, ready to speak.

And the cell door opened.

'Visiting time for Killgannon. Come on, mate. On your feet.'

44

Tom's hands clenched into fists. 'Me?' he asked the officer.

'Yeah, Killgannon, that's you.'

Any other time, thought Tom. Any other time . . .

'Who is it?' asked Tom, getting to his feet. 'Who's here to see me?'

'Scarlett Johansson. How the hell do I know? Come on.'

'I'll see you later, Noel,' he said, but Cunningham had already turned his back to him, was staring once more at the cell wall. Tom tried to quell the anger he was feeling, get his head round the trip to the visiting room, the visit itself.

He followed the officer out, watching all the time for attacks, ready to defend himself. Nothing happened.

He saw them straight away. Lila and Pearl. Sitting together. And they saw him. He could tell from the way their expressions changed on taking in his appearance. His bruises had started to heal but not quickly enough. Yellow wasn't any more attractive than purple. He felt so ashamed that they were seeing him like this. So ashamed that he actually looked like this.

'What happened?' asked Pearl as soon as he sat down.

Tom paused. Tell them the truth or make something up? He couldn't not tell them the truth but he didn't want to worry them unduly. 'I got jumped,' he said.

'Jumped?' said Pearl. 'Who by?'

'There were a couple of them. I fought them off, don't worry. They didn't really hurt me. Looks worse than it is.' The last sentence accompanied by a smile that became weaker as the words went on. 'Occupational hazard, here. Not much health and safety in the workplace.'

He glanced at Lila. She hadn't spoken, just stared at him. He couldn't tell if it was fear or disappointment on her face. Or something else altogether.

Pearl was also staring at him. He wished he had never come to the visiting room.

'It won't be long now,' he said, attempting another smile. 'He'll open up to me soon. Really. Soon.' His words faded away.

'You said that last time,' said Lila.

'Yeah I know, but—'

'About the fighting. You looked bad then. You look worse now. And about coming out soon. You said that last time. And you're still here. And now it's worse.' Her voice was slowly rising, becoming shakier.

'It'll . . . it'll not be long now. Promise.' Tom hated himself for saying that.

'Just come out, Tom,' said Pearl. 'Come home.' She reached across the table, placed her hand on his. It felt like an electric shock to his body.

He locked eyes with her. Their silence said more than words could. Lila looked away, giving them a semblance of privacy.

He took his hand away in case it attracted the attention of a prowling officer.

'I will. I promise.'

Silence fell between them. All they could hear were the hushed conversations around them, as families and friends pretended they were alone too, talking normally.

'Quint's been to see us.' Lila, recovered, spoke again.

'Quint?' said Tom. 'What for?'

'Said he was keeping an eye on us. You know, just like you asked him to.'

'Yeah, but he didn't need to come and see you. Just check you were both OK.'

'Well, he thought otherwise. I found him with his arm up the chimney in the spare bedroom.'

Both Pearl and Tom stared at her. Then both spoke at the same time.

'What?' said Tom, more a statement than a question.

'You didn't tell me that,' said Pearl.

'Yeah,' said Lila, continuing. 'Said he was checking to see if someone could get into the house that way. Making sure we were safe.' The last sentence dripped with mockery.

Tom's features hardened, his voice flattened. 'What does he look like, Quint?'

'Black guy on a motorbike,' said Pearl. 'Wears a Belstaff jacket. Nice one. Not cheap.'

'Hair?'

'Short,' said Lila. 'But not shaved. No beard or anything. And in good shape. About your age, maybe a bit less, I'd say.'

Pearl nodded in agreement. 'Why?' she asked, 'You think there's something up? He seemed fine to me.'

'It sounds like him. Just seems a bit odd, that's all.' He sighed. 'Maybe he's just doing what he thinks is best.'

'Who is this guy, anyway?' asked Lila.

'He's an old friend of mine from Afghanistan. We were on a crew together. He's a good bloke. He runs a security firm now, protecting Arabs and Russian oligarchs, that sort of thing. He doesn't get the chance to do much hands on work anymore. When I asked him to keep an eye on you two he jumped at it. Maybe I should call him. He's on my list of approved numbers in here. Yeah, I'll do that.'

Lila had fallen silent once more. The others followed suit.

'So,' said Tom, trying to be cheerful, 'anything else to tell me?' He turned to Lila. 'How's your . . . friend?'

She reddened. 'Fine. Going to bring her round. Introduce her to Pearl.'

'Must be serious.'

Lila shrugged, tried to conceal a smile. 'Yeah, you know. Is what it is.'

Tom smiled. For the first time in a long time feeling genuinely happy.

'Come home. Then you can meet her.' Steel behind Lila's words.

He knew the subtext. Just come home. I'm missing you. Not that she would ever say it. He looked into her eyes. She knew he understood.

An officer announced that visiting time was over. They stood up, embraced, Tom clinging to them both like they were life rafts and would drift away if he let go. But he had to let go.

They left. He went back to the wing.

Still watchful, still in that tiring state of perpetual readiness.

45

'Hello, Dean. I managed to get another session for you. Make your-self comfortable.'

Foley sat down in the armchair. Louisa passed him coffee. Just the way she knew he liked it. He thanked her. Took a sip. Too hot. Placed it carefully on the floor beside the chair. Looked at her. It seemed like there was something she wanted to say to him but was waiting for the right time. He blinked the thought away. Probably just being paranoid. What with everything else going on.

'So how have things been?' Louisa asked, settling back into her armchair, notepad angled away from him so he couldn't see what she was writing. 'You were very agitated last time. Wanted to meet again urgently. Has there been an event of some significance in your life since we last met?'

There it was again, he thought. Her tone of voice. That sense that she had something to say to him but was waiting for him to speak first. Perhaps he would have to be wary. Even if it went against everything that these sessions were supposed to stand for. Or maybe he should just confront her head on. Get rid of all this pissing about, get it out in the open.

He sat back. Looked at her. 'Go on,' he said. 'Say it.'

She had the good grace to look confused, he thought. I'll give her that. 'Say what, Dean?'

'That you think I had . . .' He paused. Didn't want to say a name, either real or assumed. '. . . That I had someone attacked in this prison. That I took revenge. Is that it?'

'I don't know, Dean,' said Louisa, face as unreadable as her note-pad, 'is it?'

'Well you seem to think it is. So maybe it is.'

She just looked at him. Didn't reply. He began to feel uncomfortable.

'Isn't it?' he said.

Again, she waited.

Foley sighed. Tired with all this. 'No,' he said. 'Yes, I heard there was someone attacked in this prison. Like everyone did. Like you did. But I had nothing to do with it. I never gave that order.'

He saw some kind of spark in her eye. She tried to hide it, he thought, but he had seen it.

'Do you know who did?'

Another sigh. 'Does it matter?'

She thought for a moment before speaking. 'This person who was attacked. Would I be right in thinking he was the undercover police officer you previously had dealings with? The one you blame for being in prison?'

'Yes.' Straight away. No point lying.

'And you didn't give the order to have him attacked?'

'I said I didn't, didn't I?' Voice rising with anger. He pushed it back down. 'I didn't.'

'Which implies someone else did.'

'Well, obviously.'

A thoughtful expression appeared on her face. 'And how d'you feel about that?'

He paused. That wasn't the question he had been expecting. Although thinking about it later, it was the only one worth asking. 'I . . . I haven't thought about it. In those terms. The way you're saying.'

'And what way is that?'

'Like someone else is getting my revenge. Doing it for me without me asking.'

She regarded him silently once more, face unreadable.

'I'm being honest with you. I didn't have anything to do with it. I was as surprised as you.'

'It didn't work.'

'No, it didn't. He was too good for them. I could have told them that.'

'Told who? The ones who carried it out or the ones who ordered it?'

'Both.'

'But they didn't ask you. That's what you're saying.'

'No. They didn't.' He felt anger rise within him again. This time unsure whom it was directed at.

'And how does that make you feel?'

And there it was. The question he had asked himself repeatedly since the attack on Killgannon. And he hadn't been able to give himself a satisfactory answer either. But he had to be honest now. He had given his word. Dr Bradshaw would expect nothing less. *He* would expect nothing less.

'Tired,' he said. Then reached down for his cooling coffee so he didn't have to elaborate.

'In what way?'

He replaced the coffee mug. Swallowed the last little bit down before answering. 'Just tired. Of all of it. I just want it to end, I just want some peace.'

'You want all what to end?'

He thought once more before answering, trying to articulate just what his subconscious had been trying to tell him for a long time now. 'You know who I am. What I am. In this prison and outside. If I was on the out I'd still be doing what I did and enjoying it. Loving it. Don't get me wrong. But I'm not. I'm in here. And I've tried to keep things going the way they should. Like they would if I was still outside. But sometimes . . .' He sighed, faded away.

'Sometimes what?' she prompted.

'I still want everything like it always was. The respect. The reverence. The fear, even. But I just want . . . quiet. To be left alone. And no amount of money or influence in here is going to do that. I just don't want . . . to do this anymore.'

'I see.'

'I mean, don't get me wrong, I still want everything that comes with being top dog, I'd be stupid not to. But I just . . .' He sighed. 'It's hard work, keeping this up. In here, especially.'

'Like King Lear.'

He frowned. Was she taking the piss? Was this a joke he didn't understand?

'King Lear,' she elaborated. 'Shakespeare. He doesn't want to be king anymore but still wants to be treated like a king. All the trappings that go with it.'

Is that really me? he thought. 'What happened to him?'

It looked like she didn't want to answer. 'Civil war over his empire. It didn't end well, shall we say.'

They sat in silence. Foley eventually broke it. 'Was it worth it?'

'Was what worth it?'

'This. All of this. Ending up here. My old man. What a cunt he was, pardon my French, and all that.'

Louisa shrugged.

'I was wondering what he'd have made of all this.'

'I know he's overshadowed the whole of your life, Dean.'

'Yeah.'

'And I've suggested coping strategies to deal with his pervasive influence. To try and stop you feeling you have to compete with him all your life.'

'Yeah.' Unsure of the words but understanding the meaning, he nodded. 'I've just been thinking a lot about him lately. And being inside. Questioning, like. Would he be proud of me for what I've achieved? You know, everything I did on the out, and that? Or would he think I was a failure for getting banged up all this time?' He fell silent once more.

Louisa spoke quietly. 'And what conclusion did you reach, Dean?'

Foley couldn't look up from the floor, couldn't meet her gaze. 'Failure.'

She waited. Eventually Foley spoke again.

'I'm just tired. I get no joy out of any of it. Not anymore. Like the thing with Killgannon. You may as well know his name. You probably do anyway. There was a time, not so long ago, when I could have ripped him apart with my bare hands. Happily. Got

274

right stuck in, really made him suffer for what he'd done to me. Now, when I hear that someone's had a go at doing him over I'm just . . . I don't know what to think. I mean yeah, if anyone's going to do it, it should be me. Not someone else fucking with me.'

'Is that what you think they were doing? Couldn't someone else have held a grudge against him?'

'I know it was aimed at me. I just know. Like that job on that guy in the hospital wing. Clive Bennett. That was against me, too.'

Louisa frowned. 'Clive Bennett? That was natural causes. He was in bad shape. His heart gave out.'

He gave the kind of smile that pitied her naivety. 'That what they told you? Shelley would say anything to stay in charge of his little fiefdom, even getting a doctor to lie about cause of death. No, Clive was one of mine. But it wasn't me. I didn't give the order.'

'So you're saying that your power is slipping, is that right?'

He smiled once more but there was no condescension in it this time. Just a kind of weary acceptance. 'Civil war. And it doesn't end well . . . And before you ask, it makes me feel . . . well I should say powerless, shouldn't I? Or scared. Or furious. And I was when I first heard about both things happening. But I don't feel any of that now. I just feel tired. Like I want it all over with.'

He felt Dr Bradshaw regarding him differently. Sadly? Was that it? Or compassionately, perhaps. He hoped it wasn't pity. He had never wanted anyone's pity in his life.

She leaned forwards, spoke. And before the words came out, Foley knew he had been right. He wasn't just being paranoid. There was something she had wanted to say to him. Had been since he sat down in the chair.

'Dean,' she said, 'Would it help if you and Tom Killgannon got together and talked?'

He just stared at her, didn't know what to say.

'I just think it might help you both if you found somewhere neutral to talk, away from everything and everyone else. Sorted out your differences. Just the two of you. What d'you think?'

'I . . .' He began to speak, because he thought it was expected of him. But he really had nothing to say. He hadn't finished processing her suggestion.

'Take your time.'

He did. Tried to work out for himself what he could gain from talking to Killgannon-Eccleston. Whether he would try to kill him then and there, or if he wouldn't do it, let the opportunity go to waste.

She waited.

'What are you suggesting?'

'The two of you. In this room. Talking. Seeing if there's any common ground, if you can both find a way forwards for yourselves. Put the past to rest, even.'

'Steady. That's a hell of a lot to ask.'

'Would you be prepared to do it, though?'

A smile appeared at the corners of Foley's mouth. 'Would this count towards my parole?'

Dr Bradshaw kept her face impassive. 'It wouldn't hurt it, let's say.' She waited for his answer.

'Yeah all right,' he said. 'Yeah. Let's do it.'

'Good. I'm glad you feel that way.'

'I mean,' he said with a smile that looked like it belonged to his old self, 'What's the worst that can happen?'

Louisa wondered whether she had made a very big mistake.

46

Another night in Blackmoor. And Tom was trying to chase down sleep.

Other inmates didn't seem to have a problem. Some would sleep round the clock if they could. With their bodies, their lives, rendered down to basics, being locked up for most of your twenty-four hours a day, alone with just the thoughts and impulses that had got you inside in the first place, then sleep was the only free, legalised oblivion on offer. And you took it willingly. But not Tom. His head was whirring too much.

The terror of losing control of his environment had dulled but not disappeared. He no longer lay awake worrying whether he would burn to death if there was a fire, whether they would forget to unlock his cell door in the morning. It had become part of the low-level, constant anxiety of negotiating prison life. He couldn't sleep because he was terrified he might never leave.

He worried that he might end up like Charles Salvador; in for something minor but his constant aggression ensured he would never be released, so he changed his name to Charles Bronson and styled himself the most violent man in prison. He could see how something like that could happen. Looking for threats around every corner, challenging anyone who stepped in front of him. He could understand how that would escalate, but he also worried he would be forgotten.

After returning from Pearl and Lila's visit, Cunningham seemed to have slipped back into his own sullen mind. The progress Tom had made now reversed. Tom knew why, even though neither had expressed it: because Tom had visitors and Cunningham didn't. He might consider Tom his friend, but having visits from his 'niece' reminded Cunningham he was truly alone.

So Tom hadn't pushed it. Just waited, with as much patience as he could muster, for the time to be right.

Cunningham wasn't making his quest for sleep any easier. His night terrors playing up once again.

Tom heard the now familiar wailing coming from the top bunk, accompanied by the equally expected thrashing and punching. The crying crescendoed, the words becoming clear: 'I'm sorry . . . I'm sorry . . . please, please don't, I'm sorry . . .' And yet more thrashing.

Tom lay on his side staring at the thin strip of light coming under the door, showing there was some kind of life beyond his cell, that he was still connected to it. The lack of sleep here, as well as in the seg block, had built up within him. He felt like he would never rest again. Like his body would never be allowed to recharge. And now Cunningham. He had had enough.

Anger coursed through him as he sat up and swung his legs down onto the floor. He sighed, stood up, turned to the top bunk ready to yell at Cunningham, make him shut up, just let him get some sleep for once, just once in his cretinous fucking life, just once . . .

The cell was never truly dark. There was the twenty-four/seven light from the wing coming under the door, the glow of the perimeter lights through the smudged and filthy windows. Cunningham sat upright, staring at the wall. The shadowed corner of the room, the only true darkness in the whole cell. Tom knew what was coming. Cunningham telling him there were ghosts in the shadows, that he could see them, wanting Tom to see them also. Tom didn't want to look again.

'Cunningham, listen, why don't you—'

'Look. Just . . . look . . .'

Cunningham stared at the corner, arm outstretched, finger pointing. Tom tried to fight it but couldn't. He followed Cunningham's gaze.

'There, it's . . . there . . .'

'There's nothing there, Cunningham, now—'

Tom stopped. Stared. There in the shadows, something was moving.

Like a gas trying to become solid or a dream trying to become real. A figure taking shape before his eyes. The rest of the room dropped away, the faint lights from outside and under the door dimmed. There was only the figure in the corner.

'You can see it as well, can't you?' Cunningham's voice, quieter now, almost calming.

Tom didn't reply. Couldn't. Just kept looking.

The figure became almost recognisable then drifted apart.

'I'm sorry,' said Cunningham, voice lowered, reasoning, not screaming anymore, 'I really am. Please, let me make it up to you. All of you . . .'

Tom didn't know what Cunningham was seeing. He saw only one image. One person. A young woman. And he knew instinctively who it was.

Hayley.

'I'm sorry as well,' he found himself saying. 'I really am. I wish it could have been me and not you. I want that so, so much. Spent ages thinking that after it happened, tried to make it happen . . . but it didn't. So I'm here and you're . . . there. Wherever. And I'm sorry.'

He was aware of movement at his side. Cunningham had moved his attention from the shadowed corner to Tom.

'You really can see . . . You . . . your own ghosts . . .'

'We've all got our ghosts, Cunningham.'

'Mine talk to me. I tell them sorry, I'm always saying sorry. But I think they're hearing me this time. They're telling me . . .' He cocked his head to one side, listening. 'Yeah, they're telling me . . . that they want to be put to rest. So do I . . . so do I . . .' Almost crying with those last few words. 'Yes, yes, I'll do it, I'll do it . . .'

Tom kept staring. But he couldn't see anything now. Just shadows. Whatever had been there – or he had imagined had been there – was gone. He blinked. There was nothing. Just a sleep–deprived man looking at a corner.

Cunningham was still talking. 'Yes I will,' he was saying. 'I will. I promise. And then everything will be all right. I'll make it all right.' Nodding. 'Yes. Thank you. Thank you.'

He turned to Tom, almost smiled. 'Time for sleep now.' He lay down and within what must have been seconds was out.

Tom wondered whether he had ever been awake.

Next morning, Tom opened his eyes as the lights went on. He had slept. Actually slept. For the first time in ages.

He got out of bed. Cunningham was already up. He sat on the chair watching him. Smiling.

'Good morning, Tom.'

'Morning.' Tom was instantly wary.

Cunningham stretched, smiled. 'This is a new day.'

'Isn't it always?'

He laughed. 'No. This is a real new day. The first new day in a long time. Praise God.'

Tom didn't answer. He stood up, made his way to the steel toilet. Cunningham loomed behind him.

'I'm going to tell them where they're buried, Tom. All of them.' Still smiling like he had shaken hands with God.

Tom paused, turned back to look at him.

'What?'

I'm going to tell them where the bodies are. Their souls have gone, but the bodies are still there. And I'm going to show them. Show them all.'

Tom just stared.

'And you're coming with me.'

And in that moment, Tom saw his way out.

47

'Oh, it's you. Just passing, I suppose?'

Quint stood at the door of the cottage. Lila had heard his motorbike approach and wasn't surprised to see him. In fact she was ready for him.

'Yeah,' he said, slightly taken aback at the welcome. From his expression it looked like he had expected something warmer. 'Can I come in?'

Lila stepped back to allow him to enter. She managed to make the gesture seem so offhand he hesitated, not sure whether he actually was welcome or not. That had been her plan. He followed her into the living room.

'On your own?'

'Yeah,' she said, sitting down on the sofa. The TV was on. She was watching *Pointless*. It was nearing its climax. The couple had opted for the category of American Crime Writers. She made no attempt to mute it or turn it off. Nor did she offer him anything to drink or eat.

'No Pearl?'

'At work.'

Undeterred he sat down in the armchair. 'Everything OK?'

She shrugged. 'Yeah. No problems.'

'How's Tom? Have you seen him?'

He's persistent, Lila thought. And he hasn't lost his temper yet. If I'd turned up to someone's house and they treated me like this, she thought, I'd have left by now. Or at least let them know how I felt.

'Yeah,' she said, 'Went in the other day.'

'How is he?'

She thought. This answer required some emotion. Or should have done. But she didn't want to give anything away to him.

'Well as can be expected, I suppose. We talked about you.'

Something passed over his face. Lila pretended not to be watching him, keeping her eyes on the TV, but she was studying him. She tried to catch what the emotion might have been. Fear? Apprehension? Something like that. Nothing positive.

'Jesus,' said Quint, trying to make a joke of it, 'you must have been short of conversation pieces.'

'No, we chatted for quite a bit.' Lila turned her attention away from the TV towards him. 'He told us some stories about when you two used to be together. Back in the army, was it?'

'Yeah, that's right,' said Quint, smiling. 'Plenty of stories about that.' The smile seemed superficial. Cracked ice on a barely frozen lake waiting for the slightest weight to break it.

'Iraq, wasn't it?'

'Yeah,' he said.

Lila turned away from him, back to the TV. She didn't think this couple were going to win. They had chosen the wrong category.

Lila seemed to be about to pursue the subject but Quint jumped in, changed it. 'Did he say anything else?'

'Such as?'

'How he's coping, when he's coming out, that kind of thing.'

Lila's smile was as fake as Quint's. 'He's all right, I think. You know what prisons are like these days. Holiday camps, aren't they?' She forced a laugh for his benefit. 'Probably having a better time in there than he would be out here.'

Quint nodded in agreement even though it was clear he didn't go along with her assessment.

Lila kept watching the screen. The couple failed to win anything. They were given commiserations and that was that. The credits rolled.

'Bad luck,' said Lila, pointing at the TV. 'You get all excited watching something, invested in it, and it ends like that. Nothing. Hardly fair. Although I suppose fairness has got nothing to do with it, really, has it?'

'Not really,' said Quint, unsure where the conversation was headed.

Lila stared ahead at the TV, not really seeing it, but trying not to see Quint either.

'Yeah well, if you're OK then I'd better be off.' He stood up as if he was suddenly in a hurry to be out of there.

Lila didn't move. Didn't look at him. If she was surprised at his abrupt exit she tried not to let it show. 'You know your way out, don't you? Should know your way around by now. I'm going to watch the news.'

'Yeah,' he said, although it seemed like he wanted to say a lot more. Lila kept her head angled away from him, feigning interest in the TV. She missed his look of angry exasperation as he left the room.

Lila didn't move, didn't dare breathe until she heard the front door closing, the motorbike revving away. She waited a few seconds, just to be sure. Then her expression changed. 'You can come in now.'

Pearl entered the room.

'Did you hear all that?'

Pearl nodded.

'What d'you think?'

'About what in particular, Iraq?'

'Yeah.'

Pearl shrugged, spoke like she was trying to convince herself. 'Well they might have been in Iraq together. I mean, Tom never said that they weren't. When was Iraq? After Afghanistan or the same time?'

Lila shook her head. 'Tom said Afghanistan.'

'Maybe they were in Iraq as well.'

'Then why didn't Tom mention that? He said Afghanistan.' Lila thought. 'Tom wasn't in Iraq . . .'

'But what does he want with us then? How does he really know Tom?' Pearl asked, then a sudden thought, 'He's been in this house. He knows who we are, what we look like, where we go, he's been round the house, he knows how to get at us . . .'

'I know,' said Lila, louder than she had expected, Pearl's fear contaminating her like an airborne virus.

Pearl stopped speaking. 'What are we going to do?' Almost a whisper.

'I don't know.'

And as she spoke, the carapace she had presented to Quint began to crumble.

'I really don't know . . .'

48

Dean Foley leaned back, eyes closed, body rigid, while Kim worked her particular kind of magic. He almost didn't hear the cell door open but he heard the voice when it spoke.

'Am I interrupting?'

Foley shot forwards, sent Kim spilling onto the floor. Governor Paul Shelley stood in front of them, a smirk on his lips. 'Officer Shelton. I didn't know you were so talented.'

Kim pulled her uniform together and stood quickly. She turned her back on the Governor who leered at her until she was fully clothed and, red-faced, hair dishevelled, she left the cell as quickly as possible.

Shelley watched her go, turned back to Foley who had pulled himself together and was standing up. Shelley grinned. 'Well, well, well. Who knew?'

'You did,' said Foley. 'You know exactly what happens in here and when. And who with. You probably take a cut of what I pay her. Is that why you've decided to visit me now?'

Shelley's smirk faltered. Foley continued.

'Asked her to do that for you, yeah? Know she comes to see me so you thought you'd get a bit of it for yourself, that it? But she knocked you back so you try and humiliate her like this?' He shook his head. 'Pathetic.'

Shelley stood fuming. 'You wanted to see me.'

'I could have made the journey. No hardship.'

'Neither was it to come here.'

'I'll bet. And it does you no harm to be seen on the wings, does it? Reminds them all what you look like.'

'What do you want?' More of a statement than a question. Shelley's voice flat, wanting this over with.

Foley sat back down, lit a cigarette. Shelley seemed about to tell him there was no smoking, but a look from Foley stopped him. He took a deep lungful, held it, exhaled slowly, enjoying every second. Even sitting down while Shelley stood he looked in command.

'Yeah,' he said, regarding the burning tip, 'I want to go out.'

Shelley looked like he couldn't understand the words. 'You – what? You – want to go *out*?'

'Little trip out. To the moors. Bit of fresh air. Good for the system.' Still examining the tip of his cigarette.

'That's . . . that's ridiculous. I can't let you go wandering on the moors.'

'Why not? You're letting Cunningham and Killgannon do it.'

'That's different. There's a reason for that. And you know it.'

'There's a reason I want to go out too.'

'Which is?'

Foley took the cigarette away from his mouth, stared at Shelley. Shelley flinched before the unblinking gaze.

'I want to talk to Killgannon.'

'Talk to him in here. I'm sure the lovely Dr Louisa could arrange something.'

'She's trying to. But if Killgannon's out with Cunningham I'm guessing that he's not going to be coming back. That right?'

'What d'you mean?'

'Killgannon's undercover law. If he's out with Cunningham then that must be his job. Get him to give up the bodies. Then he'll be off on his next assignment and I'll have lost him. With me so far?'

Shelley didn't answer straight away. Just stared, slightly slack-jawed at Foley.

'So is that a yes?'

'I . . . Killgannon will be back. I assure you.'

Foley smiled. 'I like my idea the best.'

He sat back, resumed smoking, dragging long and deep on his cigarette. Watching Shelley all the while. Knowing it was only a matter of time before the Governor said yes.

Foley took his silence for agreement. 'And I want to take Baz with me.'

'No. That's too much. I could find a way to explain why you were out there but no one else.'

'Baz is coming with me. End of. Do whatever you have to do, I'll pick my escort, probably Chris, he's a good bloke. Dependable.'

'When do you want to do this?'

'Same time Killgannon and Cunningham are out.'

Shelley made one last attempt at standing up for himself. 'But there might be media, TV cameras following Cunningham. I can't have them seeing you as well. What would happen then?'

Foley stood up. He wasn't very tall but he towered over the Governor. 'I run this place for you, Paul. I make sure there are no riots, that no one gets out of hand. That there are no fights over drugs or anything else. I keep a lid on everything. It's in your interests as well as mine to keep this place running smoothly, isn't it?'

Shelley nodded, dumbstruck.

'Well, that's the price you pay. Letting me have a few little jaunts. I mean, just imagine what would happen if you said no . . . couldn't guarantee there'd be a safe place for you and your staff anywhere in this prison . . .'

Shelley sighed. 'All right, then. I'll make sure you're out when Cunningham and Killgannon are out. But please keep away from any cameras. Or the police.'

Foley smiled. 'I made a career out of it.'

Shelley turned to the door, in a sudden hurry to leave. He turned. 'Why Killgannon? Why do you want to talk to him?'

'We used to be close, back in another life,' Foley said. 'And I've got a message for him.'

Shelley left. He didn't want to hear any more.

49

Dr Louisa Bradshaw drove north.

She had phoned Middlemoor police station in Exeter, asked to speak to Detective Constable Blake's superior officer. She didn't know why Shelley hadn't done that. It wasn't difficult. She was put through to a DCI Harmer, told him who she was, what the situation was.

'I'm phoning about Tom Killgannon,' she had said.

Silence on the line.

'I believe he's working for you within Blackmoor. To do with Noel Cunningham?'

More silence. Louisa felt as if Harmer was deciding whether to confirm her story. She pushed on.

'His handler was Detective Inspector Sheridan? I understand he's dead now.'

'And what can I do for you, Doctor?'

'You have a Detective Constable Blake working for you?' She made the statement a question. 'She stated that she has no knowledge of Mr Killgannon.'

'And why would my Detective Constable want to confirm or deny that?'

'I don't know. That's why I need to talk to you to get this all sorted out.'

More silence. Eventually Harmer spoke. 'Can you verify you are who you say you are?'

'I think it's best if I come and see you, DCI Harmer. That way we can get this sorted out, quickly.'

'Yes,' he said, the reluctance in his voice unmistakable, 'Why don't you make an appointment for later this week?'

'I'm afraid things have moved on and it's more pressing than that. Cunningham's confessed the location of the bodies and insists on Killgannon accompanying him onto the moor. So could I come to see you after I finish work this evening?'

They hung up and when Louisa had finished work, she got into her semi-ancient Mini and drove from Blackmoor to Exeter.

Shelley hadn't been happy at the idea of Tom Killgannon accompanying Cunningham out on the moors. Shelley hadn't been happy about anything.

'So he is undercover. And he's been operating in my prison without anyone informing me.'

'Seems that way. And now Cunningham wants him outside with him.'

'Does he now?'

'You'll get a lot of publicity from this. It'll be a vindication that your rehabilitation methods work.'

Shelley almost changed personality before her eyes. Sat up straighter, favoured her with what she supposed he believed was his good side. Vanity. That was all she had to appeal to in the man. Or most men, when she thought about it.

'But. We don't tell Cunningham that Killgannon's undercover. It might make him recant.'

'I can see that logic, yes.'

'And we don't tell Killgannon that we know either. Let him sweat a bit longer.'

'Why?'

A sly smile appeared on Shelley's lips. 'Because the bastard thought he could sneak into my prison and not tell me what he was up to. That's why.'

Petty and vindictive, thought Louisa. But understandable.

She tried to replay the day's events as she drove. Sort through everything that had happened so she could switch off and enjoy the evening. That was what she usually did, but found it different tonight as she was still working, sort of. On a normal night she would get home to her flat in Truro, kick off her boots, stick the TV on, pour herself a glass of wine, feed the cat and, while waiting for her partner Nicola to arrive home, put the day into context. She tried to do that now while driving and listening to Radio 2. It wasn't the same.

The A roads leading away from Blackmoor had, she thought, a nerve describing themselves as such. They could only be considered that in relation to where they were. They twisted round forests, went up and down hills, gave out on to both breathtaking scenery on precarious slopes and huge high hedges that hid oncoming traffic. She was on one such section now. Darkness had fallen so she should have been able to gauge headlights as they came towards her. She wasn't good at gauging distances in the dark. Her own fault, she had put off going to the opticians for new glasses. She was looking forward to getting on the straighter roads that were well lit and she could put her foot down.

She thought of Dean Foley and Tom Killgannon. Hoped she was doing the right thing by getting them together. Hoped she would get the chance to, if Tom Killgannon didn't disappear after Cunningham located the bodies. Dean seemed to think it was a good idea, although she was slightly unnerved by his final response to her. She just hoped that he was a changed enough man not to slip back into his persona. She liked to think that her work counted for something, that he had made progress. And Tom Killgannon. A wounded man. Looked like he was in a prison of his own making before he came to Blackmoor. Maybe he could—

'Jesus!'

The motorbike came from nowhere. Roaring out from a blind bend, bearing straight towards her. She pulled the wheel over to the left, felt the car shake and judder as it hit the embankment, the hedge, heard the scratching of hawthorn and bramble along the side of the car. She managed to wrestle back control, stopped the car crashing into the side.

Heart hammering, she checked round to see where the bike had gone. No sign of it. Or any other traffic. She took deep breaths, calmed herself down.

Bet that bastard's caused me damage, she thought. I'll need the paintwork looking at.

She kept going. Slightly slower now, more aware of oncoming vehicles.

The road wound out of the hedges into a forested area, began to climb steadily. The denuded trees formed a canopy over the road. She looked to her left, saw a steep drop into the trees.

And heard the powerful revving of a motorbike once more.

Headlights filled her mirror, temporarily blinding her. She squinted, tried to make out the road ahead although she could still see the image of the headlights ghosting on her retinas.

The bike overtook her. She tried to look out, see who the rider was. Couldn't make out anything. Leather jacket, full face helmet, dark visor down. He drew level with her car, began to move into her door.

'Shit . . .'

Her first response was to pull the wheel to the left, get her car away from him, but that would tip her over the edge and down the slope into the trees. She put her foot down, tried to speed past him. But her Mini was no match for the bike. Without expending much effort, he pushed his bike to match her speed, an angry roar from the engine. She felt like he was actually going slower than his bike was capable of. And at the moment, he was just keeping pace with her.

That gave her an idea. She slammed on the brakes, coming to a stop with a screech of rubber. The bike kept going. At least for a few seconds before the rider realised what had happened and swung round in the middle of the road, coming straight towards her.

Louisa started to panic. The headlights were becoming blindingly huge in her windscreen. She didn't know whether to pull forwards or to reverse. Or to just sit there. No: she couldn't just sit there. She had to do something.

She put the car in gear. Tried to swing round, go back the way she had come. The rider anticipated her movement, swung his bike out to stop her. She stepped hard on the brake, the seatbelt pulling the air from her lungs as she leapt forwards.

He turned the bike again, ready to come at her. She put her foot down and drove.

He quickly caught up with her.

Louisa was frantic now.

The bike pulled alongside her, pushed itself into her car. Instinctively she swerved again, just managing to avoid a roll down the embankment, straightening up once more.

But the bike didn't allow her to get back onto the road where she had been. It took up that position, had moved two of the Mini's wheels onto the dirt and gravel at the side of the road. The car began to skid, half on, half off the uneven surface. The front wheel hit a branch causing her to lose control. She screamed, managed to right herself again. Kept driving.

The bike pushed again. The Mini's front wheel hit a rock. The steering wheel leapt from her hands. The car began to swerve from side to side, juddering away from her control. She tried desperately to turn the wheel, keep the car upright and on the road, but the bike wouldn't let her.

All four wheels were off the road now.

A tree loomed up ahead of her.

She swung the wheel uselessly to avoid hitting it head on.

And the car rolled down the embankment into the trees.

Part Four
HUNTED

Two days after that night in Manchester

Constable Annie Blake stood at the back of the interview room, by the door, hands behind her back. Anonymous as a person, barely a presence. Just a faceless uniform. Not what she joined the force for. But observing, processing all the time.

Before her, Dean Foley, his expensive solicitor next to him, was being questioned by two detectives. Two days in custody had scrubbed off Foley's usual dangerous charm. Now there seemed less pretence about who he was or who he thought he was.

She had seen these two detectives at work before. DI Torrance and DS Sharp. Physical opposites: gravity pulled Torrance's large body downwards like a full bin bag. His hair was the colour of used tea bags, fingers also, from nicotine. Sharp's name was near literal, he was all bones and teeth. His elbows looked like they could cut. The only thing they had in common, she thought, was they were both mid-level careerists. Doing what they would call a good job, which for them meant crossing the 't's and dotting the 'i's. Putting a file together to present to the CPS. And that would be that.

I won't end up like either of them, Blake thought.

In the short time she had been on the force she had grown to detest most of her superiors. They were dull time-servers, superior in name only. She was there for advancement. In whatever way she could do it.

Foley's mouthpiece droned on, making sure he was seen to be earning his fee. The detectives nodded, answered his points briefly. Foley sat so still it barely seemed he was breathing. He looked at Blake like an animal waiting for its prey to display the slightest weakness.

The detectives started the tape, cautioned him, ran through their list of pre-prepared questions. Foley said his 'no comment's in as disinterested a manner as possible. The detectives kept going, the solicitor looked alert. Foley gave the same answer, not even changing the bored, off-hand inflection in his voice. It was a charade to be endured by both sides. *In TV dramas interviews were shown as violent confrontations, verbal cat and mouse games, even near–religious confessionals. Real life was nothing like that.*

Or so she thought.

'So where's the money, Dean?' *Torrance, the senior detective asked.*

Foley paused, didn't answer straight away.

His solicitor looked at him, waiting for an answer. Before he could give it, sensing an opening, the other detective, Sharp, jumped in.

'Come on,' *he said,* 'you've got no reason to lie about that, we've got you bang to rights on everything else. What have you done with it?'

Torrance leaned forwards. 'Come on, Dean, what you done with it?'

Foley paused again. Then answered. 'I haven't got the money.'

The solicitor started to speak. Foley waved him silent as if batting away a fly.

Torrance again. 'What you got to lose, Dean? Tell us what you've done with it.'

Foley, for the first time in the interview, displayed an emotion other than assumed boredom. Anger. He leaned forwards. 'Why don't you talk to Mick Eccleston, eh? Or whatever his real name is.'

'Why would we do that, Dean?'

'Because if anyone's got it, he has.'

The two detectives shared a glance. 'And why would he have it, Dean? Why not you?'

Foley sat back again. 'You'd have to ask him, wouldn't you? Maybe you don't pay him enough. Maybe he wanted some overtime. I mean, he's not earning with my anymore. He's going to be skint from now on, isn't he?'

The detectives kept questioning him, pushing. But Foley just slumped back in his chair, the flare of anger gone, indifference assumed once more.

He said nothing but 'no comment' *for the rest of the interview. But he didn't need to say anything more. Constable Annie Blake had heard all she needed to.*

Dean Foley, she decided, was a man she would keep an eye on.

The next day in Manchester

She had to show her warrant card to be admitted to the hospital room. Even then she had to justify why she was there. The uniform on the door was following his orders to the letter. She would have to be clever if she wanted to pass and not show up on the official log. Squeeze the tears out, pretend to be his girlfriend.

'Sorry,' he said, 'I can't let you in. He hasn't given his statement yet. He can't have anyone talk to him until he's done that.'

Turn it up a notch. 'Please, he's . . . he's all I have . . .'

The uniform checked the corridor both ways then, with a sigh that said he was charting new territory but wasn't without a heart, said, 'Go on, then. But don't be long. I'm supposed to mark everyone in and out.'

She gave him a smile so radiant the red face he was left with could have been sunburn. That's how easy it is to manipulate men, she thought. They're fucking idiots.

The only time Blake had previously been into a private hospital room was when her grandfather was dying of cancer. All the grand-kids were trooped in and presented, told to stand at his bedside looking suitably upset. The man had been an absolutely tyrannical bastard before the cancer had slowly crippled him and robbed him of his power. Most of them, those who had been on the receiving end of his wrath, including her, were there just to see that he wasn't coming back.

Then, the room had been bleak, like he was just place-holding the bed until a proper, more deserving occupant came along. Blake had managed to squeeze tears out then, too. It didn't work. He was too far gone to notice and she still got nothing from his will.

She often thought she had joined the police because of her grand-dad. Regretted he didn't live long enough to see her in her uniform. To continue his family reign of terror when she was able to physically fight back, have him arrested if necessary. Or just hurt him. A lot.

She entered the room. It was completely different from her last visit. As if she had walked onto a movie set, except in a Manchester hospital. With tubes and wires hooked up to sighing, pinging, flashing surrounding machines. Foxy lay on something more like a science-fiction life support pod than a bed. Blake was impressed. But at the centre, the recipient of all the life-sustaining attention, looked nothing like the man she used to know.

His face was mummified with bandages, tubes poking out of his nose and mouth. His arms and body were similarly covered, with plastic casts and bandages, one arm supported. His legs were under the cover. She didn't want to look. She sat down in the chair beside the bed.

'You stupid bastard,' she said, surprised to find herself crying. 'You stupid, stupid bastard . . .'

Undercover, he had said. With Dean Foley's gang. This is it. This is my glory job . . .

He shouldn't have bragged about it. Could have compromised the operation. And his head seemed to be in the wrong place from the start. The glory job. You should have just done what you were supposed to . . .

All that time spent together in the academy. They had bonded straight away. Recognised something in the other that was there in themselves. An ambition, a hunger to succeed. They almost tore each other apart, when their relationship started. They were inseparable.

Both posted to Manchester's inner city, Blake found opportunities for advancement harder to come by than Foxy did. And when he was posted undercover, part of her – quite a large part, if she was honest – resented him. The way he celebrated without taking her feelings into account.

She had watched him, preening before a mirror, trying to get his manner, his attitude, his clothing right. You've only got this job because you're black, she wanted to say. They only want you in the gang because you're officially representative of the racial mix in that area. That someone somewhere is getting a pat on the back for ticking a box on a racial quota form. But she didn't say any of that. Because that would have been the end of their relationship. And Foxy, if he stopped to think about it, might even have agreed.

At first he had been keen. Going along with the gang, delivering his reports on time, crammed with as much detail as he could manage. But he wasn't getting anywhere near the top of the organisation. He had been working his way up, trying to worm his way onto the right side of Dean Foley, when this bloke Mick Eccleston arrived out of nowhere and was fast-tracked up the promotion ladder. That was the turning point for Foxy. When he saw all his hard work come to nothing, when he mentally said fuck it and decided if he was supposed to be a gangster then it was time he made some money as a gangster. That was when he went to the dark side.

Blake noticed straight away. He changed. Became harder, more callous. He brought her gifts. She rejected them.

'What the fuck is this supposed to be?' she said, throwing some expensive, trashy earrings on the sofa while he stared at her, angry enough to punch her. 'I'm not some gangster's moll. And you're not a gangster. You're a copper. Remember that.'

They grew apart. Blake moved out of the flat they shared, found her own place. He called in fewer and fewer times, eventually stopped coming round at all. She didn't know where he was.

And then this happened. No one knew all the facts yet, but there was a dead girl involved, a crashed car, a missing gun. And, if he came round, a potentially very expensive and very ugly court case. When he came round. Keep saying that, she thought. Keep saying that.

She kept staring at him. Almost wanted to reach out, hold his hand.

She didn't know how long she sat there but after a while she realised that the room was now dark and she was holding his hand.

He wasn't going to wake up and even if he did, she had nothing prepared to say to him. So she stood up, left the room.

Thought about him lying there. Look what the job had got him. Thought of those two detectives just going through the motions with Foley. Look what the job had done to them.

301

Thought of what Foley had said about Mick Eccleston. The undercover cop was in the wind now, gone. But that didn't mean he was untraceable to police like her. And it didn't mean Foley couldn't play a part in finding the money either.

She knew what to do. It wouldn't be easy but it could be done.

Find a copper in Witness Protection with over two million of stolen money.

Whatever happened to her on the force, she wouldn't let it grind her down.

Because this would be her own glory job.

50

It was the coldest, bleakest day Tom had experienced in months. And he felt it even more keenly out on Blackmoor.

The day was in perpetual twilight. The sun absent, the wind pricking exposed skin like a fistful of needles, heavy grey clouds scudding across the expansive sky, threatening storms. Down below, Tom stood to one side while Cunningham led a team of police detectives and forensic officers as they searched for his hidden graves.

Tom stood back with a couple of prison officers who had spared no blushes telling him, and anyone who would listen, what they thought of this whole business. The whole party, leaving their parked four by fours and heading to inaccessible places on foot, looked like the most reluctant team of ramblers he had ever seen. Except for Cunningham.

Bundled up in heavy-weather clothing, he kept looking back over at Tom, waving at him, checking he was still there, like a dog not wanting to go too far from the person who feeds it. Smiling all the while. He looked like a malevolent Michelin man. He was giddy, looking round constantly as though he could barely believe he was there.

'What's he need you for then, anyway?' asked a guard, clearly unhappy at being outside when he could be on the wing with a cup of tea.

Tom shrugged. 'Hand holding, I suppose. I'm his cellmate. He opened up to me about wanting to show where the graves are. So he could visit his sick mother.'

'Cellmate, eh?' said the other officer, a suggestive leer on his fat features.

'Yeah,' said Tom, his tone of voice indicating that their innuendo or insinuations weren't welcome. 'Cellmate. The prison shrink asked for me to be put in with him. Said he would talk to me.'

'That all he's done, then?' said the first one, clearly not picking up on Tom's warning.

Tom stared at the man until he backed down, blinked.

The two officers had made a point of not sharing their snacks and flask of hot coffee with him, nor the illegal bottle of brandy they kept taking nips from when they thought he wasn't looking. They had also told him he wasn't to stray from their sight. Tom complied. He had nowhere else to go to.

At least not yet.

He was working all the time he stood there. They had parked their minibus at the bottom of the slope Cunningham and the police had walked up. It led to some rocky tor, Tom had been told. Good views for miles around. If the weather was better than this. Tom was more interested in the road they had travelled up on. He tried to get what bearings he could from the weak sunlight, tried to work out where he was on the compass, what direction his home was in. If this were going to be his only method to escape, then he would have to take it. Deal with whatever paperwork, or supposed illegalities cropped up afterwards. He could cope with anything as long as he was free again.

So far he hadn't found a way. Too many police with Cunningham, the prison officers too wary. Thankfully there wasn't any media presence. Their scrutiny would have made escape impossible. He was biding his time. He would spot the opportunity when it came.

The first prison officer checked his watch. 'Nearly lunchtime.' He turned towards Tom. 'Want yours?'

'Yeah. Sure.' He was hungry, but he wasn't about to let these two know that.

The other leaned into a bag at the back of the minibus, brought out three wrapped packages. He kept one of the two biggest for himself, passed the other big one to his partner, the smallest one to Tom.

'There you go.'

Tom opened it. Prison mystery meat on cheap white bread.

'Eat up.'

Theirs were shop bought along with a chicken leg each and a bag of crisps. They grinned as they ate.

Tom turned away, looked at the roads once more.

Made calculations.

51

DC Annie Blake waited until she heard the sound of the shower then knelt by the side of the bed, pulled something out. Opened it.

Her go bag.

Everything she had planned for led up to this moment. She had known it would come, worked for it, added to it. The bag contained everything she would need to walk out of this life, start another one. A better, richer one.

Passport, credit and debit cards with untraceable money in those accounts, clothes, even a small amount of gold that she could sell.

She had worked next to criminals her whole career. Learned from the best. The ones who never – or rarely – got caught. She had studied their methods, noted what had gone well for them, what hadn't. Vowed not to make their mistakes.

She was near to Foley's money. She knew it, could feel it. And with Killgannon now out with Cunningham, she had to move. Time for her endgame.

She took something else from the bag. An untraceable Desert Eagle XIX in .44 Magnum. It was loaded. She racked the slide. Put it down at the side of the bed on top of the bag.

The shower stopped. After a short while, DCI Harmer stepped out, towelling his hair.

'This is disgraceful, not going into the office, yet,' he said, not looking at her. 'We should have been in hours ago.'

'Didn't hear you complaining.'

He laughed, threw the towel onto the bed. 'No. You wouldn't.'

He looked up, realised that she was standing there naked. He smiled. 'Ready to go again?'

Wouldn't take long with you if I was, she thought. 'No. We'd better get going.'

He stood there, staring at her. 'God, you're gorgeous.'

'Come on. Work.'

He had come round to her flat the previous evening. He had stopped bringing wine, she noticed, and other presents. Now he just came and went. Literally, she thought. And it took about that long. Maybe he was getting bored of her. That was fine with Blake. Because his usefulness was very nearly at an end.

She had used him as much as she could. He was a good smokescreen for her activities. Even toyed with asking him to join in her scheme but ultimately decided not to. If he said no she would have had to take care of him. Just like Sheridan. And that might attract too much attention. She had also considered doing something similar to his computer as she had done to Sheridan's. But something different. Kiddie porn. That would be more his kind of thing, she thought.

But no, she would just breeze out, leaving him behind. Wondering, like all the rest, where she had gone.

'You're right,' he said. 'Killgannon's got Cunningham talking. We'd better get ready to pull him out.' He picked up his phone from on top of his neatly folded clothes. Checked the screen. 'Oh.'

'What?'

'That psychologist who never turned up last night? The one who wanted to talk about Killgannon? She hasn't turned up for work today.'

Blake shrugged. 'So?'

He kept looking at his phone, reading something. 'It's more serious than that. Her car was found off the road on Blackmoor, a few miles from the prison. That's why she didn't turn up. Why she didn't answer her phone when I called.'

Blake thought she should express concern. 'What? Is she dead?'

'Thankfully not. She was discovered in time, taken to hospital. Looks like someone forced her off the road.'

Blake tried to mask her true feelings. Bradshaw was still alive. That fucking idiot couldn't even . . .

Harmer's voice cut through her thoughts. 'I wonder if this has anything to do with Sheridan's murder?'

'Why should it?'

'One accident, one murder close together. Killgannon the common denominator. Suspicious, don't you think?'

'I've been following the investigation into his death. There's nothing there to point towards Killgannon.' I've seen to that, she thought.

'Nevertheless . . .'

'What?'

'I think we should consider it. Come on. You're right. Let's get to work.'

Blake looked down at the gun lying on top of her bag by the side of the bed. Harmer couldn't see it. But if he said anything else she didn't like, he might just feel it.

She felt as if she was having an out of body experience and was looking down on herself. Things were starting to unravel. She had to get a grip. And fast.

'I'll get dressed and go straight to Blackmoor. See what's going on.'

'No need for that. Just give them a ring. And then when – or if – Dr Bradshaw improves go and see her then.'

'It's still our jurisdiction. We should be—' The sound of a text came pinging from the burner phone in her go bag.

'D'you need to get that?'

'Dan, I should check this out. It might be important.'

He was dressed now. He looked at her. Torn about what to say. 'Go on, then. I'll see you back at the office later.'

No you won't. 'Thank you, sir.'

He crossed to her, wanting a farewell kiss. She moved forwards so he didn't see the bag, the gun. She let him kiss her. It was like having synchronised slugs running over her lips.

He left. Once she was sure he had gone she checked the phone. Saw the text:

Out of prison on the moors. Come right now.

She went. Taking the bag with her. And the Desert Eagle.

Two million was plenty if it was shared.

But even more if it was just for one person.

52

'So where are they from here, then?'

Dean Foley stood in front of the car, the prison officer's own Audi, surveyed the moor ahead of him. He was dressed for the city streets, not the open countryside. Immaculate grey chalkstripe three-piece suit, crisp white ironed shirt, tie, polished, handmade shoes. A Crombie overcoat that cost more than the monthly wage of the officer accompanying him. He knew it was impractical for where he was, but he didn't care. They were the clothes he wore entering prison, his business, cocktail reception, court appearance suit, and he wanted to wear it now. Inmates were allowed to wear their own clothes when they were escorted outside the prison and Foley wanted to feel something different to the cheap, itchy prison sweats against his skin, to remind himself of who he used to be.

Who he could possibly be again.

Baz stood next to him, shivering in his prison issue sweats and an anorak. Chris, one of his tame officers, stood with them.

'Somewhere over there, I think they said they were going,' said Chris, pointing off to a mist-shrouded rocky incline over by the horizon.

Foley looked where indicated then closed his eyes, breathed deeply down to his diaphragm. Exhaled. The air was cold, harsh, with a trace of damp. But so much sweeter than the foul stuff that came from prison. That mixture of sweat, cleaning products, bad food, cheap aftershave, bad breath and infrequently washed bodies. He would take the cold anytime.

'Wonderful, isn't it, Baz? The fresh air, the open countryside . . . You forget, don't you? Cooped up in there all the time, you lose sight of things. Forget what really matters.'

Baz looked like it was anything but wonderful. His expression was miserable, his body language turned in on himself. Like he was counting the seconds until they could get back inside. Like he couldn't function anywhere else. Foley smiled to himself. That was what he had suspected about him. It was interesting. All helping him to make up his mind, come to a decision.

He turned to Chris. 'How do I get to talk to Killgannon?'

Chris shook his head. 'Going to be risky. We can't just walk up to them, tell him you want a word. Not with all those coppers there.'

'So what do we do? You realise this may be my last chance to talk to the man before he disappears again.'

Chris pretended to look concerned. 'Let's get nearer to them. I'll see what I can do. Depends who they've sent to look after him. Hopefully someone I can talk to.' He nodded, remembering how much Foley was paying him, impressing on him his importance.

'Right,' said Foley. 'Let's do it then.' He pointed to the rocky outcrop. 'Just over there, you say?'

Chris nodded.

'Come on, then.' Foley set off walking.

'Can't we take the car?' asked Baz.

Foley turned, looked at him. He seemed to have shrunk since coming outside, his whole frame diminished. Probably more than that: his identity. He could no longer cope anywhere but inside. And to think I used to hold you in such high regard, thought Foley. Pathetic, what you've come to.

'Yeah,' said Chris. 'Might as well. Looks like rain.'

He got behind the wheel of the Audi. Baz scurried onto the back seat, grateful not to be outside anymore. Foley waited until they were both settled then slowly curled into the back of the car, like Chris was his chauffeur. Even if he did have to shut his own door.

'Right,' Foley said. 'Let's get going.'

He sat back, smiled. Tried to enjoy the journey.

53

Night rolled over Blackmoor in a series of heavier shades of grey.

Tom felt as though a mist was rolling in, making him squint to see clearly, but it was just the darkening clouds. Like they were too heavy for the sky and were coming in to rest on land. He had spent the whole day on the moor and found the environment unwelcoming. Unnerving, even. Like the place was almost sentient and didn't want anyone to walk on it, only suffered those who came onto it if they departed quickly. Rocky outcrops loomed over them like menacing ancient gods as the darkness thickened. The woods and forests thrust spiked leafless branches against the sky while their dark, black hearts were ready to absorb any unwary travellers and never let them go.

He shivered from more than just cold.

Then shook his head. He was imagining things. He had been penned in for so long, the open space was in danger of making him agoraphobic. Considering his claustrophobia he might have found that amusing. But not right now.

'Fuck's sake,' said the first officer, who Tom had discovered was called Ray. 'Aren't they back yet?'

'Coming down now,' said the second, who had revealed himself to be called Tony. 'Look, over there. You can see the torches.'

On the rocky hill ahead of them Cunningham and his party were returning. Cunningham, Tom noticed, was at the back of the pack now. Dragging his feet like the reluctant kid on the school trip.

With nothing else to do, they watched the party until they were there in front of them.

Ray crossed to the lead detective. 'Any luck?'

The detective shook her head. 'Nah. A few false alarms, but he's having trouble remembering anything.' A roll of the eyes to accompany her words told them what she thought of the whole enterprise. 'It all looks different now, apparently.'

'What, this all used to be fields?' said Tony, laughing at his own joke in case no one else did.

The detective smiled politely. 'Forensics took some readings, a couple of maybes but nothing positive. Going to be a long haul.' She looked between the two of them to Tom. 'Think of the overtime.'

Tom said nothing. There were things he wanted to ask her, one professional to another, but he refrained. He knew how it would have sounded. And knew she wouldn't have answered him.

'Right, then,' said Ray. 'Back inside for you.'

'And his mate,' said Tony. 'Here he comes now.'

Cunningham was escorted over to the two officers. He was beaming, almost manic. Buzzing with excitement.

'You had fun?' asked Tom, deadpan.

Cunningham nodded.

'Found anything?'

'Not yet, but it's just good to be back out here. Makes you feel alive, doesn't it? Like it's speaking to you, telling you secrets.' He nodded to himself, hearing something no one else was. 'I'll find them tomorrow. Tomorrow. The moor'll not let me go without them. It wants to help.'

Tom didn't look at the two officers. He didn't need to, to know what they would be thinking.

'Come on then,' said Tony, 'sooner we can get you two back, sooner we can knock off.'

Cunningham and Tom climbed into the back of the minibus. Ray took his position behind the steering wheel, Tony next to him. He started the engine, the radio blaring at the same time. Kiss FM.

'Few bangers to make the trip go better,' said Ray and drove off.

314

Tom closed his eyes.

And opened them pretty soon. There was some kind of commotion going on.

Ray and Tony were shouting, swearing. Tom saw headlights outside the bus, coming up alongside. Looked like a motorbike. Whichever way they went, the bike was still there.

'What the fuck's going on?' said Tony.

Tom knew immediately what was happening. They were being attacked. He jumped forwards in his seat. 'Keep driving,' he shouted. 'Put your foot down.'

Tony turned back to him, fear at the situation mixed with anger at Tom's interference. 'Just fucking sit down, you. We'll deal with this.'

'You haven't even got a gun,' said Tom.

The biker had come alongside them. Ray had tried to shake him off but he was keeping pace with them.

As Tom looked out of the window, the biker drew alongside the driver and, holding the speeding bike with one hand, produced a handgun, an automatic.

'Get out of the way!' he shouted, but to no effect.

The biker fired. Glass shattered and the top of Ray's head decorated the ceiling of the bus. Tony just stared, too scared to move.

The bus sped up, began to weave all over the road.

'Get his foot off the accelerator!' Tom shouted.

Tony didn't move.

'Get his . . .'

Tom leaned forwards over the front seat, ignored the blood and pulled Ray's body back. He took the dead man's hands off the steering wheel, replaced them with his own. Tried to wrestle the bus back under control.

'Get your foot on the brake,' Tom shouted at Tony but the guard didn't respond. 'Get your foot on the brake!' Still no response.

Tom looked ahead through the windscreen. Away from the direct illumination of the bus's beams everything else was pitch black. He didn't know if he was on flat land or on the blind brow of a hill with an oncoming vehicle out of sight. But he would have to take a chance.

Keeping his right hand on the wheel he reached down for the handbrake with his left, pulled it as hard as he could.

Tyres squealing, the bus skidded into a turn. Tom held on to the steering wheel with both hands. Concentrated. Ignored the smoke, the smell of burning rubber and electrics. Just held on tight as the bus gradually came to rest in the opposite direction it had been heading.

He sat back, breathed a sigh of relief.

But it was shortlived. Headlights outside told him the biker was back.

'Get out,' he shouted to Tony, but again the man didn't move.

He looked at Cunningham who had curled up into a foetal ball and was reciting a prayer to himself.

The biker pulled to a standstill, got off the bike, leaving the engine turning over. He came round to the back of the bus, ready to open the doors.

Tom got there before him. He slammed open the door, knocking the gun from the biker's hand, smashing his knuckles in the process. He didn't stop to think, just fell back into his training.

He had the element of surprise but, he knew, not for long. He kicked at the biker, aiming for his face, but only connecting with his helmet. The kick jarred him though, knocked him off balance. Tom pressed on, punching him in the stomach – once – twice – then another kick to his groin. The biker folded.

Tom looked quickly round. Assessed the situation as fast as he could.

He should find out who his assailant was, get that helmet off him. But that would slow him down. And he might get the better of him this time.

So as the biker began to come round again, search for his gun, Tom noticed his bike was standing there, still running. He made straight for it, hauled himself onto it and, without thinking or looking back, roared away into the night.

54

Blake drove her Dacia Duster over the moor, headlights full on. She was breathing so hard it felt like she was running the distance, not driving. Quint's call had just come through: Killgannon's gone, taken my bike. He had left her GPS coordinates. A good job she was already on the way.

Everything was unravelling. She couldn't stand it. Her whole plan suddenly falling apart. She had to keep herself together. Plot. Plan. Don't give in to panic, to despair. Keep calm. Think.

It had been going so well. She had managed to keep a degree of a grip on the investigation into Sheridan's death, even from a distance. The little extras she had managed to put onto his computer pointed to a completely different kind of copper than he had appeared to be, one that had shaken plenty of her colleagues. So the team had gone off in that direction, investigating things that had no bearing on him when he was alive, never mind in death. And, with subtle – and sometimes not so subtle – suggestions as to where to look, who to talk to, it would be months before they exhausted those erroneous possibilities. If they ever did. By which time she – and the money she was convinced Killgannon had been hoarding – would be long gone.

She floored the accelerator of the Duster, jumping forwards in her seat as if that would make it go faster. A Dacia Duster. She was embarrassed to own it but she had wanted a four by four. An SUV. A prestige car that put her – physically if nothing else – higher than the other drivers on the road. She had dreamed of a BMW or Porsche, or even a Lexus or a Jaguar at a push. But this was all she could afford. A Dacia. The budget brand. But even if she couldn't yet afford the thing she wanted – accent on the yet – then at least she could prepare herself for it by driving this thing.

She slammed on the brakes. Lost in her own thoughts, she nearly didn't see the figure in the road standing before her, waving both arms. Quint.

She pulled up before making contact. He ran round to the side of the car, threw his helmet on to the backseat, jumped in. She looked at him. He looked dreadful. Tired, dirty, his expensive jacket scuffed and abraded. Like his bike had been riding him, not the other way round.

'What happened?' she asked.

'Killgannon got away.'

'You said. How did it happen?'

'He . . .' Quint sighed. It was obvious from his usual demeanour that he wasn't used to failure in his work. He clearly didn't take it well. 'He overpowered me.' Said quickly, the sooner the words were out there, the sooner they would be gone. 'I forced the bus off the road, he . . . took my bike. Went off.'

'Was he the only one in the bus?'

'Another prisoner, Cunningham. And an officer. I took the driver out.'

Blake sighed. She felt like headbutting the steering wheel, punching Quint. Anything to get rid of this desperate, hopeless aggression building within her.

'He's dead?'

'Looked it. Half his head was missing.'

Blake stared at him.

'Hey, lady, you hired me for this job. You know the way I work. You know what it is I do. You've been happy with what I've done so far. Don't start with any of that fucking princess bullshit now or I'll just take the rest of my money and be off.'

Blake dropped her head, sighed once more. A mess. Nothing but a mess. But she would dig her way out of it, salvage something. She had to. Just keep her nerve.

'You're right. It's what I hired you for. I'm sure you had to do it.'

'I wouldn't have done it otherwise.'

'So where are they now? Cunningham and the other officer?'

'Don't know. I didn't hang around to find out. When Killgannon took my bike I just got out of there. There'll be police, prison staff, all sorts there by now.' He could barely contain his rage at failing at his job.

Panic entered Blake's voice. 'But that must be just round here. You can't have run that—'

'I know what I'm doing. My career's been made living in terrain like this. I got away from them. They won't find me here. That's why I told you to meet me here and not nearer to where it happened.'

Blake relaxed slightly. 'Right.' She checked her watch. This was it, the time to come up with a plan that would get everything back on track. Get her the money, get her out of here.

She looked at Quint. 'You need transport.'

'Why?'

'Because I want you to get back to Killgannon's house and tear it apart. No need to be nice anymore. We're way past that.'

'What about the women there?'

Blake shrugged. 'As you say, it's what I'm paying you for.'

'Right. So any ideas on getting transport?'

She checked her phone. Received another text. Smiled.

'Might have just the thing.'

Things might be falling back into place again

55

Tom Killgannon was lost.

He had roared off on the stolen motorbike, all attempts at location and direction gone in the adrenaline rush of the attack. He didn't know which way he was heading, he only knew that he wanted to put as much distance between himself and the bus, the rest of the hunting police force, and most importantly, the prison as he could. So he kept going in what he hoped was a straight line, off the roads, bumping over stone, splashing through mud, gorse and bramble tearing the denim of his jeans, catching his legs at high speed. He didn't stop. Just kept riding on into darkness.

As he rode he thought. Tried to order what had happened, what was happening. Formulate the best way to get out of all this. The most obvious thing to do would be to head home. That was also the most obvious thing from any pursuer's point of view. So it was the last place he could go.

Also, he had to try and think who was after him. Blake. That, he believed, was a given. And whoever owned the motorbike he had taken. Who else? Foley? That didn't make any sense. He had agreed to a meeting in prison. And when Tom's job was finished he would honour that. He couldn't think of anyone else. Not with an immediate grudge against him.

He went through his options. Find a nearby town or village, stay there the night. Too risky. That would be the second place they would look, plus he didn't have any money to pay for a room. And he wasn't going to steal some. He almost smiled at the next thought. Break in somewhere that looked deserted, keep his head down, stay there. Just like Lila had thought she was doing, all those months ago. If he did that, he hoped she would, at some point, appreciate the irony. No. That wasn't a good enough option either.

So, by process of elimination, he knew what he had to do. Find somewhere on the moor, bed down there as best he could, find out where he was in the morning, plan from there.

That was what he would have to do.

He felt the ground rising, knowing that the higher he climbed the more he could see of the surrounding area, the sooner he would know that someone had reached him. But not yet. He was quite alone.

The bike's beams alighted on a tall, rocky outcrop before him, the kind, he thought, that sheep would shelter under during winter storms. That would have to do. He pulled the bike up alongside it, cut the engine. Wheeled it under the rock. Looked to see where he was.

On a distant horizon he could see lights. He didn't know if that was the prison, a town, a village or even a city. Could be a band of villagers with flaming pitchforks, even, searching for him. He watched. The lights were unmoving. A settlement of some kind. Far enough away not to be a problem.

The moor itself was even bleaker in darkness. He had mistrusted it earlier in what daylight there was, now it seemed positively treacherous. Like there was something with him in the darkness, just waiting for him to make a mistake, to claim him for its own.

He tried to put thoughts like that from his mind. Walked about, swung his arms against his body. Tried to revel in his sudden freedom. All he could think was this: he was cold. Very cold. The temperature had dropped significantly since he had first got on the bike and it had been cold before that. He looked round for twigs, branches, anything he could use to make a fire. No. He couldn't do that. Might attract attention. He would just have to huddle up in his parka, get as near to the bike's engine as possible until it cooled, try to get some sleep if he could. Hope that hypothermia didn't set in by morning.

The wind blew sharply in his face. And with it something else. The near ice touch of rain.

With that, the storm clouds above made good on their day long threat. The rain came lashing down.

Tom got as far under the lip of rock as he could. Ready to sit out the night and everything in it.

56

'There they are.'

Blake pointed. It wasn't necessary: The only thing ahead on the moor's shingle track was a stationary car with its headlights on. She pushed the Duster harder, hoping to increase speed but in reality just rocking the pair of them backwards and forwards on the SUV's cheap suspension.

She pulled up next to the other car. Before she had time to turn her engine off Dean Foley burst from the back of his car, angry and roaring. She got calmly out, closed the door.

'I don't like not knowing what's going on,' he said, getting right in Blake's face. His sheer, physical presence was intimidating. His anger unnerving. She could understand why he was so feared. 'Baz here says we've got to wait so I waited. Now what's this all about?'

Blake looked quickly inside the car. A confused and scared-looking prison officer was behind the wheel, Baz in the back. He smiled when he saw her. She smiled in return.

'Hello Foxy,' she said. 'Long time no see.'

Baz stepped out of the car. Looked at her.

'You two know each other?' Foley, his anger unabated, stared at them, suspicious.

'Yeah,' said Baz, crossing to Blake, 'we go back a long way, don't we babe?'

He put his arm round her, pulled her towards him for a kiss. Blake resisted.

'What's the matter?' Anger in his voice. 'Don't you fancy me no more?'

Blake hadn't known how she would feel seeing him again. Hadn't prepared herself. He looked rough. And not just because of the scars. Standing there in his prison-issue best, he emanated waves of thwarted ambition, bitterness. She barely recognised him.

'That's not why I'm here and you know it. So let's get on with things.'

He stared at her, mentally adding her to the list of those who had betrayed him. She could practically feel him doing it.

'All the fucking same . . .'

Blake had tried to rekindle their relationship after the crash, more from duty or pity than anything else. But they were too different by then. She was in the ascendancy and he couldn't cope with that. He was consumed by anger and self-loathing. Blake thought he had a point to be angry with the police since they wouldn't give him the pension he thought he was entitled to. But he'd gone bad, they said. Undercover work's not for everyone. You need the right temperament. A sense of perspective. Even his union rep told him to just accept it, let it go, get on with the rest of his life.

So he took it out on Blake, initially. Shouted at her, hit her. She had never thought she would be the kind of woman to stand for that kind of abuse. Whenever she had been called out to a domestic to find a bloody, battered, broken woman crying with pain but refusing to press charges, she'd thought the woman deserved all that was coming to her. If she was too simple minded to leave then Blake had no sympathy for her. But it wasn't like that. As she found out.

It was gradual. Baz resenting her for having a career, a job, even. Letting that resentment grow. Fuelling it with drugs and alcohol. Taking it out on her. Their relationship so complicated by love and mutual desire that she didn't realise what she had become until it happened.

One of those women she had no sympathy for.

So she left him. Eventually.

'Don't start that,' she said, snapping back to the present. 'Head in the game. You contacted me for a reason. And we're here now so let's get on with it.'

Baz just stared at her.

He had contacted her out of the blue. He was in Blackmoor with Dean Foley. Had heard she was with Devon and Cornwall Police, trying to advance her career in a way she couldn't in Manchester. Guilt mingled with curiosity. She went to see him. Having the time of his life, he said, like an old boys' club. Had she tracked down Mick Eccleston yet? Did she have the money? And if so, when could he get his cut?

His words dug into her. She had tried to find Mick Eccleston – and Foley's money – but with no success. And then something dropped into her lap. The events of several months ago in St Petroc. Tom Killgannon had done his best not to get his face seen anywhere but she had spotted him. And it didn't take too long to put a plan into action.

Noel Cunningham wanted to talk. They needed someone to go inside. It was a simple matter to nudge Harmer in the direction of Killgannon. He was right in their lap. And even easier to make Harmer think he had come up with the idea himself. It was a perfect plan. She never wanted to see Baz again and wouldn't after this. She would cross him. And take great joy in doing so. Payback for all the things he had done to her.

She turned away from Baz. 'Mr Foley,' she said, smiling, 'a pleasure to meet you at last.'

She stuck out her hand, ready for him to shake. The gesture, the smile, her words, took him by surprise, stopped his rage in full flow.

He accepted her hand, more confused than angry now. 'And you are?'

'Detective Constable Annie Blake. And I'm here to help you.'

Suspicious now. 'Help me? How?'

'By taking you to meet Tom Killgannon. Or Mick Eccleston as you know him.'

Foley looked between everyone, back to Blake. 'I don't know what's going on here,' he said. He pointed to Quint. 'And who's this?'

'This is Quint,' said Blake.

'No I'm not,' said Quint.

'You are for now. I read up on Eccleston's old case files in Manchester. He often worked with some kind of backup. This, to all intents and purposes, is him.'

Dan Jameson had fallen into her lap. Ex-army, ex-mercenary, trying to make a living back in the UK. She had arrested him for attempted murder in Manchester. He was trying to carve out a career as a hitman but without much success. She thought he was the kind of person she could do business with at some point so made sure the charges against him were buried in return for a favour some time in the future. She remembered Jameson when she saw Killgannon had chosen Quinton Blair, an old friend of his. Jameson had been very thorough in assuming Quint's identity. And, as she had discovered, hadn't baulked at getting rid of anyone else.

Foley turned to Baz. 'What's going on?'

'This is the friend I was telling you about in the car. The one I texted. The one I said we had to meet.'

'She's law. And we should have been back in Blackmoor hours ago.'

Baz shrugged. 'Things have changed, Dean.'

Foley stared at him. Blake felt she was coming between these two men who had some unfinished – perhaps even unspoken – business.

'I thought you'd want to get back inside,' said Foley. 'You weren't enjoying it out here today.'

'No I wasn't. But that was then.' He smiled at Blake. She didn't return it. 'We're ready to move forwards.'

Anger came to Foley once more. 'Are you fucking me about, Baz? What's going on? Tell me.'

'We think Killgannon's got the missing two million,' said Blake.

Foley thought for a second before replying. 'You mean *my* two million.'

Blake shrugged. 'There'll be plenty to go round when we get it. We can all have a share. Call it a finder's fee.'

Foley said nothing. Didn't have to. The look on his face betrayed the fact he didn't agree with her.

'The important thing,' she told him, 'is to get it first.' She turned to her companion. 'Quint.'

'I'm not Quint.'

'Don't start that again. You know where you've got to go. What you've got to do.'

'Won't Killgannon be there?'

'Not if he wants to go back inside again, but you'd better be quick. The law might turn up at any minute looking for him. He'll have been missed by now.'

Quint nodded. Looked pensive. 'How do I get there? Your car?'

Blake looked offended at the idea. She crossed to Chris, still sitting behind the wheel of his car. Flashed him her warrant card.

'DC Blake, Devon and Cornwall police. I'm going to need your car.' He began to protest. 'It's not a debate. My associate is taking it. Now.'

He got out, stood behind the door. Looked very uncertain. Blake nodded to Quint who came over, got behind the wheel. Drove off. Chris walked towards the Duster. Made to get inside.

'Where d'you think you're going?' asked Blake.

Chris looked at her as though the question didn't need answering.

'I have official police business with these two prisoners. You're going to have to make your own way home.'

'But it's miles away. I don't even know where I am . . .'

She turned away. 'Right. You two. In my car.'

Foley looked at her, then at Baz. His attention stayed on Baz.

'I don't trust you anymore,' he said.

Baz shrugged, smiled. 'You'd be very wise not to.'

Foley kept staring at him. 'It was you, then, wasn't it?'

'What was me?'

'The attack on Eccleston. Clive Bennett's death. You did all that.'

Baz shrugged, that unpleasant smile still creasing and cracking his features. 'You're slipping, Dean, losing your power. Someone had to step up, replace you.' He spread his arms wide. 'Who better than me? Good old, loyal, dependable Baz.' He couldn't keep the hatred from his voice. 'Standing beside you all that time, doing whatever you told me to do, carrying out your every order. Well not anymore, Deano. From now on it's me in charge.'

Foley just stared at him. 'I thought you might try something like this. That's why I brought you out with me today because I couldn't trust you to stay inside without me.'

'I know,' said Baz. 'And that's what I wanted you to think. I played you, Dean.'

Foley's expression changed. He had looked like he had been about to do Baz some damage, possibly terminal. Now he wanted to listen. 'What d'you mean?'

'I wanted to be out here as much as you. I want to see Killgannon as much as you do too.'

'Why? The money?'

Baz just smiled.

'Well,' said Foley nodded, 'It looks like we're off on a little jaunt together, doesn't it?'

They all got into the Duster. Blake started up the engine, mounted her phone on a clip on the dashboard.

'You know where Killgannon is?' asked Foley.

Blake smiled. 'I know exactly where he is.'

She turned the Duster round, drove off.

The rain started.

They passed Chris as he made his long walk home.

No one acknowledged him.

57

Lila lay back, eyes still closed, sighed. Smiled. Turned to Anju, found she was smiling just as broadly, looking straight into her eyes. Neither spoke. Neither needed to.

Anju hugged Lila close to her. Curled her face into the side of her neck. Lila could feel her breath on her skin, knew from her lips that she was still smiling.

Lila sighed again. She hadn't felt this happy, this relaxed, in ages. Years, perhaps. Tom was right, she thought. Things are going to be better from now on.

They had both known this was going to happen. Ending up in bed together. Both had wanted to, but neither had planned it. Like the rest of their relationship, it had happened organically, grown out of what had gone before.

Anju had driven round to Lila's house, just to spend the evening together. Watch some TV, eat Lila's attempt at pasta carbonara, chill. Be together. But as soon as she entered they both knew what was going to happen. Looking back at that moment, both had known even before that, when the invitation was made. But neither had expressed it. Neither had needed to.

And it had felt so right. Lila didn't feel guilty. Nor did she feel like she was doing it as an act of distant revenge to spite her parents. It had been because she was falling in love with another person and wanted to express that, explore that.

She held Anju harder to her. Enjoyed the feeling of the other girl's body against her own. Could happily lie like that for the rest of her life.

Then heard a car outside.

Anju moved, made to get up.

'Don't worry,' said Lila. 'It'll just be Pearl coming back from the pub.'

Anju relaxed once more.

And stayed that way until there was hammering on the front door.

That wasn't Pearl.

They both jumped up, looked at each other. Didn't know who it was but knew it wasn't going to be good news.

'Could that be Tom?' asked Anju.

For a split second, Lila allowed herself to hope. To think that things would be alright for him too. But that soon faded.

More hammering.

'I don't think so . . .'

They both quickly got dressed, pulled on whatever clothing they found to hand. Went downstairs. Anju not letting Lila go down alone.

They stood in front of the door. Heard more hammering.

'Who is it?' called Lila.

More hammering.

'Let me in.' Muffled, urgent.

They couldn't make out the voice. Lila ran to the living room, opened the curtains, checked the car outside. She didn't recognise it. Not Quint, she thought. He would have been on his motorbike. She went back to the front door. More frantic hammering.

Lila and Anju shared a look. They both knew they were going to open it.

Quint came roaring in, gun in hand.

Anju screamed. Quint turned, knocked her to the floor with the butt of his gun. Lila ran to her.

'What the fuck are you doing?' Her anger, concern for Anju over-rode her fear of him.

He slammed the door behind him. Stared down at them.

'Get her in there,' he said, gesturing to the living room. 'Now.'

Lila helped Anju to her feet. She was bleeding from where the gun had connected with her temple.

'Move.'

Lila helped Anju to the sofa, sat down next to her. 'You OK?'

Anju nodded. 'Yeah. I think . . .'

Lila looked up at Quint who covered them both with the gun.

'Sit there. Don't move.'

Lila stared at him. 'I knew you were wrong from the first moment. Knew it. Should have trusted my instincts.'

'Yeah, well,' said Quint, looking round the room, 'bit late for that now.'

'What d'you want?'

'What I've wanted all along. The money.'

Lila frowned. 'What you talking about? What money?'

'The money Killgannon stole from Dean Foley. Don't play stupid.'

'Haven't a clue what you're talking about. Tom didn't steal any money.'

'Yeah? You think? How well do you know him?'

Lila made to stand up. Quint waved the gun at her. She sat down again. Even more angry. 'He wouldn't do that. I know him. And he wouldn't do that.'

Quint smiled. 'We'll see, won't we?'

'What are you going to do with us?' Anju's voice was weak, wavering. She held her hand to her head, trying unsuccessfully to stem the flow of blood.

'Depends how useful you're going to be.'

'Useful for what?' asked Lila, defiance still in her voice.

Quint smiled. There was no trace of the charming man who had visited them previously. Lila was angry with herself for not challenging him sooner. Letting it come to this. 'Useful to me. Can't search this whole house on my own, now, can I?'

'What makes you think we'll help you?' asked Anju, voice quiet, but as defiant as Lila's.

'Because I'm holding the gun. And you don't want to be on the wrong end of it if you piss me off, do you?'

They both stared at him.

'There's a stupid bitch policewoman out on the moors right now trying to track down your beloved Tom Killgannon. And she thinks I'm just going to roll over and give her whatever money I find.'

'There's no money here,' said Lila. 'I've told you. I would know.'

'We'll see, shall we?'

The gun seemed to loom even larger in front of her face.

Lila said nothing, just held on to Anju.

Her only slim hope was that Pearl would come home and see what was happening.

That slim hope.

Lila had learned, from bitter experience, not to believe in hope.

58

Tom didn't think it was possible but he was finding sleep even more elusive than in prison.

The rain and the cold hadn't let up, hadn't allowed him to sleep. That and the constant churn of his mind as he tried to understand what had led him to this situation and how he could get out of it.

He tried once again to put everything in place, give events some semblance of order. Sheridan was dead and with him his way out. Blake thought he had stolen Dean Foley's money. He didn't know how or why she had reached this conclusion but she seemed firmly convinced of it. Dr Bradshaw wanted Foley and him to talk, bury their differences. He didn't see that happening now. So where would he go from here, what would his future be? Assuming he had a future. Another identity since this one was compromised? Back to prison for real? Not seeing Lila or Pearl again? The last hurt the most. He had just been getting his new life established. Just about come to terms with his past, making tentative steps towards a future. That could all be gone now.

He didn't have time to think anymore. Headlights were approaching along the ridge below him.

He looked round, checked that the bike was out of sight. Hoped it was just some hill farmer checking on his errant flock. Still, he didn't want to engage with whoever it was, so tucked himself as far back into the rocky overhang as he could.

He heard the roar of an engine as the vehicle made its way up the hill. Stayed as still as he could. If it was a search party there would be more of them. Probably with dogs. And they wouldn't be able to cover the rough terrain as easily as this vehicle which, he guessed, must be some kind of four by four. Must be a farmer.

The four by four stopped, headlights still blazing. He shrank back even further into the shadows.

Heard voices. Couldn't make out the words, but managed to identify the genders. A woman. A man. No, two men. And at least one of those voices he recognised.

DC Blake.

Incredulity washed over him. What was she doing here? This was more than just coincidence. This had been planned. But how?

He thought. A GPS tracker on the bike? That must be it. The only way she could have tracked him down. Then anger: how could he have been so stupid? He should have checked. He should have known. It was what he would have done if he had been in her situation. A necessary precaution.

He tried not to blame himself any further. Needed his mind sharp, had to work a way out of this.

He listened, tried to make out what was being said but the wind and rain carried most of the sense of the words away. He heard Blake's voice:

'Get looking. He must be around here somewhere. The signal says he is.'

Tom looked round, saw the hillside illuminated once more in the glare of the headlights. Saw more outcrops of rock than he had realised were there originally. Heard footsteps approaching.

He thought of making a dash for it, trying to reach the bike, ride away before they could stop him. Quickly abandoned that idea. They had the tracker and they might be carrying guns. He had been lucky before. He might not be so lucky this time.

'Found the bike.'

That was the definite end of that plan. But did he recognise the voice? He wasn't sure. Not in this weather.

He peered closer. The figure was medium height, dressed in an anorak over what looked like prison issue gear. Very inappropriate trainers on his feet. He was examining the bike. Blake shouted something in response that Tom didn't catch.

340

Time to make a decision.

Tom felt around on the ground for a suitably sized rock, small enough to fit into the palm of his hand, big enough to inflict damage. He found one easily, weighed it, readied himself.

The man started to creep towards the overhang.

Tom barely had time to register the man's identity or what he looked like. All he knew was that he must be subdued, and in the most direct way possible.

He leaped out of the shadows, rock held high and, before the other man could turn round, brought it down as hard as he could on the side of the man's head.

'Oww . . .'

The man staggered forwards to his knees, hand to his head from the sudden pain. He looked up.

'What d'you do that for?'

Tom only had to time to register the blood on the man's face and how hideous he looked even without it. He didn't have time to think. He hit him again. This time the man went quiet.

Blake's voice drifted up from down below. 'Baz? You OK? What's happened? Baz?'

Tom lifted up Baz's body, placed it in front of him like a shield. Made his way to the edge of the cave mouth, looked down the hill. And stared, open-mouthed.

DC Blake was there, as he had expected. But she wasn't alone. Standing next to her, looking exactly like he had all those years ago, was Dean Foley. He might, thought Tom, actually have been wearing the suit he always used to wear. It was like an hallucination in the rain.

He didn't have time to be surprised, though, not if he wanted to get out of this alive. He held up Baz's body before him.

'You want him? Let's talk.'

59

'So why are you doing this to us?'

Lila and Anju were sitting on the sofa. Quint sat in the armchair opposite, still pointing the gun at them. He hadn't relaxed. Lila had no idea how much time had passed. Could have been minutes, could have been hours.

'You know why,' he said. 'And I know what you're doing. And it's not going to work. So you may as well stop it now.'

'What am I doing?'

'Trying to get me to talk. Humanise yourself in front of me. Make me feel like you matter. Save yourself the trouble. Don't bother. It won't work.'

Lila said nothing in reply. Just had a momentary flashback to a similar situation several months ago where she had tried the same thing. It hadn't worked then, either. Trying not to let that thought add to her problems, she pressed on.

'So you're going to get this mythical money for yourself and double cross your partner, is that it?'

'Shut up.' Almost yawning as he spoke.

'Is that your job?' asked Anju. The bleeding had stopped now but she still looked pale. Possibly concussed, Lila thought, desperately wanting to help her.

'Yeah it's my job.'

'So what, you're a hitman? Is that right?'

'Yeah.' He shrugged. 'Suppose that covers it.'

'How d'you get into that?' asked Anju, seemingly serious and interested.

Very clever of you, thought Lila. Ask anyone about their job and they'll always talk about it. Even people like him.

'Was in the army for a few years. Went over to Iraq, like I said. Did a few stints there. SAS. The army trains you for war. When you leave all you can do is fight. So I went back east, joined up with a few private contractors.'

'You mean mercenaries?' said Anju.

'You could say that. All those rich Arabs want their own private army. I was just hired help. Good thing was, if there was any trouble, they just waved money at the problem and it disappeared.' He smiled, almost wistfully at the memory. 'We could do whatever we liked and get away with it.'

'I can understand all that, but how did you get to be a hitman? I mean, it seems like a much more specialised job.'

'Suppose it is, really. I came back home, homesick really. Tried to go into security consultancy. Got bored really easily though. Then someone asked me to off someone. And of course, I was good at it. So someone else asked. And someone else. And word got round. I was the go-to guy. For a price, of course.'

Anju leaned forwards, the expression on her face genuinely curious. 'So why haven't you killed us yet?'

'Because you might be more help to me in looking round this house. Or you might not. Then I'll think again.'

She sat back. Thinking. 'Listen,' she said eventually.

'What?'

'You said you're going to take the money you find here and cut your partner out, right?'

Quint didn't answer.

'Well, like Lila says, she doesn't think there's any money here. And neither do I, to be honest. But I'll tell you one thing.' She leaned forwards. Lila noticed her top was gaping and she hadn't had time to put her bra back on underneath. Quint's eyes went there too.

Anju continued. 'My parents are rich. And I don't just mean rich for Cornwall. I mean very rich. They would pay you to leave us alone. Pay you really well. Honestly.'

Quint stared at her, as if seriously considering it.

It felt to Lila like the room held its breath.

'Nah,' he said eventually. 'Too much hassle.'

'What d'you mean?' asked Anju. 'I'm serious. They'd give you plenty of money to get me back safe.'

'Maybe they would. But I've heard that before. Even fell for it a couple of times, when I was just starting out. Always ended up messy. More trouble than it was worth. Either they didn't have the money when push came to shove, or they wouldn't pay up, or they threatened me with the law . . . It never worked. So no thanks.'

'Please,' said Anju, 'it won't be like that this time.'

'I said no.' Steel back in his voice. He repositioned his gun arm. Reminded them he was still in charge.

'But there is one thing,' he said.

'What's that?' asked Lila.

'I'm hungry. Make me something to eat.'

60

'OK then,' said Foley, smiling through the rain, 'let's talk.'

Tom stared at him, waiting for whatever trick he was planning. Nothing happened.

Foley behaved as if the rain, the wind, the cold, didn't touch him. Tom was certain that wasn't the case but he knew Foley. Don't show weakness in front of an opponent. And right now he was showing only imperviousness.

'Seriously,' said Foley, ignoring the water running down his face. 'Just you and me. Talking. Why don't you come down?'

Tom moved slightly forwards, still holding the semi-limp body of Baz. His human shield.

'Never mind about him,' said Foley, stretching his arms out, waggling his fingers. 'I'm not armed.'

'No,' said Tom, gesturing with his head. 'But she is.'

Blake was standing to the side of Foley, out of his peripheral vision, gun drawn, pointing it at Tom.

Foley turned to her. Irritation back on his face. 'Put that away. We don't need that now.'

She stared at him, a look of pure hatred and anger. 'I'll be the judge of that.'

Foley returned her glare, held it until most opponents would have blinked or looked away. Instead Blake held his gaze.

Foley broke first, looked back at Tom. Smiled. 'Seems we have a stand-off.'

Tom knew what Foley was up to. It was another old ploy of his. Don't show weakness. Absolutely. But only show the illusion of it if you intend to show real strength later. After you've lulled your opponent – or even your assumed associate – into a false sense of security. Let them think they have the measure of you while all the while you're taking the measure of them. Tom had never seen it fail for Foley. Except once. With him.

'Fine,' said Tom. 'I'll talk from here.' He held Baz up. 'And I'll keep him in place too. Just in case your mate gets a bit trigger happy.'

Foley spread out his arms again, as if he was some genial party host and that was fine by him.

Tom, sensing no immediate threat, turned his attention to Blake. She was still holding the gun on him. Unlike Foley, it was very clear that the weather – and everything else – was affecting her. At this moment, he thought, she was the dangerous one. The one to watch out for.

'So what's all this for?' he asked her. 'What's it in aid of?'

She smiled. 'Money, of course.'

Tom frowned. 'Whose money? What are you talking about?'

She didn't reply. Instead kept staring at Tom.

Foley smiled. 'She thinks you've got my money. My two million. I must admit, the question's crossed my mind over the years. So have you got it?'

Tom sighed. 'Why would I take your money?'

'Because two million would set you up very nicely. You and your new identity.'

Tom felt like laughing. 'The case against you nearly collapsed because of that money. The case I'd spent years working on. It could have prejudiced the trial. Sent me into Witness Protection for nothing. Why would I do that?'

Foley thought. 'I don't know, Mick. I really don't know. Unless . . .' He looked up, a thought having occurred to him. 'Maybe you just wanted me to go free.'

Tom stared at him. Wondered whether he had heard him right through the storm. 'What? Why would I do that? The case . . .'

Foley continued. 'Yeah, yeah, the case. I know. The case. But isn't it obvious? I've been thinking about this a lot. I mean, I've had a lot of time to think, haven't I? But how about this . . .' He pointed at

348

Tom, as if accusing him. 'You couldn't bear to see me behind bars. That was the main thing. Everything we'd been through, all those things we'd shared . . . part of you just couldn't let me go through with it, could you? You couldn't let all of that go. Am I right?' Foley smiled. 'I'm right, aren't I?'

Tom shook his head. 'I can't believe I'm hearing this.'

'Never mind this bullshit,' shouted Blake, making sure she could be heard over the storm, 'just tell me where the money is.'

Tom looked between the two of them. He noted Foley's reaction as she said 'me' rather than 'us'.

'So you're in this together, then?' asked Tom, knowing what the answer would be. Hoping he could drive a wedge between them.

'No,' said Foley. 'This is all her and that one.'

He pointed at Baz who was beginning to stir in Tom's arms.

'He was one of your lot once too, you know,' said Foley, smiling. 'But he turned. Came to work for me. Properly. Not pretending. Like you.' The smile faded replaced by a look of compassion.

Tom wasn't fooled for a second.

'Couldn't get any other work looking like that, could he?' said Foley. 'Poor fucker.'

'He was a good man,' said Blake, sounding even more angry about Baz than about the money, waving her gun towards Foley. 'Better than either of you two. So don't talk about him like that.'

Tom heard Baz groaning, starting to move as he came round. He held him even tighter, not letting go of his bargaining chip.

Baz opened his eyes. 'What . . .' He looked up at Tom, frowned. 'What did you do to me?'

'Hit you on the head. But you're fine now.'

'What?'

Tom stared back at him. 'I've seen you on the wing, haven't I? With Dean?'

It took a few seconds longer than usual, but Baz's thought process began to work again. 'Oh, you knew me long before that . . .' He pointed towards Foley.

Tom looked at him again. Tried to see through the blood and the rain, rebuild the face, scrub out the scars . . . 'Jesus. Foxy?'

Baz smiled. 'Yeah. Foxy. That's me. That was me. And you didn't fucking recognise me.'

'It's been a long time. I also wasn't expecting to find you here. Like this.'

'Yeah,' said Baz, the words curdling in his mouth, 'and the law looks after its own, doesn't it? Especially the white ones. The black ones can go and get fucked.'

'I didn't even know you were undercover until later,' said Tom. 'I thought you just worked for Dean.'

Baz nodded. 'That's how they wanted it. Neither of us knew about the other. But we could keep an eye on each other for them when we reported. Clever fuckers.'

'Foxy . . .' Tom's memory inevitably went back to that night.

He remembered sitting in the BMW with Foley, seeing Hayley in one of the other cars, with . . .

'Hayley,' he said. 'You were with Hayley that night.'

Baz smiled to himself. 'Oh yeah. She was your . . . niece. That was it, wasn't it? Didn't know until afterwards.'

'Yeah. My sister's girl. And she died that night.'

Tom felt his heart racing. The cold and the rain disappeared. So too did Foley and Blake. All that mattered was Foxy, Baz, and the next words out of his mouth.

'That's right. She did.'

'So what happened?'

'You mean, how did she die?'

'Yeah.' He could barely contain himself. 'They said crossfire.'

Baz didn't reply straight away. He paused. 'Bet that's been worrying you for years.'

Tom wouldn't give him the satisfaction of admitting it. 'What happened? Tell me.'

Baz turned his head away. Tom couldn't see the smile on his face. 'I mean, if it was me, if it was my niece, and that had happened to her and we were close, and that, it would have torn me up.' He turned to Tom. 'Did it tear you up? Inside? All those years?'

Tom felt anger welling up inside him. He wanted to choke Baz until he told him what had happened to Hayley. Instead he spoke with as calm a voice as he could manage.

'Yes, it did.' As much as he was willing to admit.

'So you want to know what happened to her? That night? How she died?' Baz not even bothering to hide the smile now, actively enjoying having the power over him.

'Yes,' said Tom, still managing to keep calm, but only just, 'yes I do.'

Baz laughed. 'Well, I'd better tell you then.'

61

Lila opened the fridge door, peered inside.

'Nothing hot,' came Quint's voice from behind her, 'nothing you have to cook. You might get ideas about throwing hot oil. Wouldn't want that, would we?'

'What about a cheese sandwich? Am I allowed to make you that?'

'Yeah. As long as you use a blunt knife.'

She took the block of cheese out of the fridge, closed the door. Quint stood in the doorway of the kitchen, gun held on both her and Anju. She took a dinner knife from the draining board, began to hack at the block of cheese.

She buttered the bread, stuck a few lumps of cheese on it. 'Want pickle with that?'

'If it's to hand. Not if it's miles away.'

Back into the fridge for the pickle, smeared a brown dollop on the cheese, slapped the top lid on.

'There you go.'

Quint gestured with his free hand for her to bring the plate over and put it down on the table, near to where he stood. She did, then he waved at her to walk away to the far end of the kitchen. She did that too.

He ate. Anju glanced between him and Lila, looking like she was desperately trying to come up with something that would get them both out of there. Lila hoped she wouldn't try anything that would get them killed.

'Shall I make us some tea?' asked Lila, mainly to stop Anju trying anything rash.

'What d'you think this is, some fucking tea party?' said Quint through a mouthful of sandwich.

'Don't you want some, then?'

He nodded, tried not to take his attention off the two of them.

Lila crossed to the kettle, filled it from the tap, flicked the switch. Arranged three mugs with teabags in, got the milk from the fridge, the sugar from the cupboard. She looked down at the sugar bowl.

And had an idea.

A pretty desperate one, and it probably wouldn't work, might even get them both killed, but she had to try it. The alternative wasn't looking too promising. She didn't believe for one minute that Quint was going to let them live after he got what he wanted. Even if he *didn't* get what he wanted. So a bad idea would be better than no idea at all, she reasoned.

The kettle boiled. She filled all three mugs with boiling water, turned to Quint. 'Sugar?'

'Two,' he replied.

She put two spoonfuls into his mug.

'Milk?'

'A little.'

She added a little milk, squeezed out the bag. Handed it to him.

She went back to the counter top, turned to Anju. 'I know how you like it.' She put some milk in Anju's, took the bag out. Handed it to her. 'There you go.'

Anju took it.

'I'll just do mine. Then shall we go back in the living room? Better than in here.'

'You'll go where I tell you,' said Quint, brandishing the gun.

'Fine.' Lila nodded.

She took the teabag out of her mug. Added six large spoonfuls of sugar. Anju watched her, frowning. That wasn't the way she took her tea. Lila flashed her eyes at her, hoped she remained silent. Hoped Quint didn't catch the gesture.

'Yeah,' said Quint. 'Get back in the living room. I'll decide what to do in there. Go on.'

Anju went first, followed by Lila. Quint, gun still extended, followed behind.

As soon as they reached the living room Anju stopped dead, stared at the window.

'Shit . . .'

Lila did the same.

So did Quint.

Outside, the night was lit up. Quint's borrowed car was in flames.

'What the fuck . . .'

Lila noticed he had momentarily dropped his gun arm, was no longer pointing it at them. She looked quickly at Anju, told her with her eyes that she was going to do something and to be ready. Anju looked terrified, but nodded.

It took seconds but felt like a lifetime. Lila turned on Quint and, while he was watching his car go up in flames, threw the contents of her mug into his face.

An old prison trick that Tom had told her about. Boiling hot water to burn, sugar in it to make it stick. Make it really hurt. Lila had got him right in the eyes.

Quint screamed. Lashed out.

She grabbed Anju's wrist, made for the front door.

Quint hadn't locked it behind him when he had barged in. She had remembered that. With Anju beside her, they ran into the night.

62

Tom loosened his grip on Baz, looked at him properly. The force of the rain had turned the glare of the headlights to a grainy TV static. He regarded his face without having to squint. Baz said nothing, just smiled.

'Well?' said Tom. 'Tell me.'

Baz smiled. 'You don't need to cling to me. I'm not going anywhere.'

Tom loosened his grip. Waited.

Baz smiled. 'You're not interested in me, though, are you? Where I've been, how I ended up like this.' He pointed to his face. 'Don't care.'

'What happened to you?'

Baz laughed. It was a bitter, phlegmy thing. 'Yeah, that's right. Play along, just to find out about your niece. Say what you think I want to hear. But if you do want an answer, a ton of shit. That's what's happened to me. And I ended up looking like a monster. And if you look like a monster, you may as well behave like a monster, right?'

Tom thought of Cunningham. 'Not necessarily.'

'Well, whatever. You're only interested in the pretty dead girl, aren't you? Why? Do you feel guilty about her? Think you should have been there for her, saved her?'

Tom now stood next to Baz but had trouble keeping his hands down, wanting to grab him, force him to speak. 'Just tell me what happened to her. How she died.'

Baz smiled.

And the side of his head exploded.

Tom closed his eyes as blood, brain, gore and bone smashed into him, covering him. He wiped his face, looked round, tried to make out what was going on, body now in fight or flight mode.

Blake screamed. Stared at the dead body of Baz, changed her aim to Foley.

'You haven't got the balls, love,' he said, not even looking at her, gun still outstretched. 'Anyway, you were going to get rid of him when he'd stopped being useful, weren't you? I've just saved you the effort. Don't lie and pretend you weren't.'

Blake did nothing. Said nothing.

'You said you were unarmed,' said Tom.

Foley shrugged. 'I lied. Who'd have thought?'

'Where did you get a gun from?'

'Prison officers, eh? Pay them enough and they'll do anything for you.'

Anger welled within Tom. 'He was going to tell me what happened to Hayley. He was going to tell me, and you . . . you killed him . . .'

'Yeah, I know,' said Foley, as casually as he could. 'That's why I did it.'

Tom just stared at him. Couldn't believe he could hear him say that. 'What?'

Foley shrugged once more. Tried to appear as nonchalant as he could on a moor in the middle of a storm wearing a three-piece business suit and overcoat. 'You've probably been carrying that around for years, haven't you? Her death.'

Tom said nothing. Just glared at him.

'All those years of guilt, blaming yourself. I'm sure of it. Want to contradict me? Tell me I'm wrong?'

Tom still said nothing.

'Thought so. Like I said, I've had a lot of time to think about these things. And you never knew what happened to her, did you? Not really. She died in crossfire, but whose bullet was it? Not yours, then whose? But you blamed yourself, didn't you?'

Tom just stared.

'Now maybe – as I said, I've had a long time to think, reflect on things – maybe that blaming yourself was all part of some misplaced guilt about what you did to me, how you fucked over the one man who was closer to you than even a brother. Who became family. Maybe that was all part of it, what d'you say?'

Tom spoke. 'I don't know. You'll have to ask Dr Bradshaw that one.'

'Dr Bradshaw's dead.'

They both turned towards the source of the voice. So wrapped up in their own dialogue they had almost forgotten that Blake was still there. She stood over Baz's body, the Desert Eagle pointed at both of them. She might have been crying. She might have been angry. She might have just been grimacing against the wind and rain.

'What d'you mean she's dead?' asked Foley. 'How can she be dead?'

Blake stared straight at them. 'It doesn't matter. That's not important. What is important is the money. Now I've stood here long enough. It's time we—'

Foley moved so fast Blake – and Tom – didn't see him coming. Like a human volcano about to explode, he crossed to Blake, pulled her roughly up by her lapels. The action caused her to drop her gun in the mud.

'What d'you mean, she's dead? Tell me about it.'

'She was coming to see me. And my boss Harmer. To discuss you, Tom Killgannon. She'd worked out what was going on. Knew I'd denied you were undercover after she'd spoken to Harmer. Well, I couldn't . . . couldn't let that happen, could I? No . . .'

Foley and Tom shared looks. Foley looked as angry and upset as Tom was, if not more so.

'So what did you do to her?' asked Foley.

Tom recognised Foley's quiet voice, knew what it signified. The calm before the storm.

'There was an accident. A car accident. Those country roads are treacherous at this time of year . . . Boom . . .' She smiled. 'And off the road she went.' She looked between the pair of them, as if explaining something she was sure they would understand. 'One less person to worry about.'

Foley grabbed her with one hand by the throat. Pulled the other back, still holding his gun, and slapped her as hard as he could. Then again. And again. And again. Her head went limply from side to side, the gun butt ripping at her cheek, blood arcing from her mouth, eyes rolled back in her skull, vacant.

'Stop it!' shouted Tom. 'Enough . . .'

He grabbed Foley's arm in mid slap.

'Dean. Enough.'

Foley stared at him and for a few seconds Tom wondered whether he had miscalculated and Foley would start on him next. And yes, he held the gun on Tom. Tom knew there was no way he would miss from this distance. But Foley just kept his eyes locked on Tom's while the rage inside him calmed down.

He let Blake go. She crumpled to the ground in a heap next to Baz. A puppet with cut strings. No longer a threat of any kind.

Foley kept staring at Tom. Eventually he smiled. Tom couldn't tell what kind of smile it was.

'Just the two of us now,' said Foley.

'Then let's talk. That's what Dr Bradshaw wanted, wasn't it?'

'All right, then. Let's talk.'

63

'Try and keep your head down. Come on . . .'

Lila ran away from the house, Anju with her. Quint reached the front door, cursing, firing blindly. Just my luck to be hit by a stray bullet, thought Lila, after everything we've been through to get this far.

They dodged and weaved, making as hard a target as possible for the half-blinded assassin. Between themselves and the flaming car, not to mention the still-burning sugar on Quint's face, he couldn't find them. But that didn't mean he wasn't trying.

'Lila!'

Lila turned at the voice. Pearl was crouched behind an old stone wall, her car parked behind that. Lila and Anju ran over and crouched down next to her.

'Was that you?' asked Lila, pointing towards the burning car.

'I didn't know what to do. When I drove up I saw a car outside that I didn't recognise so what with everything that's been going on recently, I parked up here and walked down. When I got to the house I looked in the window and saw him holding a gun on you both.' She shook her head. 'You were right about him, Lila. I should have listened to you earlier.'

'Never mind. So it was you?.'

Pearl's expression looked pained. 'I didn't know what to do. If I called the police they might take ages and he might hear them and keep you both locked in there. So I torched his car.'

'Why?' asked Anju.

'To get him out of the house so you could lock it behind your-selves. Then we could call the police and get them to come and take him. I didn't expect you two to come running out first.'

'Lila had a plan of her own.'

'And it was pure luck that it worked. And pure luck you did what you did, too.'

'I'll call the police.' Pearl began going through her pockets. Found her phone.

'No signal down here,' said Lila. 'We'd have to get to the top of the bank for that.'

They all looked back towards the house. Quint was still standing in front of it, some of his vision returning, scanning the area, looking for them. The flaming car burning through the storm, throwing off heat where there should only be freezing rain.

'Can we get away in your car?' asked Anju.

Pearl looked at the road up the hill, back to the house. 'It's too risky. I'd have to drive it out of where it's parked and that'll take me near to him. He might hit us.'

'Right,' said Anju. 'So what do we do, then? He'll find us if we stay here. Should we run for it?'

'There's a shortcut up that path to the top of the road,' said Lila. 'But it's on the other side to where he is. And if we get to the top of the hill we've still got miles to go to anywhere.'

'But we can call the police then.'

'If we can get up without him catching us.'

'So what do we do?' asked Pearl.

Lila looked at the house once more. Worked out where Quint was in relation to the buildings around him. Looked at the other two.

'I think I've got an idea . . .'

64

'Put it down,' said Tom, 'it makes me nervous.'

Foley looked at the gun in his hand as if seeing it for the first time, surprised it was there. 'Fair enough,' he said, tucking it inside his overcoat, 'wouldn't want it falling into the wrong hands, now, would we?'

That done, Foley looked at Tom. Taking the time to really scrutinise him.

'You look different. Well, I suppose you would after all these years. And I don't just mean the hair and beard and everything. There's something different about you. You don't look like you used to.'

Tom said nothing. Foley kept staring. Eventually he smiled.

'But there's still a bit of you in there. The old you. The old Mick. You can't get rid of it that easily.

'You look just the same,' Tom said. 'Only more so.'

Foley laughed. 'Prison tends to do that to a person, doesn't it?'

The laughter stopped. Like two gunfighters, neither wanted to be the first to look away in case the other made their move.

'So you still blame me for everything that happened to you?' asked Tom.

'Course I did. All I thought about. For years. You. What you'd done. How you'd betrayed me.' No drama in his voice when he spoke that word. Just a prosaic matter-of-factness. 'Used to lie awake at nights, planning my revenge. Picturing it in detail, real exquisite detail. Every scream, every gasp . . .' He shook his head. 'Didn't sleep for ages thinking all that. And I had people looking for you. All over the country. Even abroad. Thought you might have skipped to somewhere sunny. Spain or Florida, something like that.'

Tom almost smiled. 'Spain or Florida? Credit me with some taste.'

Foley almost returned the smile.

'Like I said, you obsessed me. I tried everywhere. Every angle. Looking for you. Searching, hunting . . . no sign of you. Eventually, I came to the conclusion that you'd probably died. And that made me even more angry. Because that meant someone else had done you in. Or cancer, something like that. And I tried to think you deserved it but it still hurt like hell that it wasn't me who'd done it. Like I'd been robbed of that satisfaction.'

Tom said nothing.

'Because, like I said, I'd planned it all. What I was going to do to you . . . Christ you were going to suffer . . .'

'And now that I'm here, in front of you? Are you still going to make me suffer?'

Tom tensed as he spoke. He was bigger in frame than Foley, but never bigger in rage. Foley was an expert at transforming that anger into physical action. Tom knew he would never best him in a fight if it was one on one.

Foley sighed. Looked up at the rain. Back at Tom. 'What's the point? Eh? What would it achieve?' He shook his head. 'You were wrong. What you said just now. That I'm not different. That I haven't changed. The Dean Foley you knew, all those years ago . . . that's not who I am anymore.'

Tom didn't know how to reply, what kind of response to give. Didn't even know whether Foley was telling the truth. Instead he gathered his thoughts. His turn to share.

'I've thought about you over the years too. A lot. Obviously. I've been living my life in hiding ever since that night. I've been living in fear that you'd find me. And I knew what you'd do if you did.'

'And here I am.'

'Here you are.'

'That why you came down here?' asked Foley.

'Yeah. Wanted to get as far away as possible. So I came to Cornwall. Lived on my own in the middle of nowhere.'

'As far away as possible. You got that right. Still in the nineteen fifties, round here.'

'It's not that bad,' said Tom, almost smiling. Despite the reality of the situation, a part of him acknowledged that it was like two old friends catching up.

'But you were right,' said Tom. 'Well, half right.'

'About what?'

'My guilt. That's what sent me down here. Away from everyone.'

'About your niece?'

'Yeah. And also about my involvement with you.'

Foley smiled, triumphant. 'Told you. What did I say? All those sessions with Dr Louisa paid off.' Then a shadow passed over him as he remembered.

Tom kept talking.

'I said half right. Not like you meant. You showed me a side of myself that I hated. Well, you didn't just show me, you allowed me to let it out. You indulged me, encouraged me. And it was a side of me that was cruel, heartless, arrogant. Took pleasure in hurting people in as many ways as I could. Enjoyed the power and fear that it brought. I could do anything when I was with you. Anything. You know you said once you could shoot someone in a pub on Deansgate and get away with it? Remember?'

'Course I remember.'

'Well so could I. I knew I could. That's how powerful I felt. And I wanted to do it, just to see what it felt like. You were the one who brought that out.'

Foley shrugged. 'Can't blame me for something that was already there in you. If you didn't like it you wouldn't have done it.'

'But I did like it. That was the thing. And it was only when I was with you that I behaved like that. I would never have done it otherwise.'

'So what? You want me to apologise for existing just so you can feel better about yourself?'

'No,' said Tom, shaking his head. 'You don't understand. I'm not explaining myself clearly. That whole side of me, all of that . . . I loved it. Really loved it. And it scared me how much I loved it. How much I didn't want it to stop. I wanted to keep going for ever. Or part of me did.' He paused. Took a deep breath. Another. 'So when it was time to do my job, to break up the gang, I was relieved that someone made that decision for me. Because it wasn't just about stopping you. It was about stopping me as well. And I don't think I could have stopped otherwise.'

Foley nodded slowly, looked down at Baz's body.

'He didn't stop. He kept going.'

'And look where it got him.' Tom looked back at Foley. 'You see what I mean, what I've been getting at? I've lived the rest of my life trying to be a different person. The person I am now, this Tom Killgannon, it's more than just a name. It's another chance. I've lived in fear, not just of you finding me, but that I'd go back to being who I was. I've worked to get rid of that part completely.'

'You managed?'

'I thought I wasn't doing so badly. Till I went into prison. Then it all came back.'

'Like I said,' said Foley. 'Prison changes a man. Or focuses them. Makes them more of what they are.'

'Don't say that.'

He held his hands up, shrugged. 'It's true, but . . . whatever.'

Silence fell between them. Foley eventually broke it.

'We were who we were.'

'What's that supposed to mean?'

'It means it was the only life we had, the only life we knew. The only thing we could do to get out of that shithole we came from.'

'There were other ways,' said Tom.

'The army? Doesn't suit everyone. University? Seriously, no matter how clever we were there was no chance of going there.

Not when we'd been to the schools we'd been to. So what else could we do?'

Tom didn't answer.

'I wanted to make something of my life,' said Foley. 'And so did you. So I did it the only way I knew how. Whatever opportunities were there, I took them. Just like you did. So don't give me all that guilt and angst and shit. We did what we had to do.'

'But did we have to enjoy it so much?'

Foley stopped himself before he could reply. Thought. Gave a small smile. 'What kind of man would you be if you didn't take joy from your work? Take pride in it?'

Tom just stared at him. Felt suddenly tired. Like everything had caught up with him. Not just the last few weeks and months, but everything. His whole life.

'You still feel the same?'

'About what? Pride in my work?'

'About what you had to do to get where you were.'

Foley thought about it. 'I've got a degree, you know. Did it inside. I knew I wasn't thick. Knew it all along.'

'No one ever said you were.'

'It's a working class thing, though, isn't it? No matter how much money you make, how successful you get, you can never shake it. So I did a degree. Prove them wrong.'

'What's it in?'

'English Lit. Hardest thing I ever did.'

Tom smiled despite himself.

'You see,' said Foley, 'this is something else I've spent a long time thinking about. All the money, everything like that, it made things easier. Money always does. But I thought doing what I did would make me somebody else. Someone better. Get me respect.'

'D'you think it did?'

'Got me feared.' Foley shrugged. 'Suppose that's the next best thing.'

'What about now?'

Foley looked directly at him once more. And Tom saw just how much his terrifying old friend had changed.

'I'm just tired,' he said. 'Really, really tired.'

'What are you going to do about it, then?'

Another shrug. 'Change. Because I'm sick of all that.'

'So what happens next, then?'

Foley smiled. Tom didn't know if it was a good smile or not.

65

'Bastard . . . bitch . . .'

Quint staggered round in front of the house, not knowing which direction to take, where Lila and Anju had gone. He was clearly torn between hunting them down and going back inside. Searching for what he had come for, then getting as far away as possible. He had to rule out the last option. And he couldn't see to ransack the house. So he searched for the girls as best he could, hoping he could find them, force them to search the house for him. And then dispose of them when they found the money. He didn't normally relish killing, seeing it only as a necessary part of his job. But in this case he would make an exception.

He didn't notice Lila as she crept back down the hill towards the house, keeping to the shadows all the time, ensuring that her path was clear, that she didn't step on anything that could give her position away.

He had found Pearl's car, was looking round for them there. Lila watched, initially scared for the other two but knowing they would have moved away by now. She saw him try to open the door, fail. Yell for them to come out, make it easy. He sounded in pain. She carried on.

The front door was locked. Lila had expected that, knew that Quint would have tried to stop them getting back in where, as Pearl had said, they could call for the police. Quietly, she crept round the side of the house to the back garden.

Tom and she had been working on it during the spring and summer, cutting back the overgrown bushes and trees, carving out a pleasant place where they could both sit, enjoy the sun, drink, eat.

She also knew that there were plenty of places where she could either trip and fall or give herself away by standing on branches or foliage. She made her way carefully forwards.

The back door was, she knew, locked, but the drainpipe beside it was old, heavy. Iron from a previous century. It clung to the outside wall of the house impervious, like nothing could bring it down. Lila hoped that was the case as she clasped it with her arms, put her legs around it and pulled herself up it.

It was heavy going. There was a time when she would have done this easily. She had always been fit, able to lift at least her body weight, but recently she had let that go. A more comfortable, settled lifestyle will do that, she thought, telling herself to get back in the gym.

It was difficult, but not impossible. She pulled herself up all the way to the first floor bathroom window. It was open. She never properly closed it. And she could fit her small frame through. Although she was settled with Tom and had found the nearest thing to contentment in her life, there was a part of her that was still wary. Ready to run as soon as things got bad. She had planned an escape route from the house just in case she needed it. It wasn't Tom she was afraid of, just parts of her past catching up with her. And if that happened she would be off. It was one of the first things she had done on moving in here. Sometimes, when she and Tom were having a particularly good time, she felt ridiculous for actually planning that. But now she was glad. Better to be safe than sorry.

She placed her foot on the narrow window ledge, balancing her weight between that and the pipe. Reached out for the open window, transferred all her weight to that. Pulled it as wide as it would go, and head first, slipped through.

She hung half in, half out of the window, as she cleared knick knacks and shampoo bottles from the windowsill, carefully placing them at the side, before hauling herself through.

She stood upright, listened for a few seconds. Nothing. She was alone in the house. She went quietly down the stairs, trying to avoid the creaking boards.

In the kitchen, the keys for Tom's Land Rover were where he always left them, in a repurposed antique bowl that didn't match the rest of the crockery but held keys for the house, the pub, their bike locks. She picked them up, careful not to jangle the others there, went to the back door. Turned the key, opened it. Stepped outside.

Listened. Nothing nearby. Quint was somewhere else.

She walked slowly round to the side of the house where the Land Rover was parked. Put the key in the lock as quietly as possible, opened it. She slipped behind the wheel. Tried to pull the door closed as well as she could. It only half caught, but that would have to do.

Now for the part where she had to make some noise. It was unavoidable. She started the engine.

It caught.

She put the headlights on full beam and saw Quint come running down the track towards her, gun pointing ahead of him.

She ducked down as a crack appeared in the glass of the windscreen. It was on the passenger side. Thank god he can't aim properly, she thought, as she put the car into gear and slammed down on the accelerator.

Quint didn't have time to move as it came roaring towards him. The front bars caught him on his left hip, sent him spinning away. His gun loosened from his hand, landed on the bonnet, bounced away into the dark.

She slammed the brakes on, got out. Looked down at him.

'Fuck . . . what've you done to me . . . fuck . . .'

His leg was twisted backwards, like the bottom part of his body faced one way and the top another. His face was seared with weeping burns.

Pearl and Anju ran from their hiding place to join her.

The three of them looked down at the broken man. No one wanted to speak first.

Anju did eventually. 'What shall we do with him?'

'Call the police,' said Pearl.

'Yeah but what do we do with him in the meantime?' asked Anju.

Lila looked over at the concrete slipway that led into the water, back to Quint.

'I've got an idea . . .'

66

'What happens next? Good question.' Foley's smile was still in place.

'You still think I've taken your money?'

Foley studied him before answering. 'No. I don't. Not if everything you've just said is true about who you were, or thought you were, back then. But to be honest, I don't care. If you took it, for whatever reason, keep it. I've got plenty of money stashed in other places. It would be nice to have, but I don't need it.'

No one had moved. Blake had come round, was cradling Baz's broken body with her own. Her face was now bloodied and ruined. She sobbed silently to herself. Tom and Foley still faced each other, ignoring the storm. Their world only as big as the two of them. Tom didn't think he was in any danger. But he still wouldn't let his guard down. He imagined Foley was doing the same thing.

'So what are you going to do now?' asked Tom. 'Go back to Blackmoor? Serve the rest of your sentence?'

Foley laughed. 'Are you?'

'I wasn't—'

'Whatever.' Foley looked round, took in the landscape as if seeing it for the first time. He put his head back, closed his eyes. Opened his mouth. Let the rain in. He licked his lips, his expression approaching ecstasy. His head dropped forwards. He opened his eyes. 'I don't think so.'

Tom waited. Knew there was more to come.

'Dean Foley's dead. He died the minute he set foot on this blasted heath.' Smiled at his own words. 'He might have stepped on to this moor but there'll be a new man walking away.'

'And what about me?'

'What about you? Are you going to walk away a new man?'

'I meant are you still digging more graves?'

Foley thought before answering. 'I reckon there's more ways than one to suffer for your actions. You've got enough going on with your guilt and everything. You've suffered as well. Maybe not as much as me or not in the same ways, but you've not been left unaffected.' Another smile. Less pleasant this time. 'And I've taken away the one thing you wanted. Closure on your niece's death. Answers. You'll never get that now. You'll only be able to guess. Crossfire'll have to do. And that might even make things worse for you to bear. So I suppose that makes us even. Or even enough.'

'So I'm safe from you? In this new identity?'

'You're safe. Until I decide you're not.'

Before Tom could reply, or respond in any way, Foley turned, walked towards the Duster and got behind the wheel. He put the engine into gear, turned it round.

Tom just watched him drive away.

For how long, he didn't know. Eventually he became aware of the sky beginning to lighten, the clouds parting. The rain easing. He looked around. Blake still cradled Baz, talking to him, stroking his face. He walked up the hill, got the bike out from under the overhang. Mounted it, ready to set off.

'What about me?' Blake had looked up, been watching him. 'What's going to happen to me?'

'Get on the back of the bike. I'll drop you off at the police station where you can turn yourself in.'

'I was going to get the money and run away. Start a new life.'

'I'm sure you were.'

'Just like Foley's done. Just like you did.' She reached her hands up to her face. 'Now look at me. At what he's done to me. I'm ruined.' She looked down at Baz once more. 'Maybe I should have stayed with him. Maybe we belonged together . . .'

Part of Tom thought he should have been more sympathetic to her words, her situation but the main part of him knew that she had tried to have him banged up in prison permanently. She had tried to hurt him.

'Ambition can be a fucker, can't it? Especially if you go after the wrong things.'

She didn't reply.

'You coming, then?'

She gestured to Baz. 'What about him?'

'Someone'll come back for the body. He won't be left behind.'

She shook her head. 'He was always getting left behind.' She gave a sound that may have been a laugh or a sob or maybe both. 'I spent years hating him. For what he'd done to me. How he'd hurt me. For the way he was. He didn't start out like that. I don't suppose any of us do, really.' She looked up at Tom. 'Six and two threes, isn't it? It's not just the things you do. It's the things that are done to you . . .'

'Suppose it is,' said Tom. 'You coming, then?'

Blake shook her head. 'I'll stay here with him. Make sure he's looked after.'

'Your call,' said Tom.

He was too tired to argue. He turned on the engine.

67

The sun was fully up by the time Tom reached home.

He was cold, soaked through to the bone, but he just wanted to get there as quickly as possible. That was the first thing. Sort everything else out after that. Just get home.

The wind and easing rain made him feel colder the further he went.

He pulled off the main road, turned down the bank. As he got closer to his house he realised something was wrong. There was a burned out shell of a car in front of it. Pearl's car was parked halfway up the hill. And his Land Rover was parked haphazardly. It had a shattered windscreen.

His heart started beating faster. He pulled up, adrenaline pumping round his body once more. Instinct kicking in. And then he saw them. Lila, Pearl and another girl standing on the concrete causeway, looking down at something in front of them. He turned off the engine.

They had already seen him, heard the bike. Pearl and Lila were running towards him, the other girl some way behind. He guessed who she was.

'Hey,' he said.

Lila was the first to reach him. She hugged him so hard he felt he would burst into tears there and then.

No words offered, no words needed.

Then Pearl reached him. The hugging started again.

They were fine. They were all fine. There was nothing to worry about. They were all right. They were all right.

Smiles and tears from two of the women. He looked at the third. She smiled at him too. He returned it. A perfect homecoming.

He made to head inside.

'No,' said Lila. 'Not yet. Here.' She took his arm, escorted him to the causeway.

There was the body of a man lying half in, half out of the water. Tied up with the tow rope from Tom's Land Rover.

'We're just waiting for the tide to come in,' said Lila. 'Or the police to arrive. See which happens first.' She looked at him, rage in her eyes. 'I know what I want to happen.'

Tom's exhaustion was coming back.

'No,' he said.

He walked down to the causeway, grabbed the ropes round the man's body. Hauled him out of the water, onto the dry concrete.

No,' he said again.

Lila stared at him. 'What are you doing? He killed your friend, Quint.'

Tom stopped, stared at her. 'What?'

'Sorry. I should have said it differently. But he did. And took his place. He was going to kill us, but we got away from him.' She looked down at the prone man. 'Why did you do that? The bastard should suffer.'

Tom looked down at the pitiful wreck of the man before him. There was no fight left in him. Either of them.

He thought of Foley. Of the man who used to be Foley. Of the man who used to be Mick Eccleston.

'Because that's not who we are. Not now, not anymore. We're better than that. We have to be.'

'But . . .'

'No. No buts. We have to be. We can't change today into tomorrow like that. You . . .'

He slumped down next to the man on the causeway, no longer able to stand up.

And began to sob his heart out.

Part Five
RENEWED

Mick just stood there, staring at the carnage. Ambulances were arriving now, their flashing lights adding to the chaos all around. He walked back to where he'd left the dufflebag. Stood beside it once more. Looked down at it.

He felt so, so tired.

Of everything.

68

Paul Shelley stood outside an unremarkable terraced house in Honiton, Devon, hoping that what he was about to do would save his career.

TV cameras, newspaper photographers, bloggers and online journalists swarmed about in front of him, like some unhealthy miasma given human form. He should have hated it but was embracing it instead. He needed this stunt to work, to deflect attention away from him and what had happened at the prison under his watch. As much publicity as he could get. With himself at the centre of it. The wise leader, the unassuming man behind this achievement. Play it that way, forget the rest, and see where his career would go next. He imagined his face on the TV screen. All fifty-six HD inches of him. Yes. This was going to work.

It had been a different story a couple of weeks ago.

DEAN FOLEY ESCAPES FROM BLACKMOOR – Just Walks Out

One of the many headlines. He had been called before his superiors, asked to give an account of himself and his behaviour. He thought the best way out was to lie, which he did. Blamed the individual officers involved in the case, particularly Chris Cartmel who had accompanied Foley on the outside. He tried to brush off questions, deflecting the blame every time. It was the staff, it was government underfunding, lack of training, sloppy wing procedure, it was anyone and everyone's fault but his.

The only thing he did take credit for: putting an undercover officer inside to get Noel Cunningham to give up the locations of his remaining victims.

That had the potential to be an ever bigger mess than the Foley debacle. So when DCI Harmer of Devon and Cornwall police corroborated Tom Killgannon's story, especially in light of the conspiratorial behaviour of DC Blake and the inmate Barry Foxton, not to mention hiring the hit man Dan Jameson, he was more than happy to take credit for it. The whole thing was an unmitigated disaster. And he knew he was lucky to still have his job. However he also knew that what had happened since, Cunningham finding the locations of his victims, made up for a lot of that.

And now he was here. Keeping his part of the bargain. Cunningham had asked to see his terminally ill mother in return for giving the locations of the remaining bodies. And Paul Shelley was a man of his word.

As he was waiting, the car drew up. Like sharks scenting blood, the media knew this was the vehicle and gathered round it, smothering it in their bid to be the first to get a photo, a quote, a piece of moving footage. The police officers present held them back, allowed the car to pull up, Cunningham to get out.

He looked terrified when he saw all the cameras, tried to get back into the car. His police escort ensured that didn't happen.

He would look very different in the papers. They had been using the same photo of him for years, the baby-faced, bow tie wearing choirmaster. Neat hair, big smile. They hadn't been expecting this dishevelled, sweating, greasy-haired obese man wearing prison-issue sweats. But, Shelley thought, they could spin that to their advantage. Write some tabloid piece about his inner degeneracy now showing on the outside. Wouldn't be the first time they had done something like that. And it wouldn't be completely wrong, either, he mused.

Cunningham was bundled inside the house as quickly and efficiently as possible. The cameras went after him. Shelley, spotting his chance, inserted himself between the cameras and the closed front door. This was the address he had been waiting for.

'I'm Paul Shelley,' he began, in what he hoped was some kind of rousing Churchillian manner, 'Governor of Blackmoor Prison. Noel Cunningham is here today because of the tireless efforts of

384

myself and my staff. And it is important that we send a message. That our rehabilitation regime works. That this is the end result of the work we do in Blackmoor. Rehabilitation. Repentance. Restitution.' He smiled once more. Why had he never thought of that phrase before? It just came to him. Clearly, he was a natural at this. He smiled, but noticed out of the corner of his eye that cameras were being turned off, journalists turning away. This wasn't how he'd planned it at all. He made one last ditch attempt.

'What you see today is the culmination of all our work at Blackmoor. All my work. I think I can take full responsibility for what you are witnessing today.'

He had lost them now.

'Thank you very much.'

He turned, knocked on the door, went inside the house.

The house was depressing. It had the stench of the old, the dying. Shabby, undecorated for years, the only new additions were council-supplied aids for movement and independence. Or at least the independence of getting to the toilet. Shelley couldn't wait to get out of there.

Cunningham was in the living room, alongside police officers. He looked up when Shelley entered.

'Hello Noel,' he said, as if bumping into him at a party, 'Everything all right?'

Cunningham stood, nodded. 'I want to see my mother now.'

'Of course.'

'That was the deal.'

'Absolutely.'

Cunningham remained standing, staring at Shelley.

'You all right, Noel?'

Cunningham moved right up close to him. Shelley could smell his unbrushed teeth. 'You tricked me,' he said.

Shelley was aware of the police moving towards him.

'I didn't trick you, Noel. How did I trick you?'

'You sent Tom in to see me. I liked Tom. He was my friend. And now I can't see him anymore. You sent him away.'

'I'm sure he'll . . .' What? He was sure he would what? 'Come and visit.'

Cunningham stared at him for a few seconds longer, turned away. 'I want to see my mother now.'

'Come on then,' said his police officer escort and began leading him upstairs.

Shelley tagged along too.

When they reached the landing, Cunningham stopped. 'I want to see her on my own.'

The police officer looked at Shelley who shrugged.

'All right then, Noel,' said the officer, 'I'll go in and check the room's secure, then I'll let you in. Right?'

Cunningham nodded.

The officer stepped inside, checked the room. Shelley peered through a crack in the door. An elderly woman, made even older from disease, lay near-comatose under the sheets. So light she was almost a skeleton.

'All clear.'

Cunningham nodded his thanks, went in. Closed the door behind him.

Shelley and the officer waited.

'How long has he got?' asked Shelley.

The officer shrugged. 'How long does he need?'

'Could be minutes, could be—'

Shouting came from behind the door. Crying.

The officer rushed towards it, pulled it open.

And there was Cunningham, bent over the still body of his mother, pillow over her face.

'I hate you . . . hate you . . . All my life I've hated you . . . what you did to me, how you hurt me . . . I hate you . . . hate you . . .'

Screaming, tearful, unstoppable.

Other officers ran upstairs, bundled Cunningham out of the bedroom. Shelley looked in. He didn't need to be an expert to know the woman was dead.

Cunningham, now sobbing uncontrollably, was taken forcibly downstairs.

Shelley watched him go.

Thought of the last words he had said to the TV crews.

Watched Cunningham leave the house.

Taking Shelley's career with him.

69

It's often said that doctors make the worst patients. But Dr Louisa Bradshaw knew that just wasn't true. Besides, she wasn't that kind of doctor.

Very lucky. She heard that a lot in the first few days after she came round and found herself in Truro's Royal Cornwall Hospital. Broken arm, broken leg, concussion but no internal bleeding and no major organ damage. You should do the lottery.

She had no memory of the crash. Or the hours that preceded it. Only that she had been told she had been going to Exeter to talk to the police. That part had come back to her but she wasn't sure if it was an actual memory or whether the doctors and police had told her so many times that it had become one. She of all people knew things like that happened.

But she could remember the previous few days at work. Talking to Tom Killgannon and Dean Foley. Trying to arrange a meeting between them to settle their differences. No chance of that now. Don't dwell on your work, she had been told, again by the doctors. Concentrate on getting well.

Nicole had been to see her several times. She had woken once to find her sitting by the side of the bed, crying silently. Asked her if she looked that bad. Nicole had replied with a hug, a weak smile and a second bout of tears.

Nicole. She had been thinking about her a lot. More so than work. About what was important in her life – who was important in her life. Despite living together neither of them had been in a hurry to make some kind of commitment. But she felt differently now. An event like this, she thought, puts the rest of your life in perspective.

So she was on the mend, trying not to think about work, when the nurse, Toni, came into the room.

'You're popular, aren't you?' she said.

She was carrying a bunch of flowers almost the same size as she was.

Louisa sat up. 'What?'

'For you. Just delivered to the nurse's station.'

'Who are they from?'

Toni laughed. 'That's for you to find out. You've got an admirer.'

She left them by the side of the bed, arranging them so they wouldn't fall over. 'Oh,' Toni said. 'There's a note. Here you go.'

She took the small envelope, opened it. Read the card.

And her heart skipped a beat.

She read:

'I WILL DO SUCH THINGS,
WHAT THEY ARE YET
I KNOW NOT'

She recognised the quote straight away. King Lear. And knew immediately who had sent it.

The signature was another quote from Lear:

'From a man more sinn'd against than sinning'

She put the card down, lay back on the pillow. Felt like the wind had been knocked out of her.

Dean Foley. He hadn't forgotten her.

She didn't know if that was a good thing or not.

No, she told herself. Of course it's a good thing. It meant that her work had value, that she had made significant breakthroughs with him. Given him insights into himself, his psyche, that he was going to carry forwards into whatever he did next, wherever he went next.

She read the card again. Studied the quote. It wasn't complete. He had only written the first half of it. Mentally she completed the whole thing:

'I will do such things, what they are yet I know not; but they shall be the terrors of the earth . . .'

She put the card down, looked at the flowers.

Her good mood suddenly gone.

70

It had turned into an impromptu party.

Nobody intended that to happen. Just a few drinks at Tom's house one Sunday night. Pre-Christmas. Tom and Lila, Anju, Pearl. And some of the new staff from the Sailmakers. Not really a party. But Pearl had arrived with a couple of boxes of beer, plus wine, and Tom had made a huge pan of chilli, so things became more festive than perhaps expected. And no one minded.

Life was good. Tom tentatively admitted that. There had been little comeback for his exploits in prison but plenty for Blake and Harmer. Neither had jobs and one was looking at a life sentence. They had cleared Sheridan's name in the process. Tom felt it was the least that could have happened.

Shelley was no longer governor and after the murder of his mother, Noel Cunningham had been moved to Broadmoor prison for the criminally insane. Tom considered sending him a Christmas card. Decided against it.

Dr Louisa was on the mend and Dan Jameson, the fake Quint, was also looking at multiple life sentences. The body of the real Quint had been found on Blackmoor days after Cunningham had shown them where his bodies lay buried. He had raised a glass or two for his old friend Quint on several occasions, felt like maybe his death would become another burden to carry round, another ghost to haunt him.

Lila had seen what he was doing and talked to him about it.

'It wasn't your fault,' she had said to him one particularly dark night after he had been released, as he was attempting to come to terms with the enormity of what he'd been through. Put his ordeal into perspective so he could carry on with his life. 'It wasn't. You said yourself Quint was a security consultant. That's what he did now. You'd have paid him, wouldn't you? For his work?'

'Yeah, I was going to. Probably not as much as he usually made, though.'

'There you go, then. It was a job. And it went wrong. You weren't to know. You can't blame yourself for it.'

He didn't talk about Quint again. At least not to Lila.

He resumed his therapy sessions. Talked about it plenty there. But that was what they were there for.

He attended Nick Sheridan's funeral. Sheridan had turned out to be a decent bloke after all. And his decency had got him killed. Seeing the turnout at Exeter crematorium, how many colleagues attended, how well his wife and children were supported, he felt like Sheridan would have been a man he could have enjoyed getting to know. He didn't speak to anyone, didn't stay for the reception and drove away afterwards on his own. He had paid his respects. That was enough.

And then there was Hayley. He had come so close to finding out what had actually happened to her, only for the chance to be taken away. For ever. He was unsure how he felt about that. Part of him was still in turmoil. But another part of him felt like that was the end of something. Nothing he did or could do would bring her back so he just had to get on with life. Let her death – and his responsibility for it – go.

His inner jury was out on which voice he would eventually listen to.

And Dean Foley was in the wind. For some reason Tom didn't feel too bad about that. He didn't think Foley would come back into his life but he couldn't be sure. Foley wasn't the type of person who could be second guessed. But he felt safe from him, for the moment at least.

Or as safe as he could ever feel knowing Foley was walking around free.

He stood in the kitchen, watched everyone enjoying themselves. Lila and Anju seemed really happy. He could tell just by watching the way they were with each other. Their happiness communicated itself. He found himself smiling.

Pearl caught him. Crossed to him.

'What you mooning about?'

'Oh, nothing. Just how happy Lila looks.'

'I know. Sweet, isn't it?'

'Yeah. I mean, just think, all those months ago what she was like. You'd never have believed she could smile like that.'

'Well that's what happens when someone shows another person kindness.'

He felt Pearl looking at him. Knew she was slightly drunk. He felt her body pushing against his.

Pearl was very attractive. And single, which he found inexplicable. But she was his boss. He also felt that if something started between them it would be serious. And he wasn't sure if he was ready for that kind of commitment. So he had kept her advances at arm's length and not made any of his own. No matter how much he had wanted to.

But now, the alcohol relaxing everyone, the ordeal of prison in the past, things felt different. Perhaps it was time to move forwards.

'You mean me or Anju?' he said.

'You just did what *you* always do.' Slightly slurring her words, hand on his arm, leaning into him.

He put his arm round her. 'Steady.'

She looked up at him, her expression unmistakable.

And they kissed.

Afterwards, neither would be able to say who had made the first move. It felt like it had been done simultaneously. But it felt so right. Their mouths locked, bodies pressed together. Arms held each other.

It was only the surrounding silence that made them both look up. The rest of the room had stopped whatever they were doing and were watching them.

They quickly pulled apart.

Lila was the first to cheer. Everyone else soon joined in.

Tom and Pearl looked at each other, smiled.

Pearl laughed. 'Well that was a long time coming. Merry Christmas.'

Tom felt himself redden. 'I . . . I just need to . . .'

He slipped out of the room as another cheer went up behind him.

He made his way upstairs, stood with his back against the wall on the landing. Took a deep breath, another. That wasn't him, he thought. That wasn't him at all. Another deep breath. Or maybe it was. Maybe this was Tom Killgannon. This could be his character, his life, going forwards. He smiled. He could get to like this man.

He knew they were thinking he had gone to the bathroom but that wasn't where he was headed. There was something he had to do, something he had to check. He had been avoiding it since he got out of prison and knew that now, with a house full of people, it was completely the wrong time. But the alcohol gave him courage. And it needed doing.

He went into the spare bedroom, looked round. It was undisturbed. Good. He crossed to the chimney, knelt down before it. Put his arm inside. Fingers searching.

Found it. Pulled it out.

The plastic brick was filthy but undisturbed. Good. The fake Quint hadn't found it. He put it on the hearth, felt inside again. The others were all there. He took his arm out, picked up the first one again. Wiped the plastic clean. Saw the notes, tightly bound, the Queen's face staring off uninterested, as if financial transactions were beneath her. He knew what denomination the notes were in. Knew how many there were.

And knew where they came from.

'Tom? You coming back down? We're missing you.'

Lila's voice from the bottom of the stairs. He looked once more at the bundle in his hands.

'Yeah. Be down in a minute.'

He put the brick of money securely back in place, dusted his hands. Stood up.

Ready to rejoin his guests.

Ready to be Tom Killgannon once more.

Acknowledgements

First of all, I should say that HMP Blackmoor is not a real place. I've worked in prisons and young offender institutions in the past and it's nothing like any of them.

Thanks as always to my agent Jane Gregory and all at Gregory and Company for always having my back.

And to Katherine Armstrong, Jennie Rothwell, Francesca Russell and the rest of the gang at Zaffre.

To all my friends in the crime fiction world. It's the best gang to be part of.

A special thank you to all the readers, bloggers, booksellers and journalists who enjoyed the last novel. You really help enormously and I can't thank you enough. Hope you like this one even more.

And lastly to my wife, first reader, co-adventurer and professional geek Jamie. You actually made me enjoy witness protection . . .

Prisons and Me

It's no secret I've been in prison. A couple of prisons, actually. I talk about it all the time at events and in interviews. Never hide it. In fact, I like saying it because it pulls people up, makes them give me a second, untrustworthy glance. Sometimes they even check their wallets or their watches. Or flinch, wondering whether I'm going to attack them. Then I go on to explain I was there for a reason. You see, I used to be a Writer-in-Residence. They relax then, a little bit. Because even though I tell people I was on the outside going in and could leave at night, there's a little bit of that word – prison – that powerful, stigmatic word that everyone has an opinion about, but most people don't actually understand, that stays there until I speak further. And sometimes, unfortunately, afterwards.

Long story short, I answered an ad in the paper from the Writers in Prison Network and ended up in Huntercombe Young Offenders Institution for two and a half years. And I loved it. It may well have been the happiest job I've ever done, which sounds contradictory at least since I was behind bars doing it. I was working with kids up to eighteen. The place I was going into had just appointed the country's first full time Arts Co-Ordinator, helping a group of inmates form themselves into a rap act – X-Konz – and perform at Capital Radio's Party in the Park that summer. The Governor came to see me (unheard of in most prions, I later found out) and gave me a two-word brief: 'Bring life'. I tried my damnedest.

Another Writer-in-Residence told me before I went in that the lives and backgrounds of the kids I would be working with were the stuff of nightmares. And straight away I found that to be true. I wrote a short story, *Let's Pretend*, about a teenage rapist who's in prison because his mother sold him to a paedophile ring and who, on being let out, can't go to his terminally ill father and instead has to become a procurer of young boys for his tormentors or they'll abuse his baby daughter. My then wife said it was the most depressing thing she had ever read. My boss called it a normal day at the office.

Some of the kids I worked with were unreachable, even at that young age. I can admit that. And it was sad. I still tried to work with them, though. Their futures weren't bright because their pasts had been so damaging but they still needed help, coping strategies, even if I was just a guy trying to get them to write stories and maybe change the endings to the ones that had led them into prison. To get them to imagine, to dream. One of my class said that when he sat down to write a story, the walls just opened up and he was free.

It was a polarising environment. There were no 'meh' days. Because I was working in such close emotional proximity to these kids, (without, as Home Office rules stated, giving too much of myself away – try making that one work) getting them to open up, talk freely, relax and know that what they said or wrote in my writing room wouldn't go back onto the wing with them and that if anyone tried to do that they wouldn't be back again; it was demanding, full-on work. And sometimes things went brilliantly. Really brilliantly. I had the privilege of helping people to turn their lives around for the better, by using writing as a breakthrough instrument. I had great poets, rappers, story writers and magazine editors. Kids who found something they were good at and could be valued for. Who were made to feel worthwhile for the first time in their lives. Later, I had a group member decide to get help for his alcohol addiction because of realisations he'd come to through his writing. A father took me out to lunch to thank me for helping him to re-establish a relationship with his son because all he talked about in their visits was writing class. Or the one guy who said he was having so much fun he didn't want to be released.

Like I said, great stuff. But, I always stressed, it wasn't me, it was the process. And by that same definition, good days would be followed by bad days. A combination of factors, the process not working, the prison system being what it is, any number of things, I felt like there was nothing I could do. Days like that I went home and drank copiously.

After two and half years of this I moved to work in an adult prison. Not Blackmoor, I hasten to add, that place is entirely made up. And then after that I felt quite burned out. I like to believe – have to believe – that what I did helped though.

Unfortunately, since 2010 the prison budget has been slashed and my kind of work – along with anything broadly rehabilitative – was the first to go. Now our prisons are overcrowded, understaffed and we recently had a moron of a Justice Minister who banned prisoners from receiving books until he was challenged in court. A far cry from my experience. Then, I felt like I was trying to grasp something that was always almost out of reach but could be found. Sometimes I managed it, other times I wasn't so lucky. I just hope there are still people within the prison environment doing that now.

Dear Reader,

Hello once again. If you've read *The Old Religion*, that is. And if you have, then thank you so much. I really appreciate you doing so and hope you enjoyed it. Obviously I'd prefer you to love it but if not then fine then I hope you had some kind of strong reaction to it rather than just, 'Meh'. Because after all, the opposite of love isn't hate, it's indifference. That's a quote from *Dynasty*.

However if you haven't read *The Old Religion* and this is your first one of mine, then welcome aboard. I'm very happy to have you. And I hope that feeling is mutual. If you want to know a bit more about me and *The Sinner* then read on. If you don't, then fine. I'm sure you've got a Netflix subscription or something.

First, here's a bit about me. *The Sinner* is my twentieth novel. Hooray. I've managed to keep going for that long. Most of the novels under my own name have been gritty (I'm contractually obliged to use that word) urban noir settings, mainly in my native North East of England. I've also written eight thrillers under the pseudonym Tania Carver. And I was chosen to write *Angel of Death* – the official sequel to Susan Hill's *The Woman in Black*. I've won awards and been in the bestseller lists, both here and abroad. *The Old Religion* was something of a departure for me. My first novel with a totally rural setting incorporating elements of folk horror. I loved writing it and a sequel was inevitable. However I didn't want to just repeat myself. I wanted something a little different. The result is *The Sinner*.

Not everyone in prison is guilty. Great tag line for the cover. (I didn't think of it, incidentally. I just handle the bits inside.) And it's kind of true. I used to work in prisons and young offenders institutions as a Writer in Residence. The first thing that struck me was just how arbitrary the justice system is. Every single prejudice and cliché that I had about was confirmed straightaway. The richer you are, the less time you do and the punishment is inversely in proportion to how much money you have or where you are on the social scale. But I've written elsewhere about that. I'm here to talk about *The Sinner*.

I was aware that it was going to be a follow up to *The Old Religion*, using the same lead character, Tom Killgannon. Whereas the first book had used all these sweeping open spaces, this one would be cramped and claustrophobic. *The Old Religion* played with folk horror. This would have the vibe of a haunted house. I wanted every character (or nearly every character) to be guilty of something. To be haunted – imprisoned, if you will – by their past actions. To be the sinners of the title. Also, and rather incongruously considering it's set in a prison, I wanted a homage, at least in part, to Geoffrey Household's classic novel of rural pursuit, *Rogue Male*. Did I manage? Read the book and find out . . .

By the way, if you would like to hear more from me about *The Sinner* and my other future books, you can visit www.bit.ly/ MartynWaitesClub where you can join the Martyn Waites Readers' Club. It only takes a moment, there is no catch and new members will automatically receive an exclusive ebook short story from my previous novel, *The Old Religion*. Your data is private and confidential and will never be passed on to a third party and I promise that I will only be in touch now and again with book news. If you want to unsubscribe, you can of course do that at any time.

However, if you like what you read then please let people know. Social media (I'm on Twitter as @MartynWaites), Amazon, GoodReads, all of that. It really does make a difference for writers.

But enough of my yakkin'. It's time to get banged up with *The Sinner*. Enjoy, dear reader . . .

All the best,

Martyn Waites

Want to read
NEW BOOKS
before anyone else?

Like getting
FREE BOOKS?

Enjoy sharing your
OPINIONS?

Discover

READERS FIRST
Read. Love. Share.

Sign up today to win your first free book:
readersfirst.co.uk